PEN

THE DR

I. J. Parker, winner of a Shamus Award for the short story "Akitada's First Case," is the author of *Rashomon Gate* and *The Hell Screen* and lives in Virginia Beach, Virginia.

For my agent, Jean Naggar,
in gratitude for her unswerving support,
her encouragement,
and her faith in me

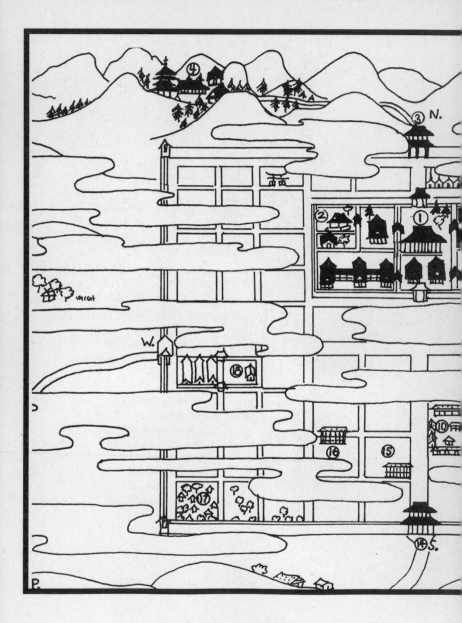

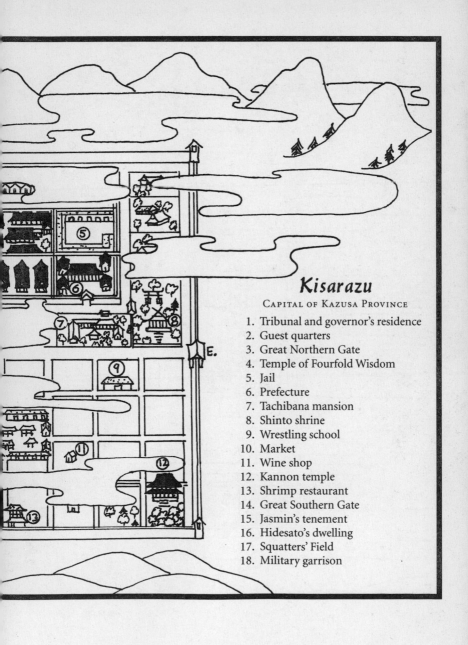

Kisarazu

CAPITAL OF KAZUSA PROVINCE

1. Tribunal and governor's residence
2. Guest quarters
3. Great Northern Gate
4. Temple of Fourfold Wisdom
5. Jail
6. Prefecture
7. Tachibana mansion
8. Shinto shrine
9. Wrestling school
10. Market
11. Wine shop
12. Kannon temple
13. Shrimp restaurant
14. Great Southern Gate
15. Jasmin's tenement
16. Hidesato's dwelling
17. Squatters' Field
18. Military garrison

CHARACTERS

MAIN CHARACTERS

Sugawara Akitada	Nobleman, presently in his mid-twenties, a minor government official on special assignment to Kazusa province
Seimei	Family retainer of the Sugawaras and Akitada's trusted companion
Tora	A deserter who becomes Akitada's servant

PERSONS CONNECTED WITH THE MURDER CASES

Fujiwara Motosuke	Governor of Kazusa province; cousin of Kosehira
Secretary Akinobu	Motosuke's right-hand man
Captain Yukinari	Commandant of the provincial garrison
Prefect Ikeda	Administrator of a local district; subordinate to Motosuke
Lord Tachibana	Retired former governor of the province

Lady Tachibana	His young wife
Master Joto	Abbot of the Temple of Fourfold Wisdom
Kukai	Deacon of the temple
Higekuro	Crippled instructor in martial arts
Ayako	His older daughter, also a teacher of martial arts
Otomi	His younger daughter, a deaf-mute painter
The Rat	A beggar
Hidesato	An unemployed soldier
Fujiwara Kosehira	Nobleman in the capital; Akitada's best friend
Takashina Tasuku	Another friend in the capital
Lady Asagao	Lady-in-waiting in the imperial household

OTHERS

Minamoto Yutaka	President of the Bureau of Censors
Soga Ietada	Minister of justice
Sato, Peony, Junjiro	Servants in the Tachibana household
Scarface, Yushi, Jubei	Three hoodlums
Jasmin	A prostitute
Jisai	A peddler
Seifu	A silk merchant

(Also assorted monks, soldiers, and townspeople)

THE
DRAGON SCROLL

THE WATCHERS

HEIAN KYO (KYOTO):
LEAF-TURNING MONTH (SEPTEMBER), A.D. 1014

*T*here were two watchers in the garden that night.

One was the old man on the veranda who leaned forward a little when he heard light footsteps on the path from the small pavilion in back.

The young woman was coming back. Alone! He feasted his eyes for a moment on the shimmer of multicolored silk gauze and the sparkle of gold in her hair. The light of the moon was uncertain under the trees, and his eyes were weak with age. It was a moment before he realized that she was weeping. She stumbled near the street gate, her full sleeve pressed to her face, a slender arm groping the way. At the gate she stopped to look back toward the pavilion; then she slipped out and was gone.

The old man grinned toothlessly. A lovers' spat. His boarder was an exceptionally handsome young man. No wonder he had been able to form an alliance with a lady of a rank so exalted that she wore fabrics and golden hairpins forbidden to lesser mortals.

He was pleased. His life had contracted to the narrow span of garden viewed from his veranda, and the vicarious enjoyment of the secret pleasures of the highborn filled his lonely hours with intriguing speculations. He looked forward to other nights and more entertainment. Sighing happily, he tottered off to bed.

The second watcher was also pleased. He had been crouching in the shrubbery, having followed the couple to their hideaway. He, too, had noted the golden jewelry in the lady's hair. When she rushed past him into the street, it was an unforeseen piece of luck. He had not expected her to leave so soon—or alone—and he followed her.

◆

The lady ran quickly through the deserted streets. She had never before passed this way, or anywhere, alone. Ordinarily she traveled by carriage or palanquin, and always with attendants, but this was no ordinary errand. Whenever they had walked this way together, she had hidden behind her veil and allowed him to lead her. Now she looked anxiously for familiar landmarks.

Once or twice she took a wrong turn. At one point she thought she heard footsteps behind her and hoped it was her lover, but when she turned she saw no one. Most of the old houses lining the streets were uninhabited and falling into ruin. Others were hidden behind thickets of dense shrubbery, their gates firmly locked against unwelcome guests.

Gradually her steps faltered. The moon silvered traces of her tears. Their meetings at the hidden pavilion had been desperately secret. Nothing had mattered when weighed against their passion. She had willingly put her life into her lover's hands, and now she was alone and in despair.

The streets lay empty, but in the trees silent shapes moved in search of prey. Somewhere a small animal shrieked and something thrashed about. She clasped her trailing skirts to her and began to run again, sudden fear of night-hunting tigers and bloody-fanged demons dogging her steps. Strange shapes loomed out of the darkness of abandoned gardens; eerie sounds came from the branches of towering trees. When a night bird started up, its wing brushing her cheek, she cried out to the goddess Kannon.

Then she saw the gilded roof ornament of the pagoda and sighed with relief. She had reached the broken wall of the old abandoned temple and knew where she was. The holy buildings lay silent and peaceful in the moonlight. The goddess, protector of the weak and troubled, resided there and had heard her cry.

◆

Just past the temple, in an open field where squatters had built their tattered shacks, the second watcher caught up with the young woman.

The human predator had expected his prey to return with her lover, whose long sword he had prepared against by positioning his men close by, but this was far better.

Grinning, he jumped into her path. She stopped and gasped. Just then the clouds parted and the moonlight fell on his face. Recoiling in horror, she screamed.

This time the goddess did not hear.

ONE

INCIDENT IN FUJISAWA

On the Tokaido:
Gods-Absent Month (November), the same year

The Tokaido, great imperial highway to the eastern provinces, was both heavily traveled and unsafe. The government had established checkpoints or barriers, staffed with military guard contingents, to examine travelers' documents and patrol the surrounding area, but they were few and far between, and highway robbery was a way of life for desperate men.

The two travelers from the capital had come far on their post horses. A tall young man in a faded hunting robe and plain twill trousers rode in front. The fact that he carried a sword marked him as one of the "good people." His servant, a slight old man in a plain dark robe, followed on a packhorse.

The young nobleman was Akitada, impecunious descendant of the famous but ill-fated Sugawara clan, twenty-five years old and recently a mere junior clerk in the imperial Ministry of Justice, a position he had won only because he had placed first in the university examination. Now he was on an official commission to investigate missing tax shipments from Kazusa province, an assignment that filled him with extraordinary excitement not only because was it his first journey from the capital, but also because he regarded it as an honor beyond his wildest dreams.

Seimei, who had served Akitada's family all his life, privately thought his young master worthy of any honor but kept this to himself. He was skilled at bookkeeping, had a great knowledge of herbal medicines, and prided himself on his familiarity with the works of Confucius, whom he often quoted to Akitada in his role of fatherly adviser.

His confidence in young Akitada's prospects was about to be severely tested.

Akitada was smiling dreamily, his eyes on a distant blue mountain range while he contemplated the honors awaiting him after the successful completion of his assignment, when a large rock struck his horse on its hindquarters. The animal screamed, tossed its rider into the dirt, and galloped off. Akitada hit the ground so hard, he nearly blacked out.

Instantly, two muscular bearded men, armed with long, stout cudgels, burst from the shrubbery by the side of the road and seized the bridle of Seimei's horse, ordering him down. The old man obeyed, shaking with shock and helpless fury, while his young master sat up, holding his head and gauging the distance to his sword, which was still attached to the saddle. One of the bandits raised his cudgel and made for Akitada. Seimei shrieked a warning and kicked the other bandit in the groin. The man doubled over, howling with pain.

Dazed, Akitada crouched and prepared to defend himself bare-handed against his attacker. He barely dodged the first swing of the cudgel and realized that an ignoble death here by the side of the road might end his chance to prove his talents as an imperial investigator.

At the moment when the other bandit recovered and raised his cudgel against Seimei, another ragged man arrived on the scene. Taking in the situation at once, he swept up a fallen branch and struck the bandit's forearm with such force that he broke it. He caught the man's weapon as it tumbled from his hand and turned toward Akitada's robber.

This man abandoned Akitada to help his friend, but the newcomer now had a comparable weapon and met the other man's whirling cudgel with such skill that Akitada watched in amazement. He had never before seen men engage in a bout of stick fighting, and while the rough cudgels were not quite as handy, long, or light as bamboo poles, both men were skilled fighters. But the new man was better. He parried even the fastest slashes, seemed to jump quicker than a grasshopper, and feinted so successfully that he inflicted several painful jabs before he saw his opening and struck his opponent's forehead with a back-handed slice, knocking him senseless. At this point the other attacker fled, and the ragged young man tied up his opponent with a piece of rope the bandit had worn around his waist.

"That was fine work you did," cried Akitada, walking up quickly. "We owe you our lives . . ." He stopped in dismay when their rescuer straightened up. He smiled quite cheerfully, but a vicious slash had barely missed his eye and opened his cheek. The blood ran freely. "Seimei," Akitada called. "Quick, your medicine box."

The young man shook his head, still grinning with a perfect set of teeth, and dashed the blood away with the back of his hand. "Don't trouble yourselves. It's nothing. I'll get your horse for you, sir." He ran off and returned a minute later, leading Akitada's mount. "If you don't mind the advice, sir," he said, "you should wear your sword. It might at least make the next robber think twice before jumping you."

Akitada flushed. For a vagrant, this young man was amazingly impudent. But he was right, and Akitada swallowed his anger. "Yes. Thank you again. I was careless. Please let Seimei tend to your face." The man's face already bore assorted bruises, but it must be handsome under ordinary circumstances. Akitada wondered if their rescuer made a habit of fighting.

But the stranger shook his head stubbornly and backed away from Seimei and his box of ointments and powders.

Akitada said reassuringly, "Don't worry. He is quite gentle."

The stranger shot him a glance and submitted.

"I suppose you live nearby. What is your name?" Akitada asked, watching the operation.

"No, I don't. I was on my way to look for farm work. You can call me Tora."

"The harvest is over." Akitada regarded him thoughtfully. "This may be a fortunate coincidence, Tora," he said. "We are indebted to you, and I need a servant. Your skill with that stick was impressive. Would you be willing to travel with us to Kazusa province?"

Seimei dropped a jar of ointment and looked at his master open mouthed. The young man thought for a moment, then nodded. "Why not. I'll give it a try. You two need someone to look after you, and if you suit me, I suppose Kazusa is as good a place to go as any." He flashed his smile again.

Seimei gasped. "Sir, you cannot seriously think of taking this person along."

"I suppose you mean him, old man?" Tora, purposely misunderstanding, gestured to the trussed-up bandit. "Don't worry. He's not going anywhere. We'll send the warden from the next village for him. He'll be glad to earn the head money."

It seemed a very fair bargain to Akitada. They had an escort and willing servant who expected no more than food and a few coppers to pay for his trouble. And, with Tora running alongside their horses at a steady pace, they made almost as good time as without him.

Crossing Narumi Bay by ferry, they reached the town of Futakawa toward evening and stopped before a large Buddhist temple with a famous Inari shrine to the fox god sacred to rice farmers. A roofed message board for the posting of official messages stood beside the temple gate.

"Look." Akitada chuckled and pointed to a fresh sheet of paper with large black characters. "'Mountain Tiger Wanted Dead or Alive for Murder and Robbery—Bandit is seven feet tall, of gruesome appearance and hairy body, and has the strength of a dragon!' Apparently there is a gang of robbers working the highway."

Tora grinned widely. "Is that what it says?" He flexed his muscles. "The strength of a dragon? That's very flattering."

Akitada turned to him, astonished. "You are this Mountain Tiger? Of course, 'Tora' means tiger."

"Well, in a manner of speaking it may be me," the young man said, flushing slightly. "But it was all a mistake."

"What? So now he's a wanted man?" Seimei cried. "A bandit and a murderer, even if he's not seven feet tall or very hairy. Pull your sword, sir! We'll turn him in."

"Whoever he is, he just saved our lives," Akitada reminded him and turned back to Tora. "Are you one of the Mountain Tigers or not?"

"No." The young man met his eyes squarely. "You don't have to believe me, but I got caught taking shelter in a cave with them. The soldiers tore up my papers, saying they were stolen. Before I knew it, they were putting chains on everyone and talking about chopping my head off. I grabbed the officer's sword and made a run for it." He waited defiantly for Akitada's decision.

Akitada looked hard at him. "Did you kill anyone while trying to escape?"

"No. Once I had the sword, they wouldn't come near me. I ran as hard as I could down the mountain, and in the next village I left the sword leaning against the warden's house."

Akitada sighed. "Very well. I believe you. But I had better get you some papers before we reach the next barrier."

Tora looked rebellious. "I'm not setting foot in any tribunal."

"Nonsense," said Akitada. "You offered to serve me. I cannot travel with a wanted man."

Seimei muttered darkly, "You'll be sorry, sir, if it turns out to be a pack of lies. A hawk does not become a nightingale, and in the service of His August Majesty one does not employ highway robbers."

Akitada ignored him.

Getting papers for their dubious companion proved surprisingly simple. The local magistrate was awed by Akitada's credentials and did not question his sudden need to hire an additional servant with the astonishing name of Tora and the appearance of a ruffian.

Tora expressed his gratitude through cheerful and eager service. He looked after the increasingly weary Seimei and found them the best lodgings at the lowest rates. This last was important, for though Akitada traveled on the emperor's business, he could not afford the usual escort of armed men and was forced to manage with a very small amount of silver and several bags of rice for provision and barter.

But the best part of the bargain for Akitada was that Tora began or ended each day of travel with a lesson in stick fighting. His belief in their new servant's good character grew by leaps and bounds.

Seimei was scandalized by these lessons, protesting that no gentleman fought with such a weapon. Ignored, he took refuge in grumbling and criticizing Tora's lack of respect at every opportunity.

The day they caught their first distant glimpse of Mount Fuji, Akitada stopped his horse in wonder. Hazy and ethereal, the great snowcapped cone swam into sight as on a cloud. His heart filled with such awe and pride in his homeland that he could not speak.

Seimei remarked that there seemed to be smoke coming from the mountain's top.

"Ha, ha!" Tora laughed. "You should see the great spirit at night. He spits fire like a dragon."

"Fire and snow," marveled Akitada, his eyes moist with emotion. "It must be very high."

"Oh, it reaches all the way to the sky," said Tora, stretching up an arm to illustrate. "People who climb to the top never return. They go directly to heaven."

"There is no medicine against foolishness," snapped Seimei, irritated beyond forbearance by the reprobate servant's know-it-all manner and lack of decorum. "Keep your tongue between your teeth until you learn who your betters are."

Tora looked hurt. "What? Don't you believe in the gods in that great capital of yours?"

Seimei did not bother to answer.

At Mishima they began the long ascent to Hakone. This mountain pass was the longest and highest on the Tokaido. The skies clouded over and a heavy silence seemed to hang in the air among the dark pines and cryptomerias.

A government barrier had been erected between the steep mountainside and Hakone lake, a desolate sheet of water mirroring sky and mountaintops. Here, for the first time since they had left the civilized world of the capital, they encountered evidence of harsh frontier justice. Displayed at eye level on shelves near the barrier were the heads of criminals, each accompanied by a plaque describing his misdeeds, a lesson and a deterrent to would-be offenders.

Akitada, though nauseated by the sight, forced himself closer to read the plaques, nearly twenty of them. Murder, rape, robbery, fraud, and one case of treason. The authorities in this eastern province took their responsibility for checking travelers seriously.

He rejoined the others, profoundly uneasy about Tora's fate, should the barrier guard decide to question his identity. There was no guarantee that his own status was sufficient to save his new servant's head, if Tora was arrested for his supposed crimes.

He looked around. About twenty people ahead of them awaited their turn. The line moved slowly. No one escaped scrutiny at the Hakone barrier.

A guard approached and asked for their papers. After glancing at them, he motioned them past the waiting line and into the inspection office.

Ducking under a curtain, they found themselves in a large room with a packed dirt floor, facing a low bench in front of a raised wooden platform. Tora and Seimei went to kneel on the bench. Akitada remained standing.

On the platform sat a uniformed and fiercely mustached captain of the guard with three soberly dressed officials behind him and a scribe at a low writing desk off to the side.

The guard handed Akitada's papers up to his commander with a whispered comment. The captain ran his sharp black eyes over Akitada, then scrutinized Seimei and Tora. Then he read all the documents, some of them twice.

Akitada felt beads of perspiration on his upper lip and his palms. This was a far cry from the deferential reception he had come to expect at checkpoints. He jumped a little when he heard a curt bark. "Approach, sir!"

Akitada's official standing meant that he should give the orders, not the other way around, but he could not risk drawing attention to Tora and so he obeyed without protest.

"I see from your documents that you are on special assignment from the capital to Kazusa province?"

Akitada nodded.

"The men with you are your servants and you vouch for them?" The captain's beady eyes left Akitada's face and rested on Tora again—more thoughtfully than before.

"Yes." Akitada tried to make his tone casual, though his heart was pounding. "The older man is called Seimei, the younger Tora."

"I see. Why did you get papers for the man Tora in Futakawa?"

Akitada felt himself flush. "Ah," he stammered, "the trip proved harder than expected and . . . er . . . Seimei is unused to traveling. We had some difficulties, and, well, it seemed a good idea to hire another servant."

The captain gave him a long look. "Difficulties?" he said with what amounted to a sneer. "No doubt you're not used to travel. You have actually come quite far without an escort. A lot of the young gentlemen from the capital turn tail long before they reach Hakone."

Akitada flushed again, this time angrily, but he bit his lip and said nothing.

"What is your business in Kazusa?"

"I travel under imperial orders, as you can see, Captain . . . ?"

"Saito is the name. You are not, by chance, looking into the missing tax shipments from Kazusa, are you?"

Akitada's instructions were to use the utmost discretion, but this man might have valuable information. "I am," he admitted. "What do you know of the matter?"

"I know that no goods from Kazusa province have passed here in years. Plenty of things going the other way—Buddhist scrolls and statuary, parcels for the governor—but no tax convoys from Kazusa for the emperor." The captain turned to one of the clerks. "Bring the ledgers for the past two years and copies of the correspondence about the Kazusa tax shipments!" Reaching for an open ledger, he turned some pages, then pushed the ledger toward Akitada. "See for yourself! When they did not show up at the usual time again this year, I reported the matter to the capital. Again."

Again? Akitada bent to read.

The clerk returned with a large document box that he set down. The captain took out two more ledgers and turned to the end of the entries. "Last year. Nothing. There you are." He pointed to a line of brushstrokes. "And here the same," he said, shoving a third ledger at Akitada. "And here are copies of the reports I sent to the capital."

Akitada looked, then looked again in disbelief. "There has not been a single tax convoy from Kazusa for three years or more?" he asked. It seemed incredible. Worse, the documents proved that no one had bothered to investigate the matter until now.

"Three years precisely," corrected the captain. "Before then everything was always in order and punctual as geese flying south in the winter."

"How do you account for it?"

"I cannot," the captain said. He appraised Akitada and compressed his lips. "I simply do my duty. My men got instructions to question everyone coming from the east about incidents on the road. There was never even the vaguest rumor of either gangs or piracy. It would take a small army to fall on a tax convoy under military escort. In my opinion—and, mind you, it is just an opinion—the goods never left Kazusa. Hrrmph." He cleared his throat and gave Akitada another of his disconcerting stares. "Confirmed by the fact that the imperial authorities have taken their sweet time to investigate." A corner of his mouth twitched. "Until now," he added with deliberate sarcasm.

Akitada felt himself flush hotly. He knew what the man thought. Nobody wanted the shipments found. By sending an inexperienced junior clerk to investigate a matter of this magnitude, the government had signaled the fact that they wished the whole thing forgotten. And for what reason but to protect the provincial governor who was a Fujiwara and a distant relative of the chancellor? Unfortunately, he also happened to be the cousin of Akitada's best friend Kosehira. They had attended the university together and become close because both had been friendless, Akitada because he was poor and Kosehira because he was short and fat.

Resenting the captain's manner, Akitada snapped, "Thank you. I must be on my way. If you are quite finished with us . . . ?"

The captain grinned. "Of course! Of course! I won't keep you. Good luck, sir." He bowed with mocking deference.

"Seimei, the bell tokens!"

A soldier received the tokens to be exchanged for two horses and rushed away.

They were headed out the door when the captain called after them, "The weather is turning. You would be well advised to spend the night in our quarters."

Akitada turned and said stiffly, "Thank you, but I think we will press on."

◆

They made the descent in daylight, but the rain began soon after they had left the lakeside barrier and fell coldly and steadily
all the way down the mountain. Its gray sheets obscured what
would have been magnificent views; its icy wetness insinuated
itself through layers of clothing to their skin. Soaked, chilled,
and exhausted, they broke their journey in Odawara at the foot
of the mountain and spent the night in an inn that was overrun
by rats, sleeping on mats of moldy, stinking straw, covered by
their own wet clothes.

The next day they awoke to more gray clouds and sheeting
rain, but set out again covered by their wet straw cloaks and
limp straw hats. The road wound through foothills until it approached the coast again. They could smell and taste the salt of
the sea on the cold wind miles before they set eyes on it.

When they emerged from the last protective belt of forest
and saw the wide expanse of open ocean before them, they were
sucked into a frigid, whirling gray mist. Above them the wind
swept ragged smoky clouds along; before them the charcoal-
dark ocean boiled and subsided with a continuous roar, vomiting up dirty yellow foam and swallowing it again; and all about
them swirled and blew the spray and the everlasting rain, tearing at their cloaks and slapping the wet, salt-laden wisps of their
hats against their stinging cheeks. Seimei developed a nagging
cough.

After Oiso the road veered away from the coast and they entered a huge plain, most of the year a rich and verdant source of
rice for the nation. Now, in this late season, the rice paddies, lying
fallow, were black sheets of water between dams, dotted here and
there as far as the eye could see by farms or hamlets huddling dejectedly under gloomy trees. The Tokaido crossed this submerged
plain on a raised dam, planted on both sides with pines drooping
mournfully under the weight of their wet needles.

Finally, toward evening of that dismal day, the rain eased to a drizzle. Battered and weary, they reached Sagami Bay and the harbor town of Fujisawa. From there Akitada had planned to journey by water, taking a boat across the bay to Kazusa province. They would save five or six days that way, arriving in the provincial capital in two days.

Fujisawa was a sizable and bustling town with its own post station and small police force. It was a major port for boats sailing across Sagami Bay, and on the nearby island of Enoshima was a famous shrine.

As soon as they entered the town, Tora left to find a room in an inn, while Akitada and Seimei continued to the post station to return the horses. Progress through Fujisawa's narrow streets was difficult on horseback. Because of the drizzle, shoppers carried oilpaper umbrellas, and the horses shied, while the Fujisawans cursed or screamed.

The post station was near the harbor. At its gate stood the usual roofed notice board. This one carried one very large and official-looking proclamation that, unlike the rest of the messages, was yellowed and torn. The writing had faded almost into illegibility, but there were faint traces of a red government seal, and Akitada went to read it. As far as he could make out, it requested information about robberies of government shipments and offered a substantial reward. The seal was that of the governor of Kazusa. Clearly no one had applied for the reward for many months, and the offer had not been renewed.

Akitada returned to Seimei. "An old posting about the lost taxes. This is looking worse by the minute for the governor. He is not even making a token effort to investigate the loss. How can we accept the man's hospitality when he is our prime suspect?"

Seimei sneezed. "I don't know, sir," he croaked dismally, his teeth chattering.

Akitada searched the old man's face. He looked unnaturally flushed and huddled in his saddle. "Are you feeling all right, old fellow?" he asked with sudden concern.

Seimei shivered and coughed. "Just a little cold. I'll be better once I'm off this horse and can stretch my legs a bit."

They turned the horses over to the post station's grooms and left their saddlebags in the office after removing their valuables.

The rain had stopped, but it was quickly turning dark because of the overcast sky. Everywhere lanterns were being lit, and fires and candles glowed from the many places of business catering to visitors. Mouthwatering smells of hot foods filled the streets. Akitada and Seimei made their way slowly through the crowds, stopping from time to time at inns to ask for Tora.

But it was as if the rain had swallowed him up.

In an unsavory and nearly deserted part of town, Akitada became aware of Seimei's lagging steps. He stopped. "Seimei," he said, "we have spent an hour searching. It is time we went back to an inn, got a room, and rested. You need a hot bath, some warm wine, and dry bedding."

To his astonishment, Seimei objected. "Please, sir," he quavered through chattering teeth, "couldn't we just try a bit longer? I have a very uneasy feeling about this. It isn't like Tora."

"Nonsense. He is young and strong. Perhaps he simply got tired of our company and took off."

"Oh," Seimei cried, wringing his hands, "I hope not. Oh, dear. It is all my fault."

"Why your fault?"

"It is said 'Cold weather and cold rice may be endured, but not cold looks and words.'" The old man hung his head. "I have been very unkind to that boy."

"Nonsense!" Akitada repeated, somewhat absently. He peered down a dark alley. At its end torches flickered and he could hear excited voices. "Something is wrong down there."

"If there are people, let's go ask one more time."

"Very well. But after that we get some rest."

When they reached the torch-lit scene, they found that a crowd had gathered because of a crime in a dilapidated two-story house with the ill-written sign "Fragrant Bower of Beauty" dangling lopsidedly from a single nail. A red-coated police constable stood guard at the doorway, glaring impartially at a knot of poorly dressed people clustered before him.

Akitada pushed through the curious and demanded, "What happened here?" Just then the door opened and two more constables appeared, bearing a body on a stretcher. It was covered by a woman's bloodstained gown.

The constable, seeing a tall, official-sounding stranger before him, puffed himself up. "A vagrant slashed a whore's throat," he barked. Then he grinned, baring crooked yellow teeth. "But he didn't get very far, and there's plenty of women left inside, so help yourself, sir." He winked, stepped aside, and strode off after his colleagues.

Seimei stumbled after him. "Constable! Wait!" he croaked hoarsely through another bout of coughing. The constable did not hear him, and Seimei returned to seize Akitada's sleeve, his face flushed and tense. "You must follow, sir. It's a murder. You know all about murder, and I have a feeling it has something to do with Tora."

"Nonsense. You are ill and exhausted, and I cannot get involved in a murder investigation here. I am on assignment to Kazusa."

"Please, sir. At least we could ask about him at the police station. It would make me feel better."

With a sigh, Akitada gave in. The police station was near the center of Fujisawa, its entrance marked by a large paper lantern bearing the characters "Police." Inside they found a lieutenant and two clerks occupied with questioning a fat man in a greasy blue cotton robe.

"I admit I was wrong about the color of his jacket, Officer," the obese man was saying, spreading small hands with fingers like fat slugs. "But you couldn't miss the scar on his face. I swear it's the same man. Poor Violet! She was just building a nice clientele, too. A big loss, that, Officer. And who will indemnify me? I paid six rolls of the best silk for that girl four years ago. I fed her, trained her, and was just realizing a small profit when . . . poof . . ." His hands flew into the air, encircling emptiness, when his eyes took in the weary, travel-worn figures of Akitada and Seimei. "It is really too bad how much riffraff is allowed to travel the great Eastern Road nowadays. An honest businessman is no longer safe in this town."

The police lieutenant turned. "What do you want?" he asked peevishly. "Can't you see I'm busy? If it's about travel permits or directions, you'll have to come back in the morning."

Akitada was tired and frustrated. He knew Seimei was feeling worse, and he had no intention of wasting any more time. "Pass the man my papers, Seimei," he snapped, and watched impatiently as the lieutenant unrolled them and paled as he read the imperial instructions to give the bearer all possible assistance. After raising the document reverently to his brow, he fell to his knees and apologized.

"Get up!" said Akitada wearily. "We sent our servant Tora ahead to arrange for lodging. He seems to have disappeared. I wish him found immediately."

The lieutenant jumped up and asked for particulars. When Akitada gave a description of Tora, his face grew longer and longer. The fat man cried out in astonishment also, and the clerks sat watching with round eyes.

"We took such a person into custody a short while ago," the

lieutenant admitted. "For murdering a prostitute. He was arrested not far from the scene of a murder on the word of this eyewitness here." He pointed to the fat man, who suddenly looked nervous.

"Well," the fat man stammered, "it was getting dark, but I recognized the scar when I saw his face at the noodle stall. Perhaps these gentlemen are not aware of the violent character of their servant."

"Can we see the prisoner?" Akitada asked the officer.

"Certainly. Right away, Your Excellency!" The lieutenant clapped his hands.

A few moments later Tora stood before them, chained, bloodied, bruised, and held firmly on either side by two brawny guards.

"Sir!" he cried, and took a step toward Akitada. The constables jerked him back by his chains.

Akitada said, "There has been some mistake. This is my servant. Set him free instantly."

"But, Excellency," protested the officer. "He has been positively identified by a respected citizen of this town. I'm afraid—"

Akitada glared. "I said, set him free."

Tora was released and came to them, rubbing his wrists and muttering his thanks.

Akitada growled, "I hope you won't make a habit of this, Tora. We've spent hours looking for you. If it hadn't been for Seimei's insistence, you might have rotted in this jail." He saw Tora's eyes moisten and relented. "What happened?"

"It serves me right, sir," Tora said humbly. "I was hungry and cold and thought there was plenty of time, you being delayed at the post station. I stopped for some noodles in hot broth. I was just finishing them when all hell broke loose. The next thing I know, I'm on the ground with four constables beating and kicking me."

Akitada turned to the lieutenant. "When did the crime take place?"

The fat man and the officer answered simultaneously, "Four hours ago."

"How do you know?"

The lieutenant scowled at the witness who subsided into a dejected lump. "She was still a little warm when we got there, and that was almost two hours ago. Toyama here is her employer and he came straight to us after finding her dead."

"But four hours ago it was not yet dark," said Akitada, regarding the fat man suspiciously. In spite of his fatigue and against his best intentions, his interest was aroused. He wished he could see the body and question the dead woman's friends. "When did this man see the murderer?"

The fat man spoke up nervously. "I saw him at the noodle stall on my way back with the constables. I knew right away he was the man. You see, the girls described Violet's customer to me. The scar on his face, that's what gave him away. The clothes . . . as I said, we could be wrong about those. Anyway, when I saw him standing there, eating noodles as if he hadn't a care in the world, I cried out and told the constables."

"Ridiculous," snapped Akitada. "If the murder happened four hours ago, my servant was still with me and my secretary several miles outside Fujisawa. I suggest you bring in your witnesses—and I don't mean this man—and have them verify that this is not the man they saw. Then I expect my servant to be released with an apology. Tora, you will join us at our inn."

"That will be the Phoenix Inn, sir. It is said to be the best," Tora offered helpfully. But Akitada was reluctant to leave. He opened his mouth to offer advice to this obviously bumbling policeman, when Tora cried out and he heard a thud behind him. Turning, he saw Seimei's frail body stretched out, unconscious, on the cold dirt floor.

TWO

PEDDLERS, MONKS, AND FUJIWARAS

For two days, Seimei was very ill with a feverish cold and a painful, tearing cough. Akitada sat by his bedside, filled with bitter self-recriminations for not having noticed his companion's illness earlier, for having pushed the old man too hard on the journey, for having undertaken this assignment against the advice of his friends. He had frightening visions of losing Seimei here, in this strange town, far from the family the faithful soul had served so well all his life.

Tora undertook the nursing duties with patience and a gentleness no one would have expected from the rough tramp. At least in this respect, Akitada did not rue his impulse to save the young man from the brutality of the constables. Except for a reluctance to reveal his real identity, Tora spoke freely about his troubles. He was a farmer's son who lost his family during the border wars and was pressed into military service. He deserted after beating up his lieutenant for raping a farm girl.

On the third day after his collapse, Seimei awoke from a deep sleep and asked for a drink. When Tora rushed up with a cup of wine, he pushed it aside and said peevishly, "You fool, don't you know wine heats the blood? Are you trying to kill me? Tea. I need tea made from steeped juniper berries, mustard plant, and yarrow root. I suppose you expect me to get up and look for those things myself?"

"Sorry, old man," Tora said meekly. "I'll get your roots and berries if you tell me where to look for them."

"Never mind, Tora." Akitada put his hand on Seimei's brow and found it dry and cool. "The local pharmacist will have all the ingredients. Take some money from my saddlebag and get what you need." To Seimei he said, "I am very glad to see you better, old friend. We have been worried about you. Tora was tireless in caring for you, keeping you covered and putting cooling compresses on your head."

Seimei looked a bit guilty. "Oh," he mumbled. "How long have I been sick?"

"Two days and three nights."

"Oh, no!" Seimei struggled to sit up. "Such a delay! We must go on immediately. I am certain I shall be able to get up after my herbal tea."

Akitada pushed him back gently. "There is no hurry. I have need of your skills once we arrive, and you must be well rested and healthy. We shall stay here in this comfortable inn until you are completely well. Tora can look after you, and I shall use my time to find out what I can about the Kazusa matter and perhaps offer my help to the local police. They don't seem at all competent to deal with that prostitute's murder."

They remained another two days in Fujisawa. Seimei improved greatly and took out his frustrations by nagging Tora. Akitada made several visits to the police station. To his regret he was given no information, nor were his questions about the murder answered. The lieutenant, scrupulously polite, assured him his servant had been cleared of all charges. The brothel keeper had quickly retracted his accusation when his girls denied ever laying eyes on Tora. His Excellency was free to travel on.

Thus, on the fifth morning, in balmy weather and with Seimei nearly well again, they took passage on a ship and crossed Sagami Bay to Kisarazu in Kazusa province. The trip by water, though dangerous in bad weather, saved them a week's hard riding across country.

Instead of proceeding directly to the provincial tribunal, Akitada took lodgings in a modest inn next to the city market. He wanted a look at the city and its people before announcing his arrival to the governor.

Leaving Seimei there to rest, he and Tora set out to explore the town.

Kisarazu bustled with activity. Akitada guessed at a population of nearly ten thousand, but there seemed to be many visitors also. Their inn had been packed, and in the unseasonably warm sun the market was bustling with vendors, shoppers, and people out catching fresh air and sunshine. The large gated enclosure of the provincial administration looked substantial, even elegant. Kazusa province seemed a very good assignment, even for a Fujiwara governor. Had the present incumbent improved it by appropriating to himself three years' worth of tax goods due to the emperor?

Around the hour of the evening rice, they returned to the inn and sat at one of the tables outside. Seimei joined them, and they ordered a simple meal from a stout, middle-aged waitress with a pronounced overbite. Tora took one look at her, grimaced, and watched the shoppers instead.

"I could swear that tall fellow lost his ear in a tangle with a chain and ball," he said, nodding toward a group of young Buddhist monks passing the inn.

Akitada followed his glance and saw what Tora meant. The chain and ball was a vicious weapon used by violent gangs. This monk shared only the saffron robe and shaven head with the pasty-faced and soft-bodied clerics Akitada had met in the capital. Tall, ruddy, and very muscular, he walked with a swagger and had the face of a cutthroat. And Akitada saw with surprise that his companions were like him. They passed through the crowds almost disdainfully, speaking to no one, their eyes roaming everywhere. People scurried out of their way.

"Hmm," said Akitada. "Odd. If he has had a checkered past, let us hope he has seen the error of his ways and chosen to atone."

Seimei, being a good Confucianist like his master, also distrusted the Buddhist religion. He looked after the monks and shook his head. "You cannot make a crow white even if you wash it for a year."

The waitress, who was serving their food and wine, burst into loud giggles and poked him with her elbow. Seimei glared at her.

"You used to say the same about me, old man," Tora reminded Seimei.

"Exactly. And look at him now!" Akitada smiled at Tora with great satisfaction. They had done some shopping. The ragged tramp was wearing a new blue cotton robe with a black sash. His long hair was pulled back neatly into a topknot tied with a black cord, and his face clean shaven except for a small mustache. The scar had faded, and Tora attracted admiring glances from passing young women.

"I may have been wrong about you," Seimei conceded. He took a bite and chewed thoughtfully. "We shall see. But remember, Master Kung Fu says that a man should be distressed by his own lack of ability, not by the failure of others to recognize his merits."

Tora reached for his bowl of rice and vegetables. "A very good saying, that," he said, nodding. "You must teach me more about your Master Kung Fu."

Seimei looked pleased. Akitada hoped that the old man was beginning to take a fatherly interest in Tora; it would be a welcome distraction if he found someone else to scold and instruct.

They ate and drank contentedly, watching the bustling crowd in the market.

"This looks like a healthy and prosperous province," remarked Seimei to Akitada, echoing Akitada's earlier thoughts. "The rice paddies and mulberry plantations we passed on the way here are well kept, and this market is selling an abundance of goods."

"Yes." Akitada had seen no signs of neglect or grinding poverty among the peasants. He knew that a dishonest administration satisfied its greed by excessive taxation and minimal maintenance of roads and fortifications.

"Something's not right here," Tora said. "I've a feeling about such things. Those bastard officials wouldn't have to rob the peasants if they kept all the taxes for themselves. The governor's palace has green roof tiles and gilded dragon spouts like a temple. Where did he get the money for that?"

"Well," said Akitada, shaking his head doubtfully, "I find it hard to associate wholesale thievery of taxes with an otherwise excellent administration."

Tora suddenly whistled.

"What's the matter?" Seimei asked, raising his eyes from peering into the empty wine pitcher.

Tora pointed. "Look at that girl! She's a beauty. What a neck! And those hips and thighs!"

Across from the inn, a vegetable vendor had set up his baskets of turnips, radishes, beans, herbs, sweet potatoes, and chestnuts. A pretty young girl, her hair tied up in the style of women of the lower class, and her slender figure wrapped tightly in a plain striped cotton gown, was bargaining with many gestures for a bunch of large radishes.

"Don't stare, Tora," Seimei scolded. "Women should neither be seen nor heard." He called for their waitress. She arrived eagerly to take his order for more wine and pickles. "And don't try to charge us for those pickles this time," he told the woman. "They come with the wine." She bobbed her head, grinned at him toothily, and padded away. He scowled after her and muttered, "Women can't be trusted. Charging for pickles and pocketing the money herself, I bet." Turning back to Tora, he said, "Mark my words and stay away from females. A young man in your position must keep his mind pure or he will be ruined by some flirtatious light-skirt."

Too late. Tora, a look of determination on his face, jumped up and disappeared in a passing group of shoppers.

There seemed to be some kind of commotion. People turned their heads to stare. But when the crowd thinned, there was no trace of either Tora or the girl.

"Well!" exploded Seimei. "Did you see that? Outrageous! He jumped up without a word to run after the first skirt that appeals to him. What shall we do now?"

"Nothing. Here's the waitress, Seimei. Let's drink our wine and eat these excellent free pickles. If Tora has not returned by the time we are done, we'll retire. You can lecture him about his behavior tomorrow."

"Hah! Trying to talk to that one is like taking the whip to the bullock's horns."

They were idly watching people again, when a peddler approached some guests at the other end of the porch. He was the first poor man they had seen in the city.

Ancient, bent, and skeletal, he was barely able to support the tray of merchandise strapped around his birdlike neck and shoulders. As he hobbled among the guests, he kept propping the tray up on tables every chance he got. Through the holes and tatters of his shirt patches of leathery skin could be seen, and he was bare-legged to his loincloth.

The guests were mostly merchants eating their rice. They made threatening noises and gestures at the peddler. But he persisted, either hard of hearing or desperate to make a sale, until one of the men became impatient and delivered a vicious kick to the peddler's backside. The old man fell face forward into the street, across his tray of knickknacks, which scattered in the mud. The merchants laughed uproariously, and some street urchins darted forward to scoop up what they could carry.

Akitada was by the side of the fallen peddler in a moment, scattering the boys. Helping the old man up, he led him to their bench. "I am sorry for the treatment you got, old man," he told him. "Here, have some wine. It will warm you and give you some strength."

The old peddler shivered and moaned, but the wine produced results, and his whimper turned into intelligible words. It appeared he was a great deal more concerned about his loss of merchandise than his injuries.

Akitada looked at him and marveled at a life where the threat of starvation was far more serious than bruises or broken bones. "Seimei," he said, "go see if you can find any of his things and bring them over here."

Seimei, his face a study in outrage, returned with the tray of muddied objects and placed it on the table next to the peddler. Taking a sheet of paper from his sash, he tore it carefully in half, wiped his hands thoroughly, and tucked away the rest.

The peddler, seeing the few grimy remnants of his stock-in-trade, uttered a string of shrill wails. Akitada rashly offered to buy what was left and the old man stopped his noise immediately. He quoted an exorbitant price, which Akitada paid. Without a word of thanks the peddler dumped the contents of the tray on the table, flung its rope around his neck, and disappeared into the crowd at a lively pace.

"Oh, the vile person was pretending all the time," cried Seimei. "What are we to do with this filthy junk?" He poked at the cheap combs and pins with his chopstick. "It isn't worth two coppers and you gave him twenty. And it's all women's stuff anyway. And dirty. No doubt we will both become ill from touching the creature and his trash."

"You might make our waitress a gift of them," suggested Akitada. "She seems to be particularly taken with you."

Seimei's jaw sagged until he saw Akitada's grin. He prepared to sweep everything onto the empty pickle tray when Akitada reached out and plucked one small piece from the pile and cleaned it off carefully. "If I am not mistaken," he said, "this is Chinese cloisonné work, a very strange sort of thing to find in a peddler's tray. Look, Seimei, it's a morning glory, and beautifully made, each blue petal and green leaf outlined with gold wire. I wonder how that old man got an exquisite thing like this." He scanned the crowd for a glimpse of the peddler.

Seimei peered at the tiny flower. "It's very small. Is it worth twenty coppers?"

"Not in its present condition. Once it was part of a hair ornament, and worth a hundred times that. But few women, even of the noblest houses, wear jewelry nowadays. It's a puzzle." Akitada frowned in concentration, then shook his head. "Perhaps it came from a temple robbery. Ancient statues of goddesses often have such ornaments. I shall keep it as a souvenir. Leave the other things for the waitress and let's go to bed."

◆

Tora had not returned by the following morning. Akitada was torn between disappointment that Tora should have left so quickly when he no longer needed protection, and fear that he had got himself into some new trouble. But either way, there was nothing he could do until he had met with the governor.

When Seimei found his master dressed in his usual hunting robe and clean cotton trousers tucked into boots, he objected, insisting that Akitada put on formal court attire for the occasion. Akitada controlled his temper because of Seimei's recent illness. He sat, quietly fuming, while Seimei unpacked and aired out his one good silk robe, white silk court trousers, and the formal hat of stiffened black gauze, accompanying his ministrations with bitter recriminations about Tora. Putting on the awkward costume did little to improve Akitada's mood, already tense in anticipation of the coming interview.

The walled compound that housed the provincial government dwarfed the adjoining district administration. Akitada and Seimei passed through a roofed gate supported by red-lacquered pillars. The two trim soldiers, standing stiffly on guard, their halberds pointing skyward, did not prevent their entry but eyed them curiously.

Inside stretched a large courtyard covered with gravel and bisected by a paved walk, about fifty yards long and leading straight to the steps of the main hall. Behind its tall, tiled roof they could see more roofs, some thatched and some tiled, no doubt offices, quarters for the governor's personal guard, prison, archives, storehouses, and the governor's private residence and guest quarters.

The reason for the complacent behavior of the two gate guards became apparent. A whole company of guardsmen was drilling, and an official in the sober dark robe of a clerk detached himself from a small group of watchers and came toward them.

"May I direct you?" he asked, bowing deeply because Akitada's silk robe and stiffened black cap marked him as a person
of rank.

"I am Sugawara Akitada, the inspector, just arrived from the
imperial capital," Akitada told him, suddenly glad that he had
submitted to Seimei's demands. "You may take me to the governor."

The other man started, then paled and fell to his knees,
bowing his head to the ground. "This insignificant person is the
governor's secretary, Akinobu. Your Excellency is expected, but
we thought . . . That is, the forerunner of an official cortege
usually arrives well ahead of the dignitary. A thousand pardons
for not being prepared to receive Your Excellency with the appropriate honors. I hope Your Excellency had no trouble on the
journey?"

Akitada noted the man's nervousness and took secret satisfaction from their unorthodox arrival. He said breezily, "None
at all. I traveled on horseback, accompanied by my secretary,
Seimei, and one servant who will arrive later. Please rise."

Akinobu rose, his thin face a study of alarm and puzzlement, but he said nothing, merely bowed and led them through
the main administration hall, a large empty space with beautifully polished dark floors and painted beams supporting
the soaring roof. This building, Akitada knew, was for official
receptions and public hearings. Beyond the main hall they
crossed another wide courtyard and entered a second, somewhat smaller hall, this one divided by tall screens into individual offices, where many clerks were busily copying records,
filing documents, and consulting registers.

"The governor's library," Akinobu said, ushering them into
an elegant room furnished with shelves of leather document
boxes, handsome lacquer desks, and paintings. The wooden
floor was covered with thick grass mats, and several silk cush-

ions rested on these. "Please be seated. His Excellency will join you immediately."

When Akinobu had withdrawn and they had sat down on the silk cushions, Seimei whispered, "Who would have expected such elegant surroundings in a province?"

Akitada did not answer. He was looking at a set of very fine scroll paintings of the four seasons displayed on a standing screen. The governor was a man of taste as well as wealth.

They did not have to wait long. Fujiwara Motosuke bounced in, fluttering his hands excitedly, a wide smile on his face, and cried, "Welcome, welcome, welcome! How glad I am to see you, my dear Sugawara! All safe and sound? What very good fortune!" He spread his arms wide to embrace his guest.

Akitada was taken aback not only by the greeting but by Motosuke's resemblance to his cousin Kosehira. Though the governor was about twenty years older than Akitada's friend, he had the same short, stout body and, apparently, uncrushably cheerful disposition. There were a few silver threads in his well-oiled black hair and his mustache was thicker and grew downward, but Akitada had an eerie feeling that he was seeing an older Kosehira.

Seimei knelt, touching his forehead to the mat in the prescribed deep obeisance, but Akitada remained seated and merely inclined his head politely and without smiling. He was intensely aware of being rude, but he could hardly allow this man, who was under heavy suspicion of having diverted three years of provincial taxes into his own pockets, to embrace him like a long-lost brother.

The governor blinked. Under normal conditions, his rank and age placed him several degrees above Akitada, but Akitada had chosen to assert his temporary status as *kageyushi*, imperial inspector charged with examining the records of an outgoing governor.

Motosuke dropped his outstretched arms and seated himself, beginning a nervous spate of more welcoming words and concerns about their journey and probable fatigue.

Akitada interrupted. "Yes, yes, Governor," he said curtly. "I will take all that for granted and am much obliged for your greeting, but my purpose here is neither personal nor ceremonial. Let us get to business without further delay. This is my confidential secretary, Scimci, who will now present my credentials."

Motosuke looked shocked but received the scrolls with proper respect, touching their imperial seals to his forehead and bowing deeply before untying the silken cords to read.

He sighed when he was done. Carefully rolling up the papers again and returning them to Akitada, he said, "It is a great shame to me that these outrages should have been perpetrated during my administration." He paused and gave Akitada an almost timid look. "My cousin wrote that you have great skill in solving puzzles of all sorts. It is my sincere hope that your inestimable experience may allow you to help me find the scoundrels and clear my record before I leave office."

Akitada frowned. Much as he disliked the role he was forced to play, he had no intention of allowing Motosuke to transform him from official investigator into his personal adviser in the situation. He said coldly, "It will be necessary that we are given access to all your files immediately. You will so instruct your staff. My secretary will keep you informed if the investigation warrants it or if your testimony is required." He rose.

Motosuke, who had paled at his words, scrambled up also. "Certainly. I shall make all the arrangements," he said, then added timidly, "You . . . you will wish to rest. I am having quarters prepared for you in my residence. May I take you there now? You will only have to tell the servants if there is anything, anything at all, that you might require."

Akitada said stiffly, "Thank you, but I should prefer to stay in the tribunal compound. Surely you have guest quarters for official visitors?"

Beads of perspiration on his brow, Motosuke was wringing his hands. He sputtered, "Yes, of course. How stupid of me! Only, the guesthouses are not nearly so comfortable. And it is getting cold. A very uncongenial season, winter. I wish you had come earlier. We could have given you some excellent hunting and fishing. Still, I hope I may introduce you to some of the important persons in town. You will not like the tribunal food. It is for the soldiers and prisoners only. My personal kitchen, my servants, and my stables are completely at your disposal." He was babbling and looked so distressed that Akitada softened.

"Thank you," he said with a formal bow. "You are very kind. I shall be honored to make the acquaintance of the local dignitaries. Now, perhaps, you might show us to the archives. My secretary and I should like to meet your clerks."

They spent the day in the archives, talking to clerks and making a superficial inspection of the records. Akitada was favorably impressed with the efficiency of the staff and the neatness of the paperwork, but he avoided questioning anyone about the missing taxes. When he had seen enough of the provincial recordkeeping, a servant led them to their quarters. It was getting dark, and a chill wind blew across the tribunal compound. The guest pavilion with its covered veranda turned out to be spacious and pleasant and had its own walled courtyard. Seimei gave their quarters a cursory glance and asked the servant for the way to the bathhouse.

"It's still early," protested Akitada. "I wanted to walk around the tribunal first."

"You forget the dusty archives," said Seimei. "Besides, who knows, the governor may call on us to make certain we are comfortable. He strikes me as a most polite gentleman."

Akitada thought so, too, but would have preferred a less likable host.

The tribunal bathhouse was large and empty except for a burly, nearly naked servant, who stoked the fire and assisted with their bath. Akitada submitted to a thorough scrubbing and then went to soak in the deep cedarwood tub filled with steaming water. They could not discuss the governor in front of the attendant, so he emptied his mind gratefully of all his doubts and worries and relaxed.

When they returned to their room, they found letters from the capital and a pot of fragrant tea with a note from Motosuke. It was brushed in beautiful calligraphy on a sheet of thick mulberry paper and explained that tea was not only refreshing to the soul, soothing to the throat, and invigorating to the stomach, but would also ward off illnesses and lift the spirit.

Seimei was delighted. Though wine was the common drink, he had tasted tea from China and believed in its medicinal powers. Filling two dainty porcelain cups, he handed one to Akitada. "You should not have spoken so rudely to the governor," he said disapprovingly. "He is clearly a very superior sort of person, not just in rank, but in his gentlemanly manners also. I was quite shocked." Akitada, who still felt deeply embarrassed by the incident, said nothing. "Ah!" cried Seimei, tasting the tea. "It is very bitter. Drink. Drink. Remember the peddler! No doubt the dirty person had all sorts of nasty diseases."

"It was thoughtful of the governor," Akitada said. He sighed and set down his cup untasted. "I may have been too abrupt. He offered us welcome and hospitality, and I treated him with cold formality—as if he were a proven criminal. Oh, Seimei, I must either clear him or place him under arrest. How am I, a mere junior clerk of the lower eighth rank, to arrest a Fujiwara who is not only older than I, but who far outranks me?"

Seimei was unconcerned. "You are sent by the emperor.

That gives you the power to act on His Majesty's behalf. The governor was very properly humble. Besides, you are very good at solving mysteries and will undoubtedly clear His Excellency."

Akitada shook his head. "There was talk at home that they sent a junior clerk because they wanted this investigation to fail. The captain in Hakone thought so, too. I shall certainly be blamed if I fail, but it may be worse if I succeed." He reached for the letters. One was from his mother; he put this aside. The other was from his former professor. "Heavens," he muttered, reading, "Tasuku is taking the tonsure?"

"Tasuku? Is that the very popular young gentleman who was always reciting poems?"

"Yes. Love poems. Tasuku had a reputation among the ladies. That is why this news seems so shocking. The professor does not know what happened. Apparently, it was all very sudden and secretive." He had seen Tasuku last at his own farewell party, where his handsome friend had drunk too much, then made a scene, breaking his elegant painted fan, and stormed away. That, too, had not been like him, but it was nothing like this.

Shaking his head, Akitada was reaching for his mother's letter when he noticed a red leather box next to the tea things. "I suppose the tea was meant to keep us awake while we study the first batch of Motosuke's accounts," he grumbled.

"Not tonight," protested Seimei. "Even the strongest ox needs his rest after a long journey."

But Akitada had already flipped back the lid. For a moment he stood transfixed. Then his face darkened with fury.

"What is it?" asked Seimei.

"Ten bars of gold," said Akitada in a choked voice.

THREE

BLACKBEARD

Tora sighed with relief and pleasure when the girl with the tantalizing hips paid for her radishes and turned around. Her face was beautiful . . . and terrified!

Two saffron-colored backs moved to block Tora's view. The monks.

Mindful only of the panic on the pretty girl's face, Tora did not pause to think that monks took vows of chastity and nonviolence. If she was afraid of the two monks, that was enough for him to rush to her aid.

He bounded into the street, dodged a passing bullock cart, made way for a pair of elderly women, jumped over a stray dog, and collided painfully with a bamboo cage full of songbirds strapped to the back of a passing vendor. Birds and man set up a loud protest that attracted a crowd, and Tora was detained until it had been confirmed that cage and birds had taken no harm.

By then the girl and the monks had disappeared. Only the

vegetable vendor remained, staring thoughtfully toward the nearest street corner.

"Where did they go?" Tora cried, shaking the man's arm to get his attention.

"Oh, are you a member of the family?" the man asked. "So sorry about the young woman. The reverend brothers explained and took her with them."

"Explained what?"

That was a mistake. The vendor frowned and asked, "Who are you? What business is it of yours?"

Tora cursed and ran to the corner. It opened on a narrow alley, made nearly impassable by the many baskets, crates, and piles of refuse that had accumulated from the market stalls; lined by a warren of tiny shops, small houses, and fenced yards; and crowded with small children playing among the debris, shop boys running with parcels, and market women hauling baskets of produce. The monks and the girl had vanished.

Taking a chance, Tora plunged in, dodging human and inanimate obstacles at a run, pausing only to peer down each cross alley as he came to it.

At the third intersection he was in luck. He saw a patch of saffron yellow disappearing around the far corner and he put on speed. When he turned that corner, he saw them. The slip of a girl was struggling frantically between her two brawny captors. One of them slapped her viciously across the face.

Tora roared and leapt. Seizing both men by their collars, he heaved backward. Caught by surprise, they ended up on the ground in spite of their size. Tora delivered a sharp kick to one monk's ribs, then grabbed the other by his robe and raised him just enough to punch him in the face. The man collapsed without a sound. But when Tora turned to deal similarly with his companion, he saw him take to his heels, yellow robe raised to his knees and sandals flapping at the ends of his long legs.

The girl was huddled against the wall of a shack, the corner of a sleeve pressed to her bleeding lip.

"Are you all right?" Tora asked, walking over to her.

She nodded slowly, looking at him with wide tear-filled eyes.

What a beauty she was! Tora put on his most fatherly manner. "It's all right now, little love. I'll look after you. Why didn't you scream for help? What were those bastards trying to do?"

She shook her head. Suddenly her eyes looked past him, widening in panic. Tora whirled about. The vicious blow, intended for his head, landed on his arm, but the pain momentarily stunned him. The monk he had knocked out had regained his senses and decided to turn the tables. Tora jumped aside and retreated to draw the man away from the girl. Then he stopped and crouched. They faced each other, the monk with a broken board in his right hand. Tora bared his teeth and roared again. Then he charged. The monk dropped his board and took off after his companion.

Shaking his head at such cowardice, Tora turned back to the girl, but found her gone, too. His disappointment was palpable. He had looked forward to showering the pretty little thing with care and attention after demonstrating his manly prowess. Impatiently he walked a little this way and that, calling out, "Hey, girl! Come back here. It's all right."

The street was in a poor quarter of one-story laborers' houses, their small storage shacks and vegetable patches enclosed by tattered bamboo fencing with dingy laundry drying on it. There were hiding places everywhere, and not a soul was in sight who might have seen the girl.

Relieving his disgust with a string of colorful curses, Tora turned back toward the market when he heard a wheezing sort of cackle, and a skeletal hand, holding an empty wooden bowl, shot out of the dark corner between a shack and a broken fence.

Tora recoiled, then peered cautiously into the dim recess. An old man, bent, decrepit, and filthy, looked back at him with beady black eyes and a toothless grin.

"Strong words, stranger!" The beggar's voice was accompanied by the same whistling sound as his laughter. "It'll cost you five coppers!"

"Don't be greedy!" snapped Tora, walking away.

"You want to find the skirt, don't you?" wheezed the beggar.

Tora went back. "Tell me first. I wasn't born yesterday."

"Heh, heh. Neither was I."

Tora took another look. The beggar sat on a basket, one bandaged leg stretched before him, the other a naked stump with grisly scar tissue where the knee should have been.

With a muttered curse, Tora reached into his sash and counted five coppers into the empty bowl.

The beggar shoved bowl and coppers into the breast of his ragged robe, said "Follow me!" and stood up.

Tora stared. The cripple was standing on two thin legs, both perfectly good, though bent like tightly strung bows. He tucked the stump, apparently a piece of painted wood, into his shirt before scooting away down the street in a lopsided scurry.

"Hey!" Tora got over his astonishment when the old rascal disappeared around the corner and went after him in hot pursuit. Five coppers were nothing to sneeze at, and besides, he refused to be hoodwinked.

The beggar moved with amazing speed on his bowed legs; he knew his way around. They passed rapidly across a deserted courtyard, past several storage houses and through a creaking gate into a back alley, which led to a small grove of trees and a Shinto shrine. Past the grove, the shrine, and its red-lacquered *torii* gates, they reached a deserted street of warehouses and walled compounds. Here the beggar stopped and waited for Tora.

"What did you run away for?" gasped Tora, skidding to a halt.

The beggar pointed at a long single-story building resembling a merchant's warehouse. "Go there and tell them the Rat sent you!"

Tora growled and seized the beggar by his ragged shirt, lifting him a couple of feet off the ground. "Oh, no, you don't! I'll walk in there and they'll slit my throat, and you'll split the proceeds. I'm not so green I don't know the games they play with strangers." He pushed his face close to the beggar's and snarled, "You fooled me once with that false stump of yours and got your five coppers. Now you either produce the girl or give them back. If you don't, I'll make an honest cripple out of you." He gave the Rat a shake that made stump, bowl, and coppers fly from his shirt and scatter in the street.

"No, no!" whined the Rat. "You got it wrong. Let me go, fool. I tell you, it's not safe to make a scene here. Those monks are still after the girl, and they won't forget you either. Go in there and tell them what happened."

Tora set him back on the ground and released him. "You saw what happened?"

The Rat nodded. "I keep an eye on her. Now go! Remember, the Rat sent you!" He ducked, scooped up his things, and scurried away.

Tora looked at the building. It had a steeply pitched, thatched roof, but no windows. A double door was in the center, and a red sign proclaimed in large black characters that this was Higekuro's Training Hall in Martial Arts.

Tora walked up to the door and pushed it open. Inside was a vast, dim hall. A few thick mats lay scattered on the floor, and a rack of oak and bamboo poles used in stick fighting stood against one long wall. Another wall held archery targets of varying sizes. Bows and quivers of arrows were hanging from pegs. There was nobody about.

Tora saw another, smaller door in the rear wall and went

through it into a dirt courtyard. It was empty also, but a short bamboo fence separated this area from a kitchen yard adjoining a neighbor's tall plastered wall. When Tora peered over the fence, he saw the girl. She had her back to him and was bending over a basket of cabbages. He would have recognized those shapely hips anywhere. Calling out a greeting, he vaulted over the fence and came up behind her.

She paid no attention to him until his foot kicked over a pail of water that spread quickly toward her. When it reached her foot, she spun around and stared at him. He repeated his greeting. Her eyes were quite large and very beautiful, but she made no sound and it suddenly occurred to Tora that she might be mentally deficient.

"Don't be afraid, little sister," he said slowly, smiling at her. "I am Tora. The Rat told me where you live."

She shook her head and backed away.

"Stop running away." Tora was losing his temper and glowered. "Why don't you answer me? You'd think you could at least say thank you."

She looked frightened and turned to run toward the house. Tora reached for her shoulder, but before he could stop her, his other arm was seized violently and he was pulled off balance; he received a very painful kick to the back of his knee and a sharp blow to his lower spine, and was then lifted, spun about in the air, and tossed. He landed against the trunk of a tree with a thud. By sheer instinct, he rolled and prepared to launch himself against his attacker, a dimly perceived shape coming at him. His lunge was met by a raised foot. The heel caught him squarely on the chin, knocking his head back against the tree, and turning day into sudden night.

When he came to, he felt, through a painful haze, gentle hands on his face. A cool, wet cloth was pressed to his lips. He licked them, tasted salty blood, and opened his eyes.

He was propped against the tree, and a girl was bent over him, not his girl, but a stranger. He looked past her for his attacker. There was no one else around.

"I am very sorry about this," the girl said in a strong, clear voice. "I thought you were annoying my sister. I keep an eye on her because she cannot call for help."

Tora recalled the ungrateful wench and glared. "What do you mean, she can't call for help? There was no need. I called out to her several times. I introduced myself. She knew me. Not to mention that I had just saved the silly skirt from being raped. Why the devil should she call for help? What's the matter with you people? And . . ." Tora pushed her roughly out of his way and got to his feet. "And who knocked me out? What, by all the demons from hell, is going on here?"

There was no sign of his attacker, but he picked up a handy length of bamboo just in case.

"I said I was sorry." The girl bit her lip. "My sister, Otomi, is a deaf-mute. That is why she cannot hear or speak. I am called Ayako, and our father is Higekuro. He teaches martial arts, and we get a lot of rough characters walking in here because of our business."

Tora noted that she was good-looking, though not the beauty her sister was. But at the moment he was too enraged to care. "Oh, so I'm a rough character now!" he snapped. "Thanks a lot! Well, you can tell your father it's customary to inform a man of the reason before knocking him out. Jumped at from the back, too! No wonder you get thugs here. No honest man would fight that way." He hit his forehead with the palm of his hand. "And to think I listened to someone called the Rat!" The girl flushed and rose to her feet. She opened her mouth to say something, but Tora was just hitting his stride. He was outraged. "And what's more," he shouted, "you would both be better employed looking after the poor girl than sending her alone to the market where any villain can lay his hands on her. Two bastards in monks' outfits grabbed her from a vendor's stall and carried her off for their pleasure. I caught up with them just in time. She could've been gang-raped by a whole cursed monastery for all you cared."

"That does not give you the right to insult my father!" she flashed at him.

"Oh, for the Buddha's sake," he muttered disgustedly and tossed the bamboo staff aside. Turning, he made for the door he had come through earlier.

"Wait!" she cried.

He kept right on going.

When he passed through the exercise hall, there were quick steps behind him and a hand pulled his sleeve. He swung around and saw the deaf girl, her face wet with tears.

"Now, then, er, Otomi," he said awkwardly, "it's all right. Just watch yourself next time," and made her a short bow.

Her sister came up, too, and knelt, bowing her head. "This ignorant person apologizes for her words and deeds. They bring dishonor on our family. Please, for the sake of my sister, I beg that you will not leave without allowing our father to express his gratitude and share a cup of wine."

Tora hesitated. He had no wish to further his acquaintance with this bizarre family, but he was curious to see the man who had floored him so efficiently. With a grudging nod, he allowed himself to be led to the living quarters of the martial arts teacher, Higekuro.

These consisted of a single room, which served as kitchen and living area, tiny but very clean, and furnished with a built-in wooden platform for sitting, cooking facilities, and a few simple utensils. In one corner, stacked wooden cupboards formed steep steps to an attic space above.

A bearded giant of a man sat on the platform in the Buddha's pose. He was occupied with weaving the soles of straw sandals. His luxuriant black beard accounted for his name; Higekuro meant Blackbeard.

"A new student, child?" he asked the older girl in a booming voice when he saw Tora.

"No, Father," the girl Ayako answered. "A friend. He saved Otomi from two monks today, and the Rat sent him to us."

Higekuro dropped his work and sat up, looking at Tora with interest. "Did he, indeed? We are deeply indebted to you, sir."

Eyeing the giant warily, Tora stepped forward, bowed, and introduced himself. Clearly this huge, muscular man was the one who had attacked him, but what game was he playing?

"Pray join me in some wine," continued Higekuro, inviting Tora to sit next to him. "Two monks, did she say? Good heavens! I see that they must have been a handful. Your face is badly bruised and cut." He waved Otomi over and said, gesturing to Tora's face, "Go get some salve, little one, while your older sister pours the wine."

The deaf girl watched his lips carefully, nodded, and scurried up to the attic.

Tora looked from the giant with the magnificent black beard to Ayako. He felt completely out of his depth. Somehow nothing was as it should be with these people. Perhaps he had wandered among the fox spirits.

Ayako saw his frown and flushed a deep red. "It was my fault, Father," she murmured, hanging her head. "I am so ashamed. I thought he was trying to grab Otomi . . . and I'm afraid I . . ." She did not finish.

"You mean it was you?" Tora was aghast. "You? A mere slip of a girl threw me? Impossible! This is a joke, isn't it? It was you all along, Master Higekuro, wasn't it?" He looked from one to the other. The girl turned away. Higekuro shook his head sadly.

"I am sorry," he said. "I know how you must feel, and it

grieves me deeply. A girl." He sighed. "Try to forgive her. She is very good, you know. I taught her myself before I lost the use of my legs. She has been helping me in the school ever since, because I can no longer stand. Ayako handles all of the stick-fighting lessons and demonstrates the wrestling holds. I am crippled from the waist down and can only teach archery and give instruction and advice in the other arts."

Tora was shaken. He avoided staring at the other man's body and instead glared at Ayako. A woman fighter! There were stories about such women, but he was deeply offended by the impropriety of it. Women were supposed to be weak, soft, pleasing, and accommodating to their men. Perhaps there was some excuse in this case. The father was crippled and had no son to take over, but in Tora's view Ayako was no longer a desirable female.

When Otomi returned with the salve and tended to his split lip with tender care and many commiserating glances from her beautiful eyes, he felt completely justified in his opinion of her sister.

Ayako handed him a cup of wine and said quietly, "My father is the best archer in the province. No one can beat him. Perhaps he could show you some of his techniques. At no charge, of course."

Higekuro said modestly, "My daughter exaggerates, but yes. Allow us to show our gratitude. When the muscles went in my lower limbs, I concentrated on exercising my arms and upper body. Bending a bow and shooting at targets is good practice. When I became adept, I took on students." He pointed to a scroll of characters hanging against the wall. "We live by those words."

Tora blinked and nodded. He could not read.

" 'No Work—No Food,' " Higekuro read. "We all work in our way, even little sister. She paints and is very good at it. After the day's labors, the girls share the household duties while I make straw sandals. But enough of us. You must think us very poor hosts. How about some food for our guest, girls?"

Tora politely refused but was pressed to stay. While the daughters busied themselves with the cooking, Higekuro asked about the incident with the monks. When Tora had satisfied his curiosity, he shook his head and said, "I don't understand it. Otomi used to visit all the temples within a day's journey to make sketches for her paintings, but recently she has been reluctant to go. I did not know she had good reason to be afraid of monks. The Rat looks out for her, but if you hadn't come along, he could not have helped her. I wonder what made those monks come after her."

Tora snorted. "She's a beauty, that's why."

Higekuro raised his eyebrows. "There have been complaints about young monks from the Temple of Fourfold Wisdom outside the city. I thought it was just youthful spirits, but perhaps we had better watch Otomi in the future."

"Is it the big temple in the hills?" asked Tora.

"Yes. My daughters say it's very beautiful. The new abbot is a great teacher. Many people travel here to hear him preach. The governor and his family, and most of the so-called good people attend his services."

Tora was listening with only half an ear, his eyes on Otomi's hips as she bent over the oven. "Those bastards!" he muttered. "I should've killed them."

Higekuro followed his glance. "Are you a married man, Tora?"

"No. Never could afford a wife. Of course, now . . ." Tora decided it could not hurt to brag a little. "I serve Lord Sugawara from the capital. We just arrived."

"Ah." Higekuro nodded. "Your master was sent to look into the missing taxes. Don't look surprised. That mystery is on everyone's mind. Three times a whole tax convoy disappears—soldiers, bearers, packhorses, bag and baggage. And without a trace, if you can believe official notices."

Tora took his eyes off Otomi and gaped at him. "How can such a thing be? It must be a lie. Do you believe it?" he asked.

"Hmm." Higekuro looked thoughtful. "The present administration has been a good one in most respects. People will be sorry to see Lord Fujiwara go. My guess is that someone with the convoy, maybe on instructions from someone else, simply took the goods to the far north. There the bearers and soldiers were paid off and are too afraid of reprisals to come home."

Tora said, "Those soldiers must be cowards and crooks, in which case the local garrison is to blame. Perhaps the garrison commander is behind it. Yes, that must be it. No wonder rowdy monks run wild in the market."

Higekuro shook his head. "We have a new commander. He is young but efficient from what I hear. Besides, it's really the prefectural police who are supposed to keep the peace in the city." He gave Tora's shoulder a friendly slap and said, "Well, perhaps you and your master will solve the puzzle for us. Here's the food."

The meal was plain but tasty, and the company pleasant, especially Otomi, who made up for her silence with the most speaking glances and tender smiles.

So much so that, when he finally took his leave, Tora promised with great fervor to return soon and often. Otomi blushed and Higekuro smiled.

FOUR

THE GOVERNOR'S GUESTS

"*H*ow dare the man offer me a bribe the minute I arrive?" Akitada was pacing about the room angrily.

Seimei knelt on the mat, looking glum. "Perhaps it was a misunderstanding," he said without much conviction.

The door opened abruptly. "Here I am," cried Tora, grinning from ear to ear. When he took in the scene, he came in. "What's the trouble?"

Seimei glared. "Where have you been? The nerve of walking in here as if nothing happened! Putting one's trust in you is like relying on the stars on a rainy night."

Tora wrinkled his forehead in an effort to comprehend that remark.

Akitada stopped his pacing and said, "Seimei is very upset, Tora, and rightly so. Why did you run off without a word?"

"Oh, is that what's bothering him? Just wait till you hear." Tora sat down and looked around the room.

Seimei snapped, "Servants do not sit in their master's presence. Get up instantly and kneel!"

"Oh." Grinning at Seimei, Tora knelt. "You'll both be proud of me. I saved a girl from being raped by two monks and picked up some very useful information." He paused. "Is there anything to eat? Maybe some wine? It's hard to talk on an empty stomach."

"No," snapped Seimei.

Akitada came over and sat down. "Just tell us what happened," he said.

Tora told his tale plainly. When he was done, he added virtuously, "I slept in the guardhouse and ran over here before my morning rice to make my report. Now, if you don't mind, I'll go get a bite in the tribunal kitchen."

"You call that a report?" scoffed Seimei. "The whole thing is a tall tale! You were chasing females, I think."

"Never mind, Seimei," said Akitada. "Tora had some strange encounters and reported them well. Best of all, he has already become friendly with a local family." He pulled his earlobe and thought. "The Buddhist presence is puzzling. I wonder what it means. These monks seem to be a strange breed."

Tora grinned at Seimei's sour face and asked, "Shall I go back to Higekuro's and ask more questions? Given a bit of time, I may be able to pick up something useful, like who's made off with the taxes."

"More likely you're going to pick up something else in that house," said Seimei. "A wrestler with two young daughters and no older female in the home? It is a known fact that martial arts schools often maintain links with criminals and prostitutes. You'd do well to beware of that company. A man's faults are measured by his associates."

Tora lost his temper and shouted, "What do you know, you stupid old man? You haven't even met them. They're better than you. They're working for their daily rice instead of living off the nobility. You're no better than a tick on a dog."

Seimei's jaw dropped. Akitada, who barely kept a straight face at being compared to a dog, knew that Seimei had somehow touched a raw nerve. He said quickly, "That is unkind, Tora. Apologize. Seimei spoke rashly because he worries about you. Go back to Higekuro if you like, but be careful about what you say until we have a better understanding of what is going on in Kazusa." He brightened. "But before you leave, let's have a short bout with the staves. You will want to stay in practice if you are going to impress the warrior maiden."

◆

During the next days, Tora spent more time in town than at the tribunal, but since he presented himself dutifully every morning for a stick-fighting lesson with Akitada, his master had no complaints.

In respect to the mystery of the taxes, Akitada made little progress and remained as much in the dark as on the day of their arrival. Although the box of gold bars seemed to prove the governor's culpability, Akitada decided against a confrontation and sent back the gold without comment. What ensued was a period of uneasy cooperation with neither man referring to the attempted bribe while observing punctilious protocol at unavoidable official meetings.

Seimei and Akitada spent every day in the provincial archives checking the accounts covering Motosuke's term of office. Akitada's youth might have made him an unlikely inspector, but both his university training and his drudgery in the archives of the Ministry of Justice had thoroughly prepared him to search out, understand, and evaluate every financial transaction, from the collection of the smallest fine to the confiscation of land and property. Seimei wrote a very neat hand and kept notes indefatigably, and Akinobu, the governor's secretary, proved a pleasant and very intelligent assistant.

But the day arrived when they closed the last box of files and Seimei made his last computation. No questionable documents had appeared and all accounts were in excellent order.

"What do we do now?" asked Seimei.

Akitada bit his lip. "Officially, my work is complete. You draw up the proper release papers, I sign and affix my seal, and Motosuke's record is clear."

"But what about finding out what happened to the taxes?"

"I shall have to report failure. Unless . . ." Akitada frowned. "Unless Motosuke's private papers account for the sums that were lost."

"Oh."

"I know. Requesting his private accounts amounts to a serious insult."

Silence fell. Seimei hunched his shoulders and sighed.

"Very well," said Akitada. "Call Akinobu."

When the governor's secretary came in and bowed, Akitada told him brusquely, "We have finished with the provincial documents and are ready to begin work on the governor's personal accounts. Please bring them to us here."

Akinobu paled. He stared at Akitada, then at Seimei, gulped, and said in a choking voice, "I shall relay your wishes to the governor, Excellency."

Akitada looked after Akinobu and said to Seimei, "That was probably the most embarrassing thing I have ever had to do. Did you see the man's face? He was shocked to the core."

Seimei looked unhappy. "Akinobu is a very loyal servant and a learned man. I cannot believe that he would willingly serve a dishonest master."

Akitada said nothing.

The secretary returned quickly. Placing two large document

boxes before Akitada with a bow, he said, "My master wishes to express his gratitude for your trouble." He paused, then continued without looking at Akitada, "I also am deeply obliged that you take such care to protect the governor, and myself as his servant, from suspicion. Please tell me how I may be of assistance."

"Thank you," said Akitada. "We will call if we have questions."

When Akinobu was gone, Seimei and his master looked at each other.

"That was very generous of the governor," said Seimei.

Akitada sighed. "I am afraid that it means there is nothing to be found, Seimei."

He was right. In spite of a most thorough analysis of the holdings, incomes, and expenditures of Motosuke and his immediate family, they found nothing. The accounts were blameless and in perfect order. Not only had Motosuke not spent provincial funds for private use, he had drawn heavily on his private purse to improve the provincial headquarters and the governor's residence.

"Well," said Seimei, "at least you can return to the capital without having arrested your friend Kosehira's cousin for fraud and treason."

Akitada clenched his fists. "I have the feeling Motosuke is laughing at us. He knew all along we would not find anything. Any other man in his position would have been outraged when I demanded his private papers. I think the goods and the gold are hidden somewhere, and there is an accomplice. I'm convinced of it. Motosuke is too good to be true."

"Let it go, sir," Seimei pleaded. "It is hopeless. You can only hurt yourself and you may hurt an innocent man."

"Remember the bribe!"

"If a man is truly guilty, his actions will return to him."

Akitada shook his head and gave Seimei a crooked smile.

"You have a saying for everything, but I still have to find the missing taxes."

"What about the local gentry? Owners of large estates keep small private armies to protect their holdings. Sometimes they turn to highway robbery or piracy."

Akitada nodded and sent the servant for Akinobu.

"We have finished with these also," he informed the secretary, pointing to the document boxes. "Perhaps you may know of landowners with large estates. Are they at all likely to keep armed retainers?"

Akinobu did not have to think at all. "We have only five families of the sort you mean, Excellency," he said. "They are all absolutely loyal. The governor visited them personally after the first tax convoy disappeared to assure himself of their innocence. Four of them had sent their retainers to Hitachi province to quell a rebellion, and on the fifth estate, smallpox had broken out. Many people died, and so did the lord and his only son. His widow became a nun, and the estate went to a cousin."

Apparently everyone had a blameless reputation in Kazusa province. "Tell me," Akitada demanded, "what *you* think. Someone here is hiding an enormous amount of gold and valuable goods. Or do you also blame it on anonymous robbers in another province?"

Akinobu flushed. "No, Excellency," he said miserably. "I think we overlooked something. The governor is really very distraught and hopes that you will succeed where we have failed." Seeing Akitada's disbelief, he knelt and said in a choking voice, "It has been a great shame to me that anyone should distrust my master, for it is I who bear the blame for not getting to the bottom of this. I am aware of my worthlessness and culpability, and shall so inform the authorities. Of course, my poor property will not make up the great sum, but I have begun to sell off my land, and by the time Your Excellency formally closes the case, I shall place all I own into your hands." Before the surprised Akitada could find his tongue, he bowed, rose, and left the room.

"After him, Seimei," cried Akitada. "Tell him to stop selling his land. Tell him we'll try to find the culprit. Tell him . . . Well, you'll think of something."

◆

The week after he finished inspecting the provincial accounts, Akitada paid visits to the lesser officials in the city. He went first to Captain Yukinari, the new commandant of the garrison. The young officer impressed him favorably. Yukinari quickly produced pertinent military records proving that all three shipments had left the province at the usual time of year and under guard. Yukinari's predecessor had committed suicide after the second incident, and Yukinari had been sent as his replacement during the past summer. This fact and his subsequent efforts to clear up the mystery eliminated him as a suspect.

Akitada's next quarry was the county prefect Ikeda, an appointed official who reported directly to Motosuke but who controlled his own staff and the constabulary of the provincial capital. Ikeda was a middle-aged man of nervous disposition with a habit of quoting statutes and regulations to support his every action. He denied any knowledge of the tax matter vehemently: it was not within his sphere of authority. He also protested against any suggestion of criminal elements at work within the city or in the surrounding prefecture. When pressed for suggestions on how the shipments might have disappeared, he mentioned highway robbers in the neighboring province of Shimosa. Akitada formed an image of the typical bureaucrat, lacking both the courage and the imagination to plan and carry out a crime of such magnitude.

By week's end, Akitada and Seimei glumly reviewed the facts.

"The convoys could have been attacked in Shimosa, sir," Seimei offered when told of Ikeda's views. "That would explain why there was no news of them all the way from the capital to Sagami province. It also would solve all our problems and clear the governor."

"Which is what everyone wants," growled Akitada. "The garrison commander, who is no fool, went himself to search the route through Shimosa without finding a trace of goods or robbers. Yukinari is young but efficient and thorough and, of all the local officials, the only one who could not have been involved. He has no motive to cover up anything and is stumped. Goods, horses, grooms, bearers, and military guard all disappeared from the face of the earth without leaving so much as a boot or horseshoe behind." He shook his head. "Since this is patently unbelievable, we must assume there is a conspiracy, and here in this very city. Whoever is behind it is very clever, well informed about dates and details, and has a large organization at his disposal."

"The governor," muttered Seimei.

There was a polite cough at the door and Akinobu bowed his way in. He presented some letters to Akitada, explaining that another government courier had arrived from Heian Kyo, then bowed again and left.

Akitada scanned the two letters from home quickly but exclaimed in surprise at the third.

"What is it?" asked Seimei.

"A supper invitation from the governor for tonight. The abbot of that large Buddhist temple stopped in for a visit, and Motosuke wants to introduce me. He is also inviting the former governor." Akitada checked the letter. "A Lord Tachibana. Nobody mentioned him to us. He seems to have stayed on here after his retirement. Curious, that. Yukinari and Prefect Ikeda will also attend." Akitada jumped up. He waved the governor's letter about excitedly. "This is fortuitous, indeed. Just think, Seimei, each of these men is in a unique position of control in local affairs. One of them may be our man, and I shall observe them all together. I am a good judge of people, I think."

"I hope you won't be disappointed," Seimei remarked sourly. "It is said that he who hunts two hares leaves one and loses the other."

"Thank you for your confidence," snapped Akitada. "Now get my court robe out. Whatever your opinion may be, I shall eventually discover who is behind the crimes. Once we have an idea of the guilty person, all we have to do is find witnesses."

Seimei looked dubious but helped Akitada dress. As he handed him his court hat, he asked, "Was there any news from home, sir?"

Akitada said, "Oh! Not much. Kosehira writes, hoping that I am making good progress. And there is also a letter from my younger sister. Everyone is well. The girls are full of the news that the emperor's favorite consort has eloped with a lover. I remember there was gossip that Lady Asagao had disappeared. It seems Lord Nakamura left Heian Kyo at just about that time to return to his home province, and so suspicion has fallen on him."

Seimei sighed and said, "You see? Even His August Majesty is not exempt from misfortune. Truly, when the moon is full, it begins to wane. Anything more from your lady mother?"

"No. Just more of the same: she expects me to remember my duty to the family."

◆

The supper party took place in the governor's private residence, in a small room decorated with elegant landscape paintings. Under carved and painted rafters a dais had been covered with thick mats trimmed in black and white silk and screened off from drafts by brocaded reed blinds on lacquered stands. Five men sat there in the light of tall candelabra, talking animatedly and sipping wine.

An abrupt silence fell when Akitada approached.

Motosuke, in a pale red brocade robe over underrobes in many shades from copper to peach, rose with a broad smile. He led Akitada to the seat of honor on his right and introduced his guests.

"This is His Excellency, the previous governor, Tachibana Masaie," he said, indicating a gaunt old man. Tachibana, who was seated across from Akitada, had a thin white beard and tired eyes.

Akitada bowed and said, "I am deeply sorry that I was not aware of Your Excellency's presence here or I would have paid my respects before now."

The old gentleman returned the bow, smiled vaguely, but did not speak.

"This province is honored by His Excellency's decision to remain after his term expired," Motosuke said nervously. "He is a great scholar and engaged in writing the local history."

"I shall look forward to being instructed by Your Excellency," Akitada murmured, thinking what a fine cover such an existence would be for a remunerative criminal organization.

Tachibana smiled again without replying. His gnarled fingers absently traced the shell design on his deep blue robe.

"And this is His Reverence, Master Joto, the abbot of our great Temple of Fourfold Wisdom," Motosuke continued, clearly uncomfortable at the ex-governor's apparent lack of interest in the imperial inspector in their midst.

The abbot had been given the other seat of honor, to his host's left. Joto was young for such an eminent position—somewhere in his late thirties. The idea that he might be a younger son of one of the great families crossed Akitada's mind. Another

Fujiwara, perhaps? More possibilities of conspiracies. Since the
religious life required cutting family ties and bestowed new
names on its members, it would be difficult to find out. Akitada
did not like the Buddhist clergy at the best of times and noted
cynically that this man, like his rowdy disciples in town, looked
strong and well fed. No ascetic life for him! The shaven head
and smooth face showed the purple shadow of heavy hair
growth, and the full, almost feminine lips were red and moist.
His clerical garb also was of the finest materials, a richly embroidered stole draped over a white silk robe with broad black
borders. On one wrist he wore prayer beads of pink crystal.

Raising his eyes from the abbot's finery to his face, Akitada
met large, hooded eyes that regarded him fixedly. To cover his
embarrassment, he said quickly, "Your Reverence's learning has
attracted an impressive following in Kazusa. I am indeed fortunate to make the acquaintance of such an inspired teacher of
the Buddha's word."

"Worldly fame has no more substance than the mist that
hangs in the mountains before sunrise." Joto had a beautiful,
resonant voice. It lent religious fervor to his words. They locked
eyes, and Akitada knew he was being mocked. Then Joto lowered his lids.

"And you have already met the captain and Ikeda, I understand," Motosuke said, waving at the remaining two guests and
saving Akitada a reply. Akitada nodded to the handsome young
officer, in plain civilian garb tonight, and to the prefect, who
was wearing a modest dark blue silk gown. He thought Ikeda,
who was said to be about forty, looked strained and older
tonight.

The food, served by maidservants on red lacquer tray tables,
was astonishing. Even in the capital Akitada had rarely been
treated so well. Fish, shrimp, and abalone appeared, cooked in
soups and stews, fried and raw. Fresh, salted, and pickled vegeta-

bles and fruits followed, and rice was presented in every conceivable form: hot and cold, dry and moist, ground or whole, boiled in gruels, baked in cakes or buns, and steamed in dumplings. Their cups were filled with a delicious warm rice wine.

Joto, obeying his religious vows, was served fruit juice and vegetarian dishes.

Akitada ate and drank sparingly. He watched and waited for wine and food to warm the blood of the others, then he entered the general conversation with a courteous question to Yukinari about his recent transfer to Kazusa.

"A good province and I am learning my way about, Excellency," said Yukinari. "But I am sure we are all very anxious to hear what's been happening in the capital."

Akitada responded with news about promotions, reassignments, contests, and marriages, adding the recent gossip about the disappearance of one of the imperial ladies for good measure.

Motosuke looked uncomfortable and said, "Of course, compared to the magnificence of the capital, Kisarazu is only a humble place, but perhaps our guest may not feel completely cheated when he visits the Temple of Fourfold Wisdom. I think it rivals even the great Pure Water Temple in the capital."

"So I have heard," Akitada said, turning to Joto. "And it is quite new. No doubt due to your brilliant leadership, Abbot?"

Joto raised a graceful hand. "Not at all. The temple was founded under our august Emperor Shomu as the guardian temple of the province, but it fell on evil times. Few subsequent emperors have been as devout as that holy man. Only recently, with the kind support of Governor Fujiwara here, has it been my privilege to revitalize the faith."

Motosuke looked pleased and said, "Oh, my dear Joto, you are far too modest. Why, the crowds that come to your readings and sermons made the building of the great hall a necessity.

And now that you are attracting so many young acolytes who wish to study under you, the monastery buildings will soon become inadequate also. You have made the temple a great attraction for pilgrims from near and far."

Joto smiled.

Akitada noted the relationship between Joto and Motosuke and decided to look into the source of the funds for the temple expansion. "How many monks live in the monastery now?" he asked Joto.

The remarkable hooded eyes fixed themselves on him. "The number is about two hundred. Your Excellency takes an interest in our faith?"

"I am astonished at your great success such a distance from court," Akitada said truthfully. "And I hear that many of the monks are young, surely a comment on your persuasiveness as a teacher. Tell me, are you a follower of the Tendai or Shingon philosophy?"

A fleeting irritation passed across Joto's handsome features. "There is too much dissension in the world," he said severely. "Though the way to the Buddha is only a single way, yet all paths lead to him. I follow no way and yet I follow all ways."

A reverent silence followed that pronouncement. Akitada considered it. Clever, he decided. If the man had rejected Shingon with its emphasis on aesthetics, he would have offended the imperial court. Yet Tendai was a far more spiritual practice.

"I shall give myself the pleasure of visiting the temple in the very near future," he announced. "In fact, far from thinking Kisarazu a dull town, Governor, I find it very lively. The market is large and busy, and there were many people about. Surely all these visitors create security problems and increase crime?"

With a sharp glance in Ikeda's direction, Yukinari said quickly, "The garrison stands ready to keep the peace and protect the people and local government even if—"

"I wonder what happened to that fellow who used to run the garrison," Lord Tachibana broke in suddenly.

There was an embarrassed silence.

"I thought," Akitada remarked blandly to Yukinari, "you told me the man committed suicide because he had lost the tax convoys."

Yukinari flushed and glanced at Motosuke. "That is correct, Excellency," he murmured.

Prefect Ikeda, on Akitada's right, suddenly leaned closer and said quite loudly, "The memory's gone, I'm afraid. Oh, don't worry. He can't hear me. Age, you know." Seeing Akitada's astonishment, he nodded and smirked. "Sometimes a man loses his life force."

Akitada drew back in disgust, but Ikeda, flushed with wine, was not at all discouraged. Seizing Akitada's arm in a familiar manner and breathing heavily into his ear, he whispered audibly, "In this case it's a female. Tachibana has a young wife. Very young and very beautiful." Ikeda licked his lips, winked, and touched his nose. "She was too much for him. He's practically senile now. What a waste."

Akitada detached himself from Ikeda's grip. He strongly disapproved of the man's words and the manner in which they had been delivered, but he welcomed the information. If Tachibana was indeed senile, he was no longer a suspect. He suppressed his disgust and searched for a reprimand that would not make it impossible to work with Ikeda in the future.

Yukinari, on the prefect's other side, saved him the trouble. "I am certain, Ikeda," he ground through clenched teeth, "that His Excellency recognized that offensive comment as typical of a certain type of low-bred individual."

Ikeda turned white with fury. Joto cleared his throat and looked at them with reproachful eyes.

Motosuke rose and clapped his hands. "Allow me to make an announcement." Everyone looked at him in surprise. Smiling at them, he said, "You are all aware that I am scheduled to depart from my post and return to the capital before the New Year." There were polite murmurs of regret. "That is why we have the pleasure of Lord Sugawara's company. He is to certify that I am leaving no debts behind. Ha ha." His laughter sounded a little forced, and all eyes turned warily toward Akitada. "But," cried Motosuke, "there is another, happier reason for my return to court." The attention swiveled back to Motosuke. "I have been," he said, trying to look modest, "immensely honored by His August Majesty. My only daughter, who spent the past four years in these rustic surroundings, will enter the imperial household. As soon as we reach the capital, I shall have the great joy of presenting her to His Majesty."

There was a sudden crash. Yukinari stood up, staring dazedly at his toppled tray table and scattered dishes. Wine and sauces were seeping into the grass matting.

Servants appeared quickly to clean up, and everyone made an effort to gloss over the incident. The captain sat back down, looking stunned, while a beaming Motosuke received the awed congratulations of his guests.

In the midst of presenting his polite wishes to his host, Akitada was gripped by icy despair. He had lost his chance—no, he had never really had one—to prove his enemies wrong, to make a name for himself against the odds. Motosuke's daughter was entering the imperial household because she had been selected as a new consort, perhaps to become empress someday. No law could touch her father now, regardless of his offense, and Akitada's report must clear the emperor's future father-in-law of all suspicion. He sat stonily through a lengthy prayer by Joto for the happiness of Motosuke's daughter.

The party broke up soon after. It was during the confusion of farewells at the door that Lord Tachibana stumbled against Akitada and clutched his arm. As Akitada reached out to steady the old gentleman, he remembered his foolish suspicions. All of a sudden Tachibana whispered something. Then he detached himself quickly and hobbled out.

Akitada stared after him, not sure if he had heard correctly. What the retired governor seemed to have said with great urgency was "I must talk to you. Come tomorrow and tell no one."

THE WINTER BUTTERFLY

*W*hen Akitada awoke, the room seemed filled with an un-earthly light. He blinked. It was not sunshine; the light was too gray for that. Then he remembered the events of the previous night, and the weight of utter failure descended again. Moto-suke, who was his prime suspect—his only one—could not be charged because of his daughter's upcoming marriage to the emperor. Akitada had been unable to sleep after the banquet, but at some point he must have dozed off and overslept, for it was daylight outside.

With a sigh he slipped from the warm cocoon of the silk quilt into the chilly room. Tossing his robe over his under-clothes, he eased open one of the shutters.

A new world met his eye. Thin layers of undisturbed snow covered the graveled courtyard, capped the earthen wall, and turned the curving tiled roofs of the halls and offices into large luminous rectangles suspended in the silver gray of an overcast sky. From the bare branches of the persimmon tree next to the

veranda a white cloud of dust descended; a pair of brown sparrows, their feathers fluffed up against the cold, eyed him with
cocked heads and beady eyes. One of them chirped, and Akitada's spirits lifted.

He turned back into the room for one of the rice cakes the
governor's servant had left. Pulling it apart, he tossed the
crumbs out into the snow. His two visitors swooped down,
chattering loudly. Within seconds their call had been heard, and
the snow below the veranda was covered with noisy, fluttering
sparrows. They fought angrily over every crumb, pushing aside
the weaker ones, pecking at the youngsters. One little fellow in
particular hovered on the outskirts, making determined efforts
to break through and snatch the food but suffering repeatedly
from the vicious beaks of his elders. Akitada aimed the crumbs
in his direction but only succeeded in causing worse hostilities.
Eventually the little sparrow flew up and landed next to the
building, practically at Akitada's feet, where a scattering of small
bits had escaped his more cowardly fellows.

Akitada watched the little bird eat his fill and smiled. Sur-
vival in nature, as in his own world, depended on determination, courage, and finding alternate solutions to problems.
Perhaps his enemies had planned to bring him to certain ruin
with this assignment. In case his youth and lack of influence
would not bring him to grief, they had assigned him to a crime
they believed was unsolvable. Motosuke could only be accused
of stealing the taxes if Akitada was willing to face imperial
displeasure. Either way he would be ruined.

But here was a little sparrow that had found a way past his
enemies. And Akitada would also seize an opportunity: Lord
Tachibana's invitation. He brushed rice dust from his hands,
closed the shutter, and turned to finish dressing.

◆

It was really too early to call on a gentleman, Akitada realized, as he strode through the snowy streets of the city, but his was no courtesy visit. The more he thought about the ex-governor's whispered words and the circumstances of the dinner, the more convinced he became that Tachibana had been afraid and had turned to him for help.

Akitada lengthened his stride. When he reached the quarter where substantial private compounds, secluded behind high walls, lined the streets, he asked directions of a beggar, tossing him a few copper coins in return.

Lord Tachibana's villa was not far, but after Akitada knocked at the fine old wooden gate, there was a considerable delay before it creaked open. He was admitted by an aged male servant, so bent and decrepit that Akitada expected him to creak like the gate. Beyond the small courtyard rose the main house, its steep roof covered with snowy thatch, and its wooden walls and shutters, blackened by years of exposure to the weather, stark in their contrast.

"I am Sugawara," Akitada told the old man, who raised a hand to his ear and blinked at him uncertainly. "Lord Tachibana asked me to call today," Akitada shouted.

Without a word, the servant turned and shuffled off down a snowy path that led past the main house into the garden. After a moment's hesitation, Akitada followed.

The garden had been laid out by a master. Elegantly clustered rocks, shrubs, and clipped pine trees, beautiful even in this season, were covered with new snow. The path wound past a stone lantern and a small pond, where, with flashes of silver and gold, carp moved sluggishly on the murky bottom.

Their path joined another, this one swept clean of snow, and they came to a small building, a secluded pavilion surrounded by a wooden veranda.

The old servant climbed the steps slowly and slipped out of

his wooden clogs. Akitada, following, bent to take off his boots. He heard the sound of the door sliding open, then a cry. Quickly pulling off his boots, he looked into a spacious studio, its walls lined with shelves of books and document boxes, and its floor covered with thick grass matting.

The servant had his back to him. "Master?" he quavered. "Oh, my poor Master! Oh, sir. Would you see if he is alive? Oh, I must run for the doctor. Oh, dear! How terrible!"

Since he seemed incapable of movement, let alone running, Akitada said, "Calm yourself," and stepped past him.

Lord Tachibana, bareheaded and dressed in a plain gray silk robe, lay facedown next to his desk and just below one of the walls of shelves. A stepping stool was beside him, on its side, and loose papers, half-opened document boxes, and rolls of records were strewn about his lifeless figure.

Akitada knelt and felt for a pulse on the old man's neck. There was none and the body was quite cold. A very small amount of blood had seeped into the matting under Lord Tachibana's head. Akitada tried to recall what the medical texts had said about timing a person's death. He touched the old man's hand, flexed the fingers, and moved the wrist. There was some resistance: the body was stiffening. It meant that death had occurred many—he was not sure how many—hours ago.

But did it really matter when? On one corner of the writing desk were traces of blood and a few gray hairs. Akitada glanced up at the shelves. One of them, quite high up, was partially empty. And there was the toppled stool and the scattered papers. Apparently the former governor had suffered an accidental fall while reaching for some documents.

"I'm afraid your master is dead," Akitada said, rising to his feet.

The old man stared at him. His eyes dimmed with tears, but he did not respond.

"There is no need to go for the doctor," Akitada said, raising his voice. "Your master died last night. He may have fallen while standing on that stool and reaching for the boxes on those shelves up there."

"Oh, dear, oh dear." The old man turned alarmingly white and clutched his chest.

Putting an arm around his shoulders, Akitada walked him to the open door. "Take a few deep breaths," he said. After a moment, recalling Lord Tachibana's stumbling the night before, he asked, "Was your master troubled by dizzy spells?"

"Never. He was very healthy." The old servant gulped and suddenly became voluble. "Oh, yes, quite energetic and agile. I often envied him. And now he is dead." A slightly smug look crossed his face as he shook his head at the unpredictability of fate.

Akitada, remembering the frail old gentleman clutching his arm for support the night before, raised his eyebrows. "But he had a doctor? You were about to call him."

"Oh, no. Not his doctor. The master never had a doctor. Not even last summer when he had that stomach complaint. He did not hold with doctors, said they just made people sicker and poisoned them with their medicines. Clean living and hard work, he used to say, that's what kept him in such good shape. He told me to eat more onions and to stop sleeping so much and my backache would go away."

Fascinated, Akitada asked, "And did it?"

"It is very hard for me to stay awake and I don't like onions. But the master cured himself of the stomach cramps. Oh, yes. He cooked his own rice with special herbs and got well right away."

"I see," said Akitada. "Well, if you feel up to it, perhaps you had better tell Lady Tachibana what happened. Then you must go and report Lord Tachibana's death to the authorities. Go to

the prefectural office. They will know what to do. I shall wait
here until they come."

The old servant cast a sorrowful glance over his shoulder
and nodded. "Terrible." He sighed. "I shall run as fast as I can,
sir."

Akitada stood in the doorway and watched him as he lowered himself painfully to the first step to put his clogs back on.
His eyes fell on a second set of wooden clogs standing near the
door. They must be Lord Tachibana's. He bent to touch them.
They were quite dry.

Eventually the old servant staggered to his feet and shuffled
off in the direction of the house. There would be plenty of time
before anyone came back.

Akitada went back inside and knelt beside the body. This
time he studied the position of the corpse carefully and then felt
the dead man's skull. Through the thinning gray hair just above
the topknot, he felt a depression the size and shape of a large
oyster shell. The bone gave under his touch, and when he removed his fingers they were stained with blood and brain tissue. He was about to wipe his hand on the grass mat when he
caught the glint of something green among the hairs of the topknot and carefully extracted a small bloodstained shard, no big-
ger than his small fingernail. This he placed on one of the
scattered sheets of paper. It was slightly curved, with a shiny
green outer side and a dull white inner one. The broken edges
were red clay. The shard reminded him of the colored tiles used
on roofs, except that commonly their color was more bluish. He
looked about the room and then stepped out on the veranda
again. No tiles in sight anywhere! Every building in the Tachibana compound was thatched.

Returning to the studio, he wrapped the shard in the piece
of paper and tucked it into his sash. Then he sat down to think.

When he had first laid eyes on the body, disappointment had struck him like a physical blow, and he had been ashamed of his selfishness. Then he had remembered the urgency of Lord Tachibana's summons, and a suspicion had taken shape in his mind that this death was too convenient to be an accident.

Had someone overheard them last night and followed the old man home?

Akitada wondered if he would find an answer among the dead man's papers. The label on the fallen box read "Agricultural Products." Akitada glanced up at the shelves. There were other boxes for "Fishing and Shipping," "Silk Production," "Local Customs and Curiosities," "Temples and Shrines" (this might contain information about Abbot Joto's temple), "Merchants and Artisans," "Plants and Animals," "Entertainers and Courtesans," and "Crime and Local Administration" (another interesting title). Akitada looked for a box that might deal with tax collection but found nothing. There was only one other box, called "Dwelling Among Frogs and Cicadas." Intrigued, he took this down and opened it.

Inside he found an odd assortment of papers. On top lay several poems praising nature—Akitada was no connoisseur of poetry and merely glanced at these; then came ink sketches of rocks, plants, and flowers, in juxtaposition and in differing arrangements, followed by notations about cultural matters, copies of various old Chinese texts describing famous people's gardens, and finally, on the bottom of the box, a treatise entitled "Dwelling Among Frogs and Cicadas." It described the pleasures and chores of making a garden and bore Tachibana's seal.

Akitada was charmed by this private passion of the scholarly man and suddenly felt a sharp sense of loss at not having had the chance to know such a man. He was sadly closing the box when he heard the sound of running steps outside.

Replacing it quickly, he turned toward the door and noticed two pairs of square indentations in the straw matting. Each pair was about two feet apart, with a distance of four feet between the pairs. Something heavy must have stood there on four square legs.

Outside someone scrabbled at the veranda steps. Akitada went to take a look.

A thin boy of about twelve or thirteen was kneeling there. He stared up at Akitada with anguished eyes. "The master? Is it true?" he squeaked, his voice breaking.

Akitada nodded. "Lord Tachibana took a fall. He is dead."

The boy swallowed, looked woeful, then said, "I am to offer my assistance."

Akitada smiled. "You are very young. Where are the other servants?"

"Aside from old Sato, there's only the women," the boy said dismissively.

"What is your name?"

"I am Junjiro, Your Honor."

Again that catch in his voice. Akitada looked at him more closely. "You were fond of your master?" he asked.

The boy nodded and ran a grubby hand over his face. "What are Your Honor's commands?" he asked gruffly.

"You can point out your mistress's quarters. Has she been informed yet?"

A stubborn look crossed Junjiro's face. "We don't go there. Only her nurse is allowed. It's that way." He flung up an arm and pointed at one of the sloping roofs among the trees.

Akitada's eyes narrowed. He could not have mistaken the animosity of the tone, nor the ferocious glare that accompanied the words and gesture.

"Do I take it that her nurse is something of a dragon?" he guessed. "I'm obliged for the warning."

The boy sniffed. "She won't try her tricks on a gentleman. It's just us servants she hates. Telling lies about us to his lordship. Saying we steal and break stuff and we don't do our work. And when we get near her ladyship's quarters, she says we're snooping. She's an evil one, that one. She got most of the servants dismissed and yesterday she was at it again, telling the master that Sato's too old for his work and sleeps all day." He bit his lip, "I don't know what's to become of us now."

"I'm sure in time things will settle down," Akitada said soothingly. "Your master will have left a will that makes provision for the household servants. Now, I am waiting for the authorities who should arrive at any moment. Why don't you go and watch for them at the gate? You can show them the way."

The boy bowed and dashed off.

Akitada returned to Lord Tachibana's studio and bent over the indentations. They were sharp and clearly defined. Whatever had stood there had been moved recently before the fibers could resume their shape. He looked about the room. The low writing desk was the only piece exactly the right size to have made the depressions. In fact, it became obvious now that the desk was placed awkwardly. A man working at it would be facing the wall. Was it likely that Lord Tachibana would turn his back on the lovely landscape outside? Why had he moved the desk? Or if not he, who had, and why?

He considered the position of the fatal wound, the blood on the corner of the desk, the whole scene of the supposed accident, and looked grim.

On the desk were the usual writing materials, a neat pile of blank rice paper with a new writing brush next to it. The ink block in its jade container was well used and the water container was full. Akitada touched the ink block. It was quite dry. More surprisingly, he saw neither lamp nor candle, not even a lantern in the room.

He was about to bend down to the fallen papers when he became aware of a soft rustling behind him. He whirled and stood transfixed.

On the threshold stood the most beautiful girl he had ever seen.

Her eyes—lovely long-lashed slanted eyes in a perfect oval of a face—were on him, studying him carefully. The childlike soft lips were slightly open. She licked them and swallowed. "Where is my husband?" The soft words were no more than a breath. A slender hand emerged from the full sleeve of the shimmering blue silk jacket embroidered with colorful flowers and brushed a loose strand of glossy hair from her cheek. "You are . . . ?"

With an effort Akitada returned to earth. He bowed more deeply than the occasion required and said, "Sugawara Akitada, your ladyship. I was calling on your husband when . . . But perhaps you will allow me to take you back to your quarters. This is no place for you."

Her eyes flickered from his to the floor. Akitada hoped his tall figure was blocking her view, but she gasped. "It is true? My lord is . . . dead?" The soft voice sounded utterly forlorn. Akitada saw that her skin was so pale, it was almost translucent and felt helpless.

"I am deeply . . . er . . . yes," he stuttered, making a hopeless gesture with his hands. "I am afraid he . . . there has been an accident. Please allow me to take you back. You should not be here. Your servants should have looked after you better." He took a few steps toward her, but she slipped past him.

For a moment she stood transfixed, much like the old servant, staring down at her husband's body. Then she began to sway. Akitada caught her before she crumpled on top of the corpse and lifted her into his arms.

Her body was quite limp, a very slight and soft burden in his arms. He caught a flowery fragrance, whether from her robe or her long silken hair he did not know. The experience of holding a female of his own class in his arms was as novel to him as it was unthinkable in their rigid society. He felt himself flush with embarrassment. What was he to do with her? He could not carry her back through the garden. If one of the servants saw them, all sorts of gossip would arise. Even worse, the prefect, that dried-up, rule-abiding, dirty-minded Ikeda, would arrive at any moment with his coroner and constables.

"Lady Tachibana," he said urgently into a shell-pink ear near his mouth. He gave her a little shake. "Please, Lady Tachibana."

She stirred. Good. He shook her again. In response, two soft arms wrapped themselves around his neck and a silken cheek touched his. She breathed a piteous "Oh" and began to cry quietly into his shoulder.

He felt like a cruel boor, and for a moment just held her close as she sobbed. Then he tried again. "Lady Tachibana? You must try to be strong. Someone may come any moment."

The arms reluctantly released him, and she slipped down to stand unsteadily on the floor. He put one arm around her to steady her.

"You are very kind," she said softly, averting her face. "Forgive me. I had to come to see for myself." Her voice broke. She detached herself gently and took a few steps toward the door.

"Let me escort you back," Akitada said, following.

"No." At the door she turned and looked at him. Her eyes were filled with tears. Akitada thought them the saddest and most beautiful eyes in the world. Then she smiled, a tiny, heartbreakingly brave smile, and said with a little bow, "I have been very honored to meet you, Lord Sugawara. I shall not forget your kindness."

Akitada took another step and opened his mouth to respond, but she had already slipped away with a silken rustle, leaving behind her only the scent of her presence.

He stood on the threshold, bemused and oddly bereft, and watched her walk back to the house, her colorful jacket and graceful movements reminding him of a gorgeous butterfly caught incongruously in a world of winter snow.

SIX

FANNING A FOG

*A*kitada turned away from the empty, wintry garden and back to its maker's corpse. Bending to the scattered documents, he began to sift through them. Not surprisingly, given his suspicions, they had no bearing on the tax thefts.

With a sigh he replaced them roughly the way he had found them and stood up to stretch. Then he heard voices outside, one of them belonging to the boy Junjiro. Apparently the authorities had arrived.

He was mistaken, for it was a uniformed Captain Yukinari who was disputing with the boy. When Yukinari saw Akitada in the doorway, he bowed with military precision.

"I came as soon as I heard, Excellency," he said, running up the steps purposefully. "It's truly terrible news."

Akitada thought Yukinari looked pale under his tan and that his eyes had a tired, haunted look. Was it grief for Lord Tachibana? Surely not. They could not have been very close. There was the difference in their ages, plus the fact that Yukinari had only been in Kazusa since summer. Yet he looked as if he had not slept at all. Akitada said noncommittally, "Yes, indeed, Captain. But what brings you here?"

Yukinari flushed. "I had business at the prefecture when Sato brought the news. Forgive the rude question, Excellency, but how is it that you are involved in this?"

"I was paying a courtesy call and found the body."

Yukinari came closer, but Akitada made no move to invite him in.

"He fell, I was told," Yukinari said, trying to peer over Akitada's shoulder. "I have asked him many times to be careful. He was becoming quite frail. You know perhaps that he had passed his sixtieth year? A very great age, that."

This made Akitada think of the beautiful young girl he had held in his arms and he was inclined to agree. He said, "You must have known him then. He did not look particularly infirm to me. Such thin, ascetic-looking people often live much longer than their more well-fed contemporaries."

The captain seemed at a loss for words. He looked nervously down the path and scratched his chin. "Ikeda is on his way. He's coming himself. If you have more important business elsewhere, Excellency, I could stay here. I daresay you would just as soon not be bothered with this matter." His eye fell on Junjiro, who was hovering nearby, listening avidly to every word. He frowned at him.

"Thank you, but no," said Akitada, pretending shock. "I feel it is my civic duty. You, on the other hand, are not at all involved, are you? Though, of course, you may wish to offer your support to Lady Tachibana."

Yukinari's head jerked around. He stared at Akitada, opened his mouth, closed it again, then bowed and strode away rapidly. Akitada watched him turn toward the gate. He was puzzled.

This was the second time in as many days that Yukinari had betrayed some strong emotion.

Akitada was still pondering the meaning of Yukinari's behavior when Ikeda and his people, led by old Sato, appeared around the corner. Ikeda wore the same dark blue silk robe from the evening before, making Akitada wonder if anyone had slept the night before. With him were two minor officials and two constables in red coats, bearing the bows and quivers of their office.

When Ikeda saw Akitada, he made a formal deep bow. The others, looking confused, followed suit.

"What an unexpected honor," Ikeda murmured, coming up the steps. "The servant told me that Your Excellency had the unpleasant experience of finding the body. An extraordinary coincidence." He managed to make the last sound like a question, as if Akitada's presence were somehow suspicious.

"No more extraordinary than your presence, Prefect," Akitada said. "Do you always investigate accidental deaths personally? Surely this is the duty of the local magistrate."

Ikeda's gray skin took on an unhealthy flush. "Our magistrate is visiting a neighboring district," he said stiffly. "Besides, for Lord Tachibana I would have come myself in any case. Out of respect." He paused, then added, "Not that we were at all close. His lordship did not encourage familiarity from subordinates."

"Oh, you served as prefect under him?"

A strange expression passed over Ikeda's face. Bitterness and resentment were there, but also a sly satisfaction. "I did," he said, then gestured to his companions. "Allow me to present my secretary, Oga, and the coroner, Dr. Atsushige." They exchanged bows, and the prefect, all smiles again, said, "Perhaps Your Excellency would share some estimable insights into this matter while my people have a look at the body?"

Akitada nodded and stepped aside. Ikeda and his team removed their footgear and entered the studio.

Akitada described his arrival, keeping strictly to matters of time, condition and position of the body, and the general appearance of the room. Ikeda looked and listened politely, then excused himself to join the coroner, who was examining the body. The secretary knelt near them taking notes. The coroner finished very quickly, but there was a lengthy whispered exchange between him and Ikeda before the latter nodded and returned to Akitada.

"Pretty clear case, as I am sure you saw, Excellency." Ikeda rubbed his hands, a gesture that irritated Akitada. "Poor old fellow was working late, climbed on that stool, lost his balance, slipped, hit his head on the corner of that desk, and died. The stool, the scattered documents, the position of the body, and the traces of blood and hair on the desk all support that. It probably happened late last night. However, my poor provincial skills are hardly a match for Your Excellency's vastly superior training. I humbly beg your views."

Akitada hesitated, then said, "It is winter and the early morning hours are chilly. Death could have occurred much later during the night or even early this morning. And the wound in the skull suggests a heavy blow to the top of the head, I think."

"Ah, just as I said." Ikeda nodded. "The servant told me his master often works quite late. The evidence speaks for itself. The old gentleman comes home from our little dinner, perhaps a bit dizzy from all the food and wine. He works awhile. Then, sleepy or light-headed, he climbs on the stool to get some documents. They fall on his head, stun him, and he slips. Nothing could be clearer. I am certainly grateful for Your Excellency's observation. Now we shall finish our paperwork, and I need detain Your Excellency no further."

Akitada glanced once more at the body, nodded to Ikeda

and his staff, and left the studio. Outside the sun had finally come out. He put on his shoes, passed the two constables, and walked up to Sato and Junjiro, who still stood on the path.

"I must be on my way," he said to Sato, "but I hope you will see to it that none of the papers in the studio are disturbed. The prefect has decided that your master's death was due to an accidental fall. He and his staff are finishing up now and should not have any need for the documents. I should prefer it if you would not mention my interest in your master's papers to anyone."

The old man bowed. Junjiro offered eagerly, "I'll stay right on the veranda and watch day and night."

Akitada smiled. "That is not at all necessary. I expect you will all be very busy during the next few days."

"Oh, heavens, yes," said Sato. "You haven't even finished sweeping the paths yet, Junjiro. Run, get your broom. I can't think how I could have forgotten. What a day!" He shook his head.

"Wait." Akitada looked at the path. "Junjiro, did you sweep here after it stopped snowing?"

Junjiro was surprised. "No, Your Honor. I haven't swept at all today. I was just going to when Sato came to tell us about the master's death."

"Well, it's time you started, boy." Sato glowered, and Junjiro dashed away.

Sato accompanied Akitada to the street. At the gate, Akitada asked him, "Did Lord Tachibana entertain many friends?"

"Not lately, sir. In the old days we had many guests. His lordship's first lady was still alive then. But that's all changed." He looked around sadly.

"I see you have served your master a long time," Akitada said sympathetically. "Nowadays it is rare to find older servants still carrying on. Most of them retire and let young people take over."

Sato sucked in his breath. "There's nothing wrong with me," he cried. "I'm as strong as an ox. People shouldn't think that an old man cannot do the same work as a young one. I've been with my master for forty-five years, sir. Since long before the second ladyship, and I've always given good service." He was shaking with emotion, and tears stood in his eyes.

Akitada remembered something Junjiro had mentioned and decided to probe a little further. "The present Lady Tachibana came recently?"

Sato took a breath and brushed at his eyes. "Yes, sir. She's the daughter of an old friend of the master's. My lord took her in as his second lady because of a promise he made to her dying father. When the first lady died, the second lady took over the household." Sato compressed his lips and shot an angry glance toward the house. He obviously had little affection for his young mistress.

Akitada said coldly, "There are always difficult adjustments to be made. It isn't easy to switch one's loyalty so quickly. Besides, so young a lady is not, perhaps, very experienced in household matters." He thought of the slender childlike creature who had smiled tremulously up at him.

"It may be so," Sato said dully. "There was gossip when her first ladyship died and most of the servants had to leave. There are only five of us left, and we mind our business. Junjiro and I are the only men, and Junjiro is just a foolish boy. I can't be everywhere at once."

"Well, I won't keep you any longer, but I shall be back to go through your master's papers. Is there some side gate I can use without disturbing the mourners?"

"We have a small gate to the alley behind the property. It's kept locked, but if you send word, I can have Junjiro let you in."

"Yes. Thank you. That will do very well."

Sato struggled to open the gate. Akitada, giving him a hand, asked, "You did not move any of the furniture in the studio recently, did you?"

"Oh, no, sir. His lordship didn't like his things disturbed. He was very particular about that."

◆

When Akitada walked into their private courtyard at the tribunal, he found Tora sitting in the sun on the veranda steps, looking glum. Two long bamboo staves were leaning against one of the posts. Tora said accusingly, "I've been waiting for hours. You are very late."

Even among equals this speech would have been ill-natured. From a servant it amounted to gross insubordination. Many another master would have had Tora beaten unmercifully. Akitada winced. He had decided to accept Tora on Tora's terms because he could not bring himself to spoil a friendship that was as strange as it was satisfying. Tora's total lack of subservience, his complete honesty, and his bluntness of speech and sentiment were more valuable to Akitada than mere obedience and submission. And Akitada was afraid that any attempt to change Tora would surely drive him away.

Now he merely nodded and said, "I left very early for an appointment with Lord Tachibana. When I got there, I found him dead and had to wait for the authorities."

Tora's eyes grew round. "Ah! Some bastard got to him before you could."

Precisely what Akitada thought himself, but he asked, "What makes you say that?"

Tora grinned. "You dashed off without telling old Seimei. I figured you were on the trail of something criminal."

"Yes, well. You may be right, though the prefect called it an accident. But let's save the details for later. If you're ready for a workout, let's have it now, and then a bath. I missed both this morning."

They stripped to their baggy trousers, tossing their outer clothes over the veranda railing. Tora took up the bamboo staves, threw one to Akitada, and they began. The air was still cold, but the sun had melted the thin layer of snow in this protected corner. After only a few bouts, sweat glistened on their backs and chests and steamed off their skin. For a span of time, they thought of nothing but the contest of strength and skill. The air rang with their shouts, the clack clack of the staves, and the crunching of feet on wet gravel. A few timid heads of the tribunal staff peered around the courtyard entrance and disappeared again. Oblivious, they advanced, retreated, slashed, whirled, collided, feinted, and parried stroke for stroke until their breaths came in gasps and their faces reddened with the exertion. Tora was, by a small margin, the stronger and able to push Akitada backward, but Akitada was agile and had learned to plan his moves. The bout ended abruptly when Akitada managed to twist Tora's stave from his grip and trip him at the same time. Tora landed with a thud on his backside and burst into a roar of laughter.

"Now for that bath," Akitada shouted, throwing his stave on the veranda and dashing off in the direction of the bathhouse. He felt wonderful, completely alive and happy. For the moment none of his worries mattered. He had finally beaten Tora. He had mastered stick fighting. The blood in his veins sang, and he leapt into the air with joy.

Tora followed with a grin on his face.

"You had me then, sir," he remarked a little later, when they were crouching naked next to each other. Two attendants in loincloths dipped rough hempen bags filled with rice husks into buckets of cold water and scrubbed their glowing bodies. "It won't be long till I'll have nothing left to teach you. I suppose you won't need me anymore then."

Akitada sluiced himself down with a bucket of cold water, gasped, and slipped into the steaming vat. The shock of the sudden heat changed to a blissful comfort. He slipped down till the water reached his chin, rested his neck against the wooden rim, and closed his eyes. He said, "Don't be silly. I can't spare you from your other duties."

"I thought so," said Tora complacently, and stepped into the vat himself. "I've got a knack for solving problems and getting to the bottom of things."

"Hmm," said Akitada dreamily. He could feel his muscles unknotting and his skin becoming soft and malleable. The steam settled in beads of moisture on his face and tickled, but he was too limp to care. He closed his eyes.

Lord Tachibana had asked him to come—asked him with both urgency and secrecy—and someone had killed him the same night. Why? Had Tachibana been killed to prevent his meeting with Akitada? Because he knew something that could not be passed on to the inspector? That something could only relate to the tax shipments. So far, so good! But there was more. Only someone who had overheard Tachibana's words could have killed him so promptly. Akitada tried to think of the men who were closest to them at that moment. Motosuke must have been nearby, for courtesy demanded that he accompany his highest-ranking guests. But who else? Yukinari? Ikeda? Joto? For the life of him he could not recall.

He decided not to force it and turned his mind instead to the Tachibana residence. It was the home of a wealthy and cultured man. The buildings, for all their simplicity, were large and beautifully designed and constructed. The furnishings and objects in the studio had been of the finest materials and craftsmanship. Akitada considered their owner. The fact that the ex-governor had spent his retirement compiling a history of his province proved he was a man who took his duties to posterity seriously. But he was also someone who loved gardening. A man of great seriousness and high moral purpose, but also of a spirituality that sought peace and happiness in the creation of beauty. In other words, a man of honor. Such a man would have abhorred the crimes against his emperor. Apparently he had waited for Akitada to arrive before speaking out. Had he also possessed wisdom? Perhaps not. For how could this aged man have taken to wife that beautiful girl-child who had stood so timidly on the threshold of that scholar's room, her eyes swimming with tears and her trembling lips so soft and moist . . . ?

A hand seized his shoulder and shook him, and his eyes flew open.

"You'll drown if you go to sleep," growled Tora. "Come on. Let's get out. I want to hear all about the murder."

They sat with Seimei around the sunken brazier in Akitada's room. A servant had brought the noon meal and they helped themselves to bowls of rice and pickled vegetables. Tora poured wine.

As soon as the servant had gone, Akitada told them about the events at the Tachibana mansion and passed around the green shard he had found in the dead man's hair. "He was murdered," he said flatly. "The body was too carefully arranged, and the murderer made a mistake when he moved the desk. Also, the head wound was on top of the head, not on the side or back, where it would have been if he had hit the corner of the desk in falling. Ikeda tried to explain that away by pointing to the document boxes. He insisted that one of them must have struck his head and knocked him out. But in that case the box would have been stained, not the desk. Besides, the boxes were not heavy enough to inflict a fatal wound. The top of Tachibana's skull was crushed. Ikeda seemed strangely eager to pronounce the death accidental."

Tora snorted. "An official! What do you expect? He's probably involved. That explains why the bastard showed up himself. Probably just sitting there in his office, waiting for the summons. That'd give him a chance to fix up any mistakes, too. He sure didn't expect you to show up."

Seimei bristled. "The great sage," he announced stiffly, "said that serving one's prince is the highest calling in the land. Those who serve in official positions do so because they have acquired an education. He also said that it is the lowest class that toils without ever managing to learn. You are a member of that class, and therefore know nothing and should keep your mouth shut when your betters converse."

Tora flushed with anger. But, to Akitada's surprise, he said only, "Let's hear your views then, so that I may learn and become a better person."

Seimei nodded graciously. "Very well. It strikes me, sir, that the prefect may be merely incompetent. Provincial officials," he explained to Tora, "are poorly trained in the investigation of crimes and he was filling in for the absent magistrate. What about the time of death, sir?"

Akitada nodded. "Yes. That may be important, and I wish I could be more certain. My guess is that Tachibana was not dead more than two or three hours when I arrived. And that, of course, means that he could not have gone to his studio upon his return from the dinner. He had changed his clothes. Also, there was no candle, and the room was without a brazier. He could not have been working on his papers when he was killed."

"But you said the body was stiffening," protested Seimei. "It must have been there all night."

"It was bitterly cold. That may have accelerated the stiffening. But whatever the time of death, I don't think Tachibana died in his studio. The murder happened elsewhere, and the body was carried to the studio to stage the accidental fall. His clogs were outside the door, but they were dry and clean. Besides, and this did not occur to me until I was about to leave, someone swept the path between the main house and the studio. The servants did not do it, so it must have been done by the murderer to remove footprints in the newly fallen snow. I wonder when it started to snow." Akitada looked at Tora.

"I think," said Tora, feeling invited to express an opinion, "that the murderer must be a strong man to have struck the old man over the head and then carried him across the garden. I hate to say it, but that prefect isn't much of a man from what I hear. Perhaps it was the captain after all. He's young and a soldier."

Akitada said, "Yes, and that reminds me. Yukinari also showed up and tried to get into the studio. And I thought he behaved very strangely when I suggested he might offer his assistance to the widow instead. Whatever happened, we forced someone's hand and that should bring us closer to the answer, but I feel as though I am groping in a fog. I know the road is there and I'm walking in the right direction, but I can't see my way."

"I can see it," cried Tora. "Remember the widow! She's young, isn't she?"

Akitada frowned. "Very young."

"And pretty?"

Akitada fidgeted. "Yes, you could call her quite beautiful."

"There," said Tora, clapping his hands, "is your motive. The handsome captain seduces the young bride. When the old man finds out the captain is mining for his treasure, having the better tools, so to speak, there's a quarrel and the captain hits him over the head."

"Nonsense!" Akitada jumped up, glaring at Tora. "Seimei is right. Your foolish tongue runs away with your dirty mind."

Seimei stared up at Akitada. "Oh," he remarked, "the boy may have a point, sir, though he puts it crudely. Not all married women are wives, you know. Such a great discrepancy in age creates disharmony in a household. But it will be easy to discover the truth from the servants. They say only a husband does not know what is going on. Women are creatures without morals."

Akitada snapped, "Enough! We are not getting anywhere on the tax thefts. Tora, you have been on your own this past week. While Seimei and I were going through the governor's accounts, you were supposed to talk to the local people. What do you have to report?"

Tora looked uneasy. "I spent a lot of time at Higekuro's, sir. Trying to get a picture of local conditions."

Seimei snorted.

"And what are the local conditions?" Akitada asked coldly.

"Well, it's a rich province. Plenty of rice, good climate, good soil. Besides, they have started making silk."

"Come, that's not news," said Akitada impatiently. "We saw the mulberry groves on our journey from the harbor. And silk was part of the tax shipments."

"Whatever it is, it's made a fortune for Higekuro's neighbor. Otomi said the fellow started out with a little shop, selling cheap cotton and hemp. Then he got to trading in silks, and before you knew it, he was a wholesaler with warehouses in the harbor and here in town. Threw up a high wall around his land and no longer speaks to his neighbors."

"Ah." Seimei nodded. "That sounds suspicious. The sage said: 'Virtue is never a hermit. It always has neighbors.' The silk merchant lacks virtue, or he would share his joy with his neighbors."

"Perhaps he's just afraid of being robbed," Akitada said dryly. "Is there much crime in the city, Tora?"

"No more than any place where there's money. Higekuro says there would be a lot more if it weren't for all the soldiers in the garrison."

"Captain Yukinari mentioned reinforcements at the garrison since the tax shipments started disappearing." Akitada pulled his earlobe thoughtfully. "I would have thought that the number of new recruits, along with the disciples Joto is attracting to his temple, must cause problems in the city."

Tora wagged his head. "I got the feeling that the people like the soldiers, and they put up with the monks because they make money out of the pilgrims. Even Higekuro and the girls are much better off now. Some of the soldiers come to the school for lessons, and Otomi does a nice little business selling her pictures to the pilgrims."

"Pictures?" asked Akitada.

"Oh, didn't I mention it? That girl's a fine painter. She paints scrolls of saints and Buddhist *mandalas,* and the pilgrims pay very good money for them, as much as a silver bar for a large one. You should see her work. It looks so real you'd think you were there."

"Where?" asked Seimei, literal-minded as always. "Saints and *mandalas* are not real. How can she paint them as real people or places?"

"Well," said Tora defensively, "maybe not those, but she did some real nice pictures of mountains and the sea."

"I should like to meet your friends sometime." Akitada smiled. "Otomi must be a remarkable artist if you praise her work, Tora."

Tora looked pleased. Casting a shy glance in Seimei's direction, he asked, "Do you think, sir, that someone like me could learn to write?" Seeing the astonished faces of the other two, he added with a blush, "I mean just a few characters. Some pleasant words a girl might like to hear?"

Seimei snorted again. "I'll teach you how to hold a brush and place the strokes," he said, "but such a skill is worth a great deal more than writing love notes to women. Women cannot read or write anyway. Their heads cannot grasp such matters."

"Oh, I promise to try very hard to learn whatever you teach me, Seimei," said Tora, "but you are wrong about Otomi. She reads and writes all the time."

"What about the other daughter?" asked Akitada.

Tora grimaced. "Ayako? She's a mannish sort of girl. Helps her father train his students in martial arts. You wouldn't like her, sir."

"Perhaps not, at least not in the way you mean," Akitada said, and thought of the fragile beauty at the Tachibana mansion. He got up, brushing down his silk gown, and said briskly, "I think I shall pay a proper condolence visit to Lady Tachibana. She is very young and inexperienced and may need some help in settling her late husband's estate. Seimei, you will draw up the final releases for the governor. And you, Tora, had better start to do some useful work talking to the people in this city."

Seimei regarded his young master fixedly and said, "More dangerous than a tiger is the scarlet silk of a woman's undergown."

SEVEN

LOW LIFE

𝒯ora decided to reassure himself of the safety of Higekuro and the girls. The day was overcast again and it was chilly, but no new snow was falling. His mind on Otomi, he strode out so briskly that he did not feel the cold.

He was passing the shrine down the street from Higekuro's when he caught sight of two saffron-robed figures and quickly stepped in the shrine entrance to watch them.

The two monks appeared to be begging for food. They knocked on a door, waited till someone opened, said a few words, and extended their bowls. The householder gave them food, and the monks moved on. Tora began to feel hungry himself. It was past midday, and his master's meals were light by Tora's standards. He was thinking resentfully of those full bowls when, to his amazement, the monks emptied the food into a patch of weeds and began the process of knocking and begging again. Could those ill-begotten monks be so spoiled that they were looking for particular delicacies?

It was not until they reached the house opposite Higekuro's school that Tora realized their true purpose. Here an elderly maid stepped into the street and pointed across the way. The monks asked questions, and the woman nodded, gesturing to her ears and lips as she spoke. After she went back into her house, the monks stood staring at the school a moment longer, then turned and quickly walked back the way they had come.

So the bastards had tracked down Otomi!

Higekuro was alone in the exercise hall when Tora burst in. He was practicing his archery with such concentration that he did not turn his head. Seated on a stool, he dispatched arrow after arrow, effortlessly and smoothly, into a series of small targets some sixty feet away, without once missing his mark. Only when the quiver was empty did he lower the great bow and look over his shoulder.

Tora applauded. "I thought I could handle a bow," he said, "but not like that. Why are the arrows so long, and how much do you charge for lessons?"

"These are competition arrows." Higekuro chuckled. "You use shorter ones in the army. And for my friends the lessons are free."

"I can pay now that I have steady work. Can we start right away?"

"Never refuse a gift from a grateful man. It diminishes him. Your lessons will be free, but today I'm expecting students. Will you mind returning another time?"

"No, but I need to see Otomi. Those monks have been snooping around again."

Higekuro raised his brows. "Really? Well, she'll be back shortly."

Tora frowned. "I'll wait for her then," he said.

"Suit yourself." Higekuro chuckled again and turned back to his practice.

Tora paced, getting upset and imagining the worst, until the door opened and Otomi and Ayako walked in, shopping baskets over their arms. He snapped, "Where the devil have you two been? Don't you know it's dangerous out there for two women alone?"

Otomi was frightened by his scowl, but her sister frowned and demanded, "What the devil business is it of yours?"

Higekuro cleared his throat. "Won't you join us for a bite now that the girls are here, Tora?"

"Thanks, but I have no time." Tora glared at Ayako. "Those damned monks found out where you live. I was worried about your sister."

"Why?" She glared back.

Her father cleared his throat again and said, "It was kind of you, my friend, but I think Ayako can handle a couple of monks quite easily."

Stung to the quick, Tora shot back, "How would you know? You haven't seen them in action. You're not safe if those bastards make a real effort. Just a couple of girls and a . . ." He stopped.

"'Cripple,' were you going to say?" Higekuro's laughter rumbled from his barrel-like chest. "My friend, I should be offended! How can you have so little faith in my skills and Ayako's? Teaching self-defense is our business. And the locks on our doors are strong. Don't worry! We will make sure that Otomi is not alone in the future. I don't think those fellows will be back. They would be very foolish to risk a bad beating just for a pretty girl." And he laughed again.

Ayako laughed also, and after a moment Otomi joined in.

Tora knew Ayako mocked him and was offended. He glowered at her and gave Otomi a reproachful look. "I'm warning you," he said, "those monks are mean bastards." This produced new gales of laughter. He snapped, "Forget it," and turned on his heel.

At the door, he collided with two of Higekuro's students, a couple of burly lieutenants from the garrison who looked scornfully at Tora's plain blue gown and swaggered past him. Tora felt like starting a fight but controlled his temper.

Outside, another saffron robe had appeared on the street. This monk made no pretense of begging but strode purposefully up the street to the large, heavy gate belonging to Higekuro's successful neighbor. His knock was answered quickly, and he disappeared inside.

Tora's ego was too bruised to go back inside with another warning and get laughed at again. Instead he remembered his empty belly and headed for the market, hoping to pick up information with a meal.

After studying the market crowd, he stopped a passing vendor and exchanged a copper for a handful of hot chestnuts. The man scooped a steaming serving into Tora's hands.

Tora howled. "May demons devour your testicles!" he cried, hopping about and tossing the hot chestnuts from one painful palm to the other.

The vendor watched with wide-eyed innocence. "You must hold them in your sleeve or you'll burn your fingers, sir," he advised.

"Thanks a lot for telling me," Tora snapped and walked away.

"One of those stupid officials," the vendor commented loudly to his next customer.

It was not a good beginning, but the chestnuts were tasty and warmed Tora as he looked for a friendly face, someone who might be inclined to chat with a stranger. He made a circuit of the entire market before deciding that Kazusa merchants were a singularly sullen tribe. Still hungry, he bought a bowl of buckwheat noodles.

"You have trouble with monks around here?" he asked the vendor, handing him his coppers.

The vendor ran an unfriendly eye over Tora. "Monks? No. They're holy men who spend their money freely." He counted the coins. "Not like some who rob a workingman of his few coppers," he added, glaring at Tora's blue robe.

"Hope your wife beats you," Tora said and strolled off. But the vendor's manner troubled him and, after a moment's thought, he stepped behind a stand to adjust his clothing. He pulled the long gown over his sash until it resembled a loose shirt and stuffed his trousers into his boots. The black cap went into his sash, and he loosened his topknot a little. Satisfied that he no longer looked like an official, he returned to his assignment.

When he overheard a fat market woman and her female customer talking about the ex-governor, he moved closer. If he could help solve this puzzling crime, his master would be very pleased with him.

"What's happened, grandma?" he asked the woman.

"Our old governor died last night," she said, running bright black eyes over Tora's tall figure. "A great man. It comes to all of us in the end, high-born or low, governor or beggar. It's all one. The Buddha himself was a prince, and he became a beggar when he learned about death."

With a familiar wheezing cough, a cracked voice asked, "But will it work the other way? I'd like to be governor for a change."

The fat woman snorted. "More likely you'll be reborn as a mangy dog."

"Well, then I'll lift my leg on you, you old turtle head," cried the Rat, and choked on a paroxysm of wheezing laughter. The old woman gasped and seized one of her long radishes.

The Rat skipped nimbly out of her reach and pulled Tora with him. "Well," he wheezed, "if it ain't the gallant hero from the tribunal. How'd you make out with the skirt?"

"Ssh!" Tora looked around to see if they had been overheard. "Come on, you old rascal. I'll trade you a cup of wine for what you know."

The Rat's eyes widened with delight. "I'll never say no to that. I know a place close by."

Even using a crutch the Rat moved so quickly that Tora had trouble keeping up. The old faker, he thought, but followed the hopping scarecrow, hoping to gather some prime information.

The Rat maintained his one legged guise until they reached a tiny wine shop squeezed between two other small businesses. It accommodated only four or five guests at a time and was without customers at the moment. A wooden platform held several large earthen wine jars and a round-faced young woman with a sleeping baby strapped to her back. The Rat perched his skinny rear on a corner of the platform, saying, "Hey, sister. Pour us some of your best. My friend here's paying." Then he unstrapped the false stump, laying it next to his crutch, and straightened his leg with a sigh of relief.

"Still at your crooked game, I see," Tora said with a grin.

The woman set out a flask of wine and two cups. Eyeing Tora, she asked, "What's a handsome young fellow like you want with a broken-down rascal like this one?" But she gave the Rat an affectionate slap on the back.

Tora poured and told her piously, "It's for the good of my soul, love! Every month I do penance by wasting my hard-earned cash on some lazy bum. It reminds me what I'll be if I don't break my back earning an honest wage."

She laughed and went back to her seat. The Rat raised his cup. "To your labors!" He wheezed and emptied it.

Tora watched the wine disappear down the stringy, dirt-grained throat and took a cautious sip from his cup. The wine was excellent. The Rat slammed down his empty cup and smacked his lips suggestively. Tora refilled it.

"And to your penance!" said the Rat, sucking down the second serving.

"After looking at you, I won't need to find another shiftless bum for months."

"Always at your service," wheezed the Rat, and went into such gasping convulsions of mirth that Tora had to slap him on his back. "Well? What do you want to know?" the Rat croaked when he found his voice again.

"I'm worried about the girl."

"Good grief!" cried the Rat. "Don't you ever think of anything but women?"

"Never mind that. When I stopped by Higekuro's a little while ago, another pair of baldpates were asking questions of the neighbors, and some old bat pointed out the school to them."

The Rat held out his cup and Tora refilled it. The Rat drank and held out his cup again. "Stop worrying," he said. "They'll be all right."

Tora felt ill-used. "Look here," he growled, grabbing the front of the Rat's filthy shirt to jerk him closer. The ragged garment came apart with a sharp rending sound. He released the beggar quickly when he saw that his bony ribs were covered with an ugly bruise. Someone had given the old man a bad beating.

"Look what you've done," whined the Rat. "I'm naked in this weather!" He shivered. "And me with my weak chest!" He coughed.

"I'm sorry." Tora dug into his sash and brought out the remnants of a string of coppers, his wages for the coming month. "Here." He counted out half the money. "Buy yourself a warm robe. That rag didn't keep your fleas warm."

The Rat scooped up the money and started hacking again. Deep, harsh coughs racked his bony frame till his face turned blue and tears ran down his face. Tora jumped up in dismay. "Some water, quick! He's choking," he shouted to the woman.

"Wine!" croaked the Rat. He coughed and wheezed. "It's the heat of the wine . . ." he coughed, ". . . that eases me." He wheezed, coughed, and watched the young woman pour his wine. "Bless you, both," he gasped, "bless you."

"Him and his fits." The young woman was unimpressed. She took her baby from its sling and began nursing it.

The Rat drank and Tora refilled his cup, waited, and filled it again. Gradually the cough improved. Eyeing Tora over his cup, the Rat croaked, "You're a good fellow. Don't you worry. Girls'll be fine. Ayako's a terror. Better leave 'em be and stay here drinking." He burped and broke into song in a hideous falsetto. Then he muttered, "Damn all soldiers," and nodded off.

"Soldiers?" Tora asked. "What soldiers?"

The woman looked up from her nursing child. "They beat him up, I think."

The Rat mumbled something, curled up on the platform, and began to snore. Tora tossed down some coppers for the wine and left.

It was dark by now, and he thought glumly that he had wasted all of his time and most of his money on two thankless women and a worthless bum without getting anywhere.

In the market, business was still brisk. Lanterns and oil lamps lit the stands and shops, and most shoppers carried their own lights. They cast a shifting, magical glow over the merchandise and customers' clothes. The food vendors were doing a lively business in the evening. Mingled smells of fried fish, spicy soups, baked dumplings, and roasting chestnuts hung in the air, making Tora hungry again. He had been quaffing wine with the Rat when he should have eaten a wholesome meal. Being an investigator was hard on one's belly.

When he caught a whiff of his favorite food, fried rice cakes, his mouth watered. He felt for his meager string of coppers and started looking.

The rice-cake vendor was a poorly dressed young man who passed through the crowd selling the tasty morsels from two bamboo containers suspended at the ends of a pole he balanced on one thin shoulder.

Tora quickly overtook him and stepped in his path. "Got you," he cried, barring the man's way. "And about time, too."

The thin fellow stared at him with a frightened expression and started to back away.

Tora grabbed his sleeve. "Not so fast, my friend," he said, peering into the bamboo containers filled with fat, crispy cakes. "So many! Business must be good."

"No, no. I hardly sold any. Let me go, please."

Tora, who really wanted some of the tasty cakes pretty badly by now, tightened his grip. "Not so quick," he said sternly. "I'm not finished with you. Where are your manners? You clearly don't know how to treat your patrons."

The vendor cringed. "Sorry, master," he muttered. "I didn't recognize you right away. It was dark last night. Believe me, I'll pay my dues. You've explained the advantages very well. I was going to stop by the Heavenly Abode on my way home." He reached into his shirt. "See, here it is! Take it! But please tell them that Matahiro paid up."

Tora was so astonished by this speech that he released the man. He felt a heavy package being pressed into his hand and saw the vendor disappear into the crowd as if he had been sucked into a whirlpool.

The package had the unmistakable feel of metal coins. The vendor had mistaken him for another man. Tora unwrapped the paper. Ten pieces of silver! A lot of money for a poor dumpling man. Perhaps it was a gaming debt.

Tora spent some fruitless time trying to return the silver, but the vendor was gone. Finally he tucked the package into his sash. Another frustrating encounter, he thought grumpily. The memory of the fried cakes lingered, and his stomach felt emptier than ever.

The name the vendor had mentioned, Heavenly Abode, sounded like a restaurant. He would leave the silver there and get a bite to eat at the same time. After the Rat's inroads on his string of coppers, he hoped it was cheap. He asked a woman for directions. She gave him a funny look but pointed down a dark alley where a dim lantern gleamed.

More like the pit of hell than a heavenly abode, Tora thought, when he fell down the steps after ducking under the torn mat that covered the doorway. Someone laughed. Tora was in a murky cavern of a room stinking of rancid grease and unwashed bodies. A few oil lamps added their own pungent stench and sooty smoke without shedding much light.

When Tora's watering eyes adjusted, he saw that the room contained a crudely made serving counter and a dirt floor where several men of the poorest class—bare-legged laborers in loincloths and quilted cotton jackets—were eating or getting drunk. They greeted his arrival as a comic entertainment.

Tora got to his feet. The food, he thought, must be cheap and decent, or the place would be empty. Besides, he was more likely to pick up useful information in a low dive than in a respectable business.

The owner, a fat, bald fellow, was leaning on the counter, looking at Tora from under bushy eyebrows.

"Salted vegetables and a pitcher of your best wine, my large friend," Tora called out to him and took a seat beside one of the other guests. His neighbor lowered his bowl and wiped his mouth with a sleeve. Tora asked, "What's that you're eating, brother? Is it good? I'm half-starved."

The man grinned. "Best bean soup in town, if you can hold

it. And if you can't, run outside. Old Denzo's stunk up the place enough." There was a burst of laughter from the others, and old Denzo stood up to demonstrate his powers.

Tora applauded, then became aware of the host's round belly looming over him.

"Perhaps the gentleman would prefer the food at the Golden Dragon," the fat man growled. "It's the big restaurant at the corner of the market."

"Why?" asked Tora, looking up at him. "If I wanted to eat there, I would've gone there. You must be all belly and no brains to tell a paying customer to eat elsewhere. I want some bean soup, and bring my friends here some wine."

Suddenly he was everybody's friend. The fat host muttered under his breath and waddled away. Tora hoped the wine would loosen tongues. "Tell me . . ." he began, when the curtain flapped back and three strangers joined them. They waited for the other men to move away, then sat down next to Tora. The room had fallen silent.

Tora looked them over: an ugly scarred brute, a fat giant, and a short, long-nosed man. He put on a ferocious scowl. "What the hell do you think you're doing?" he demanded. "Sit someplace else. I was talking to my friends."

"We like it here," said the ugly brute with the scarred face. His open shirt revealed more scars. Knife fights, Tora decided and became intensely aware of being unarmed. The scarred man bared broken teeth as his deep-set black eyes roamed over Tora. His two companions stared silently. The giant had a strangely small shaven head perched on his enormous shoulders. He had the vacuous look of a baby. Slow in the head, thought Tora, and all the more dangerous for that. The third man was middle-aged, with the sharp features and sly eyes of a weasel. All three looked at Tora hungrily.

Courage aside, Tora had enough sense not to tangle with them in this place. Any one of the other customers might join in and knife him in the back. He tried bluster.

"If you're hard up for company, scum," he sneered, half rising, "let's step outside and I'll make all three of you wish you'd never left your mother's tits."

The big oaf reached into his sleeve and pulled out a large knife. He licked his lips. "Can I cut him a little, boss?" he wheedled in a thin voice. The hair bristled on Tora's scalp.

The scarred man gave the moron a box on the ear without taking his eyes off Tora. The giant whimpered and put his knife away.

"We saw you collect our money from the rice-cake vendor," Scarface said in a flat voice. "We don't allow strangers to move into our territory and take what's rightfully ours."

So that was it. Protection money. These hoodlums collected money from small merchants with threats of roughing them up or worse. The rice-cake vendor had mistaken Tora for one of their gang and landed him in a bad spot. Even if he turned over the money, they would hardly let him walk away in one piece. His only chance lay in quick and decisive action.

Familiar with the fighting practiced by street gangs, Tora suddenly lashed out with his right arm in a backhanded sweep, letting the knuckles of his balled fist land squarely in the face of the small man. Simultaneously he rose and kicked the scarred man in the stomach. The idiot tried to get up but lost his balance stumbling over his friend. Before he could reason out the incident and reach for his knife again, Tora kicked him in the head. The idiot's face puckered up like that of a hurt child.

The small man was not moving, but Scarface was up and coming at him with a knife in each hand.

A two-handed knife fighter was the most dangerous. Tora

retreated, saw a wooden stool, and grabbed it to ward off the knife thrusts while looking for a weapon of his own. There was nothing, not even a broom handle.

Scarface slashed and Tora dodged, fending off one knife with the stool, then twisting out of reach of the other one. It was an uneven contest he had little hope of winning. He was about to try to make a run for it when someone extended a bamboo pole to him.

Tora snatched it with his free hand and immediately attacked. Scarface cursed when one of his knives skittered across the floor. His right arm hung useless. But he kept coming, his face distorted with pain, his eyes wild, the long puckered scar that ran from his hairline to his nose turning blood-red with his fury. A mad animal.

Tora dropped the stool and concentrated on working the pole. He almost enjoyed himself. The scarred man suffered a hard hit on the skull and another vicious jab in the stomach before the pole deprived him of his remaining knife, then pinned him against the wall by the neck.

Noisy applause broke out. Tora, breathing hard, adjusted the end of the pole firmly on his opponent's windpipe and looked around. What he saw almost caused him to drop his weapon.

The giant was stretched out on the floor. On his back sat a burly man with thick gray hair and beard surrounding a deeply tanned face. His eyes twinkled gleefully at Tora, and the grin showed a gap in his front teeth.

"Hito!" gasped Tora. "What the devil are you doing here?"

The other man gave a laugh. "Glad I found you in time, little brother. I was passing and thought I heard your voice."

The scarred man began to gasp and choke and his face turned purple. Tora eased the pressure on the pole a little. "Go get some rope," he told the host, who was wringing his hands and goggling at the scene.

Hidesato asked, "What will you do with them?"

Tora considered. "Turn them over to the constables?"

There was a collective gasp from the patrons. A few men began to inch toward the door. The host, coming back with an armful of rope, cried, "Not the constables! We'll take care of them ourselves."

Their disposition could wait, but they made secure bundles of the three before Tora and Hidesato sat down together to drink to their unexpected reunion.

"You've been well?" Tora asked, looking at the gray in Hidesato's hair and beard.

The other man grimaced. "Left the army a month after you did. Been knocking about since then, hiring myself out to people with more money than fighting skill."

Their fat host became obsequious, bringing a large pitcher of wine, two bowls of soup, and a platter of rice and vegetables. "On the house," he said with an ingratiating smile.

"Much obliged," said Tora, raising his cup to Hidesato. "Welcome, older brother!" he said. "It warms my heart to see you. Wait till you hear what's happened to me."

Hidesato took a sip of his soup and nodded at Tora's clothes. "You look very respectable."

"More than respectable. I'm special assistant to . . ." He leaned across and whispered in Hidesato's ear.

Hidesato stared, then raised his cup and said dryly, "I congratulate you." Turning to the host, he said, "Correct me if I'm wrong, but we got the feeling you don't like those men over there any better than we do."

"Those bastards?" The host spat in the direction of their prisoners. "Been paying the weasel and his idiot for years, and a small fortune since the ugly devil joined them. Most of my customers get knocked about every time they show up. I'd like to see them flayed alive, but we don't care much for constables here."

"They've been extorting money from the market vendors," Tora said.

Hidesato raised his brows. "You don't say. A gang."

"Tax collectors," shouted the comedian in the group. "Taking from the poor just like those cursed dogs the governor sends around."

All eyes turned to Tora and an embarrassed silence fell.

Hidesato grinned.

Tora inwardly cursed his blue robe. "I'm just a visitor," he said, "and I work for wages like you do. But if we let those three bastards go, they'll be back and take it out on you."

The host paled. "He's right. Let's kill them," he decided.

"That'll bring the constables for sure," Tora pointed out.

The host waddled behind the counter and brought out a heavy earthen jar. Delving into its clinking depth, he took out ten silver pieces. "Here," he said, counting out five each for Tora and Hidesato. "That's for you if you get rid of them."

"No," said Tora, pushing the silver back.

"C'mon! A quick slash with a knife and it's done. And we'll help you carry the bodies to Squatters' Field later. They always find bodies there. Nobody'll know the difference, and you'll be long gone before there's any trouble."

"No. We're not hired assassins," snapped Tora.

Hidesato gave him a long look, then got up to peer at the three ruffians. "You know their names?" he asked the host.

The host spat again. "Scum. The big monster's Yushi. A guy I know watched him disembowel a puppy. Yushi used to work for the thin geezer, Jubei. Jubei was a pimp for the soldiers till they found out he trained his girls to roll their customers. They beat him up and told him to stay out of that business. That's when he got into the extortion racket around the market. Then, a couple of weeks ago, the ugly guy showed up. We call him Scarface. Nobody knows his name."

"They should be in jail," said Tora stubbornly.

"Suppose," said Hidesato, "my very official-looking friend here tells the constables they attacked him, which is no more than the truth. You all say that you're not sure what happened exactly. The constables take them away and lock them up till the next court session. If no one appears against them, the magistrate will let them go, but they'll leave you alone from then on, for fear that you'll testify against them. They may even move to another province."

This was considered and met with approval. The constables arrived, listened to Tora's story, and departed with their prisoners.

Tora breathed a sigh of relief. He was going to invite Hidesato to his quarters for the night so that they could talk over old times, but when he looked around for him, his friend was gone. Without so much as a good-bye.

EIGHT

THE WIDOW

*A*kitada, neatly robed and wearing his official hat, knocked for the second time that day on the gate of the Tachibana mansion. By now the news had spread and he had an audience of a gaggle of curious idlers. This time the response was prompt and he was admitted by Junjiro, who was dressed in the hempen robe appropriate for servants in mourning for their master but also wore an expression of cheerful importance. When he saw Akitada, he straightened his back, folded his arms across his chest, and bowed deeply from the waist. In a high, penetrating voice, he sang out, "Welcome. This poor hovel is greatly honored by Your Highness's condescension."

This provoked a burst of laughter from the people in the street. Akitada stepped in quickly. "Ssh!" he said. "Close the gate."

Junjiro obeyed. "It is not the right thing to say?"

"No. Only your master and mistress can refer to their home in those terms. And if you must use an honorific, er, a title for me, you may call me 'Excellency.'"

"I am grateful for your instruction, Your Excellency," said Junjiro, then spoiled the effect by adding with a broad grin, "You missed all the fun. All those baldpates chanting and hopping about on their bare feet, the servants squalling, pulling their hair, and looking like sacks of beans in these hemp gowns"—he held out his robe and grimaced—"and outside the gate everybody's trying to see what's going on. Just like a *bon* festival."

"Aren't you grieving for your master?" asked Akitada, astonished at such callousness.

"Time enough to grieve when the mistress throws us out," said the boy. "I like to eat."

Akitada opened his mouth but thought better of it. "Take me to her," he demanded instead.

"She's in there with the corpse and the monks," Junjiro informed him crudely, pointing to the main building.

Muffled sounds of Buddhist chanting came from inside. On the veranda, Junjiro helped Akitada remove his wooden clogs and then opened the door.

The odor of incense overwhelmed Akitada. Chanting flowed back and forth across the dusky space, seemingly drawn, like a tide, by the periodic tinkling of small brass bells at opposite ends of the room: the waves of sound swelled and pulsated with the rhythmic throbbing of drumbeats. He could barely discern shapes in the thick fog of incense. It hung low over the seated figures of yellow-robed monks, the pale hempen gowns of kneeling servants, and the darker, more formal robes of visitors, all of them faceless with their backs toward Akitada, all of them motionless in respect to the dead. Wisps of incense floated about standing candles and outlined each flame in a glowing nimbus of smoke and light.

The thick scent of burning aloe and sandalwood made Akitada's eyes water and his nose burn. He blinked and perceived in the center of the flickering candles the funeral palanquin with

the shrouded body of the late Lord Tachibana seated like some
deity about to be carried in procession.

Behind and toward the side of the palanquin, a screen had
been placed. The corner of a full sleeve showed at its bottom.
The widow.

Suddenly aware that she had a clear view of him from behind the wooden lattice, Akitada approached the palanquin,
bowed, and took a seat as close to the screen as he dared.

He could now see the monks and mourners better. The servants, only five of them, were clustered about old Sato and
looked not so much sad as fearful. The visitors, all male and
strangers to Akitada, wore the politely pious expressions of
people who would rather be elsewhere. Where were Tachibana's
friends? Had he outlived them all? Where were the friends of the
widow?

Poor young girl! She had no family of her own, he knew, and
was too young and too timid to have cultivated friendships with
ladies from neighboring families. His heart went out to her and
he glanced toward the screen. He thought he heard a soft sob,
but the sound was drowned out by a renewed tinkling of brass
bells.

The monk who handled the bells was young and emphatic
in his movements, too emphatic perhaps. The drumming also
rolled along unevenly, and Akitada, who was no connoisseur in
matters of Buddhist ritual, thought the chanting lacked practice. This struck him as strange, and he studied the faces of the
monks. They were almost all young, their expressions a mix of
self-importance and boredom. They reminded him of the
young recruits to the imperial guard he had watched at their
first public parades in the *Daidairi,* the seat of the imperial administration, not sure whether they ought to be insulted or flat-
tered by the function they had been given. There was certainly
nothing monklike about these young men. Still, they did not

look quite as reprehensible as the ones Akitada had seen in the market or seem at all capable of behaving like the two who had abducted Tora's deaf girl. Perhaps their expressions and lack of expertise with music were typical of novices.

His thoughts wandered to his distant friend Tasuku, who by now must be a novice himself, perhaps chanting sutras at this very moment. It seemed to him that only great personal tragedy could make a man like Tasuku give up both his pleasures and a promising career.

This time he was certain he heard a sigh from behind the screen. When he glanced that way, the sleeve twitched a little. He bowed, trying to convey his pity with his eyes.

A silken rustling. Then the sleeve was abruptly withdrawn, followed by more rustling and the sound of a door closing softly in the rear of the hall. Akitada felt oddly bereft. Ashamed, he turned his attention back to the service.

The shape of the dead man was only a vague outline in its shrouding and looked insubstantial and shrunken. They must have broken his joints, Akitada thought, to achieve the customary seated position. The body had already been stiffening when he found it. An old man, done with life. Akitada recalled how Tachibana's skeletal, age-spotted hand had stroked the shell pattern on the dark blue silk robe he had worn to Motosuke's dinner. He had died in a different gown. What had he done after he arrived home? Had he retired but then got up again, dressed in a plain gown, and gone to his death? When had that happened? Had someone or something roused him? Where had he gone? He had not died in his study. There had not been enough blood there. Neither had there been any green-glazed splinters apart from the one found in his topknot. Akitada wondered again about the weapon. Whatever it was, it must have been made of glazed clay; it had broken or cracked on impact. No, it was hopeless. Better to think of a motive.

If Tachibana had been killed to prevent him from speaking to Akitada, then someone at Motosuke's dinner had visited during the night or sent an assassin. Once again Akitada weighed each man and what he knew of him. Motosuke, though most suspect in the tax theft, would hardly murder an old man at this point. He was about to become the emperor's father-in-law. Not, at any rate, unless he believed that Akitada and Tachibana between them could change the emperor's mind, and Akitada doubted that.

Yukinari was hiding something. The young captain had appeared too opportunely on the scene this morning. What had he been doing there? Since the crime must have happened in the dark, a murderer might have wanted to check the scene by daylight, before Akitada's visit, to make sure nothing had been overlooked. Akitada's early arrival would have surprised and dismayed the killer, and Yukinari had looked upset. Akitada recalled that the young man had acted strangely at Motosuke's. Somehow he must be connected with both Motosuke and Tachibana, and in a way that touched him profoundly and perhaps shamefully.

What about the abbot? Akitada glanced at the chanting monks and noticed for the first time an elderly man, the only old monk there. As Akitada stared at him, the man lifted his eyes and looked back. A strange expression crossed his face and he raised his hands to make the gesture of the praying Buddha before looking down again. Very odd! Everything about Joto and his monks was strange. Could Joto have sent one of his disciples to remove the troublesome ex-governor? Very possibly. The villainous monk in the marketplace would make a good assassin. Akitada decided to look into the wealth of that temple.

Lastly there was Ikeda, who had persistently called the death an accident when he should have known by training and experience that it was not. Seimei's explanation that Ikeda was a

mere provincial booby was not convincing in view of the very
knowledgeable way in which the prefect had quoted local laws
and ordinances to Akitada. But Ikeda seemed too colorless and
cautious a man to plot and mastermind criminal activities on
this scale.

Akitada shifted uncomfortably. He was stiff and cold, and
his back was beginning to hurt. How long should he remain? He
wanted to offer his condolences to the widow, to this child left
alone among servants who resented and hated her. As far as he
knew, she had no one to support her but her nurse. No relation,
no male protector, not even a woman friend of her own class.
Had anyone been to see her? Yukinari? Ikeda? Motosuke? A girl
of her tender years could not be expected to know much about
settling and managing an estate. Akitada pictured her, deserted
by the servants, cowering in the middle of this large, dark,
empty hall, without food, while rats scurried about waiting to
gnaw . . . Something tugged at his sleeve and he jerked it violently aside.

But it was only one of the servants, a large, middle-aged female wrapped in the stiff folds of hemp. She was kneeling next
to him, staring at him from eyes that looked like blackened
seeds in a large, doughy moon cake.

"My mistress begs the gentleman for a moment of his time,"
she said in a harsh whisper accompanied by a thin spray of spittle.

This must be the nurse, Akitada thought. Dabbing at his
face, he rose stiffly on feet that prickled painfully from the cold
and followed her from the hall.

Upright, the nurse was as tall as Akitada and seemed like a
giantess. She stepped along with the large, noisy strides of a
brawny laborer. They passed through a number of dim corri-
dors along wooden floors that felt and looked like sheets of
black ice. He caught occasional glimpses of rooms, sparsely but
elegantly furnished. Once he noted a beautifully written callig-

raphy scroll, another time an earthenware container planted with a miniature pine tree of perfect shape.

When the big woman finally pushed open the door to her mistress's quarters, Akitada blinked. Innumerable candles and lanterns spread light over an exotic scene that resembled a Chinese palace more than a Japanese villa. The beams overhead were lacquered bright red and green, and the room seemed filled with standing racks holding embroidered robes and brocade-trimmed curtains of state. Against the wall stood carved and lacquered tables, decorated leather trunks for clothes, and tea stands of woven bamboo with dainty cups like those Akitada had once seen in the capital in the shop of a Chinese merchant. When he stepped inside, he felt underfoot a softness, warmer and more caressing than the thickest mat of sea grass and saw that rarest of luxuries, a Chinese carpet with a colorful pattern of blossoms and butterflies. Even the sliding doors were made of lacquered latticework or covered with scenic paintings on paper. The one behind him closed with a soft swish, and he was alone with the widow.

If the room had taken his breath away, the lady who had sent for him dazzled his eyes. She was seated on a dais quite high enough for an imperial princess. The curtain stand, which by etiquette must hide a lady of gentle birth from the eyes of male visitors, was small and low. He could see almost all of her seated figure as he stood near the door.

She had covered her mourning robe with another colorful jacket, this one embroidered with plum blossoms on a sky-blue ground. Her hair framed the pale oval of her face and trailed over her narrow shoulders like liquid black lacquer. She was looking at him with large pleading eyes and softly parted lips. He stared, enchanted by her beauty, and she blushed and raised an exquisitely painted fan before her face.

"It is so kind of you to come," she said from behind the fan, bowing to him. "Please take a seat, my lord."

Akitada approached and seated himself on a cushion as close to her dais as he dared. "Although I have only just had the honor of meeting your late husband," he said softly, "I think I would have come to admire him very much. I came to express my sorrow at his passing."

"Thank you." There was a sigh and a pause. Then she cried out, "I think I hate monks. And incense nauseates me. I got quite sick and faint in the hall, sitting there for hours, hearing nothing but the chanting, the bells and drums, and always that smell. I wanted to die."

Akitada's heart smote him. This was no sophisticated woman who could be expected to deal with the rigors of public mourning. She was a child, too young to grasp the significance of the ritual, too weak for the fortitude and stoicism an older woman would have prided herself in.

"I know you must find it very difficult," he said gently. "How can I help?"

"Please, could you come to visit me sometimes? Just to talk, as you are now. It is so lonely since . . ." She choked.

Akitada did not know what to say.

"Oh!" she cried. "Forgive me. You must think me awful. You are a very important person from the capital, aren't you? I should not have asked such a thing."

"No, no. Not at all." Akitada took the plunge. "I will gladly call on you every day if you will permit it. I feel honored by your ladyship's confidence."

She gave a soft gasp of relief, and then a small hand crept out from under the hangings. Akitada stared at it. Touching a lady who was not a member of one's household was forbidden, but the hand was so small and helpless, a mere child's hand, smaller than that of his younger sister. She might be Lord Tachibana's widow, but she was still a girl, no different from his sister. Only, unlike his sister, she was alone in the world and needed reassurance, someone who could, however briefly, be to her the brother or father she did not have. He leaned forward and took her hand in both of his and held it. It was pitifully cold and curled about his warm fingers eagerly.

She whispered, "Your hands are so warm. I am nearly frozen from sitting in the hall for so many hours."

Akitada began to feel silly and intensely aware that they were alone together again. "Perhaps," he offered, "I should call your nurse and have her bring a brazier?"

Her fingers tightened on his. "No, please don't. She fusses too much."

"Then will you let me be of some assistance to you in a practical way? I have legal training and there must be a great deal of paperwork and estate business to face quite soon. Did Lord Tachibana appoint an executor?"

Her hand twitched and clenched on itself. "I have no idea what that is," she said. "I know nothing of such things. Nobody has come to see me."

"Nobody? How odd." His position was becoming awkward; he squeezed her fingers lightly and tried to disengage himself. She returned the pressure before releasing him and pulling back her hand. To his dismay, the sound of weeping now came from behind the curtain stand.

"I am sorry," Akitada said inadequately. The sobbing grew louder. He pleaded, "You must not cry. Everything will be all right, you'll see. You are young and very beautiful. Life will be happy again."

"No," she wailed. "No one will ever want me again. I wish I could die, too."

Akitada rose. She had flung herself down, a slender shape in

colored silks and glossy hair, her narrow shoulders and back
heaving with grief, and two small feet in white socks twisted
about each other in distress. He pushed the stand aside, knelt,
and gathered her against his chest as one might hold a weeping
child. Stroking her back, he buried his face in the scented hair
and murmured soothing words to her, and she held on to him
with the desperation of a lost child.

"Ahem!" The harsh, rasping sound broke into Akitada's efforts at comforting the widow. The nurse towered above them
with a disapproving frown on her unpleasant face.

Akitada released the weeping girl and scrambled up. "Oh,
good. There you are," he said. "Your mistress needs you. She is
very distressed and, er, cold. Get a brazier. And something hot to
drink!" Aware that he was babbling, he stepped aside.

The nurse grunted and moved past him to replace the curtain stand. There was a whispered exchange between the
women, then the nurse said harshly, "She needs rest. Come back
tomorrow."

Akitada turned to leave.

"No, wait," cried the widow.

He waited. Afraid to look at her behind her inadequate
screen, he stared across the room at a painted scroll of dancing
cranes between a pair of tall, carved tables, one of which held a
thin-necked jade-green vase of Chinese origin.

"My husband invited you, didn't he?"

"Yes, Lady Tachibana. I was looking forward to becoming
better acquainted with him."

"Had he anything particular in mind? Perhaps he promised
to show you something, tell you something?"

Akitada hesitated. "No, I don't think so," he said. "Why do
you ask?"

"Oh, I only thought that, if I knew what it was, perhaps I
could help you find it."

Akitada thought of the document boxes in the studio. "Your husband spoke of the history he was working on. I was interested in that."

"Then you must feel free to study his notes at your convenience. They are all in his studio."

"Thank you, Lady Tachibana. That is most kind of you." Still avoiding a glance at her, Akitada bowed and left the room.

The nurse followed him out, clearing her throat with another resounding "Ahem."

Akitada looked at her questioningly. Really, the woman was very unpleasant in her manner as well as her appearance. "Yes?" he asked.

"She's just a baby," the woman said accusingly. "Needs taking care of, not upsetting."

Akitada softened. "I have offered to help settle the estate," he explained. "Is it true that there is no one to take care of such matters for her?"

"It's true. And no wonder! Always with his nose in his books. Wouldn't have company in his house. When he wasn't in his studio, he was messing about with plants and rocks in the garden. Spent more time feeding his fish than talking with his lady. The poor child."

"Yes, she is very young." Akitada sighed. The woman deserved credit for her fondness of her young mistress, even though the criticism of her master was improper.

"Only just seventeen. For a while this past summer that young captain came to visit them. Oh, how my young lady used to laugh at his quips and stories. She was a different person then. But the master wouldn't have it. Drove him away, he did."

"Captain Yukinari?" asked Akitada.

"He's the one. And now he won't even talk to her," she said.

That explained Yukinari's reaction when Akitada had suggested a visit to the widow. Suddenly he got an image of the late

Lord Tachibana as a besotted old man who kept this beautiful child in every luxury imaginable but drove away potential rivals in fits of irrational jealousy. This thought begot another.

"Did your master visit his wife's room last night after the governor's party?" he asked.

Something flickered in her small eyes, then the woman drew herself up stiffly. "I don't speak of private things to strangers."

Against his will, Akitada felt himself flush. "Don't be ridiculous, woman," he snapped. "The prefect will ask you the same question shortly. It is customary in cases of sudden death. I only wondered if Lord Tachibana mentioned my intended visit to his wife."

She eyed him suspiciously, then said sullenly, "I don't know. I was asleep." After a moment's thought, she added, "The master rarely visited his lady's room. The age difference made him like a father to her, poor little flower. She has no one now but me. The servants in this house are all liars and thieves, but my lord always protected my young lady. Oh, what will become of us now?" She raised a sleeve to her face and snuffled.

"You will both be taken care of," Akitada said quickly and walked away.

He passed through the hall, where the monks were still chanting, and stepped outside. The broad daylight caused him to blink, but the fresh cold air was a relief after the incense-laden atmosphere inside. Putting his wooden clogs back on, he stepped down into the courtyard and turned toward the studio. When he reached the intersection of paths, he found Junjiro in conversation with a middle-aged woman. They saw him, looked at each other, and bowed deeply.

"This woman," said Junjiro, "is my mother. She works in the kitchen and has something to tell you."

Akitada remembered the animosity of the servants toward their mistress. "Well?" he asked curtly.

"Junjiro said I must speak," the woman said timidly. She had a plain, pleasant face and looked with adoring pride at her son. "It's about the honorable captain, sir. I saw him pass the kitchen window this morning before sunrise. I remember, because I was thinking the mistress will want her rice gruel now." She blushed crimson and added, "She always does right after the captain leaves."

Akitada stood frozen, his thoughts in turmoil. "What do you mean?" he asked stupidly. "Are you saying the captain was visiting Lady Tachibana before I came?"

"It was still dark," the woman said. She cringed before his angry, searching eyes.

Junjiro put an arm around his mother's shoulders. "Please don't tell the mistress we told you, sir. Mother did not want to speak, but I figured we had to, now that the master is dead. Mother once mentioned the captain's visits to old Kiku, and Kiku blabbed to the nurse. Next thing the constables came and took old Kiku away for stealing her ladyship's jacket. They found it in her bedroll. We don't think it was old Kiku who put it there, but the master believed her ladyship."

It was a bad tale and getting worse. Akitada stared at the two suspiciously. Sometimes disgruntled servants accused their innocent masters of horrible offenses. "How could you recognize the captain if it was dark?" he asked the woman harshly.

She quailed at his tone. "The light from the kitchen shone on his helmet, sir, and he was running for the back gate. That's the way he always used to come and go."

Akitada raised his head and looked past them toward the rear wall, unaware that his hands were clenched so tightly that his nails were drawing blood. "Inform the prefect when he returns," he said dully.

The light was fading. Akitada turned and walked back to the front gate. At the gatehouse he paused and knocked. Nothing.

He repeated his peremptory pounding and finally a bleary-eyed Sato opened the door and fell to his knees. "Sorry, Excellency," he cried, beating his old head against the dirt floor. "I must have dozed off. So much coming and going. All these monks. I haven't closed an eye all day."

"Never mind. I have some questions to ask you." Akitada pushed the door wider and walked in. The small room contained only a ragged mat, a pallet, and a brazier.

"But this is no place for Your Excellency," protested Sato. "Perhaps in the main house?"

"No. This will do." Akitada seated himself on the pallet. Sato closed the door, knelt, and waited uneasily.

"Did the prefect and his people remove any papers from the studio?"

"Oh, no, Excellency. I watched carefully and locked up after they left."

"When your master returned last night, what did he do?"

"Why, I think he must have gone to bed. He told me he did not need me, so I went to bed myself."

"Did you see him this morning? Did you take him his morning rice or help him dress?"

"No, Your Excellency. His lordship was much stronger than I. He liked to rise before dawn and hated troubling me. He made his own tea in the morning, saying that food did not sit well in his stomach so early. His stomach has always been delicate since his troubles last year."

"Then how did you know he would be in his studio when I arrived?" Akitada suddenly shouted at him.

Sato flinched. "But he always went there first thing every morning," he cried.

"Were you aware that Captain Yukinari was in this house before I arrived?"

The old man paled and looked away. "No, Your Excellency."

"You lie." Akitada struck the floor with his fist. "It is an open secret among the servants that the captain was having an affair with your mistress under your master's nose. This very morning he was seen leaving by the back gate. Shortly afterward I found your master dead. What do you know about the disgraceful state of affairs in this house?"

Sato cried out and beat his forehead on the dirt floor. "Forgive this worthless one, Excellency. There was some talk, but I paid no attention. Women's gossip. I thought the captain came to visit the master. They both liked to garden."

"Did you let him in last night or this morning?"

"Oh, no. He used to come and go on his own." Sato remained crouched on the floor but began to shake. "I cannot be everywhere at once," he wailed through chattering teeth, "and my memory is not what it used to be, but I try to do my work well. There is so much to be taken care of, to remember."

"You failed your master when he needed you," Akitada said in an icy voice. "Outsiders have ready access and egress by the rear gate while you lie here and sleep the day away. Your master would still be alive if you had done your duty." He rose, dusted off his robe, and walked out.

Behind him Sato wailed, "But how was I to prevent the master from falling?"

◆

Akitada returned to his quarters in a ferocious mood. He kicked his clogs off on the veranda and, hearing voices, burst in, thinking that Tora had returned with information.

To his surprise he saw that Seimei was drinking tea with the governor.

"There you are, Sugawara," exclaimed Motosuke, his round face lighting up. "I am getting some excellent pointers about herbal remedies for my back pains. Seimei is a treasure. You are to be envied. It is like traveling with your own physician."

Seimei smirked.

"What brings you, Governor?" Akitada asked curtly.

"Why so glum, my dear fellow?" asked Motosuke. "Seimei tells me that you are finished with my dreary accounts. Now we shall finally have a chance for pleasant chats about the capital and some local entertainment. What sports do you play? Football? Horse racing? Do you like games? Play musical instruments? Paint? Or would you like to meet some delightfully pretty local girls? Their manners are a bit rough, but they make up for it with other skills." He slapped his thighs and laughed.

"I have no time for such things," Akitada snapped. "You may have forgotten the matter of the missing taxes. I could use your assistance with that."

Motosuke's face fell. "You are such a very serious fellow for your age," he said, shaking his head sadly. "I shall have to call you 'elder brother' though you are not much older than my daughter. In fact, I'd like nothing better than to have you settle this nasty tax matter. It is something of a blot on my record. But it will be quite impossible, I'm afraid."

"What do you mean?"

"Dispatches from the capital." Motosuke pointed to a sealed package on the low table. "I expect yours contains the same news as mine."

Akitada snatched up the package and tore open the seal of the imperial chancery. Scanning the message quickly, he paled and let it drop from his hand.

"What's the matter?" asked Seimei.

"I have been recalled," Akitada said tonelessly.

NINE

THE DRAGON SCROLL

"*C*heer up! Cheer up!" cried the governor, seeing their long faces. "I have already dispatched a request that you be allowed to travel back to the capital in my cortege. There is plenty of time for you to explore this city and countryside a bit before we leave. The point is, you no longer need to worry about those confounded taxes. The powers in our august capital, in their wisdom, have decided to forget the matter completely." He paused and looked puzzled. "I wonder why."

Akitada stared at him. If Motosuke was involved in the crime, there was no point in playing games any longer, and if he was not, surely he could not be that dense. He said, "I assume because of the honor the emperor will do your daughter."

Motosuke looked blank. "What does that have to do with it?" Belatedly, realization dawned and he flushed deeply.

Meeting his eyes squarely, Akitada said, "Yes. Officially, you are now above suspicion." He saw the sudden pain in the round, comfortable face, but he no longer cared about Motosuke's feelings.

Motosuke sat silent, looking down at his folded hands. "You think I'm guilty," he finally said sadly. "Everyone thinks I'm guilty." He heaved a sigh.

"Face it, you always were the most likely suspect," Akitada pointed out. "However, your secretary, for one, has given you a shining testimonial of faith."

To Akitada's dismay, tears began running down Motosuke's cheeks. "Good old Akinobu," he muttered. "Poor fellow. This suspicion touches him, too. And he has no fine new career to go to. I must see what I can do for the man."

Against his will, Akitada softened and, on the spur of the moment, asked, "Tell me, what possessed you to attempt to bribe me?"

Motosuke's head came up. "Bribe you? I never bribed you."

"A matter of ten bars of gold delivered to my quarters on the day of my arrival could hardly be anything else."

Motosuke looked aghast. "It was to cover your expenses. I had precise instructions about that. You mean they did not tell you? The minister of civil affairs himself wrote to me. He said that in the rush you had not been issued any funds in the capital and that I was to rectify the matter."

"Oh." They looked at each other in mutual embarrassment. Akitada, painfully aware of the grave offense he had given Motosuke, realized that, against all rules of jurisprudence, he had built a case against this man based on a totally false impression of his character. He had prejudged him.

Motosuke broke into Akitada's frantic search for an adequate apology with a shout of laughter. "What a tangle!" he cried gleefully. "So that's why you sent back the gold without a word of explanation and glared at me every time we met. Ho, ho, ho! I thought you the rudest man alive. I even wondered if you had been sent by my enemies to falsify my accounts." He hooted with laughter. "Both of us . . ." he choked, "both of us suspecting the other . . . ho, ho . . . and all the time you thought . . ." He subsided into weak giggles.

Akitada managed a hint of a smile. "You are very good to take it so lightly. I made a very stupid mistake," he said. "I'm afraid I am new at being an inspector. No one told me that I was to be paid."

This caused more giggles from Motosuke, and Seimei, who had been listening with openmouthed astonishment, now said complacently, "There! I thought all along that you must be wrong, sir. In fact, I told you so. 'Suspicion raises demons from the dark,' I said. Isn't it pleasant to have the matter cleared up?"

Akitada gave him a sour look. To Motosuke, he said, "At least I shall have a chance to make it up to you by trying to clear your name completely. How much time is there?"

Motosuke waved a careless hand. "Oh, weeks, I should think."

"If I had not been so foolish, I would have asked you about those who might really be responsible for the robberies."

Motosuke sighed. "Don't think I haven't considered everyone already, but ask away."

"What sort of person is Ikeda?"

"Not likely, I would say. Eager, hardworking, ambitious. A thoroughly dull dog, but a good man to run the prefectural administration. A man like that would do well in the capital, but Ikeda comes from common stock and wouldn't have got this far there unless he had married well. Speaking of which, Ikeda had the nerve to approach me for my daughter's hand, but I set him right and he apologized handsomely. Even Yukinari has better connections."

"Yukinari wished to marry your daughter?"

"Oh, yes. He saw my daughter and was head over heels in love. Silver Orchid was not averse to him. He's a handsome youngster, and the military uniform turns a girl's head. It worried me no end but came to nothing. Praise heaven!"

That explained Yukinari's reaction when Motosuke had announced his daughter's future. The garrison commander certainly led a complicated love life. The thought of him as the lover of Lady Tachibana was still astonishingly painful. That weeping child! Akitada forced his mind back to the present. "And Tachibana?"

"Poor old Tachibana. Who would have thought he'd go so quickly? I liked the old man, but he kept to himself. Early on he asked permission to use the archives for his research, and I'd run across him there and invite him for a cup of wine. Then he married again, most unsuitably, and we lost touch. You met the widow?"

"Yes." Sensing disapproval of the beautiful child-wife, Akitada changed the subject. "I'm afraid her husband died under suspicious circumstances."

"Suspicious circumstances? What do you mean?"

Akitada told Motosuke of the whispered invitation and described what he found on his visit. The governor's face registered puzzlement, surprise, and horror in quick succession. "I wondered," Akitada concluded, "why Ikeda would pronounce the death accidental."

Motosuke got up and started pacing. "Murder! I can hardly believe it. You're right, it isn't like Ikeda to make such a mistake. A very careful official as a rule. But Yukinari was there. I wonder if that explains his lack of attention. They are bitter enemies, you know. There was much jealousy when they were rivals for my daughter, and Yukinari has always despised Ikeda for his background."

Akitada did not want to think about Yukinari's love life. "It occurred to me that Tachibana was murdered because he knew what happened to the taxes."

"It looks like it." Motosuke sat down again and shook his head. "He should have brought it to my attention, but then he evidently suspected me, too. If he had not spoken to you, I would have blamed his death on a burglar. That houseman of his is senile. They say anybody can walk in while the man is sleeping."

"Please keep my suspicion to yourself for the time being." Akitada paused, then said, "I've been puzzled about the abbot, though I cannot see how he is connected with the Tachibana murder. Joto's temple seems to have become very wealthy very quickly. Do you know how this came about?"

Motosuke shifted uncomfortably. "They keep their benefactors secret, especially since large donations come from powerful families. The temple is also attracting hordes of pilgrims who make individual gifts. The source of the temple's wealth is untraceable. By the way, Joto tells me that his building program is completed. The last hall has just been finished and will be dedicated in a few days. It will be a great occasion."

"No doubt. Some of his monks have questionable morals. My servant found two of them assaulting a deaf-mute girl near the market."

Motosuke sat up. "A deaf-mute? Not the painter?"

"I believe she paints," said Akitada, astonished.

"Strange. She's very good, they say. Yes, there have been reports of rowdiness. I spoke to Joto about it once, but that man always has a little sermon to fit every eventuality. Told me the way to serve the Buddha involves knowing both austerity and excess. The point he was making, I suppose, is that he has so many youngsters taking the tonsure that a few slips along the way are to be expected. The truth of the matter is that the local people are grateful to the monks for the trade they are bringing to the town, so they refuse to complain and don't want us to make trouble." Motosuke pursed his lips and shook his head slowly. "No, my dear fellow. Whatever else you try, I think you must forget about Joto and the Temple of Fourfold Wisdom."

He took his leave soon after. Akitada and Seimei were just thinking of their evening meal when Tora walked in. He looked so uncharacteristically depressed that Akitada asked him what had happened.

Tora said glumly, "A wasted day. Nothing's any good."

"Sit down and tell us."

Tora accepted a cup of wine from Seimei and plunged into an account of his frustrations.

When he was done, Akitada was baffled, but Seimei nodded with paternal satisfaction. "There is no need to feel discouraged, my son," he said. "You have gone among evil people, but you have remained honest and you have tried to protect the weak. It was good. A man's actions will return to him."

Tora shook his head and said bleakly, "No, it's no good. I just stopped in to tell you I'll be leaving in the morning."

"What?" cried Akitada and Seimei together.

Tora said, "I tried, but I cannot serve you. These clothes you gave me are what officials wear, and officials are the scum who suppress the poor workingman. You sent me to talk to people who wouldn't tell their dog's name to an official. I can't do your work and I'm tired of explaining that I'm not an official and that you, a lord, are trying to help them. Even my friend Hidesato, who's been like an older brother to me, took off when he heard who I was working for."

It was a long and passionate speech for Tora and left Akitada wordless, but Seimei looked down at his own neat blue robe and asked, "What foolish talk is this? Our clothes mark our respectable and honorable work. In the capital ordinary people look up to us. How can you wish to remain a low person all your life?"

"That is not what Tora means, I think," Akitada said quickly. "It seems people feel differently about our profession here. The honest farmer works in his paddies and the shopkeeper runs his little shop. Then the well-dressed official comes and takes their hard-earned money for the government and presses the men into military service or corvée."

Tora nodded. "He steals, you mean. By the Buddha, I would not have worked for a cursed official like you for ten bars of gold if you hadn't been a good man. You aren't like the rest of them. But I can't betray my own people. And Hidesato thinks I did."

Akitada and Seimei looked at each other.

"Tell me about your friend," Akitada said.

Tora sighed. "He was my sergeant when I was a raw recruit. Him and me, we've been through a lot together. He taught me stick fighting to take my mind off my parents dying. He also showed me how to shoot an arrow straight and how to lay my hands on a kind whore when we hadn't been paid for months. He saved my neck more than once when I was in trouble, and I covered for him when he was drunk or out of the camp to visit his girl." Tora paused and gave Akitada an apologetic look. "I know you saved my life, but that's different. It was easy for you. All you had to do was tell the bastards who you were and they let me go. You're a lord. Hidesato's . . . like a brother."

Seimei bristled, but Akitada laid a restraining hand on the old man's arm. He felt a sharp pang of envy for this stranger who had won Tora's loyalty while he had failed to, but said only, "I understand. Perhaps we can find Hidesato together and explain to him."

"You would do that?"

"Certainly. I consider you my friend."

Tora flushed and hung his head. "Your kind of people don't have friends among my kind of people."

"Why not? I look forward to meeting Hidesato and hope you will introduce me to the crippled wrestler and his daughters."

Tora's face lit up. "Higekuro? How about right now? He should be finished with his last students."

Akitada smiled. "Why not?"

◆

They found Higekuro and Otomi playing a game of *go* while Ayako was mending one of the bows.

Tora made the introductions. Akitada was astonished at the crippled man's size and muscular build. Even more impressive was the natural manner with which he received Akitada. There was nothing servile in his courteous bow or in the unaffected way in which he directed his daughters to bring some wine for his noble guest. He made no apologies for the poor offerings, and his speech was that of an educated man.

Akitada looked about the simple room with pleasure. It was clean and seemed to have everything a man might need in a home: a comfortable dais on which to rest and play a game, warmth from the cooking stoves on which simmered a savory meal, a few boxes for his belongings, and children who honored and served him.

The two young women wore the plainest of cotton gowns, but they were slender and graceful, one very pretty and shy, the other quick in her movements and openly curious about him. When Akitada gave her a smile, she tossed her head a little. The gesture was unexpectedly charming.

Higekuro stroked his thick black beard and asked about wrestling in the capital. Akitada told him what he knew, and they fell into an easy conversation about various sports and how they were played in the capital and in the provincial towns. Akitada recalled his own pastimes: football games, horse races around the imperial guard barracks, a brief but enjoyable set of lessons from a wrestling champion, and the continuous and exacting training in swordsmanship. Higekuro countered with similar childhood memories until Akitada asked in great surprise, "Do I take it that you, too, were raised in the capital?"

"Yes, but I was exiled as a young man." Higekuro smiled at
Akitada's astonishment. "Come, the story is not unusual. I was
raised in one of the 'good' families and trained for a military career. When one of my uncles was convicted of treason, all the
members of our family were sentenced to exile, their property
confiscated, their honors revoked. I was a married man with a
young family, and my only skill was wrestling. Fortunately, that
profession allowed me to support my parents till they died. I
lost my wife soon after but raised my daughters to adulthood
before I had the accident that crippled me."

Throughout this tragic tale, the smile did not leave his face,
and Akitada was deeply moved by such courage. "You have had
a very difficult life," he said awkwardly.

"Not at all. I'm a fortunate man. Ayako helps me run the
school, and Otomi is earning more every day with her paintings." He smiled with great pride and affection at his daughters.

Akitada met the serious eyes of Ayako, who had seated herself near them to listen to their talk. Her hands lay idly in her
lap, but he saw their finely drawn strength and the long, capable
fingers with their blunt nails and guessed at their strength.

Her sister had convinced Tora to play a game with her.
Otomi was smiling up at him. He smiled back in a besotted
fashion as she placed a game piece on the board with a softly
rounded feminine hand. Into Akitada's mind flashed the memory of the small cold hand of the widowed child in the
Tachibana mansion, and he was struck by the differences between the three young women.

With an effort he returned to his conversation with
Higekuro. "The governor mentioned your daughter's fine reputation as a painter. May I see some of her work?"

"The governor, you say?" Higekuro clapped his hands

sharply. But Otomi and Tora were bent over their game and oblivious to the others. When her sister put a hand on Otomi's shoulder, she turned. A series of quick hand and lip movements passed between father and daughter, then Otomi bowed and smiled at Akitada. She rose and went up the steps to the loft, returning with an armful of scrolls. She placed them on the dais before returning to Tora and the *go* board.

Akitada unrolled the paintings one by one, while Higekuro looked on and Ayako came to stand beside him. Otomi's talent was remarkable. As a classical scholar, Akitada preferred the subdued landscapes to the more colorful, but to his mind gaudy, saints and *mandalas,* although the latter were painted with great skill and a fine eye for detail and effect. He had seen enough religious paintings to know that Otomi's rivaled anything in the capital.

Ayako made herself useful unrolling and holding up the scrolls. When Akitada remarked on a rocky landscape hidden in mist, she said eagerly, "We, too, prefer the landscapes. But the Buddhist paintings bring in money from the pilgrims and from local people, too. Otomi is very careful about accuracy. She visits famous temples to copy their paintings and to receive instruction in their significance."

Akitada smiled at her. "I would like to buy a landscape painting. Do you think there is one of beautiful Sagami Bay? When I'm back in the capital, it would remind me of my journey."

Ayako looked uneasy. "There is one, but you will hardly consider it a landscape. It's a ship in a storm."

"That sounds interesting."

"Actually, it's a storm dragon picture. You know the one, Father?"

Higekuro also looked unhappy, but he nodded. "Show the gentleman the scroll," he said after a glance at the two *go* players.

Ayako went to one of the stacked chests and took out a

scroll. She unrolled it for Akitada, saying, "Otomi painted it on her last journey, but it upsets her, so we keep it locked away."

The picture showed a ship in the coils of the storm dragon. Mountainous waves, black clouds, and jagged lightning surrounded a scene of imminent death and destruction for the people aboard. The detail was as fine as in the other paintings, but the brushstrokes here were rapid, almost violent, and the painting managed to convey a sense of chaos.

Akitada bent closer. There were soldiers on the ship, perhaps a military transport of sorts. They were armed with the halberds called *naginata* and accompanied by a solitary seated monk. Strangely, they appeared completely detached in the face of impending disaster. Perhaps, Akitada thought, the scroll told a religious tale. He studied the monk's figure, trying to guess at its significance, and got the uneasy feeling that he had seen him somewhere.

"Will you ask your sister where she saw this scene?" he asked Ayako.

The girl hesitated, then went to Otomi to communicate Akitada's question. The younger girl looked up and became agitated, shaking her head and gesturing wildly.

"She doesn't want to talk about it," Ayako translated.

Akitada looked from the girls to their father. "I don't wish to distress your daughter, but I have the strangest feeling that there is something significant about this picture."

"Do you?" Higekuro's eyes lit up. "I agree. About a month ago, just after the festival of the dead, Otomi joined a local group for a pilgrimage to the Temple of Infinite Light in Shimosa province. She went there for research. The storm dragon was one of the pictures she painted on that journey. When she returned, we noticed that she was changed. She brooded a lot and had terrible nightmares. I've always thought that something happened to her on the pilgrimage and that the scroll is part of the mystery. You think that it might be connected with the tax matter? The time is right. If there is a connection, you give me hope that we may help her."

Akitada said, "You're right. The time and place of your daughter's pilgrimage roughly fit the date and route of the last tax convoy. Did your daughter take passage in a ship, or is this temple near the coastal highway?"

Higekuro stared at Akitada, then turned to Otomi and questioned her with sign language. She closed her eyes briefly and shook her head violently. He persisted, using his hands to make her look at him. Eventually she nodded. Taking a piece of charred wood from the kitchen stove, she scribbled on the hard dirt floor while gesturing to her father. Higekuro translated, "She stayed in the guest quarters of the monastery. The highway passes just below the monastery walls, and the guest quarters overlook Sagami Bay."

"Ask her if she saw a pack train passing by."

But this time, when her father communicated the question, Otomi turned pale and trembled. Clutching the piece of charred wood, she scrawled an illegible series of characters, then threw away the wood and staggered to her feet.

"Enough!" cried Ayako, jumping up and catching the shaking, weeping girl in her arms. Her eyes flashed angrily at Akitada. "You are tormenting her."

Akitada instantly revised his opinion about the sisters. Ayako was far more beautiful than the sweetly pretty Otomi. How could Tora be so blind? "I am very sorry," he said, "but surely you must see that your sister will have no peace until she shares her memory."

"My sister is an artist," flashed Ayako, "not a rough person like myself. I believe she was attacked and violated. She cannot face the brutality of that without breaking. Believe me, if I were not afraid of hurting her, I would have found out who did this to her." She took a deep breath and added fiercely, "I would have killed him!"

Otomi tore herself from her sister's arms and fled to Tora, who was hovering near them and received her eagerly in his embrace.

Akitada could not take his eyes off Ayako. "I believe you are wrong. What makes you think she was raped?" he asked.

"What else?" she spat. "Look at her! She's beautiful and men lust after her. Have you forgotten the monks who attacked her?" She glared at Tora. "No doubt your servant has similar designs."

"I do not!" cried an outraged Tora.

"Ayako!" thundered Higekuro.

She flushed and bowed to Tora. "Forgive my words," she said gruffly. "But not even in our unconventional family is it proper for you to embrace my sister."

Tora immediately released Otomi, who sniffled a little, then scurried up to the loft.

Higekuro sighed. "You must think us very strange," he said to Akitada, "but remember our background and our present life together. My daughters are everything to me. Perhaps I have been too indulgent with them, but the proprieties observed in the past have lost all meaning for the three of us."

Akitada nodded. "It's curious," he said, pointing to the scroll, "that monks should appear in both of your daughter's recent adventures. I am very interested in the Temple of Fourfold Wisdom and its abbot, Master Joto. Has Otomi visited there?"

"Yes, often." Higekuro pondered the question a moment. "She goes there to sell her pictures to the pilgrims. But surely there is no connection? Master Joto's monks have always been very helpful to her. The ones asking questions earlier today were probably just trying to send her customers."

Akitada looked at Ayako. "What do you think?" he asked softly.

She lifted her chin and met his eyes squarely. "I think you are right about the monks and Father is wrong," she said. "If you will leave my sister in peace, I'll help you investigate the monks."

Akitada laughed and bowed. "I admire your spirit. If your father permits it, it's a bargain." Turning to Higekuro, he asked, "Will you trust me with your daughter?"

Higekuro stroked his beard and looked from Akitada to Ayako and back again. "Ayako does not need my permission for anything she chooses to do. You may trust her. She knows her way about and is as useful as any man in a tight spot. Tora told us that you take an interest in stick fighting. Why not let Ayako give you a bout?"

Akitada glanced at the girl and thought he caught a look of distress, but she smiled and asked, "Are you willing, sir?"

Amused and intrigued, Akitada rose. "It would be an honor."

Taking up an oil lamp, Ayako led the way into the dark practice hall and lit the oil lamps attached to supporting beams. The hall sprang into an eerie, shadowy existence. The flames flickered in unseen drafts and familiar objects took on mysterious and threatening forms.

"Make your selection," Ayako said, pointing to a rack of staves.

Feeling a little foolish, Akitada removed his outer robe and fastened his full trousers around his knees. Then he found a weapon that felt comfortable and turned around.

Ayako had taken off her robe and wore only a pair of trousers. As he stared, she bent to tighten the strings around her knees. He had seen peasant women in the fields work barebreasted, but that this beautiful young woman should do so in front of him shocked and flustered him.

"Do you teach your lessons like that?" The words were out before Akitada could stop himself.

She straightened up slowly and looked at him. Her body was magnificent. She was as slim and muscular as an active boy, with a boy's long torso, but high, softly rounded breasts, a flat stomach, and hips tapering to slender, firm thighs. The full fabric of the trousers partially hid the shape of her lower body, but her movements left little to Akitada's imagination and he swallowed.

"No," she said coldly and turned away to reach up for a sleeveless shirt hanging on a nail. "Men dislike fighting a woman. I wear a shirt and trousers, like one of the porters on the street, and they pretend I'm a boy. Would you prefer not to engage in a bout with a female?"

"Not at all. I'm ready." Akitada hoped the uncertain light hid his flushed face.

If he had thought to prove his masculine superiority by humoring this girl fighter, he was sadly disappointed. Perhaps he had angered her, because Ayako attacked with a speed and ferocity that saw him disarmed in a minute. Wordlessly, she bent and tossed him his stave, and they began again. This time Akitada was more careful, but he lost his weapon once more. Again she threw it to him, saying, "Your technique is good, but you have been taught to attack. When you are forced to receive an attack, you have no notion how to defend yourself. This time I'll let you force me back. Watch how I counter your strikes."

Akitada bit his lip and did his best. To his surprise, even his hardest hits and quickest lunges were parried. He was about to give up before he disgraced himself completely when Ayako disarmed him for the third time.

He stood staring at his stave on the floor between them and shook his head. "You are a superb fighter," he said in awe.

"Thank you."

Her words sounded muffled, and he looked up. She had her back to him and was hanging the shirt back on its hook. Her long, slender back glistened with a sheen of perspiration that moved in patterns of light and darkness across the flexing muscles. This time she did not turn around until she had put on her long robe and tied her sash. When she faced him in the flickering lights, he thought he saw tears in her eyes.

"I expect you want to make a clandestine visit to the temple," she said, avoiding his eyes. "We could go tonight if you like."

"Yes." He agreed almost without volition. Putting on his robe, he wondered how this strange girl could have disturbed him so powerfully and why he wished to prolong their time together even at the cost of a night's sleep.

They rejoined the others. Otomi had returned, looking pale but much calmer, and was gathering up her paintings.

Akitada said to Higekuro, "Would you ask your daughter if I might purchase two of the scrolls? The dragon scroll and the mountain landscape?"

Higekuro spoke to Otomi, who nodded and brought the pictures to him. "They are a gift," her father said, extending them to Akitada.

"No." Akitada was firm. "I will pay the top price she has been getting." He looked at Ayako.

"Two bars of silver apiece," she said, tossing her head.

Higekuro drew in his breath. "Ridiculous! You know very well that was the price of a commissioned *mandala* with three hundred figures of saints."

"Four bars of silver it is," said Akitada recklessly, remembering Motosuke's gold. "The price is reasonable for good work. I will pay your daughter tomorrow." Turning to Tora, he said, "Miss Ayako has offered to take us into the monastery tonight. It means postponing the search for your friend until tomorrow."

"What's so hard about getting into a temple?" Tora asked with a disdainful look at Ayako.

"This temple is not like others, Tora, and Miss Ayako has been there before. You and I have not."

"You will need to change clothes," Ayako said to Akitada.

"Then we'll stop at the tribunal."

"We don't need Tora."

Tora's face stiffened. "I'm going!" he snapped.

Akitada hesitated, then told Ayako, "There may be trouble. Tora will be useful."

Ayako whirled to face him, her eyes fierce. "I can handle any man," she said. "What else do you want me to do to prove it to you?"

Akitada stepped back. "I did not mean . . . It was not meant as an insult. But there are so many monks there that even Tora and I . . ." Seeing the flash of anger at his use of the word *even,* he said quickly, "If we are discovered, three have a better chance of escaping. Two of us can hold off the enemy while one runs for help."

"If you're careful and don't do anything stupid, we won't be discovered." She turned away and ran up to the loft with the smooth, long strides of a large cat.

Akitada told Higekuro, "Thank you for making me as welcome as Tora. I hope he has behaved himself."

Higekuro glanced at Tora and Otomi, who were taking their time putting away the game pieces and managing to touch hands as much as possible. He smiled. "Tora's like the son I never had," he said. "I don't want Otomi to get hurt, but I won't deny my daughters some joy while they are young." He met Akitada's eyes and added with great seriousness, "Remember this: my daughters and I are outside the world you live in; we have made our own rules."

Akitada had no idea how to respond to this puzzling advice, so he thanked his host for the wine and entertainment and gathered up his scrolls.

When Ayako returned, she wore long black trousers and a long-sleeved black shirt. Her hair was bound up in a black scarf. "Do you have any dark clothes?" she asked, frowning at Akitada's white silk trousers and pale gray robe.

"Yes. Though nothing nearly as becoming as your costume," he said with a warm smile.

She looked startled and turned away abruptly. "Let's go then."

TEN

THE TEMPLE OF FOURFOLD WISDOM

*A*kitada, in his dark brown hunting clothes, joined Tora in the stable yard. Tora had brought horses from the governor's stables and wore a quilted cotton coat that was so stained and faded it was hard to tell if it was green or black. A pair of badly patched blue trousers were tucked into his boots.

Akitada stared at him. "Is there some naked beggar outside the gate?"

"What's wrong with my clothes?" Tora asked. "They're dark. Had to give that greedy bastard of a stable boy ten coppers and my blue robe for them."

The stable boy, who had saddled the three horses and was standing about yawning, decided to disappear.

"You gave him your new blue robe? I paid three strings of coppers for your clothes," protested Akitada.

Tora snorted. "You were cheated. They didn't keep me as warm as this." He patted his quilted coat affectionately, then took the bridles of two horses and headed out the door, leaving Akitada to follow behind with the third.

Ayako regarded her horse with intense dislike.

"Come on," mocked Tora. "Get up! He won't bite."

She gave him a furious look and scrambled up awkwardly. Taking the reins, she gingerly directed the docile beast onto the road. "Follow me," she said over her shoulder. "We can't use the Great Northern Gate. The guards ask questions."

They passed quickly through dark deserted streets north of the tribunal and turned down a short alley that ended at the palisade enclosing the city. Someone had broken the boards there, making an opening wide enough for a horse and rider to pass through. A well-trodden path led down into the wide ditch and up the other side. Clearly they were not the only ones who avoided official scrutiny at the Great Northern Gate.

Once in the countryside, they traveled quickly along narrow farm roads. Mulberry groves, leafless at this time of year, raised screens of fine black branches against the starry sky. The moon, nearly full, moved with them in ghostly fashion behind the lacy boughs.

It was cold, and the horses' breath hung white in the air when they snorted. They were riding single file, with Ayako leading the way and Tora bringing up the rear. Akitada's eyes were on the slender, straight back of the young woman in front of him. He wondered if she was cold in her thin black cotton shirt and trousers. Belatedly it occurred to him that, being unfamiliar with horses, she had expected to ride in front of one of them.

Bringing his horse up beside hers as soon as the road widened a little, he asked, "Are you cold?"

"No," she said curtly. "I don't like horses, that's all."

"I'm sorry I did not ask before. Would you like to ride with me?"

For a moment she hesitated, then she stiffened her shoulders and shook her head.

"Why did you offer to come? You could have drawn us a map."

"I wanted to come." After a moment she grudgingly added, "Besides, you need me. I know how to get in. When my sister was attacked, I got suspicious of the monks and paid a visit to the temple."

"And?"

"In the daytime they watch all visitors. I decided to come back after dark. The first time they almost caught me. Last time I found . . . well, something strange."

"What?"

"Wait till you see." She kicked her horse into a faster trot, and Akitada fell behind.

The mulberry groves thinned, and an icy wind began to catch at their clothes. The narrow road joined a much wider highway leading into the mountains. Akitada looked back over his shoulder. Behind him stretched the plain toward the distant bay—a thin silver line marking the separation of the night sky from the land. Between them and the sea lay the city, an amorphous mass of snow-covered roofs, pine groves, and pagodas.

Tora sat huddled into his quilted coat, staring ahead. "Looks dark in those woods," he muttered.

The mountains loomed ominously ahead, and the band of moon-silvered road led straight into them. Within minutes the pine forest swallowed them up.

The forest screened them from the wind, but small night animals frightened their horses, and many eyes, glittering sparks in the darkness of the trees lining the road, watched them pass. Tora cursed once, and when Akitada looked back, he saw in the dim moonlight that Tora was clutching the amulet he wore on a string around his neck. Tora's superstitious fears were at odds with the courage he displayed against human opponents.

The road began to climb, twisting back and forth among rock outcroppings. It was in excellent condition and quite wide, clearly a result of the fame of Joto's temple.

Soon Ayako stopped her horse and waited for them to come up. "There!" she said, pointing. The trees thinned ahead, and they saw the top of a tall pagoda stretching a graceful spire and curved roofs into the starry sky, its snowy ridge tiles and gilded eave ornaments, its bells and hanging lanterns shimmering in the moonlight. "We have to turn aside here," Ayako told them. "The gate is guarded day and night. We'll take the horses into the woods a little ways and walk from there."

She seemed to know her way through the forest, but Akitada soon became completely disoriented. They stopped in a small clearing, dismounted, and tied up the horses.

Tora looked around, glowering. "Where the devil are we?"

Ayako said sharply, "Near the western wall of the temple. When we get closer, you must stop talking and try not to make any noise. They have patrols at night, and we are passing near the stables where the horses may give us away."

A small animal suddenly shot out from under the shrub Tora's horse was sampling, and Tora cursed, tearing violently at the neck of his jacket to reach his amulet.

"Calm down!" Akitada said. "It was just a fox or badger."

"How do you know that's all it was?" Tora looked about him fearfully. "These woods are full of *oni* and *tengu*. Their hungry eyes are watching us from the darkness. There! There's one of them. Let's get out of here." He fumbled frantically with his reins.

"Stop that, you fool," Ayako snapped. "I knew we shouldn't have brought you. And I thought only children were frightened of goblins in the dark."

"Enough," commanded Akitada. "I have no intention of standing about in a cold forest in the middle of the night, listening to two children squabbling."

Ayako muttered, "Sorry!" and walked off so quickly that Akitada and Tora barely kept up with her. She moved silently, graceful and surefooted, in spite of the rocks and tree roots that caused Tora and Akitada to stumble awkwardly behind her.

They emerged from the forest at the foot of a cliff. Its top was crowned by the tiled outer wall of the temple compound. In the pale moonlight the cliff looked inaccessible.

"There," muttered Tora, "I knew it. She got us lost. That's what you get for listening to a stupid female."

"Quiet," Ayako hissed.

"Surely you can't climb up there," Akitada protested in a whisper. "It looks too steep. The monks won't worry about thieves coming from this side."

"You'd be surprised what they worry about," Ayako said darkly. "Come on. I know a way up."

She plunged into the shrubbery at the foot of the cliff, and after a moment Akitada followed. The shrubs hid a narrow crack in the surface of the rock, and now Akitada saw Ayako climbing up this fissure hand over hand like a monkey. His better sense told him to abandon the venture, but he was strangely reluctant. He did not want this strange girl to mock his lack of courage or skill. And then there was the possibility that she might get hurt. He found neither prospect bearable.

The climb turned out to be easier than he had expected—as long as he did not look down and ignored Tora's muttered curses, groans, and desperate scrabblings.

When Akitada joined Ayako on the narrow ledge at the top, he felt ridiculously proud. But before them was a wall that was the height of two tall men and topped with slippery tiles. Several pine trees grew close to it, but all of the overhanging branches had been carefully trimmed off.

Ayako made her way to one particular pine. It was farther from the wall but extended a broken branch to within three feet of the tiles. She climbed up, walked out on the branch, and then made a heart-stopping leap for the wall. She landed like a cat on all fours, crouched for a moment, then sat and looked down at him.

"All's safe," she said softly. Unwinding the black cotton scarf from her head, she lowered it to Akitada. "Grab hold of this and walk up the wall. I'll help pull you up."

Tora snorted.

"I'm much too heavy for you," Akitada told her, adding dubiously, "Climbing the pine tree is the only option."

"No. The branch won't hold you."

"Never mind," grumbled Tora. "I know a better way. Only . . ." He looked at Akitada doubtfully.

"What?" asked Akitada. "Speak up."

"I'll have to go up first, sir."

"This is no time to stand on ceremony. Go ahead."

"But I'll have to stand on your shoulders."

Akitada suppressed a laugh. More and more this excursion reminded him of a boyhood prank. "Where do you want me to stand?"

Tora showed him how to stand with his hands on his hips, back against the wall, and his legs spread a little. Then Tora vaulted upward, stepping first on Akitada's thigh and from there to his shoulder, kneeling first and then putting one foot on each shoulder and standing up. The maneuver was painful, for Tora was considerably heavier than Akitada, who groaned and held his breath, waiting for the moment when those cruel boots would leave his bruised shoulders.

The moment did not come.

Instead there was some cursing. A brief exchange followed, unintelligible to Akitada, who gritted his teeth and concentrated on keeping his knees from buckling under him.

"Get away from me, woman," Tora snarled above him. Then he said apologetically, "Sir? I can't quite reach it. But I think I can make it if I jump for it."

Akitada did not answer.

The next moment Tora pushed off. There was a brief scrabbling sound, while pain shot through Akitada's shoulders and down his back. He started to slip down the wall to his knees. His ears rang and his eyes watered from the pain, but blessedly the weight on his shoulders was gone.

"Sst!" Tora hissed from above. "Sorry about that. Now get hold of this. I'll have you up in no time, sir."

Akitada straightened his trembling legs and looked up at the end of black fabric dangling before his face. He doubted it would support his weight but had too much pride to say so. His neck and shoulders were on fire, but he raised his arms experimentally and seized Ayako's scarf, wrapped it about his wrist, and clambered up the wall to the top.

The slanting tiles were no comfortable perch. He straddled the wall and pretended to look about him while he gingerly moved his shoulders and waited for the pain to subside a little. He wondered if Tora had broken his shoulders.

The temple compound was silent under the stars, its layout apparent in the eerie moonlight: a series of quadrangles and rectangles formed by intersecting covered galleries and walls, each enclosing halls, stables, kitchen, monks' quarters, or storage buildings. The roofs of the great halls, like those of the great pagoda, were tiled. The service buildings had thatched roofs and made darker patches against the gray gravel of the courtyards. Not a soul was about.

"There's the kitchen," Ayako whispered, pointing to a long building in the courtyard below. "And back there are stables and quarters for visiting guests. We'll climb down and go through that gate over there into the next courtyard. That's where the storehouses are."

She got up and began to run along the ridge to a place where a big barrel stood against the wall. Akitada and Tora followed more slowly, unused to walking on the ridged tiles.

But just before they could climb down to level ground, they heard a faint crunching sound. Someone was walking across the gravel.

"Down!" Ayako whispered, flattening her body along the tiles.

They followed her example and watched as two dark figures detached themselves from the shadow of a wall and walked to the kitchen building. They disappeared inside, then reappeared a minute or so later, to move on to the courtyard that enclosed the storehouses.

"Now what?" Tora asked disgustedly.

Ayako gave him a look. "We wait, then follow. From what I've seen, we'll have an hour before they return on their next round."

When she gave the signal, they climbed down and crossed as quietly as possible to the gate. All was still in the next courtyard.

"Come." Ayako started toward the first and largest of the storehouses. When they reached its big wooden door, they found it was not merely latched but locked.

"You see?" Ayako asked.

Akitada nodded. Locking a storehouse in a guarded temple compound implied that the contents were either contraband or extremely valuable.

"I wish we had a key," she said. "This is the only storehouse that's locked, and I bet the missing tax shipments are in it."

Akitada looked at the building. It was large enough to hold twenty shipments of goods, let alone three.

"Here," said Tora. "Let me try." To their astonishment, he produced a thin piece of metal from his sleeve, studied the lock for a moment, and then began to bend the metal with his strong hands. Inserted into the proper opening, the hook tripped the bolt, and the door opened onto darkness. They stepped in.

"Close the door," said Akitada, moving aside and holding his breath. Tora's new clothes released an aroma of stable that was overpowering in close proximity.

For a moment they stood in the dark; then Akitada and Tora both struck flints. The momentary flashes of light revealed a large dim space containing vague piles of goods stretching far into the dark corners. Then both lights went out. Tora fumbled about on the floor. "A moment," he muttered. There was another flash of brightness, and this time Tora managed to light an oil lantern he had found near the door.

They looked around. The storehouse was large and the lantern small. Its light flickered with their every move and threw objects into grotesque relief against vast spaces of darkness that loomed above them and lurked in dim corners and far recesses behind the stacked stores. The air was musty and dry, vaguely smelling of grass mats, old wood, and spices.

As they walked slowly among the piled goods, they heard skittering sounds made by small animals, mice or rats. Akitada lifted the lid off one large barrel and found beans inside. Tora stopped before a long line of large earthenware jars. A long-handled dipper lay on one of them. He picked it up and removed the stopper from the jar. A rich, fruity odor filled the air.

"What do you know?" Tora chuckled in delighted astonishment. "The baldpates have a taste for wine just like the rest of us sinful slobs." He dipped, tasted, and smacked his lips. "Good stuff."

Akitada, still wracked with pain and exhaustion, perched on a stack of boxes and stared at the long row of wine jars. "Strange," he muttered. "Beans are a normal staple in Buddhist monasteries, but wine is forbidden."

"So is raping girls," Ayako snapped and kicked angrily at a long roll of straw matting. "Ouch!" She bent to feel the roll. It made a soft clinking sound.

"Stop drinking, Tora," said Akitada, "and see what's in all those bundles!"

Once the matting of the roll was untied and opened, a number of halberds appeared, each one new and sharply pointed.

"Holy Buddha! *Naginata!*" gasped Tora. "They must be expecting an attack. No wonder they watch this place like it was some fortress under siege."

"Let me see that." Akitada rose and held up the lantern. Roll after roll of straw matting lay stacked against the wall. He inspected the halberds and counted twenty of them in the one bundle. A quick check showed that there were nearly a hundred rolls. "Enough weapons for an army," he said with awe. The soldiers in Otomi's scroll had been armed with *naginata*. A terrible sense of unease crept over him. The idea of a whole order of monks indulging in wine and women was barely to be stomached, but these same monks arming themselves against the local government? Against the emperor? No wonder those inept monks at the Tachibana house had reminded him of recruits. They were. He also remembered vividly the rascally features of the three monks they had seen in the market that first day after their arrival. "Put them back the way we found them, Tora," he said grimly.

Ayako watched with quiet satisfaction. "I told you. I bet your missing taxes are in the rest of those containers."

She began opening boxes and barrels while Akitada trailed along behind her holding the lantern. In its light, he caught golden glints on Ayako's skin, on her eager face, on her small teeth worrying her lower lip, on the line of her slender neck, where a few tendrils of hair had escaped the black scarf. He watched her hands, long and capable, moving quickly among the tubs, boxes, baskets, and bags. But they found nothing more.

It was not until they reached the back wall that Akitada missed Tora.

"We seem to be alone," he said softly to Ayako.

She turned and looked at him.

Akitada suddenly found it hard to breathe normally. "I wonder," he said after a long moment of foolishly smiling at her, "what's become of Tora."

"Here I am." Tora belched, releasing a strong odor of rice wine. "Sir," he said, "I've been thinking. Those boxes back there? The ones you were sitting on. Did they remind you of anything?"

"What do you mean?"

"Well, you had the light, so I couldn't see to check, but I get the feeling they might be the kind you pack silver or gold in."

Akitada walked back quickly and looked at the boxes. His heart started beating faster. The lacquered containers were sturdily built of leather-covered wood, their sides and corners reinforced with metal plates, their handles and locks large and substantial. "Yes, I think you're right," he said. "These are the boxes merchants and government agents use to transport coin and bars of gold and silver."

With cries of pleasure Tora and Ayako fell upon them. But the boxes were not locked and were perfectly empty, stored apparently for some future use. If they had ever been marked with government stamps and seals, these were long gone. By the light of their oil lantern, they looked at each box carefully, but all they could discover were assorted scratches and one rather peculiar scorch mark that looked something like a fish jumping for a ball.

Akitada sighed. "They could have held precious objects used in religious ceremonies," he said. "And the rest of the storehouse contains nothing more suspicious than bales of hemp, boxes packed with brass censers and bells, and ceremonial vestments." He looked around unhappily. Wine and halberds! It just did not add up. Perhaps these items were being stored for some wealthy lay person, though what the allegedly peaceful local barons would want with nearly two thousand halberds he could not imagine.

"Shall we have a look at the other storehouses?" Ayako asked after a moment.

Akitada was tired, but he nodded. "Very well. Put out the light, Tora, but leave the door unlocked. I have a feeling we have overlooked something."

They inspected the other storehouses, all of them unlocked, without finding anything helpful. These contained the usual barrels of bean paste and pickles; bags of rice, barley, millet, and beans; jars of oil; boxes of candles; bales of silk and hemp; shelves filled with crockery, temple ornaments, and damaged statuary—in short, everything and nothing at all incriminating.

"It's getting late," Ayako urged, "and there's one more thing I want to show you. It's been haunting me ever since I first heard it."

"Something you heard?" asked Akitada.

"Yes. It's outside, in back of this storehouse."

Everything was still peaceful in the large courtyard. The stars shimmered above, but the moon had shifted slightly toward the west. To the east there was the first perceptible fading of the night's darkness.

They passed around the back corner of the building and

walked to the middle of the empty space between it and a covered gallery.

"What is over there?" Akitada asked, pointing at several low tiled roofs in the next courtyard.

"The abbot's quarters and temple administration." Ayako was moving about slowly, listening intently. She waved them over. "Listen! Do you hear it?"

Akitada cocked his head. A slight humming sound was barely discernible. "The wind?" he asked.

"No. The wind has died down. Besides, it's too regular. Like people singing far away."

"Yes, you're right. But it seems to come from the ground," Akitada said, squatting down. The sound was still very faint, but he recognized it now as rhythmic chanting. It was much like the ceremony in the Tachibana hall, except that here a sort of communal chant seemed to alternate with a single, reedy voice. "It's a monks' chant," he said, getting up with a frown.

"Coming from the ground?" asked Tora, his voice rising a little in sudden panic. "Let's get out of here. I bet this is where those cursed monks bury their dead."

"Quiet," hissed Akitada. "I want to know where the sound is coming from." He was moving again, bent over, in slowly widening loops that brought him gradually closer to the rear wall of the storehouse they had just left.

He found what he was looking for in the deep shadow of the building: a small wooden grille, slightly more than a foot square and set flush with the ground. It covered an underground air shaft from which the weak and unearthly sound of chanting came more clearly now. The hair on his scalp bristled.

Akitada knelt and bent close to peer into the subterranean darkness. He saw nothing, but a warm stench as of putrefaction filled his nose. Standing up quickly, he suppressed a rising nausea. Tora's words came back to him: This is where those cursed monks bury their dead.

"What is it?" asked Tora from a safe distance.

"I'm not sure. It looks like an air shaft to an underground room." Akitada's voice was strained and flat.

Ayako came up beside him. "You're right," she said, staring down. "I don't like this. It makes my skin crawl." She moved closer to him.

"Hey! Someone's coming," Tora hissed from the corner of the building. "I think it's the patrol."

"Let's go," said Akitada.

They retraced their steps cautiously but quickly. The courtyard remained empty. They reached the gate between the storage yard and the kitchen area safely and were about to pass through and make a dash for the rain barrel when they heard voices. Ducking into the shadow of the wall, they waited.

The two guards came through the gate. Behind them hobbled an elderly monk. All three went to the first building.

"Dear heaven!" whispered Akitada. "We didn't lock it." He suddenly realized the very unpleasant situation they were in. Until then not even the pain in his shoulders had been able to break the spell of the night and the girl. Now they were about to be discovered. Neither in his present function as imperial inspector nor as a humble clerk in the ministry of justice could he afford to be charged with unlawful entry. And then what of the case against Joto? It would be a dismal failure and end his career. No. What was he thinking? They would not be permitted to leave. With a shudder, he thought of the air shaft.

They watched helplessly as the guards rattled the door, exclaimed, and fell to cursing their elderly companion.

"Why, you senile bastard!" one of them shouted. "You left the place unlocked again. This time His Reverence will be told and that will be it for you." They punched and kicked the old monk. He cried out and started to run toward Akitada and his companions. They froze where they were, hoping that the darkness of their clothing blended with the shadow of the wall.

The old man did not get far. His tormentors were upon him in a minute, knocking him to the ground and beating him with their fists.

Tora muttered a curse, and Akitada, after the initial relief that they had not been discovered, flinched with every blow, blaming himself bitterly for his carelessness.

"Stop your noise." One of the young monks yanked the old man up. "Or we'll toss you in that shithole with old Gennin!"

The monk found his courage and cried shrilly, "You are devils! You are an abomination to the Lord Buddha, and your master grovels in the sins of flesh and corruption. You are killers and fornicators and will live in hell forever, where demons will . . . Ahh."

A fist blow full to his mouth stopped his outcry. Akitada could bear no more. He made a move forward, but Ayako snatched at his shoulder. He gasped with the pain.

One of the watchmen raised his head and looked in their direction. For a moment his glance lingered and they thought they were lost.

"You hear anything?" he asked his companion.

The other man looked up from twisting the old monk's arms behind his back and asked irritably, "What? No. Help me with this bastard."

The first monk cast another glance their way. "I thought there was something over there. Something moved."

"Probably a cat."

The two guards dragged the old monk with them and entered the storehouse, presumably to check if anything was missing. A light flickered on inside.

"Quick!" whispered Ayako. "They'll notice that the lantern is still warm. In a minute the whole place will be swarming." As soon as she spoke, there was a shout from the storehouse: "Thieves! Help! Thieves!"

They dashed through the gate, ran for the rain barrel, and clambered up the wall. Tora and Akitada were ahead, pulling Ayako up behind them. In her hurry, she kicked the barrel over but reached the top of the wall, and then they were running along the tiles to the pines. There Tora and Akitada jumped down first, landing with jarring impact and barely catching themselves from tumbling over the cliff.

In the frantic rush of their escape Akitada had ignored the pain in his shoulders, but once he was outside the compound, his knees gave way and he had to lean against the wall for a moment.

From inside the temple compound came the sounds of shouting, then the clangor of a bell. Akitada looked up. Ayako was still on the wall, preparing to jump. She pushed off lightly and landed with a cry of pain. When he reached to steady her, she clutched at his arm.

"What is it?" Akitada asked.

"My ankle." She shook him off, took a few steps, and staggered. "I twisted it," she gasped. "It will be all right in a minute. Go ahead. Hurry!"

On the other side of the wall, voices cried out. Somebody had found the overturned rain barrel.

"No." Akitada took her elbow. "It's too dangerous for you to climb down alone. We'll go together. That way, if you slip, I can catch you."

Behind the wall the noise grew. A head appeared at the top of the wall. Ayako hesitated, then nodded.

They made their way down the crevice with frustrating slowness. Akitada was unfamiliar with the footholds and he was descending blindly and backward. But mostly his attention was on guiding and supporting Ayako. The process involved, of necessity, close proximity. In spite of the difficulty and urgency of the situation, Akitada was intensely aware of her scent and her slender body whenever they touched. He felt a powerful sense of protectiveness and the stirrings of desire. When they reached the ground, she clung to him for a moment before pulling free and limping off into the trees at a half run.

They found their horses, mounted, and regained the road. Behind them, inside the temple, the bell stopped ringing, and the shouts faded away.

The ride back was without incident. They reached the city as the sun rose over the eastern hills. Akitada planned to deliver Ayako to her father's place, then return to the tribunal for a few hours sleep, but the girl, looking flushed and beautiful in the golden light of the rising sun, stopped outside a bathhouse that was already open for business.

"There won't be any hot water at my house," she said to Akitada, "and I must soak my ankle." She paused, then added in a rush, "Why don't you let Tora take the horses and join me? Your shoulders must be stiffening badly by now."

They looked at each other. Her eyes were luminous in the morning light. She smiled nervously. Akitada realized that she had known all along about his injury and was touched that she cared. It seemed natural to accept her invitation.

"Take the horses back, Tora. I'll walk home," he said and dismounted.

ELEVEN

A WORLD OF DEW

The woman who took their money led them to a small room with a large covered wooden vat. A stool served both for sitting and for climbing into the bath. There was a drainage hole in the stone floor near the vat, with two small buckets and bran bags beside it. The only other amenity was a raised platform covered with grass matting. Two faded cotton kimonos hung from a hook, and the air was moist and warm, smelling of wet wood and grass.

The woman pushed aside the heavy lid, and thick, moist steam rose against the sunlight coming from a small window. For a moment it looked as though they had stepped into a cloud of liquefying light. Akitada heard Ayako murmuring something to the attendant but was too tired and bemused to pay attention. He had not slept since the previous night. Mechanically he began to strip, dropping his clothes on the grass mat. He filled one of the small buckets from the vat, crouched near the drain, and tried to scrub himself with a bran bag, dimly aware that

Ayako was doing the same. Almost instantly a sharp pain shot through his shoulder and he gasped.

When her arm reached past him and took the bran bag from his hand to help him, he was too tired to protest.

"Now get into the water," she told him. "You will feel better soon."

"Thank you," he murmured, nearly asleep in the moist warmth of the room. Recalling himself with an effort, he peered at her through the steam. Her golden skin was luminous in the white vapor—a creature from another world. He asked, "What about your ankle?"

"Don't worry." She limped past him, glistening in the warm fog, stepped on the stool, and slipped into the steaming bath with the same smooth ease with which she had scaled cliffs and climbed walls.

He followed more clumsily, entering the water with a splash. The heat enveloped him instantly, driving hours of bitter cold winds and chill night air from his mind. He lowered himself slowly until the water lapped at his chin, his long legs pulled in to allow her room. The hot water soaked into his every pore. He closed his eyes.

But his tiredness fled; he was suddenly wide awake. Akitada had never shared a bath with a woman before, though families regularly bathed together, and bathhouses allowed strangers of both sexes to enjoy communal baths. This was unremarkable, he reminded himself.

Only it was not so in this instance. It was absurd to pretend that this shared bath was simply a practical conclusion to their shared adventure. He had desired Ayako from the moment she had stripped to her waist before their bout with the fighting sticks. Since then he had been unable to take his eyes off her for long, tracing her body through her clothes. His skin had heated to her touch, and now he was aware of his physical arousal.

Ashamed, he looked at her through the wisps of steam, wondering what to do, wondering if she would be angry or disgusted, if she would accuse him of lack of self-control or perhaps, worst of all, laugh at him.

Her eyes were closed. Beads of moisture lay like pearls upon her cheeks, her nose, her lips, and sparkled on her lashes. Her wet hair clung in black tendrils to her slender neck and softly rounded shoulders. Dimly seen through the water, one strand disappeared between her breasts. She was very beautiful. Akitada's mouth became dry. He wanted to look away but could not. There was a single drop of moisture on her upper lip that the sunlight touched with the colors of the rainbow—like jeweled dewdrops sparkling on the grass in the morning sun. He closed his eyes again.

He awoke to her touch, finding her kneeling between his outstretched legs and gently massaging his shoulders.

"Are you feeling better?" she asked, smiling a little, her breath sweet on his lips.

He panicked at their closeness and drew away, saying hoarsely, "You don't have to do this." Hoping she wouldn't stop.

"Kneading the muscles helps heal them," she said practically.

"Someone may come," he protested.

She laughed softly. "No. I told the woman not to disturb us."

Akitada's experience with public baths was limited, but he had never considered them places of assignation. It occurred to him that she must have brought other men here before him, and the thought caused his stomach to knot painfully.

She gazed back calmly, continuing to rub his shoulder muscles. Her touch was both wonderful and frustrating. Pain and pleasure fed desire equally.

"Ayako," he gasped. "You should not do this."

"Don't you want me?" she asked and moved closer, touching

him with her body. He felt her breasts, the nipples pressing against his skin, a sensation so exquisite he sighed and closed his eyes. A smooth thigh pressed gently against his groin. Her lips touched his and their breaths mingled.

"More than anything," he murmured and reached for her.

For a moment she returned the embrace, then detached herself. "Come," she said, taking his hand and rising.

Totally absorbed in each other, they left the water, helped each other into the cotton kimonos to dry their bodies, and then stretched out on the grass mat.

Ayako was experienced in the art of love. Even in his passion, Akitada noted that fact absently, yet not with reproach or distaste but gratitude. His own experience was limited. On the two occasions when he had made love to women of his own class, the business had been awkward. The women had insisted on complete darkness and on being fully clothed. A woman's gown, worn over several underrobes and tied with a sash, could become a formidable obstacle, especially when he had to contend with his own full silk trousers at the same time. Both women had maintained complete silence and lassitude throughout.

There had also been a few prostitutes in his past. They were more accommodating and talkative, but their attentions had seemed mechanical and, he suspected, forced.

Ayako was like none of them. She engaged in love play like an adversary in a contest of skill, meeting his clumsy urgency with skillful evasions, then seeking out every sensitive part of his body with caresses until he learned to reciprocate and discovered that giving pleasure was more pleasurable than taking it. She was teacher and participant and devoted herself with the same passion and skill to lovemaking as to stick fighting.

When she finally submitted to him with a little mewling cry and he took her, he knew that she was taking him also. Head thrown back, eyes closed, her face beautiful in its abandon, she cried out her triumph.

His absurd confusion of martial arts and lovemaking made him smile and he was still smiling at her when they drew apart.

"I like you, Akitada," she said in a tone of surprise.

"The feeling is entirely mutual," he said happily.

But she was matter-of-fact and explained. "I knew you wanted to make love to me when you stared at my breasts last night. Since I wanted you, too, I brought you here. Many men have looked at me in that way. Some I have brought here, but none I really liked."

Her casual admission felt like a sudden shower of icy water. He sat up, hurt that he had been no more than a convenient palliative for her physical need, and said lightly, "I gather they did not come up to expectation," then flushed because it sounded boastful.

"No. That wasn't it." Getting up, she said, "Come. Other customers are waiting."

He watched as she filled the bucket again and washed off the traces of their lovemaking without the least embarrassment. Her body, always beautiful in his eyes, was now familiar and precious to him, like a favorite possession, and the thought frightened him. He was jealous but had no claim on her. He certainly could not offer her marriage even if she were to accept it.

"We will have to walk back," he said. "How is your foot?"

She stood, looking down at her swollen ankle. He gently felt it, manipulating the joint. It did not seem too bad. "Can you walk?" he asked.

"Perfectly," she said and demonstrated, looking back over her shoulder at him.

He let his eyes travel from her smiling lips to the straight shoulders, down the long, golden back and shapely buttocks to slim thighs and legs ending in narrow ankles and feet. The water in the bath had cooled and there was less steam now, but beads of moisture still clung to the back of her neck and her shoulder blades. He wanted to taste them, taste her again. "You are the most beautiful woman I have ever seen," he told her.

She began to put on her clothes rapidly. "No," she said. "I'm too tall and too thin. I look like a scrawny boy. Otomi is beautiful. Any man would prefer her to me."

"Not I," said Akitada.

There was a silence. Then she filled the bucket again. "Come! I'll help you."

But Akitada refused her help this time. His shoulders felt much better. He dressed and said, "I'll walk you home," wondering how he was to face her father.

"No. I have an errand," she said flatly.

He was confused by her sudden distance but did not argue. They went out into the hallway. The voices of other bathers could be heard through the thin boards. The woman put her head out of a doorway, nodded, and grinned broadly. Ayako quickened her step. "What will you do about the buried monks?" she asked in a tight voice.

Ugly reality was back with them.

Akitada held the entrance curtain aside for her as they emerged into the sunny street. "I don't have the faintest idea," he said. "I suppose this is something that only the governor can handle. I plan to see him as soon as I get back to the tribunal." He paused, remembering. "Those words your sister wrote last night, the last ones, about the pack train, what were they?"

She looked away. "'Another life.' She wrote it several times, not very legibly because she was upset. I don't know what it means."

Akitada's lips tightened. "We must die in order to begin another life," he said. "I think that you must watch over your sister carefully in the future."

Her eyes flew to his in alarm.

Putting his hand on her arm, he looked at her. She was almost as tall as he. "About what has happened between us . . ." he started awkwardly, hoping for some acknowledgment of affection, but there was nothing in her expression. He dropped his hand. "I never thanked you for showing us the temple's secrets. It was a very brave thing to do."

A strange, angry look came into her eyes. She stepped back. "Yes, I know. For a girl!" she said and walked away from him.

◆

When Akitada asked to see Motosuke, he was told that the governor had left early that morning for the country to buy horses for their journey to the capital. With a sigh, Akitada went to his quarters, ate some rice gruel, and slept for a few hours.

He woke to the sound of Tora scratching himself.

Looking at his servant drowsily, he said, "Throw away those filthy rags and take a bath."

Tora grinned. "Later. You promised to help me look for Hidesato."

Akitada sat up with a groan. "Very well. But find some other clothes."

A little later, wearing clean but plain robes, they walked out through the tribunal gate and turned south into the city. It was midday, the sun had warmed up considerably, and the air was almost springlike. Akitada was silent, his thoughts on Ayako.

When they reached the market, Tora stopped a street urchin to ask where he might buy some fried rice cakes. The boy held out a grimy hand, but when Tora placed a copper coin into it, he ducked away into the crowd. Tora cursed.

"Is your stomach more important than your friend?" Akitada asked irritably. He was beginning to regret his promise to Tora.

"I'm looking for the rice-cake vendor, sir," Tora explained. "I still have his money. He looked half-starved. I'm sure he needs it back."

"Oh." Akitada was chastened. "Perhaps he only works in the evenings?" he suggested.

But he was wrong. Moments later Tora caught the familiar smell of fried cakes and took off after it with quivering nostrils. Akitada followed and found Tora in conversation with a thin young man in ragged clothes. The vendor was staring at the silver Tora had placed in his hands.

"We caught the crooks," Tora was saying, "so you don't have to pay them ever again. Next time report the trouble to the constables."

The young man gave a bitter laugh. "Thanks for the advice," he said, tucking the silver away. "You say you caught the bastards, but they're on the streets again. Who do you think the constables work for? Everyone gets a cut from the take."

"What do you mean?" Akitada demanded sternly.

The vendor gave him a startled look and muttered, "Nothing, sir." He snatched up his bamboo yoke, hooked the hampers to it, and trotted off.

Tora looked after him. "Crooked officials. Just like I told you," he said heavily. "That's why those murderous bastards are on the loose again." He spat in disgust.

"I don't believe it," said Akitada. "Ikeda seemed efficient, and the governor didn't mention any problems. It must be idle gossip. Are we near that wine shop where you met Hidesato? Good. Perhaps your friend has returned to it."

"It's not your kind of place. Only common trash like me goes there."

Akitada stopped. "As long as you work for me, you are not to refer to yourself in those terms again!"

Tora grinned reluctantly. "Sorry, sir."

The fat host of the Heavenly Abode welcomed Tora like an old friend but only nodded to Akitada. Except for a drowsy old man, the place was empty.

"What's this about those hoodlums being out of jail already?" Tora asked.

The host rolled his eyes. "The bastards! Next time they walk in here, I'll cut out their stomachs," he boasted. "I keep a sharp knife under the counter."

"I didn't see you doing any belly-cutting the other night."

The host waved a hand. "You two had things well in hand."

The solitary guest, ancient and bent almost double, suddenly cried in a cracking voice, "Amida is great. Amida saves."

They glanced at him and looked away.

"I've lost touch with my buddy," Tora said. "Has he been back?"

"No." Seeing Tora's disappointment, the fat man offered, "But if he comes in, I'll tell him you're looking for him."

"Thanks." Tora turned to go.

When Akitada saw Tora's dejected face, he followed him out and said, "I think we should try the garrison. Hidesato was a sergeant. Perhaps he put in for duty there."

Tora brightened. "You're right. He might do that."

The garrison was beside the Western Gate, surrounded by high palisades and with colorful banners flying from its large main gate. Akitada gave his name and rank to the guard and asked to see the commandant. The man looked dubiously at their plain clothes but sent a recruit to report.

The recruit returned with an older man, dark-skinned and husky, his face ringed with a graying beard. He wore short baggy pants, leggings, and half-armor over a shirt and looked sharply at them.

"Lieutenant Nakano," he introduced himself in a gravelly voice after Akitada had repeated his name and rank. "The captain's in his office."

The garrison covered a city block and contained several long, low buildings—soldiers' quarters and stables—and a large hall that served as headquarters. In the open courtyard, foot soldiers were drilling with halberds and long shields, and beyond it, mounted men circled a target at full gallop, their bows stretched, loosing arrows at it in measured volleys.

"Would you look at that?" Tora said. "For soldiers they're as good as any I've seen. That captain must be a good man."

Leaving Tora outside, Akitada followed Lieutenant Nakano into the hall. They passed busy clerks and aides to the back, where the lieutenant opened a door and announced, "Lord Sugawara."

Akitada stopped on the threshold. Captain Yukinari's head wore a bloody bandage. He rose but looked pale and seemed to sway on his feet as he bowed.

"That's all, Lieutenant," Yukinari said. The door closed.

"What happened to you?" Akitada asked.

"It's nothing. A freak accident. Please be seated, sir."

As they sat down, Akitada saw that the captain held his left arm tucked close to his chest. "Your injuries look serious. Were you attacked?"

Yukinari wiped perspiration from his forehead. "No, no. A foolish accident. I work out early every morning before the men get up. When I'm done, I ring a big bronze bell in the exercise yard. It signals the men to assembly. This morning, when I gave the bell the usual hard push, it fell. Fortunately, it only clipped my head and my left shoulder or it would have killed me. Apparently a wooden beam was rotten and gave way."

"I see. Then I'm glad you escaped. I shall be brief. Would you mind telling me exactly how you traced the most recent tax convoy?"

Yukinari nodded. "The first two raids happened before my time, but I was very careful with my orders for the last convoy. They were to proceed by land, following the coast road until it joins the Great Eastern Road. Instead of using regular bearers and grooms for the pack train, I substituted foot soldiers. In addition, the convoy was preceded by twenty mounted warriors and followed by twenty more. The men were handpicked, superb archers and swordsmen." He sighed. "Lieutenant Ono was in command, an experienced soldier who had been an aide to my predecessor. He volunteered. A brave man."

Akitada made note of this "volunteer" but said only, "I don't doubt it."

"Two weeks later I sent a scout by boat across the bay. He returned and reported that the convoy did not reach Fujisawa. I immediately set out myself with a small force and followed the route taken by Lieutenant Ono. We lost all trace of them in Shimosa province. It was as if they had disappeared into thin air. One day they were approaching a large village near the border of Musashi province; the next day they were gone. The barrier guards had not seen them."

"What about the local authorities in Shimosa province?"

"Not cooperative."

Akitada raised his brows. "Do you suspect them or the barrier guards of abetting robbers?"

"No. We raised the question of highway robbery, and they were offended. To them, we sounded critical of law and order in their province. I have no doubt they reported my insulting manner to the military authorities in the capital." He grimaced. "Frankly, I look forward to reassignment to the front," he said.

His tone was fatalistic. Akitada wondered about that. The

captain's pallid face might be due to the accident or it might have other causes. Yukinari looked like a very unhappy man. Akitada cleared his throat apologetically. "There is another, unrelated matter that you may be able to help me with. My servant Tora has a very close friend, a Sergeant Hidesato. They met briefly in this city two nights ago but lost touch again. I thought the sergeant might have reported here to offer his services. I understand he was out of work."

Yukinari's eyebrows rose, but he did not express surprise that an imperial inspector should consult him about his servant's problem. He clapped his hands and, when the lieutenant responded, relayed the question. Nakano saluted and disappeared on his errand.

Akitada wondered how he might next broach the Tachibana case. Yukinari relieved him of the problem.

Fidgeting with his writing utensils and avoiding Akitada's eyes, he asked, "Is there any more information about Lord Tachibana's death?"

"No, but I made a visit of condolence and found the widow very distraught. Apparently she has been deserted by everyone."

Yukinari's ears turned pink. "It is difficult to know what to do," he said vaguely.

"I should have thought that your friendship with both would have made it proper and dutiful to offer your services to the young widow."

Yukinari gave him a desperate look and mopped his brow again. "It . . . you don't understand," he stammered. "She would not expect it."

"Just what is your connection with Lady Tachibana, Captain?" Akitada asked bluntly.

Yukinari turned crimson. "May I ask why you are interested, sir?"

Yukinari hardly looked like a killer, but love could do strange things to a man. Akitada decided on more shock tactics. "Lord Tachibana was murdered. You were seen in the Tachibana compound the night he died."

Yukinari dropped his face into his hands and muttered, "Dear heaven."

Akitada said, "Are you admitting the murder, Captain?"

Yukinari shook his head dazedly. "No, of course not. I respected him like a father."

"Then what did you mean?"

Yukinari flushed again. "I don't know. I feel responsible. Perhaps I should have told him."

"Told him what?"

Yukinari looked distressed. "She is . . . was not happy. That is why she and I . . . we became lovers. I was ashamed to tell him. Didn't want to hurt him . . . or her."

"Your presence in the Tachibana mansion on the night of the murder makes you a suspect, and you have just admitted to a motive."

Yukinari shook his head and winced, raising his good hand to the bandage. "It wasn't me. I was out of town that night and didn't return until after sunrise. That's when I heard of his accident. Besides, the affair was brief and it ended last summer." Seeing Akitada's dubious expression, he added quickly, "Believe me, I have regretted my behavior very deeply. I looked on Lord Tachibana as the father I never knew. He was kind to me." He sighed. "I cannot expect you to understand, but their marriage was not like other marriages. The age difference made her more like an adopted daughter than a wife. In fact, she was . . . They didn't . . . There were times when I thought he might even approve."

Akitada drew himself up stiffly. Yukinari's rationalization was, to his mind, utterly reprehensible. "Did the lady break off the relationship?"

"No, I did. She was angry with me, but I had other reasons by then."

Akitada thought of that childlike creature and her tears. "I wonder that did not occur to you earlier," he snapped. "What other reasons?"

"I . . . There was someone else," the captain stammered. "It cannot matter now." He gave a bitter laugh. "The poet Narihira said that love is as short-lived and deceitful as dew. He was right." He dropped his face into his hands again.

The poetic image of dew reminded Akitada of the beads of moisture on Ayako's golden skin. He stared at the captain and wondered what to say, when Lieutenant Nakano returned to report that a Sergeant Hidesato had applied for military service the previous week. His application had been approved, but Hidesato was no longer at the address he had given. He had been thrown out for nonpayment of rent, and no one knew where he had gone.

Yukinari nodded. "Thank you, Lieutenant. Now please report to His Excellency about the incident in Hanifu village."

Nakano snapped to attention and recited, "Two days ago, after sundown, we received word about an ambush of one of our patrols. The captain set out immediately with four cavalrymen. He returned after the morning rice the following day with our men. Four of them had been wounded in a fight with a group of hooded criminals armed with swords and halberds. Their attackers escaped, but one of them was a monk." Seeing Akitada's surprise, he added, "He lost his hood."

"Thank you, Lieutenant." Akitada turned to Yukinari. "Have you had problems with the monks from the Temple of Fourfold Wisdom?"

Yukinari flushed angrily. "Have we?" he said. "There has been continuous friction between those hoodlums and my soldiers. This is only the latest incident, but this time they were armed. Every time my men encounter those baldpates, they come to blows with them. At first we punished our people severely, in spite of their protests that they had been provoked. Then I was a witness to the behavior of those monks in an incident with a local merchant. I have since complained repeatedly to Ikeda, most recently on the morning of the . . . murder, but to no avail. In my opinion, the prefect is incompetent." Yukinari stopped, swallowed, and added more calmly, "I have ordered my men to stay away from the monks. More I cannot do."

Akitada nodded. "Thank you. You confirm my suspicions. It may be that you can do something after all. We will speak of it later."

Yukinari stood and bowed, then looked at him with empty eyes. "If I can be of any assistance in the other . . . case, I would be grateful for the chance, Your Excellency."

Akitada found Tora regaling an eager group of soldiers with stories of his military exploits in the north. They parted company reluctantly.

"You were right, sir," Tora said excitedly. "Hidesato's been here. Filled out his application and left again."

"I know. And it was accepted, but when they tried to notify him, he had moved."

"Oh." Tora's face fell. "One of the soldiers said he saw him in town. In the brothel quarter. I suppose I'll try there next."

"Very well. Lead the way."

"You?" cried Tora. "In the brothel quarter? No. I'll go by myself."

"We go together." Akitada's expression allowed no argument.

TWELVE

RAT'S TALES

𝒯he brothels were in the southwest quadrant, not far from the market, but in an area of poor tenements and cheap wine shops. In narrow, dirty streets littered with human and inanimate debris, cripples and blind beggars huddled wherever they could find a sunny wall. Filthy, half-naked children covered with bruises and sores ran about, screaming. Few healthy young men were in evidence, and those had hungry eyes that watched Akitada and Tora speculatively. Now and then one would approach and offer to show them to a "love house" with "first-rate girls" or introduce them to "jesters."

"Jesters?" asked Akitada.

Tora made a face. "Pretty boys," he said.

They asked about Hidesato and twice paid good coppers to be led to him, only to discover that their guide had willfully misunderstood and taken them to a brothel instead.

Eventually the streets grew dark and chill. Here and there a lantern bobbed, marking the arrival of customers. Raucous laughter and song rang into the dark streets every time some- one lifted the gaudy curtains of wine shops and brothels. From behind bamboo grilles female voices called out to them, and when they looked, they saw behind the bars ghostly creatures, their eyes and lips garish in masklike faces turned a sickly green, yellow, or lavender by the colored lights of paper lanterns. Love was for sale in every color of the rainbow.

The thought of buying one of those grotesque females nau- seated Akitada. He thought of Ayako and how clean she was, how sweet the scent of her skin, how naturally she had come into his arms. His longing for her suddenly overwhelmed him. He stopped in the middle of the street. "Tora," he said, "I think we have done enough today. Why not stop by Higekuro's before we turn in for the night?"

Tora agreed immediately.

The quiet street of Higekuro's school was a different world. In the dusk, neighbors were having their evening chats in the street. Ayako, too, was outside her door, leaning on a broom and laughing with an elderly woman who held a small child in her arms. Ayako wore only a simple gown and had her hair pulled back and tied with a ribbon, but Akitada's heart missed a beat.

When she saw him, her face lit up. She smoothed back her hair with unconscious feminine grace and smiled shyly.

Tora whistled between his teeth. "Now there's a change for the better," he said. "I guess all that girl needed to turn her into a proper female was a man in her bed."

Akitada gave him a look of cold fury. "Ayako risked her life last night," he said through clenched teeth. "If I ever hear you insult her again, it will be the last time you will speak in my presence. Do you understand?"

Tora's chin sagged. Akitada went to greet Ayako, seeking in

her eyes what he felt in his heart, hoping that she was no longer angry. The neighbor muttered a good night and scuttled across the street.

"How are you?" Akitada asked softly.

"Very well. And your shoulders?"

"Much better. I am . . . ," he searched for words, "deeply grateful."

Her eyes softened.

"Perhaps," he suggested daringly, "we could repeat the treatment in the morning?"

She blushed. "Why not? If your shoulders still give you pain."

"Tomorrow then." He added more loudly, "We've come for a visit."

"Oh."

They looked at each other hungrily. Belatedly, Akitada remembered Tora. When he turned, he found Tora pretending to study the massive gate of the house next door. Set into a new ten-foot-high wall, it was studded with heavy iron nails and had a forbidding appearance.

"That must be the house of the successful silk merchant," Akitada said to Ayako. "Do you know the family well?"

"Not at all. He's a very unpleasant man, and his servants are rude. We don't talk to them. No one on this street does. As to his family, they never come out. It must be his wealth that has made him so suspicious of everyone."

"Perhaps," said Akitada, frowning.

Ayako cleared her throat. "Please come in. I . . . we did not expect you, but you are very welcome." Turning to open the door, she added, "I'm afraid we have one guest already. The Rat stopped by."

"The Rat's here?" Tora asked, coming up. "That old crook conned me out of half my wages for wine and new clothes."

Ayako looked surprised, then smiled. "That was very kind of you, Tora," she said, touching his arm. Tora blinked.

They passed through the empty exercise hall into the living quarters. Higekuro sat in his usual place. Otomi knelt beside him among small containers of paint, her brush poised over a sheet of paper. When she saw Tora, her eyes lit up.

A fire in the stove warmed the room, and something savory bubbled in a pot.

"Ho," wheezed an old man who huddled beside the stove, "told you, Higekuro. No time at all and both girls will bring you the sons you never had."

Ayako turned abruptly and ran upstairs.

Ignoring the Rat, Higekuro invited Akitada to sit next to him. Otomi gathered up her paints.

"You're in time to join us for our evening meal," Higekuro said cheerfully, pouring wine. "We got some particularly fine clams from a neighbor, so Otomi chopped fresh vegetables from the garden and made soup. Plain fare, but for once we have good rice with our meal instead of millet. A feast, in fact." He chuckled and rubbed his hands, adding, "Though I have a fondness for millet also."

Akitada admired this man's joy in the poorest gifts life had to offer. He felt awkward, worried that Higekuro might suspect what had happened between himself and Ayako.

"And here's the Rat, too." Higekuro laughed. "He's a great one for telling ghost stories when he's drunk. We've been filling his cup for the past hour."

"Hey, Rat," said Tora, "how come you never let on about your talent? And where are the new clothes I paid for?" The beggar choked on his wine and fell into a fit of coughing and wheezing. "I love a good tale," Tora said, slapping him on the back solicitously.

The Rat hunched up his bony shoulders. "Don't mock the ghosts!" he croaked.

Akitada laughed. He felt inexplicably happy. "Never fear," he said, "Tora has too much respect for ghosts."

Higekuro said, "It's a strange fact that the more superstitious men are, the more they want to hear about such things."

"Did Ayako tell you what we found in the temple?" Akitada asked him in a lowered voice.

"Yes." Higekuro became grave. "Not ghosts, I think. You've told the governor?"

"Not yet. He has left town."

Ayako was coming down from the loft. She had changed into a chestnut-brown silk gown and tied a brown-and-white-patterned sash about her slender middle. Her hair was loose and, though it was not as long as that of ladies of the nobility, reaching only to her waist, it was thick and lustrous and curled slightly at the ends. Akitada's eyes followed her as she busied herself gathering rice bowls and chopsticks. He was thinking how graceful and efficient all her movements were, when his ears picked up a phrase.

He looked at the Rat. "You saw ghosts in the Tachibana mansion? When? Come, speak up!" His voice was suddenly sharp and his tone peremptory.

The Rat recognized the tone of authority and cringed. "Not inside, Your Honor. Never inside. The Rat never goes where he's not supposed to be. Just in the alley. I was looking through the garbage in the alley."

"By heaven," said Akitada. "Are there people who must eat rotten food that their betters would not give to their dogs?"

The Rat was offended. "I never eat rotten food," he said. "The rich throw out good stuff. Last month I found a whole sea bream among the radish tops and abalone shells behind the rice merchant's place."

"About the Tachibana mansion," Akitada said more gently.

"Didn't have time to look properly." The Rat gave a wheeze and whispered, "Jikoku-ten struck me with his sword."

"Jikoku-ten? The Guardian King of the East?"

The Rat nodded. "That's the one. It's a miracle I'm alive to tell about it," he said darkly, wheezing a little for effect. "He was fetching the soul of the old governor."

Tora stared at him. "You don't mean it! Did he see you?"

The Rat rubbed his head. "How could he miss? There I was, by the back gate, looking up at him. He had burning pieces of charcoal for eyes and struck me with his sword—just there, feel it? I passed out. Next thing I knew, I was lying half-frozen in the snow under the kitchen window, and the maids inside were weeping and shouting about the old lord having passed away. I tell you, I haven't been myself since." He held out his empty cup.

Akitada was on his feet. Striding over to the Rat, he took his scrawny wrist in a viselike grip and removed the wine cup. "Pay attention!" he snapped. "When was this?"

The beggar cried out in pain or fear, and Ayako's hand was on Akitada's arm. "You're frightening him," she murmured. Akitada released the beggar.

The Rat shot him an aggrieved look and rubbed his wrist. "I sleep in the old fox shrine behind the Tachibana place, see. It's real quiet there. Only night before last something woke me and I crept out in the alley for a pee. It was snowing, but there was that garbage barrel by the gate. I felt a little empty, so I went to take a look. That's when the light started bobbing about." The Rat shuddered, and Tora sucked in his breath. "All of a sudden there's all this scraping and scratching and hissing like fire. Whoosh! Whoosh! Whoosh! Only no smoke."

"Go on. Go on," urged Tora, his eyes wide.

"I was bending down to look through the boards of the gate when it flew open. I saw his boots first and a bit of his blue robe.

Then I looked up and there were those fiery eyes piercing me. The last thing I remember is falling on my knees crying to the Buddha, then he struck me. I still got this monstrous pain in my head and I haven't been able to eat a bite since." The Rat glanced over at the stove and sniffed. "I'm a little better, I think."

Akitada returned to his seat. "A strange ghost story," he said with a frown.

Higekuro laughed. "The wine has done its work. Let's see if he can tell us another one. Ayako, Otomi! Is the soup ready yet?"

The soup was excellent and Ayako sat demurely by Akitada's side, serving him wine and placing choice bits of clam in his bowl. The Rat recovered his appetite and when the bowls were empty and the women were cleaning up, he embarked on another tale.

"I got a friend who watched an *oni* procession and lived to tell about it," he said, scratching his belly and belching. "It happened in the city where the emperor lives. My friend says the palaces have golden roofs there and the high-born ladies are so beautiful, you'd think they were fairies in paradise. He would have stayed forever except for the demons."

Tora shivered. "I bet he was as frightened as a mouse in the cat's paw."

Higekuro winked at Akitada and whispered, "And I bet the Rat's friend also sampled some of that strong wine I remember from my younger years."

The Rat heard him and nodded. "You're right. It was the chrysanthemum festival and my friend was celebrating, but he was sober when he saw what he saw. He'd spent his last coppers that night and had no money for lodgings, so he slept in an old temple that was all boarded up. He put down his bundle, made himself comfortable, and dozed off. Now old temples like that are regular meeting places for evil spirits, only he didn't know that. When he heard people singing and laughing, he thought it was a party and got up to look." The Rat paused to empty his cup. Then he looked around and whispered, "It was no human party he saw," and fell silent.

Tora, his eyes round with suspense, shook the Rat's arm impatiently and made him cough again. Otomi refilled the Rat's cup. He drank, wiped his mouth with the back of his hand, and continued.

"Oh, it was a gruesome sight," he said, his voice rising a little. "It was a whole crowd of *oni*, as evil a set of devils as you'll ever meet, and passing before his very eyes. There were near a hundred of them, he said, and they looked horrible. Some had only one eye in the middle of their face. Some had horns, or pointed ears and long noses, some had long red hair all over their bodies. There were some as thin as chopsticks, and some as round as chestnuts. And in front walked a giant with a face like fire and claws for hands. They all gathered by an old well in the middle of the temple courtyard."

Akitada exchanged a smile with Ayako. He enjoyed the tale and was beginning to feel benevolent toward the Rat.

"Now," continued the Rat, "what with the moon and all them torches, it was bright as day, and my friend could see they had a young lady with them. The young lady was as beautiful as a fairy and had jewels in her hair and she was crying. But the evil demons only laughed and mocked her, pulling her this way and that. They tore off her gown and ripped the jewels from her hair, and she was lying there in the dirt . . ." The Rat paused and looked at Ayako. "Storytelling is hungry work. Would there be some soup left?"

Ayako went to fill a bowl and brought it to him. He raised it to his lips, slurped noisily, chewed, and asked, "Where was I?"

Tora said impatiently, "The beautiful lady was lying there all naked . . ."

"Not naked," cried the Rat, shocked. "I never said 'naked.'

You have a filthy mind, Tora. No, she was still wearing her underrobe. But not for long . . ."

"There, I knew it!" muttered Tora.

"Will you shut up? If you keep interrupting, I'll never get done. I said not for long, because the giant with the red eyes and fiery flames shooting from his face got in a fight with the others over the jewels. He roared like the fiend he was, but the other devils were too fast for him and ran away. So he roared some more and then he saw the lady lying there in her thin gown and went to get that off her. The lady screamed, and he ripped, and she fought him. And then he took his knife, shoved it in her, and fell upon her body . . ."

Ayako gasped, and the Rat broke off and said piously, "In the presence of ladies I can't talk about what happened next, but demons are nasty creatures. Anyway, when he was done with her, he dumped her in the well and went away. My friend was frightened to death and left the capital that very night."

Tora heaved a sigh of pleasurable horror, but Ayako glared at the Rat. "I might have known you'd come up with something dirty," she spat. "I don't believe a word about this friend of yours. You made up the whole thing yourself, you and your nasty mind."

The Rat wheezed. "I saw you. You had your ears wide open, girl." He cackled. "Women act like prudes, but they talk dirt with their girlfriends."

"Why, you . . ." Ayako half rose amid the general laughter.

Akitada caught her hand to pull her back down beside him when his eyes met Higekuro's knowing smile.

THIRTEEN

HIDESATO AND
THE HARLOT

The following morning Akitada attempted to see the governor again but was told that Motosuke had returned late and was still asleep. Tora, chastened by his master's outburst the evening before, made no comment when Akitada canceled their usual workout for a visit to the bathhouse. Seimei was another matter.

"What is wrong with the tribunal bath?" he asked.

"Nothing. But the bathhouse has . . . masseurs, and since I injured my shoulder . . ." Trailing off, Akitada busied himself with his morning rice.

Seimei was distracted from the bathhouse issue. "You were lucky you only hurt your shoulder. Your ancestors must shudder at the risks you take with their good name. Stealing into a monastery with low-class companions like thieves in the middle of the night! Imagine the scandal if you had been caught. It would have been the end of your career."

"More than likely it would have been the end of my life." Akitada smiled, his mind on Ayako.

"It is no joking matter," cried Seimei. "After years of disappointment, you got this chance to make a name for yourself. Imperial inspector before your twenty-sixth year and you choose to behave in this reckless fashion! Remember, the path to success makes for a long and troublesome journey, but the way back is quick and easy." Seimei's voice broke.

Akitada's conscience smote him. "I'm sorry I made you worry, old friend," he said. "You're right, it was a very risky thing to do, but I had no other choice. Consider it part of the troublesome journey to success."

Seimei's face lit up. "Ah. You have solved the case."

"Not quite. Let's say we are closer to the answer." Pushing away his empty bowl, Akitada rose and went to keep his appointment at the bathhouse.

It was nearly midday before he got back. He took up Otomi's scrolls and walked across the compound to the governor's residence. Akinobu greeted him with a smile and led the way to the library.

They found Motosuke, sleek as usual, in figured blue silk over pale green trousers, eating heartily from a large number of dishes.

"His Excellency is here, sir," announced Akinobu, and withdrew.

"Elder brother!" Motosuke cried, apparently still enamored of his new honorific for Akitada. He smiled and waved his chopsticks in the air. "Welcome, welcome! Forgive my not rising. I got back late last night and here I am, just now eating my morning rice. Shameful, isn't it?" He pointed the chopsticks at a cushion near him. "Have a seat. Have some fish. Or some abalone? Pickled radish? Nothing? Well, then, Akinobu says you stopped by twice, last evening and again this morning. I am devastated that I missed you. What happened?"

"It's a long story. Permit me." Akitada went to hang Otomi's scrolls from a standing screen.

Motosuke peered at them, then clapped his hands. "The deaf-mute girl! You've found her. Oh, they are very nice. Very nice, indeed. And is she as pretty as they say, eh?"

"She is very pretty, yes. But that is not why I brought the pictures."

"If you say so. I am delighted you discovered a local beauty." Akitada flushed against his will, and Motosuke's eyes twinkled. "Ah! I see the way it is. Ha, ha. And I thought you a dull dog. Or worse, a fondler of boys, like our saintly abbot."

"Joto?"

"Ahem." They looked up and saw Akinobu at the door, his face expressionless. Beside him stood the abbot.

Joto came in smoothly. "Did I hear my name?" he asked, adroitly avoiding the difficult rank distinction by bowing to Motosuke and Akitada simultaneously. Without waiting for an invitation, he seated himself and looked at Motosuke's array of food. "I see I am late for the midday rice," he said with a smile.

"Merely unexpected," said Motosuke dryly. He clapped his hands. When Akinobu looked in, he said, "The abbot is hungry. Have them send in some vegetarian dishes and"—he paused and looked at Joto—"fruit juice or tea, Abbot?"

"No food, just tea, Akinobu." Turning to his host, Joto said, "I apologize for my small joke, Governor. It is too early for our only meal of the day, and besides, I have come on business." He noticed the scroll paintings. "Are these new? A local artist?" he asked.

"I think you know her," Akitada said, watching Joto's face. "She is a young deaf-mute woman who specializes in Buddhist paintings."

"Ah, Otomi." Joto squinted again at the scrolls. "Poor girl. We have given her every assistance by allowing her to copy our originals and by introducing her to wealthy visitors."

There was a scratching at the door, and a servant entered to serve tea. He departed, leaving the large teapot simmering on a brazier.

"You said you came on business?" Motosuke asked the moment the servant had gone, his brusqueness with Joto more noticeable. Akitada wondered if he just wished to be rid of him or whether there was another reason for his lack of courtesy.

Joto seemed not to notice. "I came to extend a humble invitation to you," he said, bowing to Motosuke. "And to His Excellency also." He bowed to Akitada. "We hope that you will both be our honored guests for the dedication ceremonies for our new hall. The presence of two representatives of our august emperor will lend special significance to our simple celebration and inspire the local people with due reverence. Dare I hope that you will say a few words?"

Motosuke put down his chopsticks and wiped his mouth with a sheet of soft mulberry paper he withdrew from one of his sleeves. "You may count on me," he said graciously.

Akitada added his own acceptance, hoping he would be spared the speech.

To their surprise, Joto lingered after giving the particulars. "There is another, less pleasant matter I wished to bring to your attention, Governor," he said. "It concerns a crime. Blasphemous thieves have become bold enough to rob the Buddha himself."

Akitada knew what was coming.

"Really?" asked Motosuke, astonished. "I expect word of your treasures is getting out. What did they get away with?"

Joto placed the palms of his hands together and raised them to his lips. "Nothing, thanks be to Amida. Our people kept their eyes open and surprised them in the attempt. The villains fled, but we may not be so fortunate next time."

"Shocking, if it is so," said Akitada, shaking his head. "But didn't you say that nothing was taken? Perhaps your monks simply surprised some curious pilgrims."

Joto fixed him with a cold stare. "Impossible. We have learned to be careful of those who pretend devotion for evil purposes. Pilgrims are not admitted after dark, and those who spend the night in the monastery are locked into their rooms. Besides, my disciples got a good look at the three culprits as they scrambled over the wall. Their clothing and appearance marked them as professional robbers, the kind that roam our streets and highways with such impunity."

Akitada raised his brows. "A very surprising thing for high-waymen to do, in my experience. There is another possibility, if I may make such a suggestion. Just as a criminal may hide un-der a pilgrim's robe and straw hat, the same man may shave his head and put on the habit of a monk. Is Your Reverence certain that all the monks presently at the temple are, in fact, what they appear to be?"

Joto's eyes glittered. "I cannot accept your theory," he said. "It casts doubt on our community and undermines the good we have achieved in this province. Indeed, such rumors have been spread before, but only by our enemies."

So hostilities had begun. Akitada put on a bland face. "Just a suggestion. It is equally possible that it was a prank by ghost-hunting youngsters. The temple is said to be haunted."

"I cannot imagine where Your Excellency heard rumors of ghosts. We are trained to exorcise evil spirits, not to raise them."

"Ah," said Akitada, "this is very true. But the less enlightened souls among the local people often have a difficult time distin-guishing between saints and demons. You must admit that in spiritual as well as worldly affairs things are not always as they appear to be." He had the intense pleasure of seeing Joto at a loss for words.

Motosuke cleared his throat. "Have you reported the incident to Ikeda?" he asked. "He's the man to talk to. I regret that I am already busy with travel plans. In fact, Lord Sugawara and I were in the middle of planning our route just now."

Joto compressed his lips and rose. "In that case I regret my intrusion," he said, bowing stiffly.

Akitada and Motosuke rose also. "Not at all," the governor murmured, moving toward the door.

Joto managed to pass close to the scrolls. Before the painting of the storm dragon he seemed to miss a step for a moment, but then he walked rapidly to the door and left.

"Phew," said Motosuke as they resumed their seats. "I thought the fellow would never leave. What a silly tale. Robbers in the temple. Now, what did you come to tell me?"

"That I was one of the robbers."

Motosuke's jaw dropped.

Akitada told him about their nighttime excursion and what they had found. Motosuke looked stunned, his eyes becoming rounder and rounder, and his initial amusement gradually giving way to horror.

"Holy heaven!" he cried when Akitada was done. "Do you mean to say that Joto has buried some of the monks alive? But why?"

"I suspect they refused to be converted to his teachings," Akitada said dryly. "Does the name Gennin mean anything to you?"

"Of course. Gennin was abbot before Joto. He is supposed to have retired because of ill health. Are you saying he is down there?"

"I am afraid so. And Gennin is not alone. We heard voices chanting. How soon can we move in with constables and set them free?"

Motosuke shook his head. "I don't see how . . . not with constables in any case. With that cache of *naginata* we need an army." He twisted his hands in frustration.

"The man is a threat to the country's security." Akitada gestured to Otomi's painting of the storm dragon. "That scroll is what made me suspicious of Joto and his temple in the first place. All the soldiers on that ship are armed with *naginata,* and a monk sits on the raised platform normally reserved for a captain or general."

Motosuke got up and looked. "How very odd," he said. "How did the deaf-mute girl come to paint this?"

"I think she witnessed the ambush of the tax convoy and painted the criminals. If I'm not mistaken, those soldiers are armed monks. Yukinari just reported an encounter with a small band of *naginata*-armed monks." Akitada paused, frowning. "I'm afraid that Joto may have realized just now what the scroll means."

"He's nearsighted. Besides, it looks like just another dragon painting. You did not find *any* trace of the tax goods at the temple?"

"No. They must be elsewhere. I have a suspicion about one of the local merchants, but that will have to wait. Gennin and the others must be released first."

Motosuke sighed and looked at Akitada helplessly. "I don't think you quite understand the problem, my dear Akitada. We cannot storm the temple with constables or soldiers. The local people will not permit it. They will rise up against anyone who attacks their benefactors."

Too true. Akitada realized it immediately. The frustration caused him to burst into angry speech. "Then they must be made to see that it is not saints but monsters they protect."

"But how?" yelped Motosuke.

Akitada suddenly had a wild idea and seized Motosuke's

arm. "The ceremony! The one we are invited to attend. Don't you see? There will be a huge crowd. What more perfect excuse to move in soldiers? And when we bring out our proof in the person of the liberated Gennin, the people will be convinced of Joto's guilt."

Motosuke stared. "Holy Buddha! You can't mean it. Oh, my dear friend, think of the risks."

Akitada released Motosuke. Suddenly, he saw the situation from the other man's perspective. If the Buddhist faction at court found out, as they must, that Akitada and Motosuke had disrupted a religious ceremony with arms and caused, as was probable, bloodshed, both Motosuke's career and his daughter's elevation to empress were in jeopardy. Against this the fate of a few elderly monks in a subterranean prison must weigh very lightly, indeed.

But the governor surprised him. Motosuke straightened his small, fat body and squared his round shoulders. He said firmly, "It is a brilliant idea, elder brother. We shall do it. Leave the details to me. There is only one problem. We are going to need Yukinari's cooperation."

"Yukinari will support us. As I mentioned, his patrol ran into a group of Joto's monks. There have been bad feelings on both sides for a long time."

Motosuke frowned. "When did you find out?"

"Yesterday. Incidentally, Yukinari had a strange accident before I saw him. A heavy bronze bell came off its support and nearly killed him. Such an accident could have been arranged quite easily. The monks may have an accomplice in the garrison."

"I expect you worry too much. But we still don't know Tachibana's murderer. You thought Tachibana was killed because he knew something about the robberies. Do you now suspect Joto of that crime also?"

Akitada hesitated. So much had happened. They had evidence that Joto and his martial monks were behind the theft of the tax shipments, but that did not mean they had murdered the ex-governor. The mysterious nighttime visitor still needed to be accounted for. There was also the Rat's peculiar story about Jikoku-ten. Jikoku-ten was usually portrayed as wearing armor, and he had been seen coming through the back gate. Akitada did not believe in manifestations. The Rat had not encountered an incarnation of one of the four divine generals, but a murderer, and the murderer had knocked the old beggar down, perhaps intending to kill him.

Motosuke cleared his throat.

"Forgive me," said Akitada. "I just remembered another detail." He explained the Rat's adventure and added, "Lady Tachibana may have a lover."

Motosuke raised his brows. "I cannot say I'm at all surprised. It was one of those spring and winter marriages. Tachibana gave her a home when her father, his best friend, died. She was a mere child while he was old enough to be her grandfather. Frankly, I thought he was in his dotage to do such a thing. Her background did not promise well either."

"What do you mean?"

"Her mother was a courtesan in the capital. Her father became enamored of this female on a visit there, bought her out, and brought her back with him as his concubine. After she bore him a child, he lost interest. The woman returned to her old life, taking the girl and a small fortune in gold with her. When she died, the girl was shipped back to her natural father, who, after the initial shock, ended up spoiling her terribly. Nothing was too good for her. She is said to have ruined him, and she tried to ruin Tachibana with her expensive tastes." Motosuke looked disgusted. "I never met her. Is she very handsome?"

"Oh, yes!" Akitada thought of his feelings for the lovely creature in her embroidered silks and felt a little foolish.

Motosuke eyed him shrewdly. "A beguiling flirt like her mother?"

"Perhaps." Actually, he was certain of it now that he knew her story. And—he was honest enough to admit it—because he had found Ayako and was no longer vulnerable to childlike beauties with their appealing ways. He recognized the sudden faintness, the tears, the small hand creeping into his for what they had been: the wiles of a seductress.

"Could Yukinari be the lover?" Motosuke asked.

"He was. In fact, I suspected him of the murder. His refusal to see her struck me as very strange. Then one of the maids told me of the affair. She is the woman who thought she saw him leave the night of the murder. But Yukinari was out of town the entire night and swears he broke off the affair last summer."

Motosuke scowled. "He met my daughter."

"Yes. He is very distraught."

"Infernal fool! And you think Lady Tachibana then took up with someone else?"

"Yes. Perhaps the man is another officer."

Motosuke pursed his lips. "Women are vengeful creatures. Perhaps she killed Tachibana. Wouldn't a soldier have used his sword?"

"It seems unlikely that an armed man would bludgeon his enemy to death. Tachibana was hit over the head with some heavy piece of glazed tile or ceramic utensil. I found a green shard in his topknot. That suggests an unpremeditated act by an unarmed man."

Motosuke asked, "What will you do next?"

Akitada sighed. "I promised Lady Tachibana some help in settling her estate. It may serve as a pretext to snoop a little."

"Excellent. I shall begin to make plans for the temple affair and let you know as soon as I have talked to Yukinari."

Now that he had got his way, Akitada began to feel uneasy. "Be careful," he said. "The fewer people know, the better."

◆

When he returned to his rooms, Seimei was watching Tora, who was pacing the floor impatiently.

"There you are," Tora greeted Akitada. "I found a man who knows where Hidesato eats and sent him a message. Can we go right away? It's getting late."

Akitada raised his hands. "Slowly, Tora. I have just come from the governor. There may be more urgent work."

"You'd better read this first." Seimei took a curious object from Akitada's desk and held it up: a bare branch with a slip of mulberry paper tied to it with crimson silk. "The boy who brought it is waiting for an answer."

Akitada reached for the letter, then pulled back his hand as if bitten by a snake. He knew the sender. Unfortunately, he could not avoid it. Reluctantly, he untied the note, dropping silk and branch carelessly on the floor. The paper was expensive and heavily perfumed. He read: "How sad the barren branch, the blasted flower, when friendship cools, and deadly frost kills budding love." It was a poor poetic effort, too stilted and lacking in subtlety, but she had reason to complain. He had not kept his promise because of Ayako. For a moment he stood undecided.

"What's a fornicator?" asked Tora.

Akitada started. "What?"

Seimei, always the mentor, explained, but Tora shook his head. "You must be wrong, old man. There are no women there. Was the old monk crazy, sir?"

Understanding dawned belatedly. Tora and Seimei had discussed the incident at the temple while his own mind wandered along the twisted paths of love. "No, Tora," he said with a grimace. "I expect the old monk spoke the truth. It is a practice among some monks to enjoy the love of boys."

"Swine!" Tora shook his head, then asked, "Now will you come talk to Hidesato, sir?"

Akitada let Lady Tachibana's note drop to the floor. "Yes, Tora. Lead the way."

◆

The Inn of the Eight Immortals was a ramshackle two-storied building in the brothel quarter. From its upper story eight garish banners with the figures of the sages fluttered dispiritedly in the cold wind. Tora gave his master an uneasy look.

"Go on," said Akitada, pointing at the narrow doorway covered with strips of dingy brown grass cloth. His peers in the capital would have shunned this place like a smallpox-infected house, and he wondered what Motosuke would think of his "elder brother" now.

The restaurant was large and instantly enveloped them in raucous noise and pungent smells. Four cooks, stripped to the waist and wearing checked towels around their heads, worked over the bamboo steamers, while some fifty customers were busy eating, drinking, and chattering.

Akitada's eyes followed a tray of succulent shrimp, balanced precariously on the shoulder of a youngster who stepped nimbly between the seated parties to serve a group of men.

"There he is," Tora cried. "Hidesato!"

Near the steaming cauldrons, a tall, bearded man rose, looking as if he wished he were elsewhere. He gave Tora a tight smile and bowed to Akitada.

Tora embraced him and slapped his back. "We've searched for you everywhere, Hito. Why did you run off like that?"

Hidesato's eyes went to Akitada. "Later, brother."

Akitada liked the sergeant's open face and soldierly manner, even though the feeling was not mutual. Hidesato was openly hostile. Akitada's heart sank, but for Tora's sake he would try. "I'm hungry," he said, sitting down. "Come, let's order."

Hidesato cleared his throat. "They serve only common fare here," he said.

Akitada ignored this comment and ordered three large servings of shrimp and a pitcher of wine, then said, "Tora can tell you what we ate on our journey here. This is a feast."

Hidesato muttered, "Oh." His eyes kept wandering toward the entrance.

"Are you expecting someone?" Akitada asked.

"No. That is . . . sometimes a friend stops by."

When the food and wine appeared, Akitada reached for his bowl, shelling his shrimp nimbly. Tora did the same and after a moment Hidesato joined them. Silence prevailed until the bowls were empty. Tora wiped his hands on his old robe, and Hidesato did likewise, then watched Akitada.

"Excellent," Akitada said with a sigh of satisfaction and fished a paper tissue from his sleeve to clean his hands. "Now for some wine." He filled their cups. Tora bit his lip and looked down at his clenched hands. Akitada urged, "Why don't you give your friend the good news?"

Tora looked up. "Oh. Looks like you'll be in the money again, Hito. The garrison's been looking for you. They need another experienced sergeant."

Hidesato's face lit up. "Truly? I'd given up hope. I suppose I should have gone back after I lost my lodging." His eyes went to the entrance again.

"Well," said Akitada, waving to the waitress to bring more wine, "drink up! You have something to celebrate after all. By the way, I am obliged to you. Tora has been teaching me the art of stick fighting. He tells me you taught him."

Hidesato stared at him, then at Tora, who said quickly, "He's good, Hito. I'm at the end of my tricks. Bet you'd make a better teacher."

Hidesato shot Akitada an angry glance and snapped, "You shouldn't have done that, Tora. Your master's not one of us. What need has a nobleman for the simple skills of poor people? Fighting sticks are for those who aren't allowed to wear swords."

There was a pregnant silence, then Akitada said, "Please don't blame Tora. No man could ask for a more loyal friend than you have in him. As for myself, I cannot help my birth any more than you can yours. In fact, I've had little cause to consider myself more fortunate than other men. I wished to learn your skills because I might need them someday and because I believe a man should have many skills."

Hidesato glowered silently.

"I am sorry you will not accept me," Akitada said heavily after a moment. "Tora wanted to leave my service when he found out how you felt, but I would not let him go without talking to you first. He was honor-bound to an agreement we made when we met. I mention this so you will know that he deserves your friendship. But he is free now. I won't stand between you." He fished a string of coppers from his sash and rose. "It's been a long day, and I am weary. Use the coppers to pay the bill, Tora."

"I'm tired also," Tora said, dropping the money on the mat and getting to his feet. "Let's be on our way. Good luck, Hidesato."

Akitada stopped, dismayed. He had not intended to force a choice on Tora. Before he could speak, Hidesato said, "Sit down, little brother. You, too, sir, if you wouldn't mind. It's hard to believe you find Tora at all satisfactory, but I'll take your word for it." He reached for the pitcher and filled their cups. "Now that I'm to be employed again, I look forward to returning your hospitality, sir."

Akitada and Tora sat down dazedly. Hidesato smiled and

nodded. "I'm not much for making speeches," he said to Akitada, "but Tora's judgment is good enough for me. I don't hold with the nobility as a rule, but I'll make an exception in your case if you don't mind the company of a rough soldier." He raised his cup to Akitada and drank.

It was not much, but Akitada was grateful. Raising his own cup, he said, "I'm glad and honored to know you."

With the ice finally broken, they told Hidesato about their exploits, and after some questions about the monks and Higekuro and his daughters, he offered his help whenever his military duties permitted it. This pleasant state of affairs was interrupted when a waitress whispered something to Hidesato. He rose and looked toward the entrance.

"Sorry," he muttered, "the friend I mentioned waits outside."

Akitada felt companionable. "Invite your friend to join us," he suggested.

Hidesato flushed crimson. "She'll refuse," he said.

"A lady? But I insist," said Akitada, fascinated. Looking around the room, he added, "I see other women eating here."

Hidesato said stiffly, "As you wish, sir."

He returned with a young woman who was wrapped in a quilted jacket that partially covered a soiled and garish gown. Her face wore the heavy makeup of brothel women.

"This is Jasmin," Hidesato said awkwardly.

The young woman nodded timidly.

"Come," said Hidesato. "Sit down. You must be cold and hungry." He helped her remove her jacket while Tora called for more food and wine.

Without the thick quilted jacket Jasmin looked pitifully thin. Akitada thought she was probably young and coarsely pretty under the layers of pasty white powder, but at the moment she looked merely unhealthy and pathetic. The wind had

tangled her hair, and her hands were grimy and had bitten fingernails. Yet Hidesato fussed over her with a devotion only a son
or lover could show such a woman. Akitada exchanged a glance
with Tora.

"My," the girl said in a throaty voice, looking about her, "a
woman's life's a thousand times harder than a man's. Here you
sit with your friends, keeping warm and filling your stomach,
while I'm earning a living freezing my toes on the dark streets.
In this weather there's hardly any custom. Only the poor are
out—and they like it for free." Unconcerned about their reaction, she went on, "They wouldn't let me in till you came to get
me. Oh, food!" She reached hungrily for the shrimp the waitress
set before her and began to eat so greedily that the shrimp disappeared half-shelled between her small teeth. Hidesato
watched her with a besotted smile and pushed the wine cup
toward her. She nodded her thanks, and chattered between bites
and gulps, and picked shells from her teeth. "Mmm, that's
good . . . It's been a bad night . . . only one trick, an old tight-
wad . . . carpenter from the slums. Pour me another, will you,
Hito dear? The bastard gave me ten coppers . . . can you believe
it? And not even a room! Just an alley, standing up! Ten coppers!
Roku had the rest out of my hide earlier."

She looked tired and drawn all of a sudden. Absently she
rubbed her left cheekbone with sticky fingers and dislodged
enough caked powder to reveal an ugly bruise.

"That bastard beat you again," Hidesato said hoarsely. "I
told you to let me teach him a lesson. Listen, Jasmin, I got the
job. At the garrison. I'll be a sergeant again. The money's good.
You can give up this life and get away from that brute. Move in
with me. I'll look after you."

Jasmin shook her head. "I can't, Hito. You know why. And
you mustn't touch him. Promise? If you're truly my friend?" She
looked at him piteously.

Hidesato opened and shut his big hands in helpless misery. Then he pushed the wine cup toward her again. "Well, eat and drink. You still look half frozen. I've got some money and there'll be more. So don't worry, eh?" He fished in his sleeve and brought out a handful of coppers that he pressed into her hand.

Tora was beginning to look very angry, and Akitada decided it was time to leave. Hidesato gave them a brief, distracted smile before turning his attention to the woman again.

Akitada left enough money with the waitress to cover the bill for all of them, then joined Tora in the street. "You know the girl?" he asked.

Tora cursed fluently. "I thought he was rid of her. Jasmin is from his hometown, daughter of a cousin or something. He's looked after her for years. Fool woman wants nothing to do with decent men like Hidesato. Look where it's gotten her. I bet he lost his lodging because he gave her all his money so she won't get beaten up by her latest boyfriend. It's tearing him apart."

The perversity of human relationships struck Akitada painfully. Women played havoc with the men whose hearts they touched. The burly sergeant loved a common harlot who discussed her customers and her abusive lover with him. Yukinari had succumbed twice to women and was a broken man because he had had the bad luck to fall in love with Motosuke's daughter. Lady Tachibana, like her mother before her, had manipulated men, leaving them ruined or dead. Bright butterflies were fatal. Why did men become so enmeshed in their desire for certain women that they lost all sense of proportion and propriety?

They walked home in silence.

FOURTEEN

GREEN SHARD,
BLUE FLOWER

*S*eimei and Akitada arrived at the back gate of the Tachibana mansion at midmorning the next day. Akitada's visits to the bathhouse took time not only from his practice bouts with Tora but now also from his work. Feeling both tired and guilty, he was short-tempered and hardly spoke to the boy Junjiro who admitted them.

Junjiro trotted beside Akitada toward the studio, looking up at him expectantly. When they reached the steps, Akitada glanced down and said brusquely, "We won't need you, but don't mention our presence to your mistress." He glanced nervously across to the main house lying peacefully in a deserted garden. The snow had disappeared everywhere except under shrubs and against the north side of the hall. He had no wish to see the winter butterfly.

"The monks are gone," offered Junjiro.

"Good," snapped Akitada, setting his foot on the bottom step.

"Shall I bring you some tea and a brazier?"

"No, thank you. We shall not be long."

The boy turned to go, and Akitada sat down on the veranda to remove his shoes. Seimei joined him. Below them Junjiro turned and asked, "Have you arrested the captain?"

"The captain?" Then Akitada remembered what the boy's mother had claimed to have seen. "No," he said. "Captain Yukinari was not in town during the night your master was murdered."

Junjiro's eyes grew round. "But who else could it have been?"

"Your mother made a mistake."

The boy flared up. "My mother doesn't make mistakes. I'll be back." And he ran off.

Akitada sighed and got up. "Come on, Seimei. Let's get this over with."

They were bent over the documents, sorting and reading, when Junjiro reappeared. He had a stubborn look in his eyes and announced, "My mother says it was the captain's helmet she saw. He used to wear it sometimes when he came to visit. It has red cords and big silver stripes all around it. She's sure because she remembers how the red showed up against the blue robe."

Astonished, Akitada put down an account of provincial silk production and said, "A blue robe? Why would the captain have worn his helmet with a blue robe? Surely he would have been in uniform, that is, armor." He reached up to massage his neck, which ached abominably, and tried to focus bleary eyes on the boy.

Junjiro's jaw dropped. "That's right," he said. Then he grinned. "I'm glad it wasn't him." He turned and skipped away.

Akitada shook his head, winced at the pain, and returned to

work. They finished in time to return to the tribunal for their noon rice, a meal that Akitada merely picked at. Tora came, and when they had eaten, Akitada said, "We found nothing among Tachibana's papers. Either the man was too careful to write his suspicions down, or the killer took the incriminating documents."

Tora nodded and turned to Seimei to discuss the brushstrokes he had been practicing under the old man's direction.

"Pay attention, both of you," Akitada snapped irritably, aware that this was meant as much for himself as for his companions. His head felt incredibly fuzzy, and the little he had eaten had left him mildly nauseated, perhaps due to the previous night's overindulgence in shrimp and wine. "Let's think about the murder," he said. "The sequence of events starts with Lord Tachibana's whispered invitation to me. We must assume that he had a secret to communicate, which was dangerous, and that he did not trust someone who was present. We have eliminated Motosuke and Yukinari as suspects, so that leaves only Joto or Ikeda."

"I think they're in it together," pronounced Tora. He belched and stretched out on his back, arms folded under his head. "The baldpate sleeps with boys and buries old monks alive, and Ikeda is a crooked official. That's good enough for me."

Seimei said, "You don't make sense. How could they both be guilty of the same crime?" He poured Akitada a cup of tea.

"Is there any more wine?" Tora asked him, rolling onto his elbow.

"You drink too much. Wine makes you say stupid things. And sit up properly in the master's presence."

Tora rearranged himself somewhat. "What is so stupid about the prefect and the abbot being in it together?"

Akitada was massaging his temples. A headache had joined his upset stomach. He was aware of a general soreness but was not sure whether to blame it on the nighttime exertions at the monastery or his lovemaking with Ayako. Putting such thoughts away, he said, "Tora makes sense in a way. They would make excellent allies. Joto provides the manpower and Ikeda the information about the convoy."

"You see, old man?" Tora said.

"Even a blind turtle finds a piece of driftwood sometimes." Seimei looked at him sourly.

"But," said Akitada, "it does not help us with the Tachibana murder or provide us with the proof we need to arrest the two."

"Maybe somebody used the captain's helmet as a disguise. It would be perfect to hide the shaven head of a monk," offered Seimei.

Akitada thought of Otomi's scroll and nodded. "Perhaps," he said, "the lady was carrying on with a lover and her husband surprised them. But Joto does not fit the picture of the secret lover." He rummaged in his writing box for the green shard from Tachibana's topknot. His fingers encountered another small hard object. It was the tiny blue flower ornament from the peddler's tray.

How long ago that seemed now. He wondered what had caused him to save the useless fragment. But he felt it again, that oddly unpleasant sense that the flower was significant. He picked up the fragment. Beyond the fact that it resembled a morning glory, fashioned from pure gold and blue enamel by a mysterious and probably foreign process, he had no clue what it might be. He had assumed that it must belong to a religious statue. If so, was it somehow related to Joto and the shipments of religious objects?

"Seimei?" he asked. "Do you recall this little scrap?"

Seimei peered at it. "You paid that rascal too much money for his trumpery goods."

Akitada replaced the flower in his writing box. "I want you

to go to the market with Tora. The waitress at the inn was quite taken with you, especially after I gave her the peddler's wares with your compliments. Ask her if she knows where he lives. He is probably a regular. Then find him and ask him where he got the flower."

"Sir," protested Seimei, his face lengthening with horror, "I'd rather not. Can't Tora go?"

"Sorry, old friend. You are the only one who can identify him. Tora was chasing Otomi and the two monks." Seeing Seimei's dismay, Akitada relented. "I would not ask it if it were not important."

Then he picked up the little green shard. Tucking it into his sash, he rose. "It's getting late. I'm going to call on the widow and this time I'm determined to find the murder weapon. Tachibana was bludgeoned to death somewhere in that house. It is likely that it happened in his wife's rooms and that she knows. It always seems to come back to her." He did not say that he suspected her or how much he dreaded the visit.

Akitada was crossing the tribunal compound when he remembered Ikeda and stopped. He must be unusually distracted to forget that Ikeda, who was a potential suspect in the tax robberies, must not know of Akitada's activities in the Tachibana case until after the temple ceremony. Akitada could not call on the prefectural constables if the need arose. He was tempted to postpone his plans but decided against further delay. Instead, he turned his steps to the governor's residence, where he discussed his problem with Akinobu.

◆

The Tachibana residence looked peaceful in the pale wintry sun. The sightseers were gone, and Junjiro opened the gate instantly. Beside him on the gravel of the courtyard stood a box and a bulging basket. The boy's mother and another woman, bent under large bundles of clothing strapped to their backs, came from the hall and passed Akitada with a bow.

"What is happening?" he asked the boy, looking after them.

"We're leaving. Sato's already gone. His niece came for him. The mistress sent for her. The old dragon gives all the orders now and she told us to get out."

"I'm sorry," said Akitada, and meant it. There was nothing he could do to help them. "Don't worry. Any master will be glad to get as good a pair of servants as you and your mother."

Junjiro drew himself up proudly. "We'll manage, sir. I'm clever. Perhaps we could serve you?"

Suddenly utterly fatigued, Akitada wanted to get his distressing visit over with as quickly as possible. "I'm afraid not," he said. "But you can take me to your mistress now."

There was some delay at the door to Lady Tachibana's apartments. When he was finally admitted, Akitada saw that the room was empty except for himself and the big nurse. The woman, more deferential today, took Akitada to the same low screen, placing a silk cushion for him. "We did not expect your honored visit," she said, bowing for the third or fourth time. "The mistress will come in a moment." She left by another door, presumably to help Lady Tachibana with her toilet.

The moment she was gone, Akitada searched the room. It looked unchanged from the last time he had seen it. The thick, patterned carpet was underfoot. The scroll of cranes hung between its two stands, one displaying the tall Chinese vase, the other an artificial tree with jade leaves and gold blossoms. Though, come to think of it, the tree had not been there before. Akitada went to look at it. It was a pretty bauble, but this stand had been empty on the day of the funeral. He recalled noticing the lack of symmetry and being bothered by it. Two matching stands required two matching vases.

And then it clicked. The vase was green.

He went to the remaining vase and took the shard from his sash. Yes, the same color and glaze. One of the pair had been used to kill Lord Tachibana. He hefted the vase by its slender neck. It was heavy and made an excellent club. Had not Junjiro complained that the servants were being blamed for breakage when they had been innocent? It should be easy enough to find out if someone had been accused of breaking a green vase the morning of the murder. Replacing the survivor of the pair, he got on his hands and knees to inspect the Chinese carpet. He found the spot almost immediately. Near the outside border was a rough and matted area. It felt faintly moist. He parted the thick threads. Yes, there was a brownish residue farther down. He touched his finger to it and then smelled it. Blood. Head wounds bleed copiously, and there had been only a small stain in the studio. Lord Tachibana had died here. He had his proof.

Hearing a sound from the next room, Akitada managed to reach his cushion and sit down barely in time to watch the widow enter.

Lady Tachibana tripped in. She wore a dark gray silk gown as prescribed for mourning, but over it was a lovely rose-colored Chinese jacket embroidered with butterflies. The pattern reminded him of the first time he had seen her, of his image of a poor butterfly caught in a wintry garden. Against his better judgment, he softened a little toward the small, childlike beauty as she approached with lowered lashes, her beautiful hair trailing behind her. Life with an elderly husband who devoted all his time to his garden and his studies was difficult for a spoiled young girl who had never tasted the pleasures of love.

He bowed.

Much had changed in his own life since he had seen her last. Ayako had taught him that women could be passionate and desire men. Little wonder the poor butterfly had succumbed to temptation. Her beauty was the epitome of a standard that celebrated youth and frailty in women. Many men would be attracted. Yukinari had been, and so had he himself. To his relief, he no longer felt at all tempted by the soft, perfumed creature seating herelf behind the screen.

The nurse poured wine for Akitada, then left them alone. Though he knew the wine would make his headache worse, he drank thirstily. His throat hurt, and the wine soothed it a little. He wondered for the first time if he might be getting sick—at the worst possible time.

"I am touched by your kindness," the soft voice said from behind the screen. "You must forgive my note. It was written at a moment of unspeakable grief and loneliness."

"Not at all. It was charming. I regret that important matters kept me from fulfilling my promise earlier."

"My only wish was to withdraw from the world to mourn my husband's passing, but I find I cannot do so when suspicious people raise questions about the manner of his death."

Ah. She had picked up some gossip. Probably from the servants. It would explain their sudden dismissal. He hardened against her again. Knowing what he knew now, he ignored the pretense of grief. The room seemed much too hot, causing perspiration to bead up on his face. Wishing he had remembered to carry a paper tissue, he decided that there was no sense in protracting the matter any further.

"Your husband was murdered, madam," he said brusquely. His voice sounded strangely muffled to his ears and he could feel moisture trickling down his temple.

A wail sounded behind the screen and then another, followed by a gasp. "Oh, I have been afraid of this. And I'm all alone in this evil world." She suddenly folded aside part of the screen, looked at Akitada from huge, tear-filled eyes, and stretched out her arms beseechingly. "You are my only hope, my lord," she sobbed. "I'm afraid. I'm left completely without protection. My husband's servants are gone and no one is left in this house but two weak women. What if the killer returns? Please take me away from here."

Akitada, irritated by her dramatics, gave her a long stare, watching as her lower lip began to tremble and two small teeth caught it. She reminded him of a mouse. Under normal circumstances, he might have enjoyed playing cat and mouse, but his head was aching abominably now and he wished for another cup of wine. He said, "I might be of more assistance if I knew who it is that you are afraid of."

"But I told you. The monster who killed my beloved husband," she wailed. Her small white hand touched his beseechingly. Akitada folded his arms, and she let it fall on his knee instead. "Why are you so . . . distant? You were kind to me before," she pleaded. When he said nothing, she said, "This big house is empty. You cannot be very comfortable at the tribunal. If you were to stay with me, I would feel safe." The hand squeezed his knee gently. "I would serve you with all my heart. From the first moment I saw you, I knew . . ."

If he had felt better, he might have laughed, but as it was, Akitada regarded her with rising disgust and moved his knee out of her reach.

She cried, "Why do you dislike me so? I have been told that I am beautiful to look at." She paused, then said softly, "I know how to please a man. My late lord was not interested in matters of the pillow, but you are young. From the moment I saw you I knew it was my karma to serve you or die." Crawling to Akitada, she clasped his knees, burying her face in his lap. Her action was so powerfully erotic that Akitada rose abruptly and stepped away from her. She stood up. Her eyes on his, she loosened her sash, letting both gown and Chinese jacket slip off her shoulders to reveal the nakedness beneath. "Do not abandon me, my love," she whispered.

Akitada turned away. "Cover yourself." Her body, with its small breasts and shaved pubic area, looked like that of a child of twelve. The effect, together with her overtly seductive gestures, nauseated him. He wondered what sort of man her paramour was and said sternly, "You bring shame upon yourself and upon the memory of your husband. As for your fear of the murderer, you will know best. Your husband was killed in this room by your lover and in your presence." As soon as he had spoken, he knew he had made a mistake, but he was determined to see it through.

"You must be mad," she cried, grasping her gown to cover herself.

Akitada took the porcelain shard from his sash. "This was caught in your husband's topknot. It matches the green vase over there. Your lover used the other vase to kill Lord Tachibana. It broke and you blamed the breakage later on careless servants. But by that time you and your lover had already removed the body to the studio to make the death look like an accidental fall. His wound could not have happened accidentally. Besides, Lord Tachibana's clogs were dry and unstained in spite of the recent snow. Yet someone walked to the studio, and that person or his helper swept the path to destroy his tracks."

"No!" She was sobbing now. "No, it isn't true. I swear by Amida that I'm innocent. I have been faithful to my husband. Why are you tormenting me?"

Feeling dizzy, Akitada dabbed at the perspiration on his face with a sleeve. He had to frighten her into a confession. "The servants knew about your lovers. They will tell the truth in court. The penalty for adultery and murder of one's husband is death by flogging. I suggest you tell the truth soon, before the constables strip you naked in the open courtroom and whip you with bamboo canes till you talk."

He had expected her to scream or faint, but she merely

pressed her sleeve to her mouth. Her eyes glittered strangely. Suddenly she prostrated herself before him.

"This unnatural creature confesses," she said. "I betrayed my husband, but I did not kill him. I know I must pay the price for having been unfaithful, but I am young and did not know what I was doing till it was too late. Oh, please have pity."

Her hands crept toward Akitada's feet, but he stepped away. Looking down at her, he commanded, "Tell me what happened."

In a muffled voice, she sobbed, "I was seduced by loving words. Afterward, when I realized what I had done, I wished to end the affair, but he forced me to lie with him by threatening to tell my husband. Since my husband never came to my rooms after dark, my lover visited whenever he wished. He made me unlock the garden gate for him after everyone was asleep."

Akitada's neck and back were soaked with sweat, his underrobe and collar clinging uncomfortably to his skin. "Get to the night of the murder!" he rasped.

"My husband returned late from the governor's party, and for some reason he came into my room. He found us together and threatened to expose our affair to the world. My lover seized the vase and killed him." She covered her face. "It was horrible. He made me help him hide the crime."

"Then you are as guilty as he."

She wailed, "I am not. I am not. It was he who struck him," and burst into a torrent of tears, beating the floor with her fists.

"Stop that!" shouted Akitada, and choked on the sharp pain in his throat.

To his surprise, she sat up, retied her sash, and dried her face with her sleeve. "My lord," she said quietly, "in your wisdom and generosity, you must see that a naive girl from the country would be easy prey for the sweet words of a handsome soldier. My husband encouraged our friendship. It is true I fell in love with a cruel monster, but I did not know then what he was. My lord, you cannot wish a foolish girl to suffer for a murder she did not commit?"

Akitada snapped, "If you are accusing Captain Yukinari, your lies prove you guilty. The captain was out of town during the night of the murder. You are protecting the real killer. Confess. Your lies will do you no good. Your only hope for a merciful judgment is to give evidence against your lover. It is all over."

Her pretty face contorted with fury. She jumped up and rushed at him, fingernails clawing at his face. He flung her away, then watched in disbelief as she ripped open her clothes again and viciously scratched her own neck and breasts until they bled.

Then she screamed for help.

The door flew open, and the nurse took one look at her mistress and added her own screams. The noise reverberated in Akitada's painful skull. Helplessly, he sat back down and covered his ears.

The widow stopped screaming long enough to say, "You fool. The house is empty. Quick, run to the prefecture. Get the constables. This man has violated me. Hurry!"

The woman ran, and the room became blissfully quiet. Akitada lowered his hands. It occurred to him that the nurse was probably an accessory. And she was on her way to Ikeda. Too late now to rethink the situation. Events must take their course.

"You will regret this!" the lady hissed. "We'll see who will be believed now. You're a stranger here, one of those depraved nobles from the capital we hear so much about, while I am the widow of the former governor. You'll be sorry you ever meddled with me."

Akitada cocked an ear toward the gallery outside. After a little while, he heard the expected sound of heavy boots on the wooden boards. Lady Tachibana scurried into a corner and let her clothes fall open to reveal her bleeding breasts. She arranged herself in a pose of abject terror. When the door slid open, she was sobbing pitifully.

Soldiers in the uniform of the governor's guard pressed into the room and goggled at the half-naked woman.

"Arrest that man," Lady Tachibana quavered, pointing at Akitada. "He raped me. He came here pretending to offer sympathy and then attacked me viciously when he saw that I had no protection. Oh, thank heaven there is justice for poor widows."

"Lieutenant Kenko, I believe?" said Akitada, nodding to the officer in charge, who took his eyes off Lady Tachibana's breasts and snapped to attention. "I see Secretary Akinobu has explained the matter. You have been very prompt. I want Lady Tachibana placed under arrest for the murder of her husband."

The widow cried, "How so? You have no authority here. And these men are not from the prefecture. No doubt you have bribed them. I refuse to go until the constables arrive."

The lieutenant cast an uneasy glance at Akitada. Then the door was flung open again, and the nurse ran in, followed by Ikeda and a group of red-coated constables.

"There he is," the nurse cried, pointing to Akitada.

Ikeda himself! It could not be worse. All Akitada could do now was to play the game carefully and hope his opponent made a wrong move. Easier said than done, when his head was pounding and his strategies seemed to swim about like so many slippery tadpoles.

Ikeda took in the soldiers and then saw Akitada. "Your Excellency?" he said, feigning confusion. "What happened? I was on my way to investigate a murder in the brothel district when this silly woman came running down the street screaming that her mistress was being violated. I see there must be some mistake."

"Your arrival is timely, Prefect," said Akitada, hoping his voice did not give away his nervousness. "Here, too, a crime has been committed. I am charging Lady Tachibana and her nurse with the murder of the late Lord Tachibana."

"Your Honor!" the nurse called out, trying to push past the soldiers to Ikeda. Two brawny fellows caught her around the middle and lifted her off the ground. Grinning widely, they held her as she kicked and cursed.

Holding her gown together with one hand, Lady Tachibana tripped across the room to slap her nurse soundly. "Be quiet!" she hissed. The woman closed her mouth and became limp. Her voice trembling with fury, the widow turned to the lieutenant and said, "Lord Sugawara told a pack of lies to escape a charge of raping a defenseless widow. My nurse is a witness to his depravity. Release her immediately!"

Akitada felt his control of the situation slipping. The pounding pain in his head and the soreness of his throat had been joined by more nausea. With an effort he turned to Ikeda. "I'm afraid the evidence of murder is incontrovertible. A vase just like the one over there was the murder weapon. Lord Tachibana fell there, bleeding into the carpet. The stain is still visible. Lady Tachibana, her nurse, and a male visitor carried the body through the garden to the studio and arranged it to suggest an accidental fall. Then one of them swept the path. One of the maids and another witness saw the male accomplice escape into the alley behind the house."

Swallowing nervously, Ikeda looked around the room. The pause stretched as he weighed his options. "Who is this alleged accomplice?" the prefect finally asked.

"Lady Tachibana has refused to identify the man. She briefly tried to blame the murder on Captain Yukinari, but I happen to know that he was not in town the night of the murder."

Ikeda stared at him, then cleared his throat. "Horrible," he said. "Murder. Who would have thought? I don't see how I could have missed . . ."

Akitada's stomach churned as nausea threatened again. He had to get away from here, get outside into the clean, fresh air. He glared at Ikeda. "Well, what are you waiting for now, man?" he snapped. "This crime is heinous. It touches the most sacred foundations of our nation." He knew he sounded pompous but did not care. "Respect and duty to husband and master have been foully perverted by these women. Or don't you agree?"

"Oh, yes. Absolutely!" gasped Ikeda, glancing nervously at the women. Lady Tachibana stared back at him. He cleared his throat again. "For a wife to raise her hand against her husband or for a servant to assist in the killing of her master is frightful indeed. The most severe penalty permitted by the law must be imposed." He waved to his constables. "Arrest these women!"

The nurse began to jabber wildly.

"Gag her!" snapped Ikeda. With the help of Kenko's soldiers, the constables subdued the maid. Lady Tachibana wept softly but offered no further resistance.

It was over.

Akitada stumbled up. He managed to nod to the lieutenant and Ikeda before walking quickly out of the door. The icy air hit his sweat-covered face like a burst of cold water. For a moment he stood swaying, breathing in deep gulps of it. Then the nausea rose again, and he staggered down into the garden to vomit.

He did not know how he managed to get back to their quarters, but he found them dark and empty. Dimly recalling that Seimei and Tora were still on their errand, he lay down on the floor as he was and closed his eyes.

Later he roused himself. He was burning with fever. Tearing off his clothing, all but the thin silk underrobe that clung to his wet skin, he crawled over to his desk to drink the remnants of cold tea from Seimei's teapot. Then he collapsed into uneasy sleep again.

When he awoke a second time, he was shaking with cold. He

tried to call for Seimei, but his voice was gone and his teeth chattered so badly, he gave up. The room was completely dark. He got up and attempted to reach the trunk that held the bedding but was unable to control the trembling of his arms and legs. Dizziness caused him to sit down abruptly, and he vomited up the tea. Though his throat still felt as if he had swallowed hot coals and his head pounded like a drum, the nausea was gone. Covering himself with his clothes, he lay back down.

Strange dreams and nightmares filled his sleep. Lady Tachibana hovered above him, eagle's talons instead of hands ripping open his throat while her butterfly wings gently fanned his burning brow. Ayako appeared and disappeared in clouds of steam, beckoning to him, while he groped blindly and futilely for her. At one point the green shard in his fingers turned into a leaf and fluttered away to join a blue flower: *asagao*, he thought, the morning glory. It nodded in the moonlight, and the dewdrop on its petals turned to blood.

FIFTEEN

THE BLOOD-RED CURTAIN

𝒯he stout waitress recognized Seimei immediately. Her pock-marked face split into a grin flashing crooked yellow teeth the minute she saw them at the door. "Master Seimei!" she shouted, plopping down a flask of wine so suddenly between two customers that most of it spilled. "Master Seimei!" She started toward them with flapping sleeves.

Seimei shot behind Tora's broad back with a gasp. "We cannot stay, Tora," he hissed. Someone in the room burst into laughter.

"Come in, come in," the woman cried, reaching around Tora and pulling Seimei out by his arm. "It's cold outside and I've a good seat for you by the fire. What will you eat? Some fine *kisu* fish stewed in wine and soy sauce? Salted mushrooms and pickled eggplant? We have boiled sweet potatoes I could mash for you with a little honey if you have a sweet tooth."

"No, no," gasped Seimei, pulling away from her grasp. "We

are in a great hurry. Isn't that right, Tora? No time at all. We just stopped to ask you a question."

She bared her teeth again. "No need to ask." Without letting go of his arm, she playfully poked Seimei's bony chest with a stubby forefinger. "I'm free in another hour." Seimei looked blank. She pursed her lips over her buckteeth in disappointment. "Well, come in and sit down at least," she pleaded. "Just to rest your legs. You're not as young as you used to be." Looking at the grinning Tora, she added, "You should look after your uncle a little better. It's hard on a man his age when he has no wife to see to his comfort."

Seimei glared. "I am not at all tired," he snapped. "And it is not polite to call people old."

Chuckling, she patted his cheek. "Oh, there's lots of life left in you yet," she said. "You're just the sort of man I like."

Seimei retreated behind Tora again, to more laughter from their audience. "You talk to her, Tora," he yelped.

Tora stopped grinning and put on a ferocious face. "Pay attention, woman!" he growled. "We're here on official business."

She cocked her head at him. "Go ahead, ask."

"There was a peddler here selling his wares the day you served us. He got knocked about a bit and spilled all his stuff in the street. Do you remember?"

Her eyes suddenly moist with sentiment, she peered around Tora. "Do I! It was so sweet of you, Master Seimei, to make me a present of the peddler's things. See here?" She raised a hand to pat her hair. "That's the pretty comb you gave me. I wear it every day and think of you."

Someone applauded and shouted some lewd advice.

Seimei made a choking sound and clutched convulsively at Tora, who said, "Never mind that now. Where can we find the peddler?"

She said slyly, "I'll tell you if Master Seimei comes back."

Tora elbowed Seimei, who croaked, "Yes. As soon as we can."

"Jisai hasn't been back since your master paid him, but you can ask his friend."

The friend turned out to be the Rat, who was taking his ease with a cup of wine.

"Getting drunk already?" Tora greeted him.

"Just keeping out the cold," wheezed the Rat, looking at Seimei. "Who's the old geezer?"

"I'll wait outside," Seimei snapped and turned to leave.

Tora caught his sleeve. "We're all going. The Rat's going to show us the way to Jisai's place."

"Jisai?" The Rat looked interested. "What's he done?"

"We just have some questions," Tora said. "You coming or not?"

"What's it worth to you?"

"We'll pay your tab if you're quick about it."

The Rat jumped up, grabbed his crutch, and hopped off toward the street.

The bucktoothed waitress grinned. "He's had three flasks of the best wine and a platter of pickled plums," she informed Tora.

Tora whispered in her ear, "Your boyfriend here has the cash. But you'll have to be nice to him. He hates parting with it." Aloud he said, "Pay her, Seimei. A promise is a promise, and the master's in a hurry."

Eyeing the woman warily, Seimei pulled out a string of coppers. "That man was a walking lesson on why drinking is a shortcut to poverty," he said. "How much does he owe?"

"Forty-five coppers."

"Forty-five . . ." Seimei blanched and clutched the money to his chest.

She leaned forward to tap his cheek playfully. "But for you, my dear," she murmured, batting her eyes flirtatiously, "I'll make it a special price." Seimei stared at her teeth like a drowning man at a shark's jaws. "Make it ten coppers, love," she cooed, "and we'll spend the rest together."

Applause and shouts of encouragement broke out all around them.

Seimei counted out ten copper coins with trembling hands and ran.

"Don't forget your promise!" she called after him.

"Only ten coppers for all that wine!" Tora said outside, slapping Seimei on the back. "You'll have to tell me your secret with women, old man."

Seimei glowered at him and then turned his wrath on the cheerfully whistling Rat. "Start walking! Even a dog that wags its tail can be beaten," he said.

The Rat pulled in his tail. Hopping along on his crutch and complaining of the cold, the long way, and his indifferent health, he took them through dirty alleys, a derelict burial ground, and the courtyards of several tenement buildings where frozen laundry drooped from lines and women emptied their slops into the yard. Eventually he dispensed with his fake handicap, leaving the crutch in a hollow tree. Seimei maintained a disapproving silence.

Thoroughly chilled and frustrated, they reached an area of open ground near the southern palisade of the city. Among a scattering of bare trees stood the makeshift tents and grass-covered huts of squatters. Black smoke rose against the twilight sky from open fires. Ragged women and children tended to their families' dinners, while the men huddled near the warmth, drinking and rolling dice.

Exchanging cheerful greetings, the Rat dodged a line of frozen rags strung between two trees, kicked a snapping dog, and stopped in front of a particularly depressing hovel.

A ragged mat covered its entrance, and broken cooking utensils littered the ground. Flicking the mat aside unceremoniously, the Rat ducked in and Tora followed. Seimei, wrinkling his nose at the stench released from inside, stayed outside. A spate of excited talk came from the hut.

A group of dirty children quickly gathered around Seimei with pitiful wails: "Give us a copper." "Just a copper for a bowl of soup, master." They pushed against him, fingering the fabric of his robe, pointing at his black cap, feeling his sleeves, and inserting inquisitive hands under his sash. Seimei slapped the hands away and shouted, "Be quick about it, Tora!"

Instead of an answer, Tora's arm shot out from behind the mat and pulled him inside. Seimei choked. Blinded by the sudden murky darkness, he felt as if he had been swallowed by some large, foul-smelling creature. Then he made out a human being cowering on a pallet covered with ragged blankets. The blankets had long since faded to the grayness of dirt, and the frail creature was of the same hue: gray skin, thin gray hair like cobwebs on a pale skull, grayish layers of clothing. Deep-set black eyes stared at Seimei with dull curiosity.

Thinking they were in the wrong place, he was backing out again when Tora moved and he saw that the frail figure was an old woman and that the peddler Jisai sat cross-legged beside her. He wore the same rags, probably, thought Seimei, still caked with the same mud. Between them stood a cracked brazier that produced more acrid smoke than warmth.

Seimei held a sleeve over his nose and mouth and told Tora, "That's the man. Ask him and let's go."

"Where's your manners, old-timer?" sneered the Rat, who seated himself on the bare dirt floor near the peddler. "We just got here. Sit down and be sociable."

Seimei cast a pleading glance at Tora, who ignored him and settled down also. After a moment, lifting the back of his blue robe carefully above his hips, Seimei lowered himself to the floor.

What followed next, to the extreme frustration of the fastidious Seimei, was a leisurely discussion of the weather and conditions among the squatters. Then the ill health of the peddler's wife was examined symptom by symptom. Seimei was consulted about medicines and thawed a little. He was urged to take the old woman's pulse and look into her eyes. Teas, ointments, and plasters were weighed for their efficacy, and anecdotal evidence of local curatives—frog skins, charred mole meat, and powdered cockroach featured in these—heavily laced the conversation.

With weak quavers from the patient, a shrill whine from the peddler, Tora's deep voice, and the Rat's wheezing commentary, the dissonant but cozy chat proceeded in unhurried fashion without the least reference to the purpose of their visit.

When Seimei's store of advice was as exhausted as the old woman's litany of complaints, the conversation began to lag. Tora stretched and said, "Well, it's good to see old friends again, Jisai. Our master sent us to make sure those bastards that tripped you up did no permanent damage."

His words were ill-advised. The peddler and his wife now fell to reciting a whole string of Jisai's physical problems, supposedly incurred during the incident. His back ached, one hip was out of joint, a knee inexplicably refused to bend, and he had terrible headaches followed by bouts of dizziness. In short, he was totally disabled, could not work, did not sleep well at night, was in constant pain, would never work again. Doctors' bills were mounting, what with two patients, and they had had nothing to eat for days.

Seimei gave a snort and lifted the lid of a pot that stood on a rickety bamboo stand beside him. "Bean soup?" he asked, wrinkling his nose.

"A kind neighbor brought it," said the peddler. "A waste! The wife's too sick to eat it cold, and I'm too weak to build a fire to heat it." He sighed deeply and added, "Even if I had some wood."

Seimei snorted again.

Tora said, "Maybe we can help." He stretched out his hand for Seimei's string of coppers. "Our master's a very charitable man. He would wish us to leave a little something."

Seimei, muttering under his breath, counted out a coin at a time until Tora withdrew his hand and placed a small stack of money before the old woman. She gave them a toothless smile and said, "A great man, your master. You're blessed to be working for such a saint."

"And you're a wise woman, Auntie," said Tora. He rose. "Well, we'd better go." Seimei opened his mouth in outraged protest when Tora added casually, "By the way, there was a little blue flower among the stuff you sold the master. You remember it?"

The peddler nodded. "A fine piece." he croaked. "Pure gold. Worth a whole string of coppers."

Tora ignored this. "Remember where you got it?"

The peddler's eyes narrowed. "Couldn't say. I picked it up someplace. What's so special about it?"

"Nothing. My master was going to throw it away, so I took it to give to my girl. Now she wants more stuff like it."

"Would you spend some real money, say a silver bar?" the peddler suggested.

"That much? No kidding? Well, that's too bad. My girl will be disappointed," said Tora calmly, and stooped to gather up the coins he had laid before Jisai's wife. "We're on our way then. My master will be glad to hear that you've recovered and how good your business is."

"Wait, wait!" cried the peddler, jumping up with astonishing agility. "I just remembered. I got it from one of the whores. She wanted drink money for her man. I don't know where she got it. I don't ask questions."

"Who is she and where does she live?" Tora let the coppers jingle in his hand.

"Her name's Jasmin. Lives near the market, I think."

Surprisingly, the Rat grunted, "That's Scarface's slut. I know her."

Tora stared at the Rat, then tossed the coins to the peddler. "There, you old rascal," he snapped. "You'd better use the money to get back in business, or both you and your old woman will have your backbones poking through your navels."

Outside Tora grasped the Rat by his bony shoulder. "What's this about Jasmin and that Scarface bastard?"

The Rat twitched his shoulder free and whimpered, "Is that the thanks I get? I help you get what you want and you knock me around for it?"

"Sorry." Tora let him go.

"I'm cold again." The Rat shivered. "And thirsty."

"No more wine," warned Seimei.

Tora took Seimei's arm and walked him a few steps away. "Look," he said, "this guy needs wine to go on. You've got your work, and your proper robe and hat, and your medicines, and your master and me to nag. He's got nothing. Wine is all he lives for. Not everybody's as lucky as we are."

Seimei blinked. Then he said, "But wine has ruined him. It will kill him. Look at the pathetic creature. And he calls *me* an old geezer!"

Tora sighed. "Dying is easy; it's the living that's hard. Wine makes him forget a little."

Seimei stared at the Rat. "How old are you?" he called to him.

The Rat cocked his head. "Fifty-two. And you?"

"I shall be sixty," Seimei said proudly, straightening his back and giving the Rat a pitying glance. "You look worn out, poor fellow. Let's go find some warm place where you can rest a little before we go on."

The Rat knew all the wine shops and led them to a place where they could warm their backs near the cooking ovens and their stomachs with a flask of warm wine.

"All right," said Tora. "Start talking!"

The Rat drank deeply and said, "Far as I can tell, this Scarface showed up a couple of weeks ago and started working the street girls. Then he got to collecting from the vendors. They say he takes in a lot of money, but he gambles. Jasmin, the stupid skirt, is besotted with him." The Rat shook his head and drank again. "He's ugly enough to scare a ghost and he beats her."

Tora nodded. "We met. He had a couple of thugs with him, a big drooling idiot and a short weasel of a guy."

"Yushi and Jubei. Better watch yourself. They use knives and they don't ask 'May I?'"

Seimei did not like the sound of this. "Who is this Jasmin?" he asked nervously.

"A friend of a friend," Tora said. "I guess we'd better go ask her about that flower. You've had enough wine for today, Rat. Let's go."

Outside, darkness had fallen. A bitter wind whistled through the narrow streets and blew bits of refuse and dead leaves along. They passed through dark alleys where rats scurried away and drunks and vagrants were curled up in corners. Gradually the glow of lights rose above the dark roofs.

"The market," said Tora.

Seimei shivered, more with dread than cold, for he wore a quilted gown under his blue robe. He was not used to seeing so much filth and misery in one day and worried about meeting Scarface and his friends. The market seemed to lie at the center of all their troubles. They had started their ill-fated visit there

and kept returning to it. Each time it led to greater unpleasantness. It was almost as if he were trapped in some sort of maze
from which there was no escape.

Just then there was the sound of running feet, and he swung
around with a gasp. But it was only some boys. They shouted as
they ran past.

Tora frowned. "Something's happened ahead," he said.
"They've sent for the prefect."

"Must be a murder," cried the Rat, hopping about excitedly.
"We don't call the prefect for a fight or an accident. Let's go see!"
He disappeared around the next corner, Tora hard on his heels.

Seimei strongly disapproved and followed more slowly. His
day had been bad enough already. When he reached the corner,
he saw a crowd at the end of the street. Lanterns bobbed, casting shifting shadows. People pressed around a narrow passageway between two old houses with cracked windowless walls,
their rotten thatch mottled in the eerie glow from the market
beyond. Tora and the Rat were pushing through the chattering
crowd and disappeared into the dark passage.

Panic seized Seimei. They had abandoned him among harlots, thieves, and murderers, in a place where people did not
bother to call the constables until it was too late. There was a
killer loose, perhaps close by, and Seimei had no idea how to get
back to the tribunal by himself.

He nervously approached the outer fringes of the crowd. A
slatternly-looking young woman with a bawling child was talking to an old crone. "Serves the whore right," she said with callous satisfaction. "One of her tricks, I bet. Filthy harlots. Women
like her go after every man they can grab, even perverts."

"They say he slit her throat from ear to ear," said the crone.

Seimei shuddered. A very low crime. But he had no choice.
He had to find Tora. He cleared his throat nervously.

The woman with the child turned, saw his blue robe and black hat, and said, "It's the prefect! Let him pass!" The crowd parted and Seimei walked forward quickly, trying to look as official as possible. He scurried through the dark passageway and came to a torch-lit courtyard.

It was quieter here. More lanterns gleamed and dim lights shone from doors on the upper and lower floors. People were leaning on the railings and sitting on rickety stairs. They gave Seimei curious stares but quickly lost interest. The courtyard was covered with garbage, and ragged clothing dried on the railings. The air was smoky and odorous from cooking fires.

In the middle of the yard, a small group of people was looking up at a door on the second floor. Someone had hung a lantern near it. Its light shone on the red-patterned curtain.

Tora was not in sight, but the Rat stood leaning against a post. Seimei joined him. "What happened?" he asked. "Where is Tora?"

The Rat looked uncharacteristically glum. "Gone up for a look," he wheezed, nodding toward the red curtain. "Looks like somebody finally did for the poor skirt."

A fat woman in a dirty black silk dress was sitting on the steps gasping for breath and moaning. Two female friends supported her on either side, fanning her face and taking turns talking earnestly to her.

"Was that woman attacked, too?" Seimei asked.

"No. That's the landlady. Nosy female came home and noticed the red curtain, so she went to look. Hah! Did she get a surprise, old cat!"

"She found the dead woman?"

"Yeah. She also found out what made the curtain red."

Seimei looked up at the curtain and gulped. The cloth flapping heavily in a gust of icy wind had left lurid stains on the plaster of the wall.

Tora came down the stairs, his heavy boots echoing hollowly across the courtyard. He walked over to speak to the landlady.

Seimei had had enough of this nightmare assignment. Now Tora was getting them involved in this disgusting crime. Walking across the yard, he seized Tora's arm and shook it. "Come along, Tora," he said sharply. "We have no time to waste on sordid murders that don't concern us. Let us go this instant!"

Tora looked at him blankly. "In a moment," he said and turned back to the landlady. "On the next major street, you say, but one block over?"

"Tora!" Seimei stamped his foot and raised his voice. "You forget your place. We have no business with these people. No doubt this sort of thing is common around here. Foul-smelling things attract flies, they say. Let's finish our assignment and return to the tribunal, where our master is waiting. I am worn out with all this walking around slums."

Tora flung around. Taking Seimei by the shoulders, he lifted him off the ground. Seimei's eyes grew large with shock at the fury in Tora's face. "You silly old fool," Tora hissed. "You worthless official and servant of worthless officials! What do I care if you're tired or if you're too good to rub shoulders with low people? That dead woman up there is Hidesato's girl, Jasmin, and they'll arrest him for her murder as soon as they talk to the landlady. I've got to go warn him. Now do you understand?"

Seimei nodded several times, and Tora dropped him. "Go back to your precious tribunal. I don't care," Tora flung over his shoulder and walked out of the courtyard.

Seimei looked around at the hostile eyes watching him. The Rat turned his back. He had chosen to stay. "Wait, I'm coming," Seimei shouted and ran.

He had to trot to keep up with Tora's long strides. After a few minutes, he asked timidly, "What happened to the girl?"

Without slowing down, Tora said hoarsely, "Cut up! Her

throat slit all the way to the neck bone. The rest of her . . ." He
glanced at Seimei and said, "Well, she's been cut all over. The bastard tied her up and stuffed her shift in her mouth first to keep
her from screaming while he had his fun. There's an awful lot of
blood. Puddles of it. Smeared all over the walls and soaked into
the curtain! She was bleeding to death before he cut her throat."

"Horrible!" gasped Seimei. "But why are they saying your
friend did it?"

"Because the landlady saw Hidesato with Jasmin. They had
a fight. She says the last thing she heard when she was leaving
was him shouting, 'Then you're better off dead!'"

"People say such things without meaning them."

"Tell that to the constables and the prefect," growled Tora.
"Officials don't waste time on dead whores and common soldiers." They had reached a quiet street, and Tora stopped in
front of another tenement. "I guess this is the place. The landlady says Hidesato paid up Jasmin's rent because she was moving in here with him."

They found Hidesato sweeping the floor of an empty room.
Some rolled-up grass mats stood near the door, and his clothes
chest, with his armor and sword lying on top, was pushed
against a wall. A brand-new roll of bedding lay in a corner.

"Tora!" Hidesato dropped the broom to embrace Tora, giving Seimei a nod and a smile. "Come in. How'd you find me so
quick?" He unrolled the mats and spread them out for them to
sit on. "Sorry I haven't got anything to offer you. I'm getting the
place ready for Jasmin!" He smiled happily. "Guess what, Tora.
Now that I've got a sergeant's pay, she's finally given in. I'm going to be a married man."

Tora looked around the bare room and bit his lip. "Her
landlady said you had a fight with Jasmin. Did you tell her she
was better off dead?"

"So that old bat was snooping again. Well, you know how

women are. Jasmin was hard to convince. I guess I lost my temper a bit. But she came around in the end."

Tora looked down. "Hidesato, Jasmin's not coming."

Hidesato's grin faded. "You're joking and it's not funny. It *is* a joke . . . isn't it?"

Tora shook his head without looking up. Hidesato's eyes went to Seimei, who began to inch out the door.

"What happened?"

Tora said, "I'm sorry, Hito. I wish I didn't have to tell you."

Hidesato turned pale. "That bastard hurt her again."

"She's dead, Hito."

"She's dead? Jasmin's dead? It can't be. I just saw her a couple of hours ago."

"Someone got to her, cut her up, and left," said Tora. "The landlady thinks it was you."

Hidesato was on his feet. "Cut her up? I've got to go to her. Maybe she's just hurt."

Tora clasped his arm. "No. I saw her."

With a wild look, Hidesato shook him off and made for the door. Tora tackled him, and they both fell to the floor. "She's dead, Hidesato!" roared Tora. "You can't go back there. They've called for the prefect and you'll be arrested!"

The fight went out of Hidesato abruptly. He rolled onto his stomach and sobbed, pounding the floor with his fists.

They watched him in silence. Finally Tora put his hand on his friend's shoulder. "You can't stay here. The old bat has this address. I'm taking you to Higekuro's for a few days till we get this cleared up. You remember my mentioning the crippled wrestler?"

Hidesato sat up. He looked dazed, his face wet with tears.

"Put a bundle together," urged Tora.

Hidesato shook his head. "Why bother? Just let them arrest me. Nothing I touch ever turns out right. You'll just get yourself and your friend in trouble."

"Shut up and move!" snapped Tora. Hidesato stumbled up and looked vacantly around the room. Tora cursed, kicked the trunk open, found a large kerchief, and started tossing clothes into it. When he had enough, he knotted everything into a bundle and handed it to Hidesato. "Go take a look outside, Seimei," he said, "and call if the street's clear."

Seimei rushed to obey. It was quite dark by now, but the street was empty. He gave the signal that all was safe.

Tora stopped on the way to buy two cheap paper lanterns from a vendor near the market before heading north. Between the blind walls of tenements and private homes, they passed side streets that opened like black tunnels into the unknown. At one of these they turned off toward Higekuro's neighborhood. None of them felt like talking.

When they reached the wrestling school, Hidesato stopped. "I'll kill the bastard, if it's the last thing I do!"

Tora said quickly, "No, brother! That's not the way. My master and I, we'll find who did this. Why pay with your life for his?"

After a moment Hidesato nodded and allowed himself to be led inside.

To Seimei's relief they did not stay after the introductions and explanations. He met the crippled wrestler and his daughters and thought it was as strange a household as he had ever seen and well suited to accommodate a fugitive like Hidesato. As for himself, he wanted nothing so much as to be in the familiar surroundings of their tribunal quarters.

But when they reached the tribunal, Tora walked right past it. Seimei cried out, "Where are you going? We're home."

"I'm going to talk to that prefect."

"The prefect? Not now, Tora. I'm worried about the master. Or at least . . . couldn't you go without me?"

Tora was immovable. "No," he said. "You're coming with me.

Your proper robe and hat will get us past the constables and clerks."

"Surely the prefect won't be back yet." Tora did not answer, and Seimei gave in, muttering merely, "So now you see how important a person's clothes are."

But the clerks and constables at the prefecture were too busy to be impressed by Seimei's appearance. They were running about, shuffling Seimei and Tora from one brusque clerk to another. Finally a thin and tired-looking young man said, "It's been such a night! First a maniac loose in the prostitution quarter, then the Tachibana case. I'm afraid the prefect will not be back for a while. Can I help?"

Painstakingly, Tora told the story of his encounter with Scarface and his thugs, then mentioned the Rat's story about Jasmin being beaten by Scarface. The young clerk's eyes narrowed as he listened. He said, "That does sound like very important information. You were quite right to come here immediately. If you will sit down over there, I'll see to it that His Honor is informed as soon as he returns."

Seimei and Tora sat. And sat. And finally fell to dozing. Some time much later the thin young clerk came and shook Seimei's shoulder. "The prefect has retired for the night," he said, looking apologetic. "He will want to talk to both of you, but I thought you might like to go home for a few hours' sleep and come back in the morning."

Tora staggered up. "In the name of a thousand demons . . ." he started furiously. The young clerk backed away and two drowsy constables came wide awake, reaching for their chains.

"No, Tora!" said Seimei. "Remember what you told Hidesato. The master will take care of it."

Muttering curses against all lazy, crooked officials, Tora submitted.

Their quarters were dark when they got back. Seimei kicked off his shoes and opened the door quietly, shading his lantern. Tora was still taking off his boots when he heard Seimei cry out.

"The master! Quick, Tora! Something is wrong with the master."

SIXTEEN

AWAKENING

Akitada was ill for three days. During this interval he was watched with the greatest anxiety by Seimei, Tora, and Motosuke. Servants and physicians came and went. The prognosis went from desperate to hopeful, and still the three watchers persisted, leaving only for meals or urgent business.

When Akitada finally came back to full awareness of himself and his surroundings, he happened to be alone. Sunlight filtered through the wooden lattices and fell in broad rectangles across his chest and bedding. Faint, pleasant traces of incense lurked in the air and dust motes danced in the sunlight.

Akitada's first sense of himself was one of lightness, of floating almost. Intensely aware of the pleasurable warmth of the bedding and of the sun on his chest, he sighed. He had woken from a dream, one of many, he thought, but in this one he had been walking with Ayako, first in a mountain meadow, then through the grounds of a temple. Their hands had touched, and she had smiled at him.

The sun! It must be midday already, and he had missed their regular meeting.

Akitada sat up too suddenly, and the sunlit room turned black. Falling back with a groan, he remembered his illness the night before. He clearly was still in no condition to go to Ayako. Tora would have to take a message later.

He lay wondering idly where Tora and Seimei were and looked around the room. It had been cleaned, for he recalled vomiting before he had fallen asleep. Perhaps Tora had already gone to Higekuro's and told them of his illness.

She would worry about him. The thought pleased him, and he smiled, wondering if what he felt was love. Their lovemaking had become more passionate each time they met, and they had fallen into an easy, affectionate familiarity with each other. The thought of parting from Ayako terrified him. For a foolish, dizzy moment, he imagined himself settling down here, as a judge perhaps, and raising a family with Ayako.

But he knew he had a duty to his mother and sisters and could not choose this happy exile, for exile it would be when neither Ayako nor their children could ever return to the capital. He closed his eyes and remembered their last meeting. She had leaned over him, both of them naked, their skin moist from steam and their passion. Her eyes had been dreamy, half-closed, and she had bent down till her lips had touched his face. She had placed kisses, light as the touch of a petal, on his closed eyes, his nose, his mouth. Then with the tip of her tongue she had traced the lines of perspiration to his eyebrows, hairline, ears, and when she reached his lips, she had teased them open to plunge her tongue deeply into his mouth in passionate imitation of his own act of love earlier. Akitada had never been loved by a woman before.

The door slid open with a soft swish, and Seimei tiptoed in, carrying a teakettle.

"Where is everybody?" Akitada asked, his voice thin and hoarse to his ears.

Seimei almost dropped the kettle. His lined face broke into a wide smile. "You are awake," he crowed. "We have been so worried. Oh, you must be hungry. Just let me start this tea and I'll run and make you some good rice gruel. The governor will be so pleased, and Tora, too. Tora's beside himself, what with your illness and Hidesato's trouble, and the governor has done nothing but wring his hands. A very good-hearted person in spite of what you thought of him . . ."

"Seimei, calm down, please!"

Seimei put the kettle on the brazier. Next to it rested a curiously shaped incense burner, the likely source of the faint fragrance in the room. It was a bronze orb with a pierced design of interlocking circles, leaf shapes, and flower petals.

"Where did that come from?" Akitada asked.

Seimei followed Akitada's glance. "The incense burner? The governor brought it from his own library when he saw that you had none. The air was so bad from your illness."

"That was kind. What is this about Tora and Hidesato?"

Seimei sat down. "Ah! That was the worst day of my life," he said with feeling. "First that bucktoothed female at the inn made the most embarrassing scene, then we found your nasty peddler and his wife living in a hut of rags and filth, then the murder—oh, that was frightful!—and we had to rush to hide Hidesato at Higekuro's. And as if that weren't enough, we were kept waiting in the prefecture until all hours. When we finally got back, we found you lying on the floor at death's door."

"Slowly, Seimei. One thing at a time. There was a murder?" Akitada listened, astonished and appalled, to Seimei's highly colored account of Jasmin's murder and the lesser events of that fateful day. He frowned. "I don't understand. All this happened yesterday?"

"Yesterday? Oh, no. It happened four days ago. You have been very ill."

Akitada rubbed his head. "Four days?" Dismayed, he thought of Ayako. How she must have worried! He felt a surge of tenderness and gratitude for her. "I'm glad Hidesato is there. He will protect them from those monks." He hesitated, then smiled. "Let's hope it won't cause trouble for Tora. Otomi is a very pretty girl."

"Oh, Hidesato cares nothing for *Otomi*," said Seimei, and closed his mouth abruptly, busying himself with the teapot and some cups.

Sitting up gingerly, Akitada accepted a steaming cup of tea and sipped and thought about poor Jasmin. "About that murder," he said, cradling the warm cup in his hands. "Was there really so very much blood about?"

"I saw the curtain myself. It was as big as that door over there, and it was soaked. Tora said the killer must have taken it down to sop up the blood and then hung it back up. Imagine!"

Akitada nodded. "Yes, very strange. Where *is* Tora?"

"He went to check on Hidesato but should be back soon. Shall I go get you some rice gruel now?"

Akitada nodded and Seimei bustled out. Feeling a little light-headed, Akitada lay back down and stared up at the ceiling. He considered the possibility that the blue flower fragment was somehow connected to Jasmin's death but could not imagine any connection between a cheap Kazusa prostitute and that delicate piece of jewelry.

Feeling thirsty again, he got to his feet and took a few wobbly steps to fill his cup. He was amazingly weak and rested for a moment near the desk. The incense burner had no stand. When he touched it with his finger, it rolled about, though a hinged center tray for the incense remained horizontal. Clever craftsmanship! Taking a sip of his tea, he played with the orb. The pattern seemed strangely familiar. He sat down and took the burner into both hands, turning it this way and that. Bronze circles, flowers, and leaves shaped the orb. The cutout spaces of the pattern allowed the incense to escape into the air. As he looked at the openings, another pattern stood out, one that he had seen in the temple storehouse, a fish shape jumping for a ball. His heart began to beat faster.

"Heavens! What are you doing out of bed?" cried Motosuke, bustling in. "Quick, quick! Lie back down before Seimei catches you."

Akitada chuckled, put down the orb, and went to sit under his quilts. "I am glad to see you," he said.

Motosuke hitched up his gown and knelt next to him. His round face puckered with sympathy. "Thank heaven you are recovered. You can have no idea how worried we all have been." Then he threw his arms around Akitada.

Touched, Akitada returned the embrace warmly. "Thank you for your care, brother," he said. "I trust your preparations for the temple festival are progressing satisfactorily?"

"Very nicely." Motosuke rubbed his hands. "And now you will be able to attend after all." He studied Akitada's face anxiously. "You *do* think you might be well enough by day after tomorrow, don't you?"

"Day after tomorrow?"

"Have you forgotten the date? While you were lying here these past three days, Akinobu, Yukinari, and I have been slaving like mules to get all the arrangements worked out." He smiled. "If I do say it myself, I'm a brilliant organizer. I cannot wait for you to hear the details."

"I am very sorry. I had forgotten all about that."

"No wonder. You were hallucinating most of the time. We took turns watching and wiping your brow."

"I am very grateful."

Motosuke's face became serious. "Did Seimei tell you that the Tachibana woman and her nurse are both dead?"

"What?"

Motosuke nodded. "Double suicide in jail."

"I don't believe it," cried Akitada. "Ikeda must have killed them . . . and it's my fault."

"No. Ikeda's gone, and from what we could make out, he left before they died."

Akitada's head spun. He realized now the grave mistake he had made when he had allowed Ikeda to take the women to his jail. The fact that he had already felt ill at the time was no excuse for such carelessness. The image of the butterfly caught in the snow flashed again through his mind. It had been prophetic. He grimaced. "Do you know any details?"

"I have all the details because I sent Akinobu over to investigate. It happened two nights ago. Apparently, Ikeda left the night before, not long after you had the women arrested. There was a message on his desk that he had been called away to a case out of town. So far he has not returned, and I have arranged for Akinobu to take over his duties temporarily. Anyway, Lady Tachibana demanded to speak to Ikeda, and when the head clerk informed her that Ikeda had left town, she became frantic and sent for Joto."

"Naturally," groaned Akitada, clenching his fists. "What a fool I have been."

Motosuke gave him a questioning look. When Akitada did not explain, he continued, "Well, the head clerk assumed that she wanted spiritual comfort in view of the charges against her and he allowed the visit. Joto did not come himself, but he sent his deacon Kukai and two other monks the same evening. According to the guards, they prayed with her and then left. She settled down quietly for the night. In the morning, the warden found her hanging from a beam. She had taken off one of her silk gowns, twisted it, and used it for a rope. When they checked on the nurse in the next cell, the older woman had done the same, using her sash."

"They killed them," Akitada said. "The women knew too much."

Motosuke shook his head. "I don't think so. But whatever happened, it saves us unpleasantness."

It sounded callous, but Akitada knew that women who committed adultery and then killed their husbands could not hope for mercy. They were made to suffer harsh and public torture, as did servants who raised their hands against a master. Public morality demanded it. But this case involved Lady Tachibana. Stripping this beautiful child in open court and flaying the skin off her back to assure a speedy confession would shock even the most callous and prurient crowd. From Motosuke's point of view, Lady Tachibana and her nurse in court presented a problem. Being dead, they satisfied the demands of justice. And chances were that they had themselves sought an easier end. Yet Akitada did not share Motosuke's relief.

"This is my fault," he said again. "When she insisted on sending for him, I should have suspected that it was Ikeda who was her lover."

"Ikeda? Are you sure?" Motosuke looked shocked.

"It fits. When I charged her with her husband's murder, Ikeda surprised me by taking my side, even though she had accused me of trying to rape her. He ordered both women arrested, and she meekly allowed herself to be taken away to the prefectural jail. She would not have done so if she had not expected Ikeda to get her out." Looking at Motosuke, Akitada said, "And now everything points to both of them having been Joto's accomplices. That is why she sent for the abbot when Ikeda decided to flee. I should have listened to Tora."

As if on cue, Tora strolled in. Unabashed by the presence of the governor, he seated himself and, recalling his manners be-latedly, bowed to Motosuke, saying, "Hope to see you well, sir." To Akitada he said, "Thank the gods, you're better! Did Seimei tell you about Jasmin?"

"Yes, but there is no need for concern," Akitada said. "I know who killed Hidesato's girlfriend."

"Yeah. That bastard Scarface. He's beaten the poor thing all along. This time he just decided to butcher her."

Akitada shook his head. Seeing Tora's expression, he said, "Come on, Tora, surely you can work it out. Think of all the blood! It was you who told us about the bloodthirsty cretin with the knife."

Tora's eyes widened. "Yushi!" he breathed.

"Yushi. Though Scarface may well have had something to do with it." Akitada looked at the governor. "It seems a gang of three—a scarred man everyone calls Scarface, a giant by the name of Yushi, and a third man . . ."

"Jubei," Tora supplied.

". . . and Jubei—has been taking protection money from small merchants in the market and from prostitutes. Tora had them arrested, but Ikeda let them go. I suppose Akinobu will have to be told. Perhaps this time we can put the whole gang away for good."

Motosuke rose, shaking his head. "Such shocking news all around. Horrible," he said. "You must tell me all about it some other time. I had better go talk to Akinobu about the murder. You need a little more rest, elder brother. I'll return later to dis-cuss the festival."

When Motosuke had left, Akitada turned on his side and propped himself on an elbow. He smiled at Tora. "My compli-ments. It seems you were absolutely right about Ikeda and Joto being accomplices."

Tora tried to look modest and failed.

"And how is Hidesato getting along with Higekuro and the girls?"

Tora's face lengthened. He looked away. "Fine."

"Did you tell them about my illness?"

"Yes. They sent best wishes for your recovery."

Taken aback by such indifference, Akitada tried again. "What did Ayako say?"

Tora poked at the incense burner, rolling it about on the desk. "Oh, the same," he said, scowling. "They are all very busy, what with a houseguest and everything."

Akitada thought he knew the cause of his depression. "Otomi is a very pretty girl," he said gently. "It's only natural that Hidesato should think so, too."

Tora swung his head around to stare at him. "Otomi? Hidesato's not looking at Otomi. It's Ayako he's after, curse him!"

"Ayako?" Akitada blinked, then laughed. "Heavens," he said. "I forgot. They are both masters at stick fighting. No doubt they found much to talk about. Relax, Tora. I'm glad Hidesato is staying there. Otomi is in real danger now that Joto has seen the dragon scroll. I'm convinced he sent his people to cause the death of Lady Tachibana and her nurse, and there is nothing to prevent him from doing the same with Otomi. With Hidesato there, at least they will think twice before attacking her."

Tora got to his feet. "Hidesato's not there. He and Ayako went off to the bathhouse this morning." As soon as he said it, he flushed crimson. "That is, he went to the bathhouse. I don't know where she went." He took a deep breath. "If you don't need me," he said, "I guess I'd better get over there quick," and ran out.

The room seemed to dim, as if a large cloud had passed over the sun. Akitada sat back up. For a long time he just stayed there, hunched over, twisting his hands. What was it that Seimei had said? "More fearful than a tiger is the scarlet silk of a woman's undergown." He had been warning him against Lady Tachibana at the time. Ayako was not the type to wear a scarlet undergown. She was no pampered, perfumed seductress. Ayako was clean and natural as life itself. But Ayako had betrayed him.

When the pain hit, it was sharp as a sword thrust into his belly. He cried out and doubled over, hugging himself and rocking back and forth.

"Sir? Sir? What's wrong?"

Seimei's voice, frantic with worry, penetrated the fog of grief and pain. Akitada opened his eyes and willed himself to relax his body and unclench his hands. "Nothing," he croaked. "A cramp. My empty stomach rebelling."

Relief washed over Seimei's anxious face. "Is that all? I brought the gruel. Boiled it with herbs. That's what took so long." He pressed a bowl into Akitada's hands and watched him as he sipped the thin gruel. It tasted like bile. "You don't look well," he said dubiously.

Somehow Akitada managed to force the food down and, surprisingly, felt slightly better. He lay down and closed his eyes. "I'm tired, Seimei," he said listlessly.

"Yes, yes. You sleep a little. Later I will bring you more food, some nourishing fish broth with noodles perhaps." Seimei quietly gathered the dishes and tiptoed from the room.

The pain returned. Not so sharply perhaps, but as a dull soreness seeping from his belly into his head, like thick black ink soaked up by a sponge. And with it came a sense of profound loss—as if he himself had been swallowed up by this dark flood.

Too much had happened. He was no longer the same man who had relished this ill-omened assignment in hopes of serving his emperor well and finally fulfilling his mother's expectations. It seemed to him now that that Akitada had been a foolish dreamer, that nothing was as he had thought, least of all himself.

This made him angry, but his anger was not directed at Ayako or, he thought, at the scruffy sergeant. Would not any sane man take such a gift if it were offered? And why should not Ayako, for whatever reasons motivated her—pity, curiosity, or affinity—offer herself to Hidesato as readily and naturally as she had given herself to him? No doubt Akitada, too, had aroused feelings of pity or curiosity in her. She had probably thought him a pathetic weakling, much like Tora once had. Or perhaps she had taken him to the bathhouse to find out how noblemen from the capital made love.

Ayako had always lived by her own rules and never promised him anything. It was he, in his arrogance, who had believed that she must feel for him what he had felt, no, was still feeling, for her. Ayako belonged to no one, not even Hidesato.

This thought made him feel a little better until it occurred to him that Hidesato might like such an arrangement. What if this rough soldier took his pleasure with Ayako and afterward simply walked away without another thought, treating casually that which had been offered casually? He pictured the two of them on the grass mat together, and a desperate rage seized him.

There was a scratching at the door.

"Are you awake, my dear Akitada?" asked Motosuke, peering through the opening.

"Yes," said Akitada, sitting up and rubbing his eyes. "Please come in."

"I brought Akinobu and Yukinari. You do not mind?"

"No, no. Come in and sit down."

Yukinari and Akinobu filed in slowly, bowing and casting dubious glances at him. Yukinari's head was without its bandage, but a thick scab had formed near his hairline and most of his forehead bore a purple bruise.

"I think there is some tea left," said Akitada, "or would you prefer wine?"

Nobody wanted anything. They seated themselves. Yukinari and Akinobu asked politely about his health, then fell silent.

"The governor told me that you are filling in for Ikeda," Akitada said to Akinobu, trying to banish the image of the lovers from his mind. "It will be difficult to carry out both responsibilities, especially since the matter of the tax conspiracy is complex and time-consuming."

Akinobu bowed. "I was fortunate in finding a number of bright and reliable people in the prefecture," he said in his dry voice. "Once order was established, the normal routine could be resumed. I expect to leave prefectural matters in the capable hands of the head clerk when I have other duties. Just now I have given him full instructions about the criminals named by Your Excellency. A special team of constables familiar with the local underworld is searching for the three men, and I hope to report their arrests by tonight."

"Thank you. Well," said Akitada, looking at the others, "arresting Joto and his supporters during the temple festival will be more difficult. We must at all costs avoid bloodshed. Our man has proven again and again that he can act swiftly and decisively, and that human lives mean nothing to him. The temple enclosure will be packed with townspeople and pilgrims, and his monks are trained fighters who have an armory of halberds in one of the storehouses. No doubt other weapons are hidden elsewhere on the grounds. We have only the element of surprise on our side."

Yukinari spoke up. "What sorts of weapons and how many?"

"I only know about the *naginata*, but in the capital there were rumors of weapon shipments to the east. On the journey here, I had occasion to see the barrier logs at Hakone. They showed an unusual number of religious objects passing along the eastern road in this direction. It is likely that those objects were, in fact, arms destined for the Temple of Fourfold Wisdom. A man like Joto would have little compunction about causing a bloodbath on the temple grounds or of plunging the province into civil war to preserve himself."

Akitada looked at the three men and wondered how each would act under the stress of the coming days. Yukinari's fists were clenched. He muttered something under his breath, but Akitada judged him to be above average in courage. Besides, his conscience would spur him on to give his life, if necessary, to atone for his affair with Lady Tachibana.

Motosuke, normally buoyed by high spirits, looked drawn and grave, but Akitada knew now that Motosuke was his friend and committed to their undertaking. While Motosuke had much to lose if they failed, he would also gain enormous prestige by subduing an incipient rebellion.

"I blame myself," said Motosuke when their eyes met, "that this conspiracy should have grown to such proportions without my knowledge."

Akinobu said quickly, "You could not have known, Governor. Buddhist clergy are revered and protected from the normal checks and searches we carried out everywhere else. Besides, Ikeda seems to have covered up all misdeeds by Joto's monks."

Akinobu's loyalty to Motosuke was as impressive as his sense of personal honor. He had been ready to sacrifice his family property to make some sort of restitution for thefts he had not been responsible for. Had Motosuke still been a suspect, Akinobu might have been his accessory, but that possibility had been eliminated long ago.

"I knew it!" muttered Yukinari. "Ikeda's been involved all along. That's why he ignored all my complaints."

"Yes." Akitada sighed. "I hope we find him alive."

Akinobu cleared his throat. "I am, no doubt, very obtuse," he said apologetically, "but may I ask what caused Your Excellency to identify Joto and Ikeda as the conspirators?"

It was a reasonable question from a man who was used to accounting for the smallest detail in the documents he had been handling all his life, but the new Akitada was impatient with details. With an effort he dragged his thoughts from his troubles and said, "I started my investigation with the usual questions. When someone acquires sudden wealth as the result of a major robbery, there are signs in the local economy unless the person resides outside the province. I found many such signs here. The economy had improved dramatically recently. Merchants prospered, at least one of them beyond all expectation. Rapid new building was under way everywhere, most strikingly in three places, at the Temple of Fourfold Wisdom, at the governor's residence, and at the garrison."

"I used personal and discretionary funds to strengthen the garrison and add to my residence," Motosuke said defensively, "and I assumed Joto's preaching attracted large donations."

"I have seen your accounts," Akitada said with a smile. "But the temple prospered too quickly. Its fame had not reached the capital, and there was not enough money in local coffers to pay for its expansion. Seimei and I studied the historical records in your archives and in Tachibana's library. Joto started his building program shortly after the first tax convoy was ambushed."

"I should have made the connection," said Yukinari, "but when I arrived, there was a general mood of enthusiastic support for the temple."

Akitada nodded. "Exactly. Why investigate good fortune? I'm afraid the people will not like what we are about to do. But their good fortune also brought crime, violence, and corruption to this city. Everywhere Tora and I went, there was dissatisfaction with the local administration. We were told that calling the constables was useless, because the appointed officials themselves took bribes. This first alerted me to Ikeda. From what I had seen of the man, it was not incompetence or dereliction of duty that had caused the breakdown of trust between prefect and citizen. That left greed, and I came to suspect him. My servant Tora first linked Ikeda to Joto. He had an instinctive dislike for both men. As it turned out, Ikeda and Joto are perfect allies. Joto had the men and means to carry out the robberies, and Ikeda, as the local prefect, provided the details about time, route, and military strength for each convoy."

Motosuke and Akinobu exchanged looks. "Impossible," said Motosuke. "Ikeda was not involved in the planning of the tax convoys. He could not have known those things."

"Are you certain?" asked Akitada, astonished.

Motosuke nodded. "Akinobu and I always met in my library with the garrison commandant. Only the three of us knew precisely the circumstances and details of the shipments. Only we three checked the goods in the tribunal warehouse and only we counted the gold and silver bars before packing them in boxes and sealing them."

Akitada's eyes went to the incense burner. "By any chance," he asked, "did you pack the boxes near your elegant incense burner?"

Akinobu gasped. "Yes. How did you know, Excellency? We had a little accident the last time with that incense burner. It rolled against one of the boxes, and before we realized it, it had burned the leather."

Akitada smiled. "We found a leather box with an odd burn mark on it in the temple storehouse."

"The box was at the temple?" cried Motosuke. "But that proves the monks got the gold. Perhaps we will find the other goods there also."

"Much of the rice will have been traded," Akitada said, "but I have a good notion that some of the silk is stored in town, in a certain silk merchant's house. The merchant became wealthy overnight, it seems, built a wall around his compound, and is visited regularly by monks from the temple." Akitada looked at Akinobu. "On the day of the temple festival, I think you had best send your men there for a thorough search."

Akinobu bowed.

The sun had moved. Where it shone on the teapot and brazier, a drop of water at the end of the spout sparkled with a burst of colors, and in a moment grief returned. Just so had the beads of moisture glistened on her golden skin in the steam of the bath, just so had the water sparkled like a net of jewels on her cheek.

"But how did Joto find out about our plans?" asked Motosuke.

Akitada forced his mind back to the business at hand. "If Ikeda had no information about the tax convoys," he said slowly, "we may have overlooked another accomplice. Did any of you discuss the plans with others?"

Yukinari and Akinobu shook their heads. Yukinari said, "When I sent off the convoy in my charge, I gave my lieutenant sealed orders, to be opened only after they had passed the border."

Akitada looked at Motosuke, who flushed.

"I consulted Tachibana early on, before the first convoy," he said. "He took a great interest, especially after it disappeared. But I cannot believe that Tachibana would stoop to such a thing."

"No. But Lady Tachibana would." Suddenly that murder made sense. The idea that Tachibana had died because he was a jealous husband had never been entirely convincing. "I think this knowledge cost him his life. He walked into his wife's room that night to inform her of his decision to speak to me about the possibility that she had passed on the information about the tax shipments. He found her with Ikeda. You may imagine the ensuing scene. No doubt Ikeda killed him."

"So that's how Ikeda fits in," said Yukinari.

"Yes," said Akitada tiredly.

For the next hour they went over every last detail of their planning. Seimei came in once, cast a worried look at Akitada, and made more tea for everyone before withdrawing again.

They were nearly finished when Motosuke stopped and said, "Enough for today. You look terrible, elder brother. We should not have troubled you with all this when you are still so weak."

"Not at all," lied Akitada. He felt a profound indifference about his condition or their elaborate plan to catch Joto.

Motosuke rose and the others followed. They were still looking with concern at Akitada when the door flew open and Tora burst in.

He glanced around wildly, his clothes and hands stained with blood. "They've slaughtered Higekuro," he gasped. "And now they're after the girls. We've got to get the soldiers. Hurry or they're dead."

"Who is 'they'?" asked Akitada, pushing back his covers.

"Those cursed monks. The neighbors saw them, and some brainless female sent them after Otomi and Ayako." Tora seized Yukinari's sleeve. "Get your soldiers. Quick. They've got to scour the city."

"No, Tora," said Akitada. "No soldiers or constables. We'll have to go ourselves." He got to his feet. "Hand me my robe and boots."

SEVENTEEN

THE TEMPLE OF
THE MERCIFUL GODDESS

𝒯he sun had set by the time they jumped off their horses in front of Higekuro's school. Across the street a gaggle of frightened-looking neighbors stood in the dusk. Akitada shivered with nerves and weakness as much as with the cold. He crossed the road to the onlookers and snapped, "Which one of you saw the girls leave?"

A short, elderly woman stepped forward timidly. He recognized her as the neighbor who had been chatting with Ayako on his last visit. There were traces of tears on her round cheeks.

Akitada gave her a nod and said, "Tell me what you know quickly. They are in great danger."

"About two hours ago," she said. "The monks at the temple had just rung the hour of the rooster. I was looking out for my son because he was late for his dinner and saw Ayako and

Otomi walking over there." She pointed down the street. "At the corner they turned south."

"Do you know where they were going?"

"No, but Otomi had her painting things."

"Are there any temples that way?"

"Only the Sun Lotus temple is still open. Since Master Joto has come, everybody's been going to the mountain temple. The other temples have closed, even the big temple of the goddess Kannon."

"I was told that the girls were followed by some men. Did you see them?"

The old woman shook her head emphatically. "Not me. And I would have known better than to send them after Otomi. It was this foolish female." She dragged a trembling white-faced young woman from behind the others. "Go ahead, tell His Honor what you did."

The younger woman started to cry.

"How many men were there?" Akitada snapped.

"I don't remember," the woman quavered.

"You said ten, stupid," the older woman said, giving her a shake.

"That was before. Only five when they stopped to ask." The young woman wailed, "I'm sorry. They came from the school and I thought it was all right. I thought they were students of Master Higekuro."

Akitada stared down at her, then turned on his heel and strode back across the street. "Come," he said to Tora, who was waiting by the horses. "Maybe we can find something inside that will tell us where the girls went."

The heavy door opened onto darkness. Akitada was aware of the smell first—warm, sweet, and metallic. Then he heard a faint dripping sound. It was getting dark outside but enough light fell from the door that he could make out several motionless shapes strewn about the exercise floor.

Blood. It was the smell of fresh blood—and a great deal of it. Akitada stepped into the hall, Tora on his heels.

Thinking of the women outside, Akitada said, "Close the door and strike a flint!" He did not know whether his rising nausea was due to the smell or his condition, but he started to gag.

Tora closed the door and fumbled about for some light, saying, "Higekuro's over by the pillar."

Suddenly, fear seized Akitada. How many bodies had there been? What if the women outside had been wrong? What if Ayako had not left but had died here, defending her father and sister? He took a step in the dark, slipped, and fell heavily onto his side.

"Sir?" A flint rasped. Light flickered on and went out again. Tora's anxious voice came from the right. "Are you all right? There's a lot of blood on the floor."

"Yes," said Akitada, getting to his knees. His head was swimming, and he was shaking with cold and weakness. "For heaven's sake, get some light." He wiped his hands on his trousers and stood up.

Tora was noisy in his groping around. He cursed once or twice, things fell with a clatter, then the flint flashed and one of the oil lamps on the wall lit up. Tora went to light another.

Akitada slowly turned and looked around. As the lamps came on, his first impression was of a battlefield after incredible carnage. Deep, dark red, glistening blood was everywhere. The bare floor was covered with puddles of it, the exercise mats were soaked in it, and somewhere it was dripping ponderously like a slow heartbeat. Akitada counted six bodies altogether, Higekuro's among them. All of them were men.

The crippled wrestler lay slumped against the center pillar, one hand clutching a short sword covered with blood, the other his great bow; his fixed gaze was turned upward, toward the ceiling—or toward the weapon that had descended on his head and left the two terrible gashes, one reaching almost to the bridge of his nose, the other slanting toward the left temple, exposing part of his brain. Blood still oozed from the terrible head wounds. It had soaked the magnificent black beard and puddled on one shoulder, from where it fell, thickly, drop by drop, into his empty quiver.

Akitada controlled his rising nausea and went to touch Higekuro's pale cheek. It was cool. Then he felt the blood and found it thick and sticky. "It must have happened shortly before you got here," he said.

"Higekuro was still warm then," said Tora. "I rushed through the place looking for the girls and then ran all the way back to the tribunal." He glanced around the room. "He took five of the bastards with him."

"Yes. The woman mentioned ten men, then later five," said Akitada. "I think she saw them arrive and go into the school. Higekuro killed five, but the other five left to look for Ayako and Otomi."

He moved among the dead assassins. They were all strangers to him, young, muscular, dressed neatly in dark cotton gowns, with scarves covering their heads like middle-class shopkeepers or artisans. Akitada stripped off the headgear and exposed the shaven heads. "Monks," he said without surprise.

They had paid a heavy price. All of them had two or more arrows through their bodies and one, closest to Higekuro, had died in agony from a sword thrust into his bowels. It had been Higekuro's final act against the man who killed him.

When they looked into Higekuro's private quarters, they found trunks and boxes gaping, their contents strewn about the floor, curtains slashed and screens torn from the windows. Outside, in the small kitchen yard, a fire had been lit in an empty rain barrel. Tora stirred the smoldering ashes and pulled out a charred dowel with remnants of paper and silk attached to it.

"They burned her paintings," Akitada said. "Come. There is nothing left to find. We are wasting time."

On the way out, Tora snatched up one of the heavy staves from its rack on the wall. Outside the neighbors had dispersed, but someone was coming down the street, whistling. Tora cursed under his breath.

Akitada, worried about an unarmed Ayako facing five murderous monks, was swinging himself on his horse when he saw the whistler.

Hidesato.

In a moment he was out of the saddle again. In another, he had reached Hidesato and flung him against the wealthy neighbor's plaster wall. Seizing the neck of his robe, Akitada bashed the sergeant's head into the wall, punctuating each thrust with an accusation. "You worthless dog!" he snarled. "Where were you when you were needed? Is this how you repay kindness?" Akitada choked on the thought that the kindness had included the use of Ayako's body. "What kind of low animal are you to do this to her?" he groaned, suddenly dizzy from his outburst.

Tora pulled him off. Akitada leaned against the wall, taking rasping breaths of air, trying to control his shaking limbs.

"What's wrong with him?" croaked Hidesato, holding his head. "Has he gone mad?"

Tora said bitterly, "While you were enjoying your bath, those cursed monks came back. They killed Higekuro and went after the girls. Thanks to you, they're probably dead by now."

Hidesato dropped his hands. He stared from Tora to Akitada, saw the blood on Akitada's clothes, and ran to the school. Flinging open the door, he disappeared inside.

Akitada came away from the wall and staggered to his horse. He dragged himself into the saddle, kicked the horse in the flank, and galloped off. Tora followed, ignoring Hidesato's shouts behind him.

They looked for pagodas rising above the low-slung dwellings and pine groves. The first temple they found quickly. A battered sign on its gate spelled out the name "Sun Lotus Temple" in characters that had once been brilliantly red but had faded to a pale brown. An ancient monk was sweeping dead leaves from the steps.

"You there. Have you seen two young women?" Akitada shouted from his horse.

The old man peered up nearsightedly and bowed. "Welcome," he said in a cracked voice and put his broom aside. "Would Your Honor like to buy some incense to burn before the Buddha?"

Seeing his age, Akitada brought his horse closer and repeated his question.

A pleased smile crossed the old man's face. "Do you mean Otomi and her sister? They came by. After they had left, some young men asked for her." He smiled again. "She's a very pretty girl."

"What did you tell them?"

"I said we were all well and thanked the girls for their concern."

Akitada gritted his teeth and found they were chattering again. He looked at Tora, who bellowed, "What did you tell the men?"

"Oh. Why didn't you say so? I told them where the girls went, of course."

Akitada groaned. "Where?" he shouted, twisting the reins between his clenched fists.

"You don't look at all well, sir," said the ancient one, peering worriedly up at Akitada's face. "Please honor our poor temple for a short rest. If you like, Kashin, our pharmacist, will brew you one of his herbal teas."

Akitada took a deep breath, fought down his desperation, and managed to say more calmly, "Thank you. Some other time.

We're in a hurry. Those men you sent after Otomi and her sister mean them harm. Where did the girls go?"

The monk's chin sagged. "Harm? Oh, dear. I hope you are wrong, sir. Otomi told me she wanted to paint the Kannon, so I sent the young men to the old temple in the southeast corner of the city. There's a lovely painting of the Goddess of Mercy enthroned on a large lotus blossom in the main hall. The temple is locked, but there's a back door—" Akitada and Tora were already galloping down the narrow street.

They clattered through quiet neighborhoods where curious householders peered out of lit doorways at the sound of their racing hoof beats. The light was failing quickly. Clouds moved in like black curtains drawn across the opalescent sky.

"It'll be dark soon," shouted Tora to Akitada, "and we've brought no lanterns."

"Quiet!" Akitada reined in his horse. Before them rose a dark mass of curved temple roofs and trees. A three-storied pagoda loomed like a dark sentinel beside the black rectangle that was the main hall. Tile-topped walls enclosed the temple buildings and a whole city block of wildly tangled shrubs and trees.

Akitada dismounted and tied his horse to a bare willow tree at the street corner. Shivering in the cold wind, he stood listening until Tora joined him.

"Did you see someone?" Tora whispered.

Akitada shook his head. "Ssh!"

The wind rustled the dead leaves, and branches rubbed together. Somewhere in the distance an owl hooted.

Akitada moved. "I thought I heard voices," he said. "Come. We'll have to find a way in. The front gates will have been nailed shut. Be quiet."

Tora gripped his stave more fiercely. "I look forward to getting my hands on those butchers."

They crossed the street and moved along the shadow of the wall, looking for broken masonry. When a curious hissing noise came from the other side, they froze. Nothing else happened, and they were about to move on when there was a suppressed curse and the sound of breaking shrubbery. A muffled male voice in the distance shouted something that sounded like an order, and the rustling receded.

"They're here," said Tora.

Akitada nodded. "It sounds as though they're searching. We may be in time."

They continued to inspect the wall. It was in frustratingly good condition. There was not so much as a foothold to climb over, and Akitada was not about to propose another attempt by Tora to scale a temple wall via his shoulders. In his present weakened state, he could not support a small child, let alone a full-grown man.

"Let's try the main entrance," he said finally. At that moment, the silent air was rent by a woman's scream.

"They got the girls," said Tora, staring frantically at the top of the wall.

"That was Ayako." Akitada was already running toward the roofed gatehouse. Both wings of the ornate gate gaped wide, and they ran inside.

The courtyard was empty, silent, and vaguely ominous. To their right, the pagoda roofs spread their dark wings; to the left crouched a small reliquary; and before them loomed the vast shape of the great hall whose immense curving roof they had seen from the road. Its doors stood open on a darkness as absolute as the gaping maw of death.

"The cry came from the back of the hall," Akitada said. "The fastest way is through it."

They ran up the steps of the hall. The official seals on the massive doors had been broken. The anteroom got some light from the outside and was empty. To its right was the office of the temple custodian, a monk who accepted donations from worshippers and handed out incense sticks. Ahead lay the vast interior of the temple hall. They stopped to listen and heard nothing.

"Come," said Akitada. "They are in the garden in back."

"We can't see anything without a lantern," Tora muttered under his breath. "I bet I'll find some in that office."

"No. There's no time and we can't show a light."

They went into the pitch-black hall, sliding one foot in front of the other and feeling their way with outstretched hands. Akitada tried to remember temple construction and hoped to gain the rear wall. Something fell with a clatter.

"What happened?" Akitada asked.

"Caught my foot on something and lost my stave."

Akitada heard Tora's hands scrabbling across the floor. "Let it be," he said, moving on. Tora abandoned the stave and joined him. When Akitada's hands finally touched the rear wall, Tora cursed. There was a dull thud, then silence.

"What's the matter now?"

No answer, just a slithering sound coming closer. Before his better sense could prevent him, Akitada had moved toward it. A viselike grip seized him around the knees, jerked, and then he fell backward, barely remembering to twist to keep his skull from striking the floor. The fall knocked the breath out of him.

Then his assailant was upon him, trying to pin his arm while fumbling for his throat. The move was a standard form of attack among wrestlers. Akitada had never been in worse shape to fight off a murderous thug, but his wrestling experience came to his aid. He reacted instinctively with the correct defensive move. But the other man, though thin, fought desperately and was quicker than Akitada. They rolled about on the rough planks of the floor, fighting silently for their lives.

Fortunately, Akitada's assailant was also handicapped by the darkness. He could not always find the right hold immediately and gave Akitada time to twist out of his reach. Eventually Akitada had enough purchase for a hard kick. Somewhat to his surprise his foot made contact. The body slid across the floor, hit a column with a soft thud, and was silent. Akitada rose to his knees and called out to Tora. No response. He debated checking on his attacker, then felt around for Tora. He found him breathing and brought him around by shaking him. Tora groaned, sat up, and almost immediately lashed out, knocking Akitada into a pillar.

"Ouch! It's me."

Tora croaked, "What . . . ? Oh! Sorry. Somebody grabbed my foot." Then fury seized him. "Where are the bastards?" he growled. "I'll tear their heads off and kick them around this infernal pit of hell."

Rubbing his bruised shoulder, Akitada felt like laughing despite their danger. "Calm down. There was only one. He tried the same thing with me, but I got in a lucky kick and knocked him out. That leaves only four outside. We'll have to tie this one up and gag him. Give me your belt."

But when they groped their way back to where Akitada had left their attacker, he was gone. They felt around for a few seconds, then Akitada put his hand on Tora's arm. They listened. A soft noise moved away from them toward the entrance. Akitada made out a shadow against the faint light from the outside and leapt after it. Wrapping both arms around the other man's body, he brought him down and landed heavily on his back.

But the cry of pain was female, and Akitada's hands under the slim body confirmed the fact. Akitada rolled off. Then recognition came: Ayako!

He opened his mouth to speak her name, shaking with the relief of having found her safe and sound, and reached out to gather her into his arms, when some heavy object struck the side of his head. The darkness flashed into burning light and then vanished.

◆

Tora had heard Ayako's cry and Akitada's fall. He, too, rushed across the intervening space and collided violently with a large unfamiliar body. Cursing, he pulled back his fist to lash out at the new enemy when Hidesato's voice asked, "Tora? Is that you?"

Tora lowered his arm. "Hidesato! What are you doing here?"

"I followed on foot. Good thing, too. I think one of the bastards got hold of Ayako. Ayako? Where are you? This cursed darkness. A man can't see what he's doing."

Tora struck a flint. In the brief flash, he saw Hidesato with a long, heavy bamboo stave in his hand and Ayako crouching on the floor over Akitada's prostrate figure. Then the light went out again.

"You fool." Ayako sounded bitter. "You hit Akitada and probably killed him."

Tora left them, groping his way toward the entrance. He returned a moment later carrying an ancient lantern that shed a flickering light. "How bad is he?" he asked.

"He's breathing." She held up a bloody hand.

"Where's Otomi?" Tora asked.

"I made her hide. Tora, there's so much blood."

Tora was on his knees, tearing strips of fabric from his shirt for a bandage. "He shouldn't have come," he muttered, looking at the pale face of the unconscious Akitada in Ayako's lap.

"I didn't know," Hidesato said miserably.

Ayako said scornfully, "You're a stupid, bumbling fool who can't do anything right."

Hidesato sagged to the floor and put his head in his hands. The other two ignored him. Around them heavy columns rose into the distant darkness. The enormous painting of the Goddess of Mercy seemed to float in space, and the reds, pinks, and soft browns of her robes shifted and trembled in the unsteady light of the lantern flame, while the gold of her jewelry and halo flashed like fire in the gloom.

"If you'll stay with him till he comes around," Tora said when they had put a bandage on Akitada's head, "Hidesato and I'll go out and get those cursed bastards before they find Otomi."

He expected an argument, but Ayako merely nodded.

Hidesato looked at her. "I'm sorry, Ayako," he said hoarsely, brushing at his eyes. "I didn't mean to do it. It was dark. I know I've been worse than useless. He nearly killed me because what happened was my fault. I swear I'll try to make it up to you. If it's the last thing I do." He turned away.

Tora scooped up his bamboo stave and followed Hidesato out. Ayako, in the dim circle of lantern light, looked after them with a puzzled frown, then turned back to the unconscious Akitada, cradling his face in her hands.

◆

Outside, the darkness was less opaque. From a far corner of the garden came a crashing noise and someone cursed.

"Thank the gods. They haven't found her yet," Tora said. He leaned his stave against the railing. "Too many trees to use these. I guess it'll have to be our bare hands."

Hidesato put down his own bamboo pole.

Their quarry was making so much noise thrashing through the shrubbery that they did not have to be very careful. The monks had separated to cover a larger area in their search, and Tora and Hidesato surprised two of them. Tora knocked out his man with a handy piece of broken roof tile, while Hidesato produced a length of thin chain from under his jacket and threw this over the other man's head, snapping it back so suddenly that they heard his neck snap. The monk dropped without a sound.

"Your master won't be able to talk to this one," Hidesato said. "What about yours?"

Tora shook his head. "I hit him too hard."

Both dead men had shaven heads and both carried short swords. Tora and Hidesato helped themselves to these.

They found their next victim because he was cursing loudly, trying to disentangle himself from a thorny vine. He broke off abruptly when Tora appeared before him with a drawn sword. His eyes started from his head in shock.

From somewhere close a voice called, "Daishi? What is it? Have you found her?"

Tora put his sword to the monk's throat and shouted back, "No! Twisted my ankle. Who's with you?"

"Hotan. Where are the others?"

"Coming." Tora grinned and knocked his prisoner out cold.

Hidesato joined him. "Two more? That should be all."

Tora nodded. "I told them we're coming."

They ran along the overgrown path and came face-to-face with two husky men in the same dark clothes and head scarves as the others. But these drew their swords and charged.

Tora had never used a sword before and managed to survive the attack only because he jumped about like a monkey while slashing wildly in all directions. Hidesato knew the rudiments of sword fighting but was badly outclassed. He tossed his sword aside in favor of the chain. Letting out the chain and swinging it until it wrapped itself about his adversary's sword and sword arm, he was able to jerk him forward and disarm him. Tora prevailed only by kicking his man in the groin. When he screamed and dropped his sword to clutch himself, Tora jumped him.

They tied up these two, but when they turned back to do the same with the unconscious man in the brambles, they discovered him gone. A quick search brought them to an open gate in the wall, but the road outside was empty.

"Damnation! The bastard's gone to warn Joto," Tora said ruefully.

They collected their prisoners and dragged them back to the temple hall.

"Hey, Ayako. All's safe," shouted Tora.

Ayako appeared on the veranda and scanned the shrubbery. "Where's Otomi?" Tora asked. "She can't hear us."

Ayako did not answer. She came down the steps, her eyes on Hidesato. "You're hurt."

Hidesato looked down at himself. A large dark stain was spreading across his chest. "It's nothing," he said.

"Oh, Hidesato," Ayako said. "Sit down and let me see."

A rustling sound came from under the veranda steps. Tora reached for his sword, but it was Otomi who crept out, her eyes huge in a dirt-smeared face and her clothes covered with dead leaves, cobwebs, and twigs. Tora's mouth widened into a smile. He dropped his weapon and went to scoop her into his arms.

Ayako found a flesh wound in Hidesato's shoulder and untied her sash to bandage it.

"Please forgive me," he begged, stumbling to his feet.

Her face softened. "There's nothing to forgive. I am sorry I blamed you," she said, rising. "It was too dark for you to see, and I made the same mistake myself."

He looked at her searchingly. "I would not have you think badly of me," he said awkwardly. "I've never known anyone like you and I'd rather die than . . ." His voice faltered.

Ayako smiled and took his hand. "I know," she said softly.

◆

Akitada staggered out onto the veranda in time to take in this tender scene. His face hardened. "Tora," he snapped.

Tora jumped to attention. They all looked up at Akitada, who stood clutching the balustrade, his face as pale as the bandage against his black hair.

"I see you've managed by yourselves. Did you inform the young women about . . . what happened?"

"The young women?" Ayako took a few steps toward Akitada. Their eyes met briefly, but he glanced away. "What are you talking about? What happened?"

Tora and Hidesato exchanged stricken looks. Akitada slowly descended, supporting himself on the railing. He gave Ayako an impersonal nod and said stiffly, "I am afraid it falls to me to inform you that your father died this afternoon."

Ayako became very still. Her eyes were on his lips, waiting.

"He was murdered by the men who attacked you and your sister," Akitada continued in the same tone, "but he fought bravely, killing five of his assassins before succumbing to the sword of another. I regret extremely to be the bearer of such tragic news."

Ayako straightened her slim body. "I am greatly obliged to Your Excellency," she said. "My sister and I shall always be in your debt for coming to our rescue." She bowed deeply, then turned her back and went to Hidesato.

Akitada's heart contracted. He felt tears rising to his eyes. With sheer effort of will, he made himself climb the stairs again and walk back into the temple hall.

The lamp still burned before the image of the goddess. Otomi's painting gear lay nearby. Akitada paused, clutching a pillar like a drowning man, and looked up at the inscrutable face in the painting. The lines of the painted image blurred until it seemed to him that the Goddess of Mercy's face was Ayako's. The lustrous eyes looked at him with cold detachment, and the soft lips wore a sneer.

He turned away and walked unsteadily out of the temple hall and into the night.

EIGHTEEN

THE FESTIVAL

The governor's palanquin was comfortable and elegant, but on the steep mountain road it began to list precariously. Riding in such a conveyance was a new experience for Akitada, who decided that he much preferred the back of a horse. He lifted the bamboo curtain and looked out.

They were in the thick pine forests mantling the mountainside. The bright sunlight splashing the road and forest floor was at odds with his gloomy disposition. He watched as one of the outriders passed the curtained window on his right. The governor's personal guard accompanied them in the full flourish of polished armor, snapping red banners, and high-stepping mounts dripping with red silk tassels. Self-consciously Akitada tugged at his old court robe, hoping it did not make too poor a showing next to Motosuke's splendor. The governor sat across from him in a crisp new gown of figured green brocade over his voluminous trousers of deep red silk.

Motosuke also peered out. "We are almost there," he said. "I can see the top of the pagoda. Heavens, have you ever seen so many people?"

The closer they got to their destination, the more spectators lined the side of the road. As soon as the governor's cortege passed, they fell in behind to join those waiting at the temple for the dedication ceremony. Akitada exchanged looks with Motosuke. All those people. The responsibility was frightful. Anything might go wrong in spite of their careful planning.

Akitada, for one, was convinced that it would. Everything he had touched so far had turned to grief. He had brought death wherever his feet had carried him. Since their frightful discovery of Higekuro's murder, Akitada's thoughts rarely strayed from that memory. Higekuro's blood tainted every aspect of his present life. The only exception was the memory of Ayako, and her he banished firmly from his thoughts.

As if reading his mind, Motosuke said, "I shall never forget the sight of all that blood at the wrestling school. This Higekuro must have been a most remarkable man."

Akitada nodded.

"It is a mercy that the young women are safe. The deaf-mute girl is a very fine artist."

Akitada nodded again. Would Ayako be safe with a man like Hidesato? Would Hidesato take her father's place in the school . . . as he had taken Akitada's place in her arms? Aloud he said, "Luckily I was lying unconscious inside the temple hall when Tora and Hidesato tangled with Joto's men. The monk who escaped could have spoiled our plans if he had recognized me."

Motosuke rubbed his pudgy hands together and smiled. "Yes. A good omen. The Goddess of Mercy is on our side."

She was nothing of the sort, Akitada thought bitterly, remembering Kannon's sneer.

"Why the long face, elder brother?" Motosuke asked. "Is your head still painful?"

"No." This was, surprisingly, the truth. He was perfectly fit again in spite of his fever and Hidesato's blow. The same could not be said for his mood. "I envy you your good spirits," he said sourly. "Once we are inside the temple, we are sitting ducks, you know."

"Don't worry. All will go well. We are guarded by my own men and Yukinari's. The soldiers assigned to the inner court-yard and the great Buddha hall are absolutely loyal."

Akitada fell silent, ashamed of having sounded cowardly.

"And only think," Motosuke continued, "at this moment Akinobu and his constables are raiding the silk merchant's property and warehouses. When the day is done, we will have our prisoners, the evidence, *and* the loot." Motosuke rubbed his hands again and chuckled. "Won't they be surprised in the capital to get three tax shipments they had written off as lost?"

"They won't get it all back," grumbled Akitada. A temple bell began its booming call. The palanquin jerked and veered suddenly to the right. At Motosuke's window appeared the great gate of the Temple of Fourfold Wisdom, its blue tiles sparkling in the sun. On both sides of its steps stood saffron-robed monks.

"I wonder if Ikeda is here," Motosuke said.

"I wonder if he is alive. He is a danger to Joto." Akitada reached for the small silver mirror that hung on one of the hooks and checked his court hat, a black pillbox of starched silk with a loop in the back. He scowled at his long face with its heavy brows and passed the mirror to Motosuke. The palanquin finally stopped and came to rest on solid ground. "Are we supposed to get out here?" Akitada asked.

Motosuke pushed the woven bamboo curtain a little farther aside. "No. Just some formalities to welcome us. Ah, here we go again." The palanquin lurched up, and both men reached for their hats. Motosuke peered around. "I see Yukinari has posted men at the gate. Clever fellow. I think that affair with the Tachi-bana woman was a hard blow to him."

"I almost had him arrested. Both the Tachibana maid and a beggar said the killer was wearing a helmet."

"Oh," said Motosuke. "I had meant to tell you, but your ill-ness and Joto drove the matter from my mind. The young fool confided that the lady became so violent the day he ended their relationship that he ran from the house leaving his helmet behind."

The palanquin suddenly tilted back as the bearers ascended the steps to the gate.

"Yes, that explains it." Akitada snatched at a silk loop to keep from falling back and crushing his headgear. "My guess is that Ikeda used it as some sort of disguise. I thought something like that must have happened when I was told the man wore a blue robe. No military officer would wear his helmet without the ar-mor." The palanquin tipped forward as the bearers trotted down the steps on the other side of the gate. When it leveled out again, Akitada released the loop and continued, "I should have thought of Ikeda earlier. He wore that blue robe to your party."

They became aware of a sound like the buzzing of a giant beehive. Akitada lifted his curtain. They were passing down the center of a large courtyard filled with people. On either side of the palanquin, yellow-robed monks were swinging incense burners and chanting softly. Behind them pressed the local people, chattering and trying to snatch a glimpse of the pomp and circumstance of the arriving dignitaries.

Their bearers, conscious of all the eyes on themselves and their burden, trotted briskly until they reached the steps of the great Buddha hall, where they deposited the palanquin with a flourish that rattled their charges' teeth.

Egress from the palanquin was fraught with difficulties; first Motosuke, then Akitada emerged, their voluminous robes, trains, and stiffened silk trousers gathered to their bodies, their heads inclined to squeeze out without knocking their hats askew.

The next problem was ascending the broad stairs to the veranda without falling over trousers that extended almost a yard beyond their feet. Fortunately, the waddling gait adopted by high court nobles in full ceremonial garb was considered elegant. Akitada was sweating by the time he reached the high veranda. His inferior rank in the capital had not exactly accustomed him to such occasions. Motosuke, he noticed, managed with ease despite his greater years and weight.

The reception committee was headed by a middle-aged priest with a pale face and sunken eyes. Motosuke addressed him as Kukai. So this was the deacon who had been sent to give spiritual comfort to the jailed Lady Tachibana. Feeling an almost physical aversion, Akitada turned away to look out over the courtyard below.

Visitors, monks, and soldiers milled about everywhere. A number of raised platforms had been erected in front of the new hall, and the carriages of wealthy and influential families were lined up along the far galleries. Screens hid upper-class women and their maidservants from the curious eyes of strangers. And everywhere were uniforms and armor. Yukinari's soldiers stood discreetly in the galleries, clustered about the gates, and hovered near the Buddha hall.

Reassured, Akitada joined Motosuke for a guided tour of the new hall.

It was vast and beautifully constructed, but Akitada listened with only half an ear to Kukai's descriptions. They paused for the required obeisances before a large gilded bronze figure of the Buddha. A group of elderly monks chanted softly, reminding Akitada of the prisoners in the subterranean pit. Then a long line of beautiful boys, none older than ten or eleven, passed through. They wore the most splendid silk gowns of all colors and carried golden chimes. Each time the clear tones rang out, there were smiles or giggles from the younger ones. Their innocence struck Akitada as incongruous and surreal as they disappeared into the silvery haze of incense surrounding the great Buddha. He stared after them in bewilderment.

"Our youngest novices." Kukai's voice startled Akitada from his reverie. "Their families placed them in our charge."

Akitada remembered the old monk's accusations against Joto and felt sickened. The monastic life forbade relations with women, and monks were known to turn to each other for affection, but children? And what of his friend Tasuku, who had loved women all his young life? How had he managed to turn his back on them forever?

When they reemerged from the hall, Kukai led them to one of the viewing platforms, explaining that the other platforms, spaced some fifty feet apart from one another, were reserved for the reader, the abbot and temple administrators, and the dancers.

Their viewing stand was covered with thick grass mats bound in brocade, and their cushions were of silk. A brocade awning shielded them from the glare of the winter sun. Akitada had the seat of honor, with Motosuke slightly to his left. The cushion to Motosuke's left had been intended for the missing Ikeda. Yukinari seated himself to Akitada's right. The other members of the official party, several judges and the senior secretaries of the provincial administration, with Seimei in the lead, filed up and took their places behind them.

Akitada nodded a greeting to Yukinari, who looked splendid. His present responsibility had done much to bring color to his face and assurance to his bearing.

Below them an orchestra of drums, flutes, and zithers struck up, and costumed dancers appeared on the platform in the center to perform the measured movements of sacred dances. Akitada kept glancing at the empty stand reserved for the abbot.

At long last the dancers ceased and the music ended. An anticipatory silence fell. Then a silvery tinkling of small bells drew every eye to the doors of the new hall, where the children were gathered. The panels opened slowly, and Joto appeared. The crowd burst into welcoming applause.

He stood for several long minutes as they shouted and waved before advancing to the top of the steps. Here he paused again, waiting for silence, then raised folded hands to his lips and forehead in greeting and benediction and descended. His robe was made from silk dyed in two contrasting shades of purple that shimmered and shifted hue with every movement. Gold embroidery and pearls encrusted his stole.

Two long lines of monks emerged from the hall. Each monk carried a staff with colored silk streamers. Joto, joined by Kukai and other monastic officials, took the lead as all the other monks, novices, and acolytes, in their best robes and with colorful stoles about their shoulders, fell in behind. Chanting "Amida! Amida!" the whole gorgeous stream flowed around the great courtyard and out through the main gate to perform the ritual perambulation of the temple.

Motosuke leaned toward Akitada and said, "Have you ever seen such showmanship? I think we have just watched three tax shipments of gold and silk walking out that gate."

"There will be something left," Akitada said, adding grimly, "A man of Joto's flair has greater plans than a mere temple dedication." He turned to Yukinari and said in a low voice, "This is surely the time to release the prisoners. I haven't seen Tora around."

Yukinari murmured, "He's taking some of my best men to the storehouses. If they can find the access to the underground prison, they should have plenty of time before the monks return. Tora will signal when they have been successful."

The planning so far had been flawless. From beyond the

temple walls drifted the sounds of chanting and ringing bells. Akitada guessed that the perambulation might take half an hour, considering the size of the compound and the terrain. Still, he was nervous.

To keep the crowd from becoming restive, the musicians and dancers began their performances again. Some of the child novices brought fruit juices to the official party. The boy who served Akitada could not have been more than six or seven. He was beautiful as such young children often are, and when he managed to fill the cup without spilling a drop, he chuckled in delight and gave Akitada a gap-toothed grin.

Eventually the head of the procession reappeared. The long snake of monks wound to the other viewing platform. Joto and the temple dignitaries ascended it, but Kukai climbed to the speaker's stand and, as soon as the abbot and his officials had taken their seats, began the sutra reading. The rest of the monks dispersed to various positions, where they joined with periodic choral responses.

The congratulatory addresses by the representatives of the emperor were next. Both Akitada and Motosuke were to express their happy thoughts on the occasion. Their official gifts, in the form of rolls of silk, robes, sutra boxes, and prayer beads, stood neatly wrapped and decorated at the foot of their viewing stand. As imperial emissary, Akitada was to congratulate Joto first. His actual intentions were altogether different.

But everything depended on Tora's prior release of Joto's prisoners. Where was he? Akitada's stomach lurched unpleasantly as the worm of fear twisted its coils. Unable to contain his worry, Akitada turned and nodded to Seimei. As prearranged, Seimei rose quietly to make his way to the kitchen courtyard and the latrines.

◆

Seimei walked purposefully, like a man on his way to the con-
veniences. There were few people in the kitchen enclosure, and
he saw no monks at all. Trying to remember the temple layout,
he turned to the gate in the northern wall.

The next courtyard was deserted. Seimei tentatively identified the large low building before him as the storehouse with the
hidden halberds. This must be the enclosure where Tora and the
soldiers were supposed to release the buried monks, but there
was no one about. As Seimei approached the large storehouse,
he heard a noise inside. Tora, he thought with a sigh of relief
and pulled open the door. A shadow moved inside.

"Who's there?" Seimei whispered nervously, no longer sure
who lurked inside.

No answer.

It occurred to Seimei that his errand might be dangerous.
Some vicious monk, perhaps a whole gang, could be behind
those barrels and bales and jump out to kill him. For a moment
he considered slamming the door shut and locking in whatever
was lurking there, but he remembered his instructions. He was
to find out what had gone wrong and warn his master.

Gingerly he stepped inside. He scanned the long line of barrels and baskets and saw that the bundles of *naginata* had been
unwrapped and some of them had rolled out onto the floor.

Creeping forward on trembling legs, he reached the barrels
and peered over them. Crouched behind the farthest barrel was
a man wearing a blue robe like his own. Tora also wore such a
robe, but this could not be Tora. Tora would not be hiding from
him . . . unless he was up to one of his childish tricks.

Seimei crept a little closer. Then, gathering all his courage,
he pounced forward, grasped the other man's collar, and demanded, "What are you doing? Didn't you hear me—" He
broke off in astonishment. "I beg your pardon," he gasped, releasing the man.

Prefect Ikeda stood up. He was pale, but he measured Seimei's thin, bent figure and white hair calmly. "Oh, it's you," he said, inching along the barrels toward the door. "I was just leaving. It seems Joto's been storing contraband here. Your man Tora and some soldiers were here a moment ago. I was just making sure they had not overlooked anything."

Seimei regarded him through narrowed eyes and stepped in his way. "I don't believe you," he said. "You are hiding here because you are wanted for the murder of Lord Tachibana."

Ikeda stopped and smiled. "Oh, that. That's all been cleared up."

"It has not," cried Seimei. "You need not take me for a fool. In fact, I happen to know that you have been declared a fugitive from justice." The moment he uttered the words, Seimei realized with a sinking heart that he was now obligated to raise the alarm so that Ikeda could be apprehended. But an alarm was the last thing his master would wish at this moment. Drawing himself up importantly, he glared at Ikeda and said, "You are under arrest."

Strangely, Ikeda said nothing. He just stood there, smiling and seeming to wait for further developments.

Seimei was at a loss. "I'd better find something to tie you up with," he muttered, looking around. He saw a coil of rope near one of the barrels, but when he bent to pick it up, Ikeda made a rush for the door.

Fortunately, he had miscalculated his distance. Seimei flung himself forward and met Ikeda's charge in a bone-crunching collision. They both fell back, gasping.

"Oh, no, you don't!" wheezed Seimei, feeling his left shoulder for damage. "You aren't getting away so easily."

"Get out of my way, old man," Ikeda snarled, rubbing his arm.

Seimei was desperate. If Ikeda escaped, he would warn Joto.

What had happened to Tora and the soldiers? Seimei decided to play for time. "I thought you wanted a chance to explain," he reminded Ikeda.

"You're a fool," said Ikeda. "I had to kill Tachibana. He was about to ruin us." Looking Seimei over, he smiled unpleasantly. "Old age is no guarantee of wisdom. It seems I'll have to kill you, too." Taking the cover off the barrel beside him, he stuck his arm in and felt around. A shower of beans spilled over the rim and scattered across the floor.

Clearly nothing good was hidden in those beans. Seimei swallowed and moved toward the door, eyeing Ikeda warily. Ikeda grunted with satisfaction and drew forth a sword, its new blade gleaming wickedly in the dim light. Then he started toward Seimei.

Seimei glanced about desperately and found one of the *naginata* at his feet. Snatching it up, he staggered under its weight. He had no idea how to use this long pole with the sharp blade at its end but thought that it was meant for stabbing or slashing an enemy from a safe distance. Since Ikeda's sword was much shorter, the *naginata* would give him an advantage. Unfortunately, it was too heavy for him. As he watched Ikeda approach, the long pole tipped and wobbled in his grasp.

Ikeda sneered, "What are you trying to do with that, old man?"

Seimei gripped the *naginata* tightly. He tried to recall some of the moves he had watched during his master's stick-fighting practice. If he could not slash or stab, perhaps he could at least hit or whirl around.

Grasping the pole with both hands, Seimei hopped aside a few steps, slid on some beans, and sat down hard on the floor. Ikeda laughed. Seimei, flushed with anger, scrambled up. Gathering all his strength, he swung the halberd back in a wide sweep. To his surprise, the force of this motion and the weight of the weapon spun him around like a top. He staggered, stopped dizzily, and looked for Ikeda.

Ikeda, who had watched, round-eyed, now burst into gales of laughter, doubling over with hilarity.

This was too much for Seimei. Heaving up the halberd, he charged.

Ikeda stopped laughing and jumped out of the way. He raised his sword, but at that moment someone stepped into the doorway, blocking the light. Ikeda turned his head.

Seimei awkwardly corrected his aim and brought the *naginata* down with all his force. It caught Ikeda's head with the wooden pole instead of the sharp blade and knocked him to the floor, where he lay, limp as a sack of grain, a trickle of blood seeping from his nostrils.

"Holy Buddha!" gasped a voice. "Did my eyes trick me or is that you, Seimei?"

Seimei dropped the halberd from his slack fingers. "Tora," he whispered. "Where have you been? I . . . had to knock him out. He was about to kill me." Suddenly faint, he sat down on a barrel. "The master sent me to see if everything was all right. You weren't around, but I found him." He looked at Ikeda's inert form and shuddered.

"By the great Amida," Tora said, "that was the finest thing I ever saw. Who would've thought you had it in you? Let me congratulate you." He bent, seized Seimei's limp figure in a bear hug, and lifted him off the barrel.

"Let me go." Seimei kicked his shins. "Tie him up quick or he'll come around."

Setting him back down, Tora said, "Well, you can tell the master we got the prisoners out." He walked over to Ikeda and gave him a kick in the ribs. When this produced no results, he bent to put a hand to the other man's throat. "Looks like you killed the murdering rat," he said, straightening up. "You used that *naginata* like a born soldier. How come you never let on that you know about fighting?"

Seimei had blanched. "He's dead?" His eyes went to the dead man's face and he felt his stomach rise into his throat. "I must get back," he mumbled and made for the door. Outside, knees shaking, he vomited.

Tora followed, still grinning, Ikeda's sword in his hand. "I don't believe it," he said. "They hid the swords in those beans, and we missed them."

Seimei shuddered. "Let's lock up and go," he said, dabbing at his mouth with a sleeve.

Tora slammed the door shut. "You'd better go first," he said, suddenly grave. "I'll give the fellows a hand with those poor wretches."

Seimei looked across the yard and saw five or six of Yukinari's soldiers carrying or supporting several filthy, ragged creatures who looked more like walking skeletons than living human beings. "Oh, how pitiful," he cried, his own encounter with death momentarily forgotten. "Yes, go help them."

He walked back unsteadily, sick at the thought of having killed a man.

◆

Akitada gathered his robe and rose. The winter air felt cold on his perspiring face. On the abbot's stand, Joto was speaking to an agitated monk. The monk looked like the brute with the deformed ear who had swaggered across the market with his tough-looking companions on their first day here. Joto looked across at Akitada, and the other man's glance, in equal parts triumph and mockery, felt like a physical attack.

A movement near the gate meant that Yukinari's soldiers prepared to block all the exits. Below him the governor's guard drew closer to their platform. It was time. Akitada must go forward with the plan or lose his only chance.

One of the guardsmen marched up with the imperial banner and stood directly below him. Joto was watching the soldiers now, clearly puzzled by their behavior. The crowd began to whisper and hum, and Akitada was in an agony of indecision.

Then Seimei emerged from among the spectators. The old man looked up and nodded. Still Akitada held his breath. After a moment, Yukinari rose behind him and left the viewing stand. It had begun.

Gradually silence fell over the courtyard. Akitada pulled from his sleeve the imperial decree and raised it above his head so that everyone could see the golden seals and purple cords. Below a drum began its rhythmic beat.

"Prepare to hear the august words!" thundered the banner bearer.

The people in the courtyard fell to their knees and bowed to the ground.

Akitada read the imperial instructions, which gave him the power to investigate and prosecute, in a reasonably steady voice. Then he rolled up the scroll and said, "You may rise. The investigation I was charged with is complete. The villains who raided three tax shipments and brutally murdered those who guarded them are known."

A ripple of excitement passed through the crowd.

Akitada looked across to the other platform and faltered. Kukai was there, but Joto had disappeared. Suppressing this new worry, he said, "The guilty are hidden in this temple." After outlining the case against Joto and his supporters, he paused.

They had listened in silent shock, but now panic spread through the crowd. Some of the monks tried to leave and were restrained by soldiers. Minor scuffles broke out.

"Silence!" the banner man thundered. It had little effect.

Motosuke came to stand beside Akitada, his face tense and serious. And then, finally, Akitada saw Yukinari and next to him Tora. Yukinari raised an arm, and a double line of soldiers marched forward. The crowd fell back, suddenly quiet when they saw the sad, pitifully small group of released monks. Two of Yukinari's men brought up the rear carrying the abbot on a stretcher. More soldiers followed them.

The imprisoned monks were covered with filth and sores and staggered from weakness, shading their eyes against the sun. When they reached Akitada's stand and the soldiers set down the stretcher with the semiconscious abbot, the crowd had become still.

"There you see how Joto treated the temple's holy men," Akitada told them. "As His August Majesty's representative and with your support and that of your governor, I shall see to it that justice returns to the people of this province and to this temple. Joto, his deputy Kukai, and all their accomplices are under arrest."

A soft moan went through the crowd. Many had lost relatives with the tax convoys.

Suddenly a shout came from the other platform. Kukai stood there, his arms raised. "Don't trust the enemies of Buddha. They have come to destroy the true faith and cast you back into poverty. This is a plot to get rid of our holy abbot." He swung around and pointed an accusing finger at Akitada and Motosuke. "There are your criminals! There is the man who has kept your hard-earned taxes to fill his own chests and buy his daughter a place as the emperor's concubine. There is the official sent from the capital to hide the crimes of the nobles under the mantle of official sanction. He even uses a sick and senile monk against us. Are you going to permit this evil thing to happen, or are you going to defend your faith?"

The crowd wavered. Somewhere a woman screamed. The

soldiers sprang into action, and the sea of people began to roil like boiling water. Aghast, Akitada attempted to raise his voice again, but it failed him. Motosuke shouted, "In the name of the emperor, clear the courtyard!" The banner bearer below repeated, "Clear the courtyard!" Motosuke bellowed, "Return to your homes to mourn the deaths of your sons and fathers, your brothers and husbands, who were foully massacred by Joto and his followers, and leave the authorities to bring justice to this province!"

For a moment the outcome hung in the balance, then a woman's voice began to wail softly. Others joined her. The crowd broke part. People on the periphery headed for the gate. Those who had pressed forward fell back. Soldiers dispersed groups and rounded up monks.

Tucking the imperial decree back into his sleeve, Akitada turned and sat down, his hands and knees shaking. Motosuke watched a moment longer, then joined him. They were both silent. Yukinari was in the crowd, directing his men. Provincial guardsmen escorted women and children through the gate. As the courtyard cleared, the soldiers began to herd the monks into one corner. Yukinari and his men were placing Kukai and Joto's staff under arrest. There was still no sign of Joto.

Then Seimei stumbled to them. Akitada rose and asked, "Seimei, are you ill?"

Seimei wiped his face with a shaking hand. "No, sir. I . . . I caught Ikeda . . . I had to kill him, or he would have warned the abbot."

Motosuke gaped. "You killed Ikeda? By yourself?"

"I couldn't help it, sir. I struck him on the head with a halberd." Seimei shuddered. "I never killed a man before. It was horribly easy. May the gods forgive me."

Akitada put an arm around his shoulders. "You did what had to be done. We are grateful," he said. "Ikeda was a killer and a traitor. If you had not stopped him, many innocent people would have died today. Thanks to you, we stopped a dangerous conspiracy."

"Indeed, indeed," said Motosuke, patting Seimei's back. "What courage! You will be the talk of the town. And I shall mention you in my report to the emperor."

Seimei blinked. "Thank you sir," he murmured. "It was nothing."

NINETEEN

PRAYER BEADS

*T*he small group of officials followed Akitada and Motosuke on their inspection tour of the temple courtyards and galleries. They visited the storehouses and peered down the shaft into the underground prison. Everywhere they went the military was in full control, saluting as they passed from enclosure to enclosure.

Yukinari and Tora waited outside the abbot's quarters. Akitada let the others precede him, then asked, "Has Joto turned up?"

"Not yet." Yukinari bit his lip. "I'll never forgive myself, Excellency. If I had kept my eye on the man, this would not have happened. The guards at his viewing stand were distracted when some citizens attacked them. During the scuffle nobody was watching the stairs behind the stand."

"Never mind! He cannot have gone far. Any other news?"

Tora said, "You've heard about Ikeda?" When Akitada nodded, he grinned. "How about old Seimei? Didn't blink an eye and let him have it. Smack on top of the skull." He laughed out loud. "And we've caught the brute with the missing earlobe. He was lurking about the back of the compound. Turns out he's the bastard that got away over the wall at the Kannon temple, so he's one of Higekuro's killers. Quite the big wheel around here, it seems. He may know where Joto is."

"They talked earlier during the ceremonies." Akitada frowned. "What about the old abbot and the buried monks?"

Tora's cheerfulness faded abruptly. "Poor bastards. I'd like to get my hands on that smooth-faced devil Joto. They're only half alive. Some of them haven't seen the sun in years. They were so blind we had to lead them. Some couldn't walk at all. And they're the lucky ones. The place was full of graves the living dug with their hands. The old abbot is in bad shape, too weak to talk. The rest are a little stronger, but not much. I found three who'll tell their story."

Motosuke joined them. "Horrible!" he murmured. "And to think that none of us knew."

Akitada sighed. "I suppose we'll talk to them later. What has been done about the children?"

"Joto's pretty little boys?" Tora rolled his eyes in disgust and jerked his head in the direction of the building before them. "I expect they're playing at tops in the abbot's quarters."

"Their families must be anxious," Motosuke said.

Akitada shook his head. "A little late," he said bitterly. "They should have thought before giving them to monks." Seeing Motosuke's surprise, he amended his words. "I realize it is common practice, but it seems to me that at that age . . . a little more time in a loving family . . ." He broke off awkwardly. His own childhood had hardly been spent in a loving home. Besides, revealing a personal prejudice against Buddhism was politically unwise.

Tora slapped his back. "Cheer up! We pulled it off. They're going home, and we'll drink to our luck later."

Motosuke took Akitada's arm and pulled him aside. "I

know, elder brother, that your man is very capable, but he has the most peculiar manners. I'm sure the others must be shocked. No kneeling, not so much as a bow, no idea how to address you properly or how to acknowledge an order. Hadn't you better mention it to him?"

Akitada found the thought amusing. "I doubt I could change Tora," he said. "Besides, all that protocol wastes a great deal of time."

At that moment one of the soldiers ran up to Yukinari. After a brief exchange, Yukinari turned to Akitada and Motosuke. "Forgive the interruption," he said, "but there seems to be a problem about releasing the boys to their parents."

"What do you mean?" asked Motosuke.

"They are locked in and nobody has a key. The parents are angry and threaten to break the door down."

"Locked in?" Akitada got a hollow feeling in his stomach. "When was the last time someone checked on the children?"

"I don't know, Excellency. I told one of my men to take the boys there as soon as we started rounding up the monks."

Tora joined them and Akitada exchanged a glance with him. "Dear heaven, let me be wrong about this," he muttered, feeling suddenly sick. "Come, Tora."

They ran down a covered gallery toward the abbot's private quarters. Before a pair of doors a small cluster of people stood shouting, pounding, and scratching at the heavy wooden panels.

When they saw Akitada and Tora coming, they fell back, their faces anxious.

Akitada told them, "We'll have the door open in no time and your children will join you, but please wait outside the enclosure."

"I'm not going anywhere," blustered a young man with angry eyes. "I want my son and then I'll kill every baldpate bastard who laid hands on him."

Some of the women began to wail.

Akitada sighed. "Very well," he said. "Stay here but keep quiet. Tora? Can you pick the lock?"

Tora nodded, pulling his wire tool from his sash. "Almost left it behind this morning," he said, setting to work, "as not fitting with all this finery." The lock clicked, and he opened the door.

A strange scene met their eyes. Joto, still dressed in his purple silk robe and the embroidered stole, was seated in the abbot's chair on the dais. Around his slippered feet clustered the boys, who stared at them from round, startled eyes. On Joto's lap sat the smallest boy, the one who had served Akitada juice during the festival. Joto's prayer beads, a string of rose-colored quartz, were twisted around the child's neck.

Before anyone could speak, the irate father pushed Akitada and Tora out of the way and made for Joto, shouting, "You devil, I'll show you—" Akitada and Tora lunged quickly to snatch him back and restrain him. Behind them, the other parents crowded into the room, and Akitada regretted bitterly his earlier permission to let them stay.

"Very wise," came the odiously smooth voice of the false abbot. "I see that you understand the situation." Joto's hand moved behind the small boy's head, and the pink beads tightened around the child's throat. The boy uttered a frightened cry. Joto said, "I shall kill this child if any of you come closer."

Behind Tora and Akitada were gasps, and the father in their grip squirmed. "Tosuke," he shouted. "Come here."

A boy got up slowly, then ran to him. He clutched his father's leg and burst into tears. "I want to go home!" he howled.

In a moment, the other children, all except the one on Joto's lap, were also running to their parents. In the ensuing tumult, Joto rose, clutching his struggling hostage more tightly, and retreated a few feet.

Akitada let go of the father, who scooped up his son and ran.

Joto had lost his calm demeanor. His face was flushed, and his free hand was clamped tightly around the struggling boy's neck. "I'll kill him," he mouthed over the noise of howling boys and shouting parents.

Akitada called to Tora, "Get everybody out! Close the door and guard it!"

Tora moved quickly, gathering the boys and their parents and pushing them out. In a moment, the room was silent and empty except for Joto, the child, and Akitada. Joto returned to his chair and sat down again.

"Let the boy go," said Akitada. The child's face had turned alarmingly red. Joto was twisting the beads until they cut into the soft throat. "He is not responsible for your predicament."

Joto's eyes narrowed. "And then you will arrest me?"

"You will have to answer certain charges, yes."

"I have no intention of accommodating you." Joto took his hand from the boy's neck. The child gasped for breath, coughed, and then whimpered. Suddenly he let loose a shriek that made Akitada's hair stand on end.

"Be quiet, little beast!" Joto slapped the boy hard with his free hand. The boy gasped and fell silent, his eyes wide with shock. Joto's fingers had left white marks on the soft, tear-blotched face.

"You're worse than an animal," Akitada cried, clenching his fists.

"Let us say that I have weighed my life against his," Joto remarked coldly, rearranging his hold on the child and getting a grip on the string of beads again, "and I found that my claims outweigh his. What does he have to offer humankind with his seven years of existence? In a few years he will even lose the beauty that makes him attractive now." He twisted the boy's face toward himself. "His skin will grow coarse and those soft cheeks will lose their fullness. The red lips will no longer offer affection, and the charming voice will become gruff and common. He will be useless. I, on the other hand, have yet to leave my mark on this nation. If it had not been for your rash and untimely interference, I would be well on my way to power now, the spiritual counselor and adviser of the nation."

"His August Majesty does not deal with monks who bear arms, rob his treasury, and kill his subjects."

"As I said, if it had not been for you, I would not be in this position. But you had to meddle in my affairs. We only sacrificed a few bearers and soldiers, an insignificant loss of life in any undertaking of this magnitude. But then you arrived, and Tachibana started making trouble. Even then, if Ikeda had not been careless in silencing Tachibana, the women would not have become a problem." Joto let his voice trail off, then said abruptly, "But all is not lost. I have friends everywhere. I shall leave Kazusa for the time being and after a few years' travel and meditation, who knows?"

"Don't be ridiculous. You will not be permitted to leave."

Joto smiled unpleasantly. "You are unusually fond of children, I think. Take this little fellow, for instance. While I was hiding here among the boys, he told me that you had smiled at him. He seemed absurdly proud of this. Isn't that so, Tatsuo? You like the gentleman, don't you?"

The boy gulped. His large eyes filled with tears, and he whispered, "Please take me away, sir. I'll be a good boy, honest."

"Let him go!" Akitada said harshly. "I'll do what I can for you."

Joto laughed softly. "No, no. You will set me free. And you will give me safe conduct out of the province."

"I cannot do that."

"Then he dies." The beads jerked tight, and the boy's mouth flew open. His hands scrabbled in the air.

"No!" screamed Akitada, taking a step and stopping. He would not be in time.

Joto loosened the beads slightly. The child gasped for air, his hands clawing at the beads. Joto laughed softly. "Why do you prolong his agony?" he asked.

Akitada thought frantically, but no solution came to him. "Very well," he said, defeated. "I agree. Now let him go."

"Come," said the other man, "do not take me for a fool. He and I will be inseparable until I am safe."

"Let the child go. He is ill. I will be your hostage instead."

Joto shook his head.

Hopelessly, Akitada turned to make the arrangements, trying not to think of the report to his superiors in the capital, thinking instead of ways to free the child somehow later. Before he could open the door, it burst open. On the threshold stood a wild-eyed young woman, her face pale and frightened. When she looked past him and saw the boy, she screamed, "Tatsuo."

The boy wailed, "Mother."

Then things happened with incredible speed. The woman rushed past Akitada. Joto rose, causing his armchair to topple, and shouted, "Stay away!" Akitada reached out to stop the woman and caught her sleeve, but she pulled away so violently that the fabric ripped. Joto backed all the way to the wall. "Stay away or he dies," he snarled to the mother.

But she was past hearing. The moment her hands touched the child's body, Akitada saw Joto's arm jerk. There was a snapping sound, and rose-colored beads hit the grass mat with the sound of hailstones on a thatched roof. The child fell limply into his mother's arms. She stood, cradling him against her and whispering endearments.

For a moment, Akitada felt only relief, an enormous gratitude that fate had saved the child by breaking the string of prayer beads. Then he saw the way the boy's head fell back, saw the lifeless eyes turned upward. In a blood-red fury of grief, he flung himself at Joto and seized his throat.

Joto gagged. Their eyes met and held for what seemed an eternity. And Akitada knew he could not kill this man and saw that Joto also knew it. "Why?" Akitada sobbed, shaking the abbot in helpless grief. "Why? I would have let you go." The other man said nothing, merely stared back at him. With an exclamation of disgust, Akitada flung him aside and turned away.

The mother was still rocking her child, humming a tune and cradling his head against her breast. But her brows contracted with worry. "Tatsuo?" she pleaded. "Don't go to sleep now, my little sparrow. Speak to your mother."

Dear heaven, thought Akitada, what have I done? He ran to the door to call for assistance.

Outside a small group of people waited. The other parents had left with their children, but Tora, Motosuke, and the officials stood there anxiously, their relief fading when they saw his face.

"He killed the boy," Akitada told them harshly.

Tora was the first to react. He took a sword from one of the soldiers and went to Joto, calling over his shoulder, "We'll need chains."

The mother suddenly screamed, only once, but it was a sound Akitada would never forget. Laying the dead child tenderly on the floor, she staggered toward Tora and Joto. Halfway there, her steps faltered, she swayed and began to fall. Tora jumped to catch her.

He was not fast enough. Ducking under his arm, she snatched the sword from him and raised it with both hands. Joto shrieked and lifted his arms to shield his face as Tatsuo's mother struck. The sword severed his forearm but glanced off his head. Blood spurted everywhere. Joto screamed. This time she plunged the blade deep into his chest. The abbot's eyes opened wide, he made a gurgling sound, and then his body, in purple silk and pearl embroidery, convulsed and fell. Blood bubbled from his mouth and his eyes glazed over.

Before Tora could stop her, the mother pulled the weapon from his chest and raised it to stab the corpse again.

◆

When Tora found him, Akitada was standing before the great Buddha statue in the dim temple hall, staring up at the smooth, golden face with its remote expression.

"Sir?"

Akitada made no answer.

Tora sighed and shuffled his feet. "There's a Lieutenant Nakano who wants to talk to you."

"Tell him to go away."

"Nakano's recognized one of the monks."

"Tora, leave me alone!"

Tora hesitated, then blurted out, "The man he recognized is the former garrison lieutenant. A fellow called Ono. He led the two convoys before the last one. After the first one, he said he barely escaped with his life when highway robbers attacked them. The second time he did not return and was presumed dead. Now he turns up in Joto's gang."

Akitada turned around. Tora's eyes were anxious. "Tell the governor," Akitada said, his voice flat, "but by the Buddha, by the souls of your parents, leave me alone now!"

He returned to his contemplation of the statue. After a moment, he heard Tora's steps receding. Silence fell in the dusk of the great hall.

The lips of this Buddha were soft, full, and finely shaped, like the child's. But the Buddha did not smile. No gap-toothed boy's grin here! The Buddha's eyes looked downward, vaguely toward Akitada, but their glance was immeasurably remote.

The flickering light from candles and oil lamps created the illusion that the Buddha was breathing.

"Amida?" whispered Akitada. "Why the child? Why destroy the seed before the plant blossoms and bears fruit?"

There was no response. Some people believed that the Buddha was everywhere, in all creatures, even in man. Others spent hours calling his name to force his manifestation or to reserve a place for themselves in paradise. The child had chanted all day. Was he now in paradise? Was Joto, who had also chanted? And what was this place, this hell, where people struggled and loved so painfully, praying to indifferent gods for a better life?

A moth appeared from nowhere, flew into the flame of the candle before the image, and, with a dry hiss, perished, leaving behind charred wings and a small trace of smoke.

They would prosecute the poor woman for Joto's murder. Perhaps, in her grief, she did not care, but her husband had come to stare at the body of his son, tears silently streaming down his cheeks. He had put his arms around his wife with a look of love and despair on his face. He had whispered endearments, begged her to consider the other children, himself, their old parents.

But she had remained stonily silent even when the soldiers took her away.

Women could be fierce creatures who lived by their own rules, incomprehensible to their men. Men followed simple laws, their own ambitions, their duties as they saw them, considering their power over others their birthright. So what if the women and children suffered the consequences of their failures?

Akitada raised his eyes from the burned moth to the golden face again. All representations of the Buddha were male. They had large ears, signifying their ability to hear prayers, and a rounded prominence on top of the skull, signifying omniscience. Perhaps Amida could read his thoughts.

A sudden movement of air disturbed the candle flames and caused a shadow to cross the golden face. For a moment, it seemed as if the heavy-lidded eyes looked into Akitada's and the Buddha inclined his head.

"Sir?" Tora had tiptoed in again. "The palanquin waits. It's time to go back."

Akitada heaved a long sigh and turned away from the statue. "Yes," he said. "I must go back. That poor woman. We will tell them that Joto attacked me, and she took your sword to save my life."

Tora opened his mouth, then nodded.

◆

Back in the official palanquin on their way to the city, Motosuke gradually lost his look of distress. Eyeing Akitada's pale, set face nervously, he said, "I know how you must feel. The poor little child—a thing you really could not have foreseen. But you must think of the good that has come out of this day. And you must think of the future. You have conducted this entire investigation brilliantly. I shall make a point of telling His August Majesty so myself. I know you will go far in the service of our nation."

Akitada lifted the curtain. They were entering the city. People lined the road, bowing their heads respectfully as the palanquin passed. What price authority?

Motosuke gave him another anxious look and continued his false cheer. "On the whole, we really have had some splendid luck. Those evil females hanged themselves, Ikeda was killed by your admirable Seimei, and that poor demented creature took Joto's life. Heaven knows what trouble all those murderers might have caused if they had lived."

Akitada said nothing. His hand slipped into his sash and touched some small, smooth pellets. Cool, rose-colored quartz. Prayer beads.

TWENTY

THE HEARING

𝒯he following day they met in the governor's residence for an informal preliminary hearing.

Akitada and Motosuke were seated on the dais of the reception room, with the local officials to either side of them. These were the provincial police commissioner, the senior magistrate, the mayor, and the chief of the local guilds. Seimei and two clerks from the governor's office had their places below, behind low desks with paper and writing utensils. The witnesses in the case against the renegade monks were about to be interviewed.

Akitada had not slept. He doubted that he would ever find peace of mind again. Red-eyed and drawn, he was going through the motions of what remained to be done. He read out the charges against Joto and his followers and asked the senior magistrate to hear the cases against all the accused.

The senior magistrate, a large man with a full black beard, balked. "Your Excellency must be aware that the abbot has many staunch friends in Kazusa," he pointed out. "I also know that the

Buddhist clergy is much admired in the capital. In fact, several imperial princes are abbots themselves. Who is to say that we shall not all be called to account severely over this affair?"

"Joto is dead," Akitada said, "and if you will be patient, you will hear the evidence against him and his followers. Their crimes are of such magnitude and nature that no one in the capital will be able to gloss over their misdeeds, not even the Buddhist hierarchy."

The senior magistrate cleared his throat nervously. "I hope Your Excellency will not take it amiss," he said, "but there seem to be an awful lot of prisoners, and my court docket is already rather full with two murder cases. Should we not send to the capital for additional magistrates and judicial staff?"

Akitada made an effort to feel some sympathy for the man. The judge had just been handed a very complex and politically dangerous case and feared the bureaucratic repercussions as much as the heavy workload. But it could not be helped and he had no assurances to soothe his fears. "There is no time," he said. "The governor's staff will assist you and the other judges. Much of the paperwork has already been completed and witnesses will be made available to you. The charges are, in any case, nearly identical for most of the defendants."

The judge bowed wordlessly.

The three monks entered to a murmur of pity. Two looked seriously ill. Old, rheumy-eyed, and wobbly on their thin legs, they tottered in, blinking against the candlelight. They had washed, shaved their heads and faces, and wore clean robes, but they looked in confusion at the row of officials on the dais. The third man Akitada recognized as the elderly monk from the night of their clandestine visit. He looked better than the others but still wore the bruises of his beating. Motosuke sniffled and dabbed at his eyes with his sleeve.

"Please be comfortable and take your time," Akitada told the monks as they knelt. "We understand that you have charges to bring against the monk Joto."

The monk from the storehouse spoke up. "This insignificant monk is called Shinsei," he introduced himself. "We are greatly indebted to Your Excellencies for releasing us from our grave to charge the monster who buried us alive. I served as deacon of this temple under Abbot Gennin. Joto was one of the monks then, a recent arrival. When he took over, I was away visiting another temple, but my friend Tosai sent me a warning. I returned, passing myself off as a cook. I hoped that way I would be able to move about more freely and be of some use to His Reverence Gennin and the senior monks who were already confined in the underground cellar." The old man sighed deeply.

"Alas, I could do little more than smuggle some food and a few medicines to them. The devils watched too closely. His Reverence was already ill. I was, of course, known to my brothers, but they were loyal and kept my secret, though they pretended to obey Joto. Then, one night, I spoke carelessly in anger and was buried myself."

"But how could Joto have made himself abbot?" asked Motosuke.

The old man looked at him sadly. "We allowed it to happen, Excellency. When Joto arrived, his manners and talents, and above all his learning, seemed to us superior to our own. Our prior Kukai was particularly impressed. On his advice, Abbot Gennin made Joto lecturer. When people came in droves to hear him, we were so pleased that we urged the abbot to appoint Joto assistant high priest. I left soon after."

"I hope His Reverence Gennin will recover and explain more fully how Joto seized power," Akitada said, "but for the present, can you tell us about any specific crimes committed by this man and his followers?"

"Crimes?" Shinsei cried. "They broke every law of Buddha,

they corrupted his teachings, they perverted the faithful who came for instruction, and the children who were given into their care as acolytes they seduced with their filthy lust. But you wish to know about secular crimes. I suppose you can charge them with theft, for they certainly took the treasures of the temple; you may charge them with kidnapping and assault, for they abducted and imprisoned our abbot and his faithful fellow monks; and with murder, for nine of us died from lack of food and medical attention while buried alive in that underground chamber. And one of us, Kukai, joined them in their outrage."

The officials on either side of Motosuke and Akitada broke into excited questions and comments.

After a moment, Akitada raised his hand for silence. "Gentlemen," he said, "what you have heard so far is a most heinous crime deserving the full severity of the law. But it is not, as you shall see, all that the monk Joto is guilty of."

"Yes. Let's get to the tax robberies," Motosuke said.

But Shinsei and his companions knew nothing of this, so Akitada let them go.

When the door opened again, Tora brought in a leather box.

"Ah, yes," said the governor. "That is one of our boxes and here is the mark." He pointed to the burn mark on one side and explained how it had got there.

"Tell us where you found this, Tora," said Akitada.

"In one of the temple storehouses. The same one where they hid all those halberds. And the bean barrels were filled with swords. A whole arsenal."

Of course there should not have been bean barrels in both storehouses when only the second one was used for foodstuffs. Overlooking the swords was an embarrassment to Akitada, but he had made graver mistakes than that.

The officials passed around the leather box, peering and muttering.

The senior magistrate asked, "What happened to the gold? And how did the monks get hold of it?"

"The gold may have been spent on temple buildings and other expenses," said Akitada. "And the monks attacked the tax convoys. We have an eyewitness to their last raid. Seimei?"

Seimei unrolled Otomi's scroll and hung it on a nail. Then he went to the door and admitted Ayako and her sister. Dressed in their best gowns, they knelt before the dais.

Seeing Ayako's slender figure and her narrow, pale face with those compelling eyes was almost more than Akitada could bear. He clenched his hands as he told the officials, "These are the daughters of Higekuro, a well-known wrestling instructor in this city. The younger is called Otomi. She is the artist who painted the scroll you see before you. Unfortunately, she is a deaf-mute. Her sister, Ayako, will interpret for her by using sign language."

Then he took both girls through their testimony carefully. Both sisters identified the scroll as a scene Otomi had witnessed while visiting a temple in Shinano province. As Ayako translated her sister's signs, telling of the raid on the convoy and the subsequent massacre, the officials looked profoundly shocked.

"But," said the senior magistrate after whispering with his neighbors, "that will mean that the victims' families will demand justice."

"And they shall have it, Judge," Akitada said tiredly. "It will be your duty to give it to them."

"You misunderstand, Excellency," said the man. "I referred to civil unrest. Rioting. Attacks on civil authorities who attempt to protect the prisoners."

"Your fears are unwarranted," snapped Akitada. "Put your trust in the garrison, sir. Captain Yukinari has already demonstrated his ability."

The magistrate subsided with a red face.

Akitada was conscious of a profound sense of inadequacy. He had lost his temper, and his feelings for Ayako troubled him deeply. When they came to the slaughter of Higekuro and the subsequent hunt for the girls, he knew his questions and comments were too blunt, too abrupt and unfeeling, but he pressed on to get finished. Ayako remained calm and answered patiently, but she avoided looking at him.

The hardest part was yet to come. He must prove to the officials that the two young women were reliable witnesses, but springing a surprise on Otomi, who was very pale already, was both cruel and dangerous.

He said, "I should like you both to identify someone, if you can."

"Of course," Ayako said.

What enormous presence she had. From the moment she walked in, she had behaved with a nobility of manner and spirit he had not expected in a commoner or a woman.

"The night you and your sister were attacked," he said, "one of your assailants escaped. He is in custody and will be brought in momentarily."

Ayako's eyes widened briefly, then she said, "If he is the one who is missing part of an ear, Otomi will identify him as the monk in charge of the attack on the convoy." She went to the scroll and pointed to the figure of the seated monk. "If you look closely, you can see his maimed ear."

She had made it easy for him. Akitada said gratefully, "I hope she will recognize him, but it may be too much for her."

"My sister will do her duty," Ayako said stiffly.

Two soldiers dragged in a tall man in bloodied monk's robes and tossed him down before the dais. The man raised himself slowly on muscular arms and assumed a kneeling posture.

"Turn around," said Akitada.

When the prisoner turned, Otomi gave a strangled sob.

Raising a shaking finger, she pointed first to the prisoner and next to the scroll. Then she fainted.

Catching her, Ayako said, "Otomi identifies this person as the one on the ship, the one who led the attack on the tax convoy." She bent over her sister, attempting to bring her around.

The prisoner jumped up and shouted, "I didn't hear her say anything."

"Kneel and state your name," snapped Akitada.

"Daishi," spat the man in his hoarse voice. "Not that it's any of your business. You have no right to arrest the disciples of the holy Joto."

One of the soldiers pushed him down and took a leather whip from his belt, looking at Akitada hopefully.

"Neither you nor Joto is a legitimate member of this temple," Akitada told the prisoner. "I want your real name."

The prisoner stared back defiantly. "Daishi."

The soldier raised the whip.

Akitada said quickly, "Very well. It is immaterial at the moment. You and your friends are under arrest for treason and murder. In a short time, all of you will undergo questioning until each of you has confessed fully. I trust you understand how this is done?"

"You can do nothing to me." The words were defiant, but a faint sheen of perspiration appeared on the man's face.

"You may be able to suffer repeated floggings without confessing, but I assure you that your fellow conspirators will be quick to place the blame on you. Their confessions will corroborate the other evidence, such as the painting done by this young woman who was an eyewitness to your raid on the tax convoy. Look at it closely. The figure on the raised platform of the ship is missing part of his ear."

The man turned his head and saw the scroll on the wall. His hand went to his right ear. The lower half of it had been torn or cut off, leaving an ugly red scar behind. He looked shaken. "It's a trumped-up lie," he said. "She wasn't there. That's just a picture of a storm dragon. There was no storm"—he corrected himself—"that time of year."

Motosuke snorted. "You heard him. He's like a cat protesting innocence with a fish tail hanging from its mouth."

"In addition to leading the tax raid," Akitada went on, "you led the nine assassins who slaughtered Higekuro and attempted to kill his daughters."

Tora called out, "Remember me, bastard? We saw you in the temple garden. And we caught two of your gang that night."

"Yes. He was there. I saw him, too," Ayako said in her clear voice.

"Do you want any more proof that you are lost?" Akitada asked.

For a moment, the false monk's eyes searched the room like a cornered animal. When they fell on Otomi, he jerked his chains from the hands of the astonished guards and rushed forward.

Ayako was still kneeling, holding her sobbing sister in her arms, when the wild-eyed brute attacked, howling, cursing, his chains flying, his clawlike fingers reaching for them.

Tora snatched up the small writing desk in front of Seimei and threw it across the room. It caught the monk between the legs. He fell, crushing the desk. The guards, awaking belatedly to their duty, pounced on him.

Seimei cursed for the first time in his life. When Akitada turned disbelieving eyes on his proper old servant, Seimei glared at his scattered papers, his brush still poised in his hand, ink spattered over his gown and the tip of his nose, and an expression of outrage on his face. After a moment, he raised his eyes to Akitada. "Ah," he said. "Hmm. Is there another desk? That is, if you intend to continue this . . . ah . . . unusual interrogation, sir." With the blame neatly shifted to Akitada, he sniffed and dabbed the ink off his face with a piece of paper.

"Never mind. We are finished," said Akitada, and added to the two soldiers who had jerked the limp figure of the monk into a kneeling posture again, "Take him away."

Ayako helped her sister up. Bowing slightly toward the dais, she said, "If you have no further need of us, we will leave. My sister is not very strong."

Akitada did not know what to say to her, but Motosuke told her, "You have performed a great service for this province and nation, both of you. We shall not forget what we owe you."

Ayako inclined her head a fraction. "Thank you, Excellency, but that is quite unnecessary. Our family has always honored its obligations to this country." Without another glance at Akitada, she led her sister from the room.

Akitada sat, lost in silent misery.

Motosuke cleared his throat. "Well?" he asked. "Is there anything else?"

"No. That is all."

TWENTY-ONE

SNOWFLAKES

*L*eaden clouds hung low over the tribunal compound. Already a few snow flurries teased the snarling clay dragons guarding the curved eaves of the governor's residence and danced around Akitada as he dodged the many carts and porters who were loading Motosuke's household goods for the journey to the capital.

Outside the gate, Akitada turned left and walked to the prefecture. Tucking his chin into his collar against the wet flakes, he considered sadly how differently his great adventure had turned out from what he had hoped. Only a few weeks ago he had looked forward to the journey here, to meeting people in the provinces, to learning much and achieving more. All of these things had happened, but the price had been human lives. Far from bringing him pleasure and satisfaction, his assignment had left him humbled and distraught. He had lost a priceless thing: faith in himself. All that was left was the sense of duty his parents and teachers had instilled in him, and duty to his emperor and to his family overruled any private desires and was, in and of itself, sufficient reason to carry on. The prospect was a bleak one.

Duty had brought Akitada out on his last day in the city. The prefecture, his first stop, was much smaller than the provincial headquarters, consisting only of a modest administration hall, a jail, and barracks for the constables. He found Akinobu bent over a desk piled high with documents. The new prefect greeted Akitada with a tired smile.

"I am sorry that I cannot offer Your Excellency tea," he said. "I doubt our budget permits such a thing in any case. But perhaps a cup of wine?"

"No, thank you. I have had some of the governor's excellent tea. Besides, I am not exactly accustomed to luxuries myself. My assignment, along with its honorifics, ends as yours begins. My heartfelt congratulations on your appointment as prefect."

Akinobu grimaced. "To tell you the truth, I'm merely the clerk in charge, and the work is very similar to my duties for the governor." He nodded at the towering stacks of documents on his desk.

"Surely the present crisis is abnormal," Akitada said. Then he sighed. "At the moment I feel that I have brought nothing but trouble to this province."

"No, Your Excellency. Our trouble has found you. We are very grateful for your help. I intend to pay a formal farewell visit before your departure tomorrow morning."

"Please call me Akitada. And there is no need for a special visit. You must know how grateful I am for your assistance. I have the highest regard for your ability." The two men smiled and bowed to each other. Akitada continued, "But there is another reason for my coming. I want to speak to one of your prisoners, the man called Scarface."

Akinobu raised his brows. "Is he connected to the tax case?"

"No. A different matter altogether. You are holding him in the murder of the prostitute Jasmin. I suspect him of having killed two other women."

"Here? He only arrived on the fifth day of this month."

"No. These are two murders of young women in the capital and in Fujisawa."

"But . . ." Akinobu hesitated, then asked, "Forgive me, but why are you only now sharing this information?"

"I did not know until this morning. Or rather I did not understand what I knew until then. And I'm still merely guessing at the details. I need to speak with the man to confirm my suspicions."

"I'm afraid you don't know Scarface very well. He has steadfastly denied all charges against him. In the murder of the woman Jasmin he accuses his associate, a half-wit, of committing the crime."

Akitada nodded "Yes, he almost fooled me with that. But considering the murder of the prostitute in Fujisawa and his motive in Jasmin's case, I now believe it was Scarface who killed Jasmin. On the day of the murder, she told him that she was leaving him for another man. I believe he slashed her throat, then turned the corpse over to his mentally unbalanced follower for some additional mutilation. The second man has a fixation with blood and knives and is dangerous on his own account, but he did not kill the woman."

Akinobu said, "I suspected as much. What are these other murders you suspect Scarface of?"

"I believe that during the night of the Chrysanthemum festival he killed a young noblewoman in Heian Kyo for her jewelry." Akitada took the blue flower ornament from his sash and laid it on Akinobu's desk. "This is part of it. The woman Jasmin sold it to a local peddler, who, in turn, sold it to me the day I arrived here."

"Extraordinary!" Akinobu leaned forward to pick up the small object. He looked at it, then at Akitada. "I always thought such jewelry was worn only by the imperial women," he said. Akitada met his eyes and held out his hand without answering. Akinobu returned the flower ornament and reached for a document roll. "He left Heian Kyo on the tenth day of the leaf-turning month and spent the next two months traveling east along the Tokaido highway."

Akitada nodded. "The dates fit. He must have left the capital immediately after the killing. By the beginning of this month he was in Fujisawa. The Fujisawa victim was also a prostitute who had her throat slashed. We were passing through Fujisawa at the time, and my servant Tora was mistakenly arrested for the murder because his face was badly bruised and cut."

"Ah!" Akinobu sat forward. "Then there were witnesses?"

"Yes. In both cases. In Fujisawa, the murderer was seen by other women in the brothel. In the capital, he was observed by a vagrant. In both instances the witnesses described a man with horribly scarred features."

"You must be right." Akinobu rose. "Let me warn you, though, Scarface has been interrogated without confessing to any of the charges against him."

Akitada knew what that meant. The man had undergone questioning while being flogged with fresh bamboo whips, a particularly painful, lacerating form of torture. It rarely failed to produce positive results.

They walked across the courtyard in the wet cold to the small jail. The roofs of the buildings were already dusted with snow, and here and there patches were beginning to stick to the gravel underfoot.

A guard sat in the chilly anteroom, warming his hands over a brazier. At a word from Akinobu he got up, reached for his ring of keys, and unlocked a heavy door. Beyond lay a narrow hallway, dimly lit by flickering oil lamps attached to the walls. To the right and left were cell doors, their bars opening on darkness beyond, but directly ahead lay what appeared to be a fiery furnace. As they came closer, Akitada found that it was merely a small room with a stone pit in its center, where a large open fire burned, its black smoke rising toward a hole in the pitched roof, where it whirled away into the steel-gray skies. The rafters were blackened with soot, the walls scuffed and stained by dirt and generations of bloodied bodies, the air stifling with heat and smoke. It reminded Akitada vividly of those lurid paintings of hell displayed in Buddhist temples as reminders to sinners of what awaited them in the hereafter.

Heads appeared behind the bars of two cell doors, one a moon-faced goblin, the other the predatory beak of a vulture. The guard selected another key and unlocked a third cell. "Get out, scum!" he bellowed. "Visitors."

The figure that emerged from the darkness, rattling chains on its feet and arms, fit the place. Such faces gave the faint-hearted nightmares. Akitada, who had been prepared by Tora's description of the man, took a step backward. The prisoner saw it and grinned maliciously.

In the flickering firelight, the man's face no longer appeared quite human; the raised purplish scars distorted his features grotesquely. Bloodshot eyes blazed with some hidden excitement, and his lips, swollen and discolored from torture, stretched into a grin that bared teeth like yellow fangs. He stood, tall and broad-shouldered, with an easy arrogance, grinning, mocking, a devil in human shape.

Akitada looked back at him silently, confirming to himself that the killer of Jasmin matched the demonic creature of the ghost story told by the Rat. That murder had really happened, almost three months ago, in another city and to another woman. Strangely, here and now the three murders finally met through an extraordinary set of coincidences.

In spite of the heat from the fire pit, Akitada shivered. His hand closed around the tiny flower fragment in his sleeve. Who knew by what strange and bizarre ways the ghosts of victims found their revenge? The blue flower had accompanied the killer here, the witness had traveled the same route, and Jasmin, the latest victim, had passed it on until it reached the only person who would understand its meaning. But he had come to that knowledge slowly, resisting the signs when they were given to him. He had dreamed of a morning glory dripping with blood. He had received a letter from home, telling him of the disappearance of Lady Asagao, the emperor's favorite. Asagao meant morning glory. And there had been another message: Akitada's handsome friend Tasuku had abruptly renounced the world and become a monk. Tasuku, the notorious ladies' man whose affairs with the women of the court had been the talk of the town. Perhaps Akitada would learn the truth of that when he got home—or perhaps he would never know what had happened.

Akinobu touched his sleeve. "Are you feeling well, Excellency?"

Akitada nodded. With an effort, he asked the prisoner, "What is your name, and where were you born?"

The man bowed. "They call me Roku, short for Heiroku, of the Sano family, at your service, my lord," he said in a surprisingly cultured voice. "Please forgive my appearance. These stupid dogs of provincial officials have mistaken me for some low killer. Perhaps Your Honor can clear up the matter?"

The nerve of the man was astounding. Faced with a long list of charges and more torture, he was yet trying to brazen it out. Akitada decided to play along. "Your speech tells me that you were raised in the capital and well educated. How does a man like you come to be here and in this condition?"

A shrewd, calculating look came into the grotesque face. "Ah," Scarface said, "one can always tell a fellow gentleman. As you say, I was raised in the capital. And attended the Buddhist academy near Rashomon. My parents wanted me to become a schoolmaster, but my spirit was too ambitious for that. I took up the sword and trained at several fencing academies. When I was just beginning to make a name for myself, I ran into trouble. My skill had made me enemies, and when one of my competitors challenged me, the bout turned ugly." The man raised a hand to his scarred face and smiled crookedly. "I killed him after he cut me up. His friends charged me with murder. I had to seek my fortune elsewhere and made my way here. Unfortunately, I found myself almost immediately arrested for the murder of a local whore. Some demented maniac has confessed, but the authorities refuse to believe him and try to beat a confession out of me." Scarface glanced pointedly at Akinobu, who gazed back calmly. When Akitada made no comment either, the prisoner turned around. His white shirt was dark with dried blood across the back. He lifted it to show the swollen and oozing stripes of the whips. Then he bent and raised his stained rouser legs. Boh calves were a mass of raw flesh.

Akitada was sickened. It was surprising that the man was able to stand. He reminded himself that Scarface's deeds had been far worse than anything he had suffered, and said, "As I am about to return to the capital, I will take you along. The authorities there will sort out the charge quickly enough."

The man flung about to face him. "No. Don't trouble yourself. It would embarrass my clan. Only put in a word for me here."

"Nonsense. I can do nothing here, but I'll have you on the road in no time. The Sano clan is not important enough to be embarrassed." Akitada waved his hand dismissively and turned to go.

Behind him, Scarface cursed loudly until the sound of the guard's whip caused him to suck in his breath with a moan.

Akinobu followed Akitada outside. "You cannot be serious about taking him, Excellency," he protested. "He lied."

"I know and I am absolutely serious," replied Akitada, gulping the clean air and tasting snowflakes on his tongue. "I shall send my report ahead by special courier today."

"But what of his crimes here? What of the murder in Fujisawa? He's a dangerous character."

"He will travel under heavy guard." Akitada's expression was bleak and weary. "The crime he has to answer for in the capital will result in a secret and speedy trial and execution, which is more than you could get here without a confession."

◆

Akitada's last errand was also the hardest. His steps slowed when he turned the corner and saw Higekuro's school ahead. Flakes of snow touched his face like a cold caress. He did not bother to take his hands out of his sleeves to wipe them away. As he passed the house of the wealthy neighbor, he saw that its gate was scarred from the constables' axes, its lock broken and replaced by the paper strips and seals of the provincial administration. How much chaos and tragedy this one small street had seen in the last few days! Akitada looked up at the heavy clouds. The snow muffled sounds and blurred sharp edges. A quiet peace had returned to the street, but for him it was a joyless peace.

The front doors of the school stood wide open. As he approached, Hidesato emerged with a broom and dustpan. He emptied debris in the gutter and, turning back, caught sight of Akitada. The expression of happy contentment on his face changed to anxious concern.

"I came to say good-bye," said Akitada.

Hidesato's relief was painfully obvious. He looked around, then placed broom and pan against the wall of the building and bowed. "I hope Your Excellency will have a safe journey home," he said.

"Thank you. I see you're lending a hand here."

Hidesato flushed. "The girls needed some help," he said, adding, "Tora's inside."

This news was no surprise, but it hurt nevertheless. Akitada had expected that Tora would stay with Otomi. He thought back to their first meeting. What he felt for the rough ex-soldier and farmer's son would have seemed inconceivable then.

Hidesato fidgeted. "Er," he mumbled, "I'm very grateful for your help, sir. I understand you cleared me of the murder charge."

"It was nothing. Sooner or later you would have been cleared without me."

Hidesato shook his head. "If it hadn't been for you and Tora, Ayako and I would not be together. I'm not a young man and never hoped to find a home and a family, let alone a girl like her. I shall never forget what you've done for me."

Hiding his pain and rage, Akitada turned his back on Hidesato and stepped into the exercise hall.

The doors to the backyard were wide open. Outside, snowy bundles of mats and broken blinds were stacked against the fence. Just inside, in the gray light of the morning, Tora sat on the floor near a hot brazier, cleaning Higekuro's bow. Perhaps Hidesato would be using it soon. From the private quarters came the delicious smell of cooking.

Tora greeted Akitada with a wide grin—another happy man!—and said, "The place looks nice again, doesn't it?"

Akitada looked around and nodded. Gone were the bloody mats. The floorboards and pillars had been scrubbed and polished till they shone. All the weapons were hanging neatly against the wall or resting in their racks. "You have done a fine job," he said listlessly and turned toward the kitchen.

He had expected to find Ayako at the stove, but only Otomi was there. She crouched over a silk scroll on the floor, unaware of Akitada, absorbed in painting the image of the Goddess of Mercy. Akitada's eyes went to the raised platform under the window. It was empty except for a pair of half-finished straw sandals.

A great sadness for Higekuro filled him suddenly. The fact that such a man should have died when far less worthy men lived was utterly unacceptable. In its own way, it had been as shocking a death as that of the child. Yet he at least had not died in vain. What Higekuro had wanted more than anything else in life had been to find husbands for both of his daughters. He had achieved that. Life would go on here. Tora, Hidesato, and Ayako would carry on with the school, Otomi would paint, and the two couples would raise their children here. Their happiness would soon erase the memories of blood spilled across the hall next door.

He turned away. "Where is Ayako?" he asked Tora.

"No idea." Tora tried to evade, but when he saw Akitada's expression, he bellowed, "Hidesato?"

The sergeant came in immediately, as if he had been waiting outside, impatient for Akitada to leave.

"Where's Ayako gone off to?"

Hidesato's eyes flew to Akitada's face. He hesitated, then said, "To the temple of the Kannon . . . like every day since . . . since her father died."

"Thank you." Akitada asked Tora, "Will I see you tonight?"

"Of course." Tora was depressingly cheerful. "We're just about done here. Tell Ayako dinner's ready."

The distance to the temple took longer on foot, but Akitada

was in no hurry today. How different everything seemed. People walked about in straw boots and colorful scarves and jackets. The muted sound of children's laughter came from backyards, and plunged him into a deeper depression. Smoke from cooking fires rose from chimneys, mingling with the white haze of falling snow. His steps inaudible in the white softness underfoot, Akitada felt as if he were walking through a cloud.

The sensation of unreality intensified when he reached the deserted temple. All was silent here. The buildings seemed surreal, a fairy palace inhabited by celestial princesses. He remembered how ominously the dark roofs of the hall and pagoda had risen from the black wilderness of trees the other night. Now a silvery blanket of snow covered the roof tiles and wrapped the curving eaves in feathery white so that they appeared to rise into the swirling air above like the wings of snowbirds. Behind the magic palace, trees made a filigree of white and black branches, silent guardians of the place. Akitada stopped. It seemed that no mere human could pass into that unearthly world without becoming irrevocably lost.

But he had obligations. Crossing the street quickly, he passed between the red-lacquered pillars of the gate into the courtyard. On the snowy ground, a single set of footsteps led to the main hall and up its stairs. He followed, careful not to mar them with his own large boot prints.

She was not inside, though a candle still burned at the foot of the goddess painting and a thin white spiral of incense curled from a censer she had placed before it. Akitada walked through the hall and stepped out onto the rear veranda.

Ayako was leaning against one of the pillars, soberly dressed in a dark quilted robe, looking out at the silent, snowy grove below. "I knew you would come eventually," she said without turning her head.

"I have been very busy." He was not really aware of his

words, so intent were his eyes on her, memorizing the curve of her cheek, the graceful column of her neck, the way she held her shoulders straight and proud. Guessing at the rounded hips tapering to long thighs, he undressed her in his mind one more time, seeing the golden skin, touching its smoothness, breathing her scent.

She turned. "I have waited here every day." Her eyes moved over him slowly, tenderly.

Akitada gazed back. "Everything has changed," he said.

She nodded. Then, surprisingly, she said, "You are still angry with me. And with Hidesato."

"Yes. I know I have no right."

She turned away again. "You think that I took him to the bathhouse and made love to him where you and I used to lie together."

He was ashamed of his jealousy but could not lie. "Yes," he said softly.

"You are wrong." She sighed. "Perhaps that will make you feel better. I don't know. It makes no difference, because you and I are of different worlds. Although my father once held rank, we have become nonpersons in this nation, neither noble nor common. My father accepted this and taught us that human relationships depend on qualities rarely found in your world. He believed in honor, but by his standards even the Rat has honor, perhaps more honor than a high-ranking nobleman from the capital."

Rage seized Akitada. "How dare you accuse me of lacking honor?" he snapped. "You who gave herself to a mere sergeant who had wandered in off the street looking for a place to hide from the law. How can you think that he will not discard you when he gets the urge to move on? To a man like that you are just a convenience, a livelihood, and a warm bed at night."

She flinched at his anger and turned to face him. "Forgive

me," she said sadly. "I had not meant to hurt you so." Her voice was thick with tears, and she pulled her robe around her more tightly as if to fend off the coldness of his contempt. "I heard about the child and wished I could help you."

"Ayako," he begged, immediately contrite. "It is not too late. Come with me." He paused fractionally, then added, "Be my wife."

"No. It is much too late," she said. "It was too late when we first met. I knew it, but I could not help myself, and for that I ask your forgiveness. I can never live with you as your wife without forcing you to become as we are. That is why I must choose Hidesato."

"No!"

"Yes." She stood, sharply defined against the snowy world beyond, black hair framing the narrow pale face with its strange eyes. Her body was tense, the shoulders squared, the hands clasped so tightly around the red-lacquered balustrade that he could see the bones through the skin. But her voice was calm and very clear in the silence of the place. "Hidesato is a kind man with more honor than you allow him, for he has never touched me. I shall become his wife after you leave, because it would have been my father's wish, and so it is mine. Together we will make a home for Otomi and a life for ourselves."

Akitada stood in silence, looking at her. Snowflakes gathered in her black hair, turning to beads of crystal. Then he nodded, defeated by her firmness, her sense of duty.

"You must go now," she whispered. "Please, Akitada! Please go quickly!"

He stretched out his hand to brush away her tears, then dropped it and left.

◆

For the remaining daylight hours of this, his last day, Akitada walked the streets of the city. From the Temple of the Merciful Goddess he wandered to Squatters' Field, then drifted northward to the garrison, where he stood at a distance, watching Yukinari drilling a troop of foot soldiers. The captain would see them off the next morning, and Akitada left without speaking to him.

He went to the residential quarter of the wealthy, turning into the alley behind the Tachibana residence. The back gate of the empty mansion swung loose in the wind, and he stopped in for a look at the garden. The studio slept under a mantle of white. At the small pond, Tachibana's fish rose from the black depths at his approach, still expecting their owner's hand dispensing food. But only snow fell and melted on the black water. One by one the silver and gold shapes turned and sank again to the bottom. When Akitada left, he looked back. His steps marred the pristine white paths, perhaps never to be swept again. He latched the gate behind himself.

In the gathering dusk, Akitada drifted toward the colored lights and bustle of the market, uncaring that his feet had become numb from the cold. He went down a street of pleasure houses, of powdered faces and smiling eyes, of inviting fingers on his sleeve, barely answering the offers whispered to him. In the falling snow he heard the music of zithers and lutes, the thin, reedy voices of the women and the rough laughter of their customers. Then he walked the poorer streets, where urgent couples ducked into alleys or embraced furtively, leaning in the covered doorways of closed shops. And he felt like a ghost watching the living.

It was dark when he finally returned to the tribunal—wet, cold, and too tired to feel.

Tora and Seimei were packing boxes. Tea simmered on the

brazier, and on his desk stood a tray with covered dishes of food. Akitada realized he had not eaten since morning.

"Have you been waiting long?" he asked Tora.

"Don't worry. Seimei's been telling me all about your mother and sisters."

Akitada winced. What awaited him in the capital was the life he had sought to escape. His widowed mother ruled him and his sisters with an iron hand and a bitter tongue.

"You look tired," Seimei said sympathetically. "Paying farewell visits is always depressing. I saved your food for you, in case you were not invited to dinner."

"Later, Seimei. I must settle with Tora first." Akitada looked at Tora sadly. How handsome he had become. He suddenly noticed that Tora was wearing his blue robe again. "I thought you traded that away," he said, nodding at Tora's clothes.

Tora looked down at himself. "I decided to get it back. The color and cut suit me pretty well. Besides, there's something to be said for making an impression." He winked at Seimei, who chuckled.

"I see," Akitada said heavily. "You will do very well whatever you do and whatever you wear, Tora. I shall miss you." He turned away to hide his emotion. Opening his document box, he muttered, "Here are your wages. I have added a bonus for your efforts and advice in solving the tax case. And there is a present to help you get started in your new life." He held out a package to Tora.

Tora stared at it, making no effort to take it. "You don't need me anymore?" he asked tonelessly.

"I told you once before that you are free to leave at any time. Now that you have plans and my work here is done, I will not hold you any longer."

"What plans?" Tora's voice rose angrily. "You're still sore because of what I said about officials. And I thought you'd given me another chance." He snatched the money from Akitada's hand, tore open the package, and glanced at the contents. "Very generous," he sneered, then flung the gold bar and silver coins at Akitada's feet. "Take care of yourself, old-timer," he called to Seimei and stalked out the door.

Akitada stared after him. "What . . . ?" he began.

"He was hoping you'd take him back with you," said Seimei, dropping dejectedly onto a cushion. "That is all he has been talking about, wanting to know about the capital, about the family, what kind of house you live in, what kind of work he would do. He was afraid you might let him go, but I told him you would never do that, that you would find a way to keep him. It was wrong of me to give him hope." Seimei wiped his eyes with his sleeve. "Such a short time we had together," he said. "It is true what they say: 'Every meeting is the beginning of a parting.' I shall miss that boy."

Akitada shook his head. Had he missed something? Then hope sprang suddenly, and he ran after Tora.

He caught up with him just outside the tribunal gate. Tora stood in the swirling snow peering at the message board, his wide shoulders in the blue robe hunched up. He seemed to be checking the notices.

"Tora," said Akitada, "I did not know you wanted to come."

Tora did not turn. "Don't let it bother you. I see they aren't looking for me anymore. I'll find other work. There's a lot of fighting going on. Maybe I'll go back to the army."

"But aren't you marrying Otomi?"

Tora swung around, astonished. "Me, marry?"

So much for love! Relief washed over Akitada. Otomi's loss was his gain. "In that case," he said, "perhaps you would consider returning to the capital with me. It's not very interesting work, I'm afraid, and I can't pay you much, but there are some very pretty girls there."

TWENTY-TWO

MORNING GLORY

*I*n an austere office of the Bureau of Censors, two middle-aged men faced each other across a desk with neat stacks of documents. The desk and office belonged to Minamoto Yutaka, the feared president of the censors, a personage so powerful that he reported directly to the chancellor. He was a tall, almost cadaverous man, his sparse hair graying, his nose sharp, and his lips thin and permanently turned down at the corners. He sat stiffly upright, hands tucked into the sleeves of a dark green brocade robe, and watched the man opposite him from slitted eyes.

Soga Ietada, the current minister of justice, wore a lighter shade of green and was physically Minamoto's opposite. Almost obese, he had abundant, bristling hair on his head, eyebrows, mustache, and the backs of his hands. At the moment he was occupied with a fan and a cup of tea.

"There are those at court who predicted a different outcome to this matter," Soga said, putting down his empty cup. He spoke with a slight whine, as if he were complaining.

The president turned down the corners of his mouth a little more. "The Fujiwaras are blessed by Buddha. Motosuke emerged from this regrettable affair not only with a clean record but as the man who uncovered a dangerous conspiracy."

The minister waved his fan agitatedly. "We should have stopped Moto—" He broke off, his mouth frozen open in mid-speech.

The thin man had opened his eyes wide and raised a hand. "You are confused, Soga. It is naturally with great relief and pleasure that we have received the news of Fujiwara Motosuke's return from Kazusa and his appointment as senior councilor in the Great Council of State. Equally delightful is the news that his daughter has entered the imperial household."

The minister found his voice again. "If she produces an heir, Motosuke may become the next chancellor."

"Quite possible." The president pursed his thin lips and smiled sourly. "And in the fullness of time, your junior clerk Sugawara may become minister of justice."

The minister blanched. "This development was completely unforeseen. Sugawara was a mere nobody, and now everyone talks of his brilliant future. The worst thing is that we are thought to support the Fujiwara faction becuse I recommendd Sugawara to you."

The president smiled unpleasantly. "If you intended a different outcome, you should have chosen a different man. Not even you could have been blind to this man's ability. I have reviewed Sugawara's background and read his reports. He took top honors from the university in both Chinese studies and the law, no mean feat, which should have secured him a promising position in the administration. Instead he ends up in your dusty archives. His reports are more than competent and reveal an intelligence unexpected in one of your clerks. Such a man should have been watched more carefully."

The minister wailed, "That is precisely what I did. But he began meddling in murder cases, stirring up trouble for everyone and making himself a reputation. Finally, in desperation, I suggested him for this assignment. Your Excellency told me yourself that whoever went would fail. Failure would have removed him forever to some remote provincial administration."

The president leaned forward, fixing the minister with a cold eye. "Do not dare to shift the blame! Regrettably, you miscalculated. I had nothing to do with your private vendetta, although I may regret having put my trust in you."

The minister paled. "I . . . I . . . It was not my intention . . ."

"Enough," said Minamoto coldly. "The matter is closed."

As soon as his visitor had bowed himself out, the president clapped for his clerk. "Send in Sugawara," he ordered.

Akitada stumbled over the threshold, lost his balance, and reached up to steady his court hat, while sinking to his knees clumsily. He had been waiting outside for over an hour, during which his superior, the minister, had arrived, walking past him without so much as a nod. Just now Soga had reemerged, mopping his face and giving him a look of such open fury that Akitada had gaped after the minister in shocked confusion.

Now here he was himself, prostrated before one of the most powerful men in the government, a man who was said to have neither friends nor enemies because he was so widely feared. Akitada quailed at the thought of what was about to be done to him.

"Approach," ordered the thin voice, icy as the floor Akitada knelt on.

He slid closer to the desk and stole a glance at the great man. It was not reassuring. Cold eyes, reminiscent of a snake's unblinking inspection of a mouse, measured him from half-closed lids.

"You are the person we sent to Kazusa as inspector to the outgoing governor?"

"Yes, Your Excellency."

"I have read your report. As regards the taxes, it reveals incredibly lax standards of investigation, a rashness of action that borders on madness, and an appalling lack of concern for the most fundamental rules of behavior. You succeeded in your assignment only because of amazing luck and favorable circumstances. What do you have to say?"

"I regret extremely my foolish mistakes and shall endeavor to learn from them."

There was a moment of silence. When Akitada glanced up, the president's eyes were looking into the distance, as if Akitada were no longer worthy of regard. "If you are implying," Minamoto finally said flatly, "that you expect a similar assignment, or any other position of responsibility, you are even less intelligent than I thought. We cannot afford to employ bunglers."

Akitada turned cold with apprehension.

"Still, you write clearly and seem to have handled the review of provincial accounts well enough. Those skills are of some use in the administration. Because others seem to be more impressed with your activities in Kazusa than I am, I am recommending your transfer to the Ministry of Ceremonial. The position of senior recorder has fallen vacant. This amounts to a promotion in rank by half a grade and an increase in salary. In my opinion, you do not deserve either."

Akitada's heart froze. The Ministry of Ceremonial? He would be keeping the records of all officials, their ranks, offices, appointments, and dismissals. During palace ceremonies, he would be responsible for program, entertainment, attendance, and protocol. The post provided status and income without challenge or future.

He rebelled. Meeting the president's eyes, he said, "I respectfully decline, Your Excellency. My training is in law, not ceremonial. I had hoped for another assignment within my expertise. If this is not feasible, I should prefer to return to my old position as clerk in the Ministry of Justice." As soon as he had spoken, he was aware of having committed an unheard-of breach of etiquette. In his confusion he prostrated himself.

For a while there was no sound but the president's breathing and the tapping of his fingernails on the desk. Both sounds conveyed suppressed anger.

When the president spoke, his voice dripped icicles of derision. "So you refuse a promotion? You cannot be fully cognizant of your offenses," he said with exaggerated patience. "Let me point out merely a few of your errors in judgment. You were sent to investigate a shortage, a mere accounting matter. Instead you took it upon yourself to employ military and civilian forces to uncover certain irregularities in a local temple. In the process you seem to have left a trail of murders and a mountain of paperwork." He thundered suddenly, "Look up!" Akitada jerked upright. The president pointed to the stacks of records. "These documents are a small sampling of what your visit to Kazusa has wrought. Here are reports from four separate ministries you managed to involve in the investigation. These are the files pertaining to confiscated temple properties, accompanied by petitions from Buddhist clergy both here and in Kazusa. This stack is private correspondence from highly placed nobles and officials, either demanding that we outlaw Buddhism altogether or that we exile you as an enemy of the true faith." The president's cold eyes bored into Akitada. "Clearly you have exceeded your responsibilities. What can you possibly say in your defense?"

Akitada swallowed. He was only too aware of his many blunders, of his responsibility for the deaths of innocent and guilty alike. But his intentions had been pure, so he said, "I am afraid, Your Excellency, that I judged the activities of the monk Joto to be a threat to our government. In my subsequent decisions I acted at all times within the oath of office I swore when

I became a servant of His August Majesty. Anything less would have been a dereliction of my duty."

"You dare defend yourself?" The president leaned forward with a sneer. "You had neither the maturity nor the experience to make such a judgment. It was ridiculous! No mere provincial monk could pose a threat against our government. The proper move would have been to lay immediate charges in the local courts against this man and his supporters. Instead you waited, no doubt to win personal acclaim, and the criminals had time to kill more people."

It was true. Higekuro would still be alive if Akitada had acted sooner. The child would be playing with his New Year's gifts if Akitada had not put him and others at risk. The matter weighed heavily on his conscience, and he prostrated himself again.

"I mentioned earlier," continued the president, "that you succeeded only by chance. Perhaps you need to be reminded that it was mere accident that the blind girl's painting fell into your hands. You had the good luck of clearing up the murder of Lord Tachibana because of the incredibly careless manner in which his killers had left the body. Happily for you the garrison commander had an alibi, or you would have had him tried for murder. And the arrest of Joto's supporters was only possible because of a convenient temple festival that allowed you to hide a whole garrison of soldiers in the temple grounds. An idiot would have succeeded. As it was, you managed the matter so badly that the fellow killed a child and attacked you. When the child's mother had to kill this renegade monk to save your life, it cost us the testimony of the prime suspect."

Akitada knocked his forehead against the floor mat. Seeing the justice of the president's strictures, he was ashamed of the hopes for reward that had accompanied him on the long journey back to the capital. He sought for words of apology.

"Since you insist, you may return to your former duties in the Ministry of Justice. Naturally they do not justify a rank increase. You may go."

Akitada rose, making a series of formal deep obeisances as he retreated backward to the door. When his heel touched it, he cleared his throat. The great man looked up impatiently from the document he was reading.

"I beg Your Excellency to forgive my impertinent curiosity," Akitada began nervously, "but I had wondered about the disposition of the case."

"It is hardly your business any longer, but we ordered that the guilty monks be defrocked and assigned to hard labor at the northern frontier. If they behave themselves, they will be allowed to enlist in the frontier armies. The former leadership of the temple has been confirmed, and a new prefect has been appointed to the district." Noting Akitada's dismay, the president added grudgingly, "The high praise of former governor Fujiwara for two of his people has resulted in their promotions. His secretary, Akinobu, will become assistant governor. Of course, the governor's post itself will go to His August Majesty's brother, who will remain in the capital. The other promotion concerns the garrison commander Yukinari, who will join the imperial guard. I believe that is all."

Akitada was happy for Akinobu and Yukinari, but there was the other matter that troubled him more. "I brought a prisoner to the capital, Your Excellency," he said. "He is charged in another case, in the disappearance of Lady—"

"Silence!" roared the president, jumping up. He pointed a quivering finger at Akitada. "You are to forget that matter or risk permanent exile. You are to ask no questions, mention no part of your investigation, nor contact anyone remotely connected with it, ever. Do you understand?"

"Yes. Forgive me."

"Dismissed."

Akitada fled out of the dim halls and into the graveled courtyard, where he took a deep breath of cold air and then passed quickly through the roofed gate into the street. To his right lay the vast enclosure of the Palace of the Eight Ministries, where the emperor presided over his administration to rule his people. Beyond it was another large enclosure, the Palace of Court Festivals. And beyond that, among many smaller courts, was the Ministry of Justice. It was his duty to go there to report his return immediately, but the look of loathing on Soga's face was still vivid in his memory. He turned his steps toward the great gate and the city beyond.

A dusting of snow covered roofs and streets. Pine-bough decorations marked the coming new year. People on elevated wooden sandals hurried along with an air of excitement and happiness. Tomorrow the emperor would announce new assignments and promotions. Customarily, the happy recipients of the august benevolence would then celebrate their good fortune by inviting all who had not fared so well. Akitada himself was expected at Kosehira's mansion for a great party given by his cousin Motosuke, who was staying there until his own residence was ready to receive the new councilor.

Turning his steps homeward, Akitada considered how to break his news to his mother. She would be very angry with him for failing again. They had barely enough to support themselves, and he had returned with another mouth to feed. Lady Sugawara's reaction to Tora had been mixed. After expressing her displeasure privately to Akitada, she had taken Tora as her personal attendant.

The thought of Tora cheered Akitada a little. Perhaps it would all work out. They would have time for their morning exercises again. And today he was going to show Tora the city. Akitada smiled. At least he would not have to transfer to the Ministry of Ceremonial.

◆

The following evening, considerably the worse for a night on the town with Tora, Akitada approached Kosehira's mansion. Introducing the "Tiger of the Tokaido" to the pleasures of the capital, not the least of which were the wine shops, had finally blotted out the image of Minamoto's reptilian eyes, but it was exacting its price now, for his head hurt and there was a dull ache behind his eyes.

Akitada was probably the only guest who arrived on foot for Motosuke's celebration. Torches lit Kosehira's street and his courtyard, where at least fifty carriages of all types had been crammed together. The oxen had been unhitched and stood about, munching hay, while their drivers sat around small fires, talking or throwing dice.

Akitada knew his way and went to the main hall with its reception rooms. Servants were everywhere. Someone helped him remove his boots, someone else took his quilted outer robe, and a third man held a mirror so that he could adjust his hat.

Loud talk and laughter came from the rooms beyond. Akitada looked in each of them for Kosehira's familiar round shape and cheerful face. The company was intimidating. To judge from the colors of the court robes and the rank ribbons on the hats, Motosuke had illustrious friends. Perhaps, thought Akitada, still smarting from his meeting with President Minamoto, he should just send a message of congratulation to Motosuke and leave quietly.

Too late! Kosehira had spied him.

"Here is the man of the hour!" he cried. "Come in, Akitada. Everyone's been waiting to meet you."

Akitada flushed with embarrassment. He cast an anxious look around and recognized three imperial princes, two ministers, several imperial councilors—Motosuke's prospective colleagues—and one of the sovereign's uncles. Kosehira bounced forward and pulled him into the room by his sleeve. His good cheer was infectious; Akitada met with smiling faces everywhere. He was asked questions, which he answered briefly and cautiously, hoping he was not breaking some rule he had not been warned about.

His head still felt fuzzy and, worried that he might say the wrong thing, he refused the offered wine. It was ironic that so many people of rank appeared pleased with his success while the two men who held his future in their hands regarded him as a fool and a bungler.

Kosehira steered Akitada through the throng into the next room. There, in the place of honor sat Motosuke, resplendent in purple and flushed with wine and happiness. When he saw Akitada, he jumped up to embrace him and led him to a cushion next to his own.

"This is the man to whom I owe my good fortune," he announced. "If you ever get yourself into deep water, call on him and your fortune will be made."

That caused laughter and more questions. This time Akitada's reticence about the events in Kazusa was futile, for Motosuke took it upon himself to give a detailed and colorful description of everything that had happened, interspersed with such highly flattering comments about Akitada's brilliance that the latter wished the floor would swallow him.

Kosehira eventually rescued him. "Enough babbling, cousin," he said irreverently to the new councilor. "There is someone who wants to see Akitada."

They left the main hall by one of the covered galleries, walking toward Kosehira's private quarters. Akitada was curious, but

Kosehira maintained an air of secrecy. The sound of voices and laughter faded, trees blocked the light of the torches and lanterns, and the quiet of the wintry garden surrounded them.

Akitada saw the lake where Kosehira had given him his farewell party before his departure for the east. "How different the garden looks," he said. "Is there really someone waiting, or are we just having a quiet chat?"

"You will know in a moment," said Kosehira mysteriously. They entered the dim corridor that led to Kosehira's study. Before the door, Kosehira put his hand on Akitada's sleeve. "He is inside. Join us again when you can." Then he left.

Akitada slid the door open. The room was lit only by the moonlight and the snow outside. On the veranda sat the still figure of a young monk in a black robe. His back was to Akitada, and a string of prayer beads moved slowly through his fingers.

There must be some mistake. What business could he possibly have with a monk? He was about to withdraw quietly when a soft voice asked, "Is that you, Akitada?"

Recognition came suddenly and painfully. "Yes, Tasuku. Kosehira sent me."

The other gestured toward a pillow lying near him, and Akitada went to sit down.

Now that he could see his friend's face, he was shocked. It was not merely that the thick, glossy hair had been shaved off, leaving nothing but a naked skull tinged an unearthly silver-blue in this light. Tasuku's once handsome face looked almost emaciated. Gone was the youthful roundness of cheeks, chin, and lips, and gone was the healthy tan. The eyes still burned darkly, but the full lips were compressed. Worse, the bones in his friend's wrists stood out, and his once muscular shoulders drooped as if the thin black hemp of his robe were too heavy to support.

"Tasuku," Akitada cried, "have you been ill?"

"My name is Genshin now." He smiled a little, sadly. "I am well. And you? You have returned to great honors, I am told. It seems we were all wrong when we tried to dissuade you from your journey."

Akitada glanced across the snow-covered garden to the lake, where they had sat composing their poems so many months ago. If he had known then that he would meet violent death in so many dreadful forms, he would have accepted the conditions of his life. He saw again, in his mind, the broken body of the child, Higekuro's split skull and the carnage around him, Joto's blood bubbling from his lips, the frail corpse of Lord Tachibana.

On the large terrace of the main house, Motosuke's guests strolled about admiring the moonlit scene. Someone was leaning against the balustrade to look out over the trees. Just so had Ayako stood.

Akitada sighed. "No. You were right after all. It was the most difficult thing I have ever done."

His friend glanced at him, then looked up at the moon. "The same moon," he said, "but, oh, how changed we are."

The old Tasuku would have composed a long poem on the subject of lost happiness. Yes, they were both changed forever.

"You don't ask why I have renounced the world?"

"No, Tasuku. Forgive me. Genshin. It makes me sad, but I understand."

The burning eyes sought his. "How so?"

Instead of answering, Akitada took the blue flower fragment from his sash and passed it to his friend.

He heard the in-drawn breath and saw the slender fingers close around the flower.

"Forgive me," said Akitada, "for causing you pain."

"I have been making progress in my discipline. Soon, I hope, matters of this world will no longer touch me. I have asked to see you to bid you farewell. And to lay to rest all that troubles me still. I heard you were the one to bring her murderer back."

Akitada's stomach lurched a little as he remembered the president's warning. "I don't want to add to your distress," he said evasively.

The pale monk smiled. The sweetness of that smile recalled the old Tasuku. "Only in forgetting is there freedom from pain," he said. "And only the truth can help me forget."

Akitada acquiesced. "You and the Lady Asagao were lovers?"

The other man nodded. "I have no excuses for what I did, but Asagao and I grew up together. Our parents were neighbors. I loved her then, but she was sent to serve the new empress. From time to time I used to visit her, bringing her letters from her family. I knew she was unhappy. One day she told me that the emperor had honored her with his . . . attention." He closed his eyes.

After a moment, he took a deep breath and continued. "I was filled with jealousy and turned my anger against her. Poor girl. How could she have helped herself?" His burning eyes sought Akitada's. "I seduced her, Akitada. We met secretly in the summer pavilion of an old villa in a deserted part of the city. She would take a palanquin from the palace to the house of her former nurse, and I would meet her there to take her to our secret retreat." He sighed deeply and looked out over the snowy garden shimmering in the moonlight. Akitada waited.

"I was not worthy of her." His anguish sounded strange coming from the lips of this pale monk. "The risk she took was enormous, her gift of love to me. She imperiled her reputation and her family's future to be with me, but I was not satisfied. I wanted her for myself. I demanded she prove her love for me again and again, while I strutted like a peacock in the knowledge that the emperor's favorite preferred me. But it was not enough." His voice broke.

Akitada shivered. The winter cold seeped through the thick planks of the veranda. He wished they could move inside or that at least he had his quilted outer robe. Strangely, his companion seemed untouched by the frigid air, though his clothing was pitifully thin.

"That final night I demanded one more proof. I insisted she stay with me through the next day and night. I knew it would mean discovery. She wept on her knees. She swore that she cared nothing for her own life, but she could not hurt His Majesty, who had shown her nothing but kindness. I was adamant, but she remained firm. When she left, she asked for my escort. I refused."

There was a long silence. Akitada reached out and put his hand on the sleeve of his friend's rough robe. The arm beneath the poor fabric felt thin. "I am sorry," he said softly. "It must have been terrible. That night of our farewell party . . . you carried her fan, didn't you?"

The shaven head was bowed and nodded slightly. "She forgot it. It was all I had of her, for I never saw her again. Weeks passed. I assumed she had returned to the palace. Then I heard the first rumor that she had disappeared. I was beside myself with uncertainty, not knowing what had happened to her. That was the state of my mind the night you saw me."

"How can you bear to hear what happened?"

The monk raised his face. "I watched her murderer die."

"What?"

"The man died horribly. His was the death I should have died. I was the one who had offended. I was the one who put temptation in his way. But I was spared. Spared in spite of the fact that they knew. Spared because I had become a monk." He paused to look up at the starry sky. "But not spared all. The emperor's personal secretary paid me a visit in the monastery. He informed me that the murderer of Lady Asagao had been sentenced and that he had requested a priest prior to his execution. I was to be that priest."

Akitada said, "Tasuku, I did not tell them about you."

His friend smiled. "I know, but they found out. I think she kept some poems of mine. And the man whose summerhouse I rented for our meetings identified me. In any case, I refused the killer's request, claiming my lack of experience, but I was told that the condemned man had insisted on me by name. That was when I realized they knew. The emperor's secretary told me when and where Asagao had died and then left me to the agony of my guilt."

"It was cruel."

"Cruel? No. I told you I watched the poor wretch die. It took a very long time. No one touched me."

Akitada said angrily, "They may not have touched you, but it was a terrible vengeance nevertheless. And don't waste your sympathy on that animal. He killed two poor women after using and abusing them and might have continued his bloody career if I had not guessed that he had murdered Lady Asagao."

"You guessed?" The luminous eyes probed Akitada's.

"Perhaps the Lady Asagao had a hand in it." Akitada shivered again. "The blue flower fragment came into my possession in Kazusa."

His friend opened his hand and looked at the tiny ornament in his palm. "It was part of her hair ornament. A gift from the emperor."

"Her murderer gave it to the woman he later killed. She sold it to a peddler, who sold it to me. At the same time, a strange ghost story was traveling around the city, a story of a demon with a flaming face who killed a noble lady in an abandoned temple in the capital. He robbed her of her jewelry, then slashed her throat and threw her down a well."

Tasuku shuddered.

"Somehow the mystery of her disappearance and the flower

fragment became fused in my feverish dreams with the strange ghost story. Later, I noticed similarities between the ghost story and a local murder. I reported my suspicions to the emperor and brought the prisoner back with me. But at no time did I think they would involve you. I am sorry." Akitada searched his friend's face anxiously for some reassurance.

To his relief, the other had regained his calm and smiled his sweet smile again. He said, "Thank you, my dear Akitada." Tucking his hands into his sleeves and looking up at the moon, he murmured, "Like snowflakes melting in the moonlight, like the call of the owl fading at dawn, so ends this dream we live." Then, with a sigh, he rose, bowed to Akitada, and slipped soundlessly from the veranda.

Akitada remained where he was. Tasuku had unknowingly reopened the wound. He closed his eyes, and the wintry scene shifted to the veranda of the Temple of the Merciful Goddess. Somewhere in the winter night an owl cried with a lonely, mournful sound. In the garden below a woman stepped into a man's embrace. Then night passed into day, a gray and misty day when snow swirled, danced, and settled on her hair like an ornament of crystal beads. Or drops of dew.

"There you are! All alone in the dark?" Kosehira put his hand on Akitada's shoulder. "Has Tasuku gone? Poor fellow."

"Yes, Kosehira." Akitada rose slowly, feeling like an old man with his cold-stiffened limbs and his thoughts of death. "I must be on my way, too. It has been a long day."

"Nonsense, my friend." Kosehira looked at him anxiously. "You mustn't let Tasuku's decision get you down. He was tired of the world and chose another life. You, on the other hand, have a great future ahead. Everybody says so. You will do great things someday. I feel it in my bones." He firmly grasped Akitada's arm and pulled him back toward the voices and the laughter, the sounds of zither and flute, and the world of men.

HISTORICAL NOTE

*D*uring the Heian period (794–1185), the Japanese government still loosely resembled the centralized empire of Tang China. Japan was ruled from the capital, Heian Kyo (Kyoto), by an emperor and an elaborate bureaucracy of court nobles. Outlying provinces were administered by governors who were dispatched from the capital every four years with their own staff to oversee law and order, as well as tax collection. At the end of their tenure, an inspector *(kageyushi)* would make sure that their accounts were in order. But the distances were great and transportation still in its infancy. Bandits and pirates roamed the land and the seas. Provincial landowners, including the great monasteries, set up their own armies to defend their property. Toward the end of the Heian period the military power of these private interests became a danger to the governors and to the empire.

The events in this novel are fictional, but they play out against the politics and culture of the eleventh century. Akitada is a member of the ruling class and serves in the central government in the capital, but he is on the very fringes of their slowly eroding power. He is well born, university educated, fluent in the Chinese language of government, imbued with Confucian ideals, and struggling to climb the administrative ladder of rank, power, and privilege. Unlike most of his peers, he consorts with the common people, is inept at poetry, and dislikes the Buddhist faith.

Early Japanese culture was based on that of ancient China. Thus, the calendar followed the sexagenary cycle, and era names were periodically designated by the court. To simplify greatly, there were twelve months and four seasons as in the West, but the year began about a month later. In the eleventh century, a workweek lasted six days, starting at dawn, and was followed by a day of leisure. As in the Chinese system, the day was divided into twelve two-hour segments. Time was kept by water clock and announced by guardsmen, watchmen, and temple bells. Generally only the upper class and some of the clergy could read and write. For the government official that meant being able to read and write Chinese in addition to Japanese. Upper-class women and others read and wrote in their native language. These women particularly were responsible for the rich and beautiful literature of the time. Lady Murasaki, a lady-in-waiting to one of the empresses, wrote the first novel in the world, *The Tale of Genji*.

By the eleventh century, Japan had two religions, Shinto and Buddhism. They coexisted peaceably. Shinto, the native faith, venerates the *kami*, divine forces in nature that assure good harvests. Buddhism, imported from China via Korea, became ex-

tremely powerful through the court aristocracy. Shinto is responsible for many taboos. Buddhism stipulates a hereafter in-
volving both hell and paradise. There were many well-endowed
Buddhist temples, monasteries, and nunneries throughout the
country.

Much of life during these times was restricted by innumerable superstitions, ranging from belief in ghosts and supernatu-
ral monsters to directional taboos that forbade certain directions
on certain days of the year. Medicine was primitive in many
ways and practiced both by university-trained physicians and
monks or pharmacists. It involved herbal medicines, acupunc-
ture, and moxabustion (the burning of herbal cones on the
skin), as well as yin-yang correspondences and the sexagenary
cycle.

Buddhism dictated a meat-free diet consisting mostly of
rice, other grains, fruit, vegetables, and fish. People still drank
rice wine in preference to tea. Men did not shave the top of their
heads and wore their hair long and twisted into a topknot;
women wore theirs loose, trailing to the floor, or tied with a ribbon. Upper-class women blackened their teeth. Depending on
class, clothes were made from either silk or hemp. The upper
classes layered their simple kimono-style garments lavishly,
while peasants made do with short pants and shirt, or even just
a loincloth. This was not yet the time of the samurai, but martial arts of all sorts were gradually becoming important. Nobles
were certainly taught to ride, use a bow and a sword, and engage
in battle, but most preferred writing poetry and participating in
court ceremonial. Fighting with wooden swords *(kendo)* was
known, but for the common man the weapon of choice was the
staff or pole *(bo),* which was readily available and less expensive,
hence Tora's stick-fighting skills *(bo-jutsu).*

The role of women in early Japanese society was restricted.
Upper-class women spent most of their lives in the inner apart-

ments of their parents' or husband's home, while the middle class and poor worked alongside their men. Upper-class women in the eleventh century could own property, but they were under the control of the men in their family. Lower-class women had more freedom but little leisure to enjoy it. Ayako is, of course, not typical of the women of her time, though sexual favors were freely given and taken in all classes, and noblemen not only practiced polygamy but conducted affairs on the side.

The issue of law and order is important for crime and detective fiction. In some ways, eleventh-century Japan was quite modern in this respect. It had a police force, judges, prisons, and a set of laws pertaining to crime and punishment. However, since Buddhism forbade killing, the worst that could happen to a murderer was that he would be condemned to exile at hard labor and his property and that of his family be confiscated. Interrogation permitted torture, since confession was necessary for conviction. Prisons were generally full but emptied periodically through general amnesties. As a result, crime of all sorts tended to flourish, to the great frustration of law-abiding citizens.

Kazusa province was part of what became modern Chiba prefecture, and the famous Tokaido highway, linking the eastern provinces to the capital, already existed, but much of the detail for Akitada's journey and for life in Kazusa is fictional.

Some of the plots in *The Dragon Scroll* are loosely based on ancient Japanese tales. The pirate plot and the case of the missing lady-in-waiting were suggested by episodes in *Uji Shui Monogatari*, and the story of the three monks has its source in *Sannin Hoshi*.

ACKNOWLEDGMENTS

I am indebted to a group of wonderful friends and fellow writers, Jacqueline Falkenhan, John Rosenman, Richard Rowand, and Bob Stein, for reading drafts of this novel. Their help has always been generously given and is greatly appreciated. In addition, I have a gentle and caring editor, Alicia Bothwell-Mancini, whose clear eye helped me tighten and polish the novel further. Last but not least, my thanks go to everyone in Jean Naggar's office for working so very hard for me in foreign sales, contracts, and everything else I might need. No author could have better representation. Jean Naggar is, of course, the best.

FOR THE BEST IN PAPERBACKS, LOOK FOR THE 🐧

In every corner of the world, on every subject under the sun, Penguin represents quality and variety—the very best in publishing today.

For complete information about books available from Penguin—including Penguin Classics, Penguin Compass, and Puffins—and how to order them, write to us at the appropriate address below. Please note that for copyright reasons the selection of books varies from country to country.

In the United States: Please write to *Penguin Group (USA) Inc., P.O. Box 12289 Dept. B, Newark, New Jersey 07101-5289* or call 1-800-788-6262.

In the United Kingdom: Please write to *Dept. EP, Penguin Books Ltd, Bath Road, Harmondsworth, West Drayton, Middlesex UB7 0DA*.

In Canada: Please write to *Penguin Books Canada Ltd, 10 Alcorn Avenue, Suite 300, Toronto, Ontario M4V 3B2*.

In Australia: Please write to *Penguin Books Australia Ltd, P.O. Box 257, Ringwood, Victoria 3134*.

In New Zealand: Please write to *Penguin Books (NZ) Ltd, Private Bag 102902, North Shore Mail Centre, Auckland 10*.

In India: Please write to *Penguin Books India Pvt Ltd, 11 Panchsheel Shopping Centre, Panchsheel Park, New Delhi 110 017*.

In the Netherlands: Please write to *Penguin Books Netherlands bv, Postbus 3507, NL-1001 AH Amsterdam*.

In Germany: Please write to *Penguin Books Deutschland GmbH, Metzlerstrasse 26, 60594 Frankfurt am Main*.

In Spain: Please write to *Penguin Books S. A., Bravo Murillo 19, 1° B, 28015 Madrid*.

In Italy: Please write to *Penguin Italia s.r.l., Via Benedetto Croce 2, 20094 Corsico, Milano*.

In France: Please write to *Penguin France, Le Carré Wilson, 62 rue Benjamin Baillaud, 31500 Toulouse*.

In Japan: Please write to *Penguin Books Japan Ltd, Kaneko Building, 2-3-25 Koraku, Bunkyo-Ku, Tokyo 112*.

In South Africa: Please write to *Penguin Books South Africa (Pty) Ltd, Private Bag X14, Parkview, 2122 Johannesburg*.